TITAN

Dean Crawford

ISBN: **1535296852**
ISBN-13: **978-1535296854**

I

Tethys Gaol,

Saturn

Xavier Reed could feel sweat building beneath the rough fabric of his clothes and a prickly heat tingled painfully at the back of his neck as he awaited his fate. The sound of metal against metal clattered around him, a mournful chorus of chains that manacled dozens of ankles and wrists, and the air was stale with the stench of unwashed bodies.

Xavier did not look to either side or behind him. Instead he sat in absolute silence and stared straight ahead down the interior of the shuttle's drab gray metal cabin. Ahead, rows of equally still heads stared toward an uncertain future, watched over by a pair of robotic drone guards armed with high–precision rifles charged with rounds designed not to kill but to incapacitate.

Behind metal grills at the front of the cabin sat two human guards, this time armed with assault rifles and grim expressions. There were no windows, nothing for the rows of convicts to look at as they sat in silence and awaited the green overhead lights above the guards to turn red, signalling the landing sequence.

Xavier swallowed thickly, his throat dry and his vision blurred. A brief vision of his wife Erin and their daughter flickered behind his eyes and he felt a black wave of anguish, hate and helplessness rise up, threatening to engulf him and send him screaming into an abyss of desperation deeper than anything that he had ever known. Nobody noticed his silent battle of will as he forced the black wave down, closed his eyes and trembled with the effort of controlling his emotions, burying them inside some deep neural tract where they could no longer bother him.

The lights in the cabin changed to red and a harsh alarm buzzed around them, breaking Xavier out of his painful reverie. The convicts around him shuffled in their seats, some fearing what was before them, others sitting in fearless silence, enveloped within a force–field of restrained violence as though they welcomed, yearned even, to finally reach their destination.

The shuttle's hull vibrated as retro–rockets fired into the frigid vacuum of space outside, the craft manoeuvring and slowing as Xavier imagined it easing into the landing bays of the Tethys Gaol. He had seen the process once as a young recruit fresh into the prison service, had watched in awe as the tiny shuttles landed inside the huge prison, the immense backdrop of the gas giant Saturn and its vast and peaceful rings belying the hate and the violence that festered inside this most feared of gaols. He recalled how overwhelmingly relieved he had been that he was not aboard such a craft, not facing the terrible fate that those prisoners had been so long ago.

And yet, here he was.

A deep thud echoed through the cabin as the shuttle landed inside the bay, and Xavier could imagine the doors closing behind them and the atmosphere being altered inside the bay before the interior doors opened and the shuttle advanced on its landing pads into the prison proper, ranks of heavily armed guards and drones in position to quell even the slightest protest or disturbance.

The shuttle moved for a few moments more, and then it settled again and Xavier heard the faint sound of its engines whine down as the pilots shut down the shuttle's systems. A deep dread rose up in his chest and threatened to break free from his lips as a cry of despair as the seat beneath him folded automatically away, forcing him to stand on legs that seemed barely able to take his weight.

The shuttle's main exits opened on either side of the cabin and a guard's voice boomed like cannon fire.

'Out, all of you, single file!'

The prisoners shuffled out, their chains rattling as Xavier walked among them. The air was thick with loathing, the shaming stench of fear permeating it seemed not just their clothes but the very atmosphere within the prison as he stepped down off the shuttle's ramp and got his first look at Tethys Gaol.

The prison was located in orbit around Saturn's moon Tethys, with only the largest military base in the Solar System for company, Polaris Station. Considered one of the worst of the *"Seven Circles of Hell"*, as the various orbital prisons were described by former inmates, it was surpassed only by Io Five, another maximum security facility in orbit around the Jovian moon of Io, an intensely volcanic world that offered no means of escape even if a prisoner was able to break out of the facility, as Jupiter's immense gravity could only be escaped by military grade vessels.

Tethys' structure was of hatched barred steel, the prison a former mining colony that had drawn from Saturn's rings water ice for sale to passing vessels making their way toward the edge of the solar system, or harvested ammonia and ammonium hydrosulphide from Saturn's atmosphere for fuels and orbital agriculture. Xavier could see immense and aged pipes running overhead the landing bay that had once contained pressurized gases destined for immense spacecraft docked alongside the mine.

The prisoners were arranged into two lines, thirty four men in all, no women. Xavier found himself in the front rank as a tall, powerfully built man with a shock of red hair that glowed in the harsh light as though it were aflame approached them. His beard likewise glistened with photoluminescence, a recent craze on the colonies, the short lived bacteria implanted into hair. The man was evidently the warden, his belly vast, his arms thick and leading up to a bull neck and cold, almost malicious blue eyes.

'Gentlemen,' he growled as he spread his enormous arms to encompass the prison around them, 'welcome to Tethys Gaol. I am Arkon Stone, the warden, and I sincerely hope that you do not enjoy your stay, which will likely be extended for as long as possible due to your innate inability to conform to the simple rules of society.'

Arkon seemed to peer into their eyes one by one, seeking weakness, like one of the ancient lions that roamed the African veld in search of prey. His brittle gaze settled briefly on Xavier, just long enough that it made him feel uncomfortable.

'There are two simple rules in Tethys Gaol,' Arkon went on. 'First: you do everything that we say or you will be punished in ways more painful than you can imagine. Second: neither I nor my guards are required to obey any rules at all. You will suffer here, both for your crimes and for our pleasure. We do not care about your welfare. Society does not care about your welfare. You have been chewed up and spat out, abandoned here to dwell on your crimes and the pain that they have caused your victims. Now, those crimes shall cause you that same pain.'

Arkon walked along the line of prisoners, dwarfing many of them and glaring down at each as he passed by and moved closer to Xavier.

'You may believe that you have rights, but you do not,' he growled. 'You may feel that you can complain or seek assistance, but you may not. You may even be innocent of any crime, but we do not care for it is not our job to care.'

Arkon walked up to Xavier and glared at him. Xavier held that glare as best he could, knowing that to show fear was to accept your doom. Arkon peered at him as he walked by but then moved on, and Xavier felt his own shoulders sag slightly with relief.

'There are those among you whose crimes would appall any sane human being,' Arkon boomed as he walked down the line behind Xavier. 'Serial killers, rapists, armed robbers and cop killers. But I personally reserve my greatest hatred for the *latter*.'

Something slammed into Xavier's kidney with the force of a fallen angel and he cried out in agony as he dropped onto his knees, his eyes bulging with pain that soared through his body as tears spilled from his eyes. He gagged with the force of it, then felt a heavy boot slam into his spine and he jerked forward and his face smacked down onto the cold metal deck.

From the corner of his eye he saw Arkon glaring down at him as a heavy boot slammed between his shoulder blades and pinned him in place. Xavier felt his guts convulse as he heard from high above the cackles and cheers of dozens, hundreds of criminals all cheering and pointing as Xavier squirmed beneath the warden's boot and heard Arkon's enraged cry echo across the entire landing bay.

'Especially when he himself was a *prison officer!*'

The cheers and the calls died down and Xavier felt the cold dread return, the sudden silence even worse than the cacophony. Now he could feel in the stale air a growing resentment, a hatred that could only boil over as soon as he reached the cell blocks. Arkon was setting him up for death, and Xavier knew why.

'Enjoy your stay,' Arkon growled, and then yanked his boot from Xavier's spine as he whirled away and yelled at the guards surrounding them. 'Put them in their cells!'

A blast of murderous cheers echoed through the landing bay as Xavier was hauled to his feet and dragged along with the other prisoners toward the prison's main entrance, half of them glaring at him with murder in their eyes.

Xavier thought of his wife and daughter one last time and then fought back his tears as he was swallowed whole by the gaping black maw of Tethys Gaol.

***

II

New Washington Orbital Station,

Earth

Nathan Ironside was in another world, yet that world was the one he knew best.

The acacias of Aurora gusted in the gentle breeze and whispered to him of the nearby deserts of Colorado in one breath, the busy streets of Denver in the next. The sound of his daughter Amira's squeals of delight echoed eerily through the warm summer air as she was pushed back and forth on the garden swing, his wife's voice tinkling nearby.

Nathan stood on the lawn, a hose in one hand that sprayed glistening water like a shower of diamond chips across the perfect grass. The sound of traffic whispered nearby and he could hear other children in their own gardens or riding their bikes on the streets beyond the lawn. Everything was perfect, and yet he stood and stared into the middle distance as though in a trance.

'You okay, honey?'

His wife's voice reached him from afar and Nathan managed to shake himself from his gloomy reverie and nodded, smiled.

'Sure, I'm fine.'

Amira smiled and waved. 'Come and push me, daddy!'

Nathan dropped the hose without question and made his way across to the swing, but then he hesitated as he looked at the two people he loved more than anything in the world. Angela, his wife, reached out for his hand, concern in her green eyes.

'What's wrong?'

Nathan blinked away tears that stung the corner of his eyes as he sucked in a ragged breath. 'I'm sorry, I just can't keep doing this.'

Angela frowned and Nathan saw confusion and concern in Amira's eyes as she stopped swinging and looked up at him. 'Daddy?'

'I'm sorry honey,' Nathan replied. 'Really I am.'

Nathan reached up to his temple and pressed gently, and the bright sunlight and fresh scents and his wife and child and their home vanished instantly. Nathan blinked and sucked in another breath of air as he leaned back on the couch and stared vacantly across the lounge to where broad windows overlooked New Washington's west quarter.

The perfect blue vault of the heavens was laced with speckles of distant cloud, and he could see through the windows their shadows beneath them on the surface of the ocean far below. The panoramic view above spanned only a fraction of Earth's surface, in this case the Pacific Ocean as it passed by three hundred kilometres below. Nathan could see tiny island chains scattered amid the vast blue oceans, and across the view stretched immense girders that supported New Washington's vast ray–shielding that kept warmth in and the radiation and vacuum of space out. As the surface of the Earth drifted by below it also rotated in a dizzying effect as New Washington spun in space, the motion producing the natural gravity felt by the population occupying the inside of the station's disc–like ring.

Nathan sighed, rubbed angrily at a stray tear on his right cheek as he stood up and removed from his head a thin silver object that looked much like a hair band but for the slim blue light traversing its length. The *Lucidity Lens* was a device that allowed dreams to become reality, giving the wearer the ability to produce what were known as lucid dreams at will – a virtual reality indistinguishable from true reality because it was generated by the brain itself. But the device created a four hundred year old reality that only haunted Nathan, teased him and kept him trapped between two worlds, neither of which always felt entirely real.

Nathan tossed the device onto the couch and ran his hands through his hair as he glanced at the Optical Data stream in his right eye. *10.42am, Geo–stationary Orbital Time.* Despite his initial resistance, it had been required of him by the New Washington Police Department to install an ID chip, which came with the Optical Stream as standard.

The Implanted Designator, or ID for short, was fused into the bone of his skull while the optical data display was a biomechanical electrode resting against the inside of the lens of his eye. Updated every time he moved through one of the city's myriad checkpoints, every human being was implanted at birth with one of the personalized chips. A liquid–cell quantum storage device, everything about Nathan and every other person was recorded and stored if needed for future use. The law stated that no ID chip was ever to be tampered with, but a vibrant market existed for those able to afford tinkering with their ID and evading the law.

Nathan closed his eyes briefly until his grief had passed and then he tightened his belt, buttoned his shirt and grabbed his badge and his weapon from a table alongside the couch. He was due for duty at 11am, the precinct just around the block from the small apartment he had been gifted by the city's governor as a reward for his *"heroic efforts"* of just a few months before. The invasion of the Ayleean warrior ships and their colluding with the Director General, Franklyn Ceyron, had created a tremendous conflict into which Nathan had been hurled, despite being awoken so recently from a cryogenic slumber that had lasted four centuries. The world he had known had long ago succumbed to an alien virus and was long gone, as were five billion souls who perished before a cure was found using his own body's preserved immune system.

Nathan walked across his apartment, grabbed a sip of stale coffee and then walked for the door. As was his unbreakable habit, he paused as the apartment door dematerialized before him before walking through and heading for the elevator. Hard–light, one of the strangest and most bizarre technologies that Nathan had encountered since he had awoken in the twenty fourth century, allowed for light to possess mass and thus had changed the very nature of many cities. Doors were opaque or transparent and elevated walkways were walled with invisible barriers meaning that nobody could fall from them. An unforeseen consequence of this freedom of visibility was that Nathan was frequently confronted with vertigo–inducing chasms between buildings to which he had not yet become accustomed. Most all folks in the city thought nothing of a six hundred foot drop just inches away from where they walked.

Nathan travelled down in the elevator that clung to the outside of his apartment block and then joined The Belt.

The New Washington Beltway, or simply The Belt, was a conveyor system that ringed New Washington with multiple routes and carried commuters and pedestrians along at a spritely pace without the need for the flying vehicles humming through the skies above. As The Belt carried Nathan away from the apartment block so he got a panoramic view of the sky above the city.

Built before the scientists who designed such cities had been able to grasp the fundamentals of the Higgs Boson's control of mass and gravity, New Washington relied instead on good old–fashioned centrifugal motion: the orbiting platform spun at a rate sufficient to generate one–G of acceleration on the inside of its outer ring, The Belt, thus providing natural gravity for those living there. In the center of the station the docking and loading bays allowed visiting spacecraft to land without worrying about gravity – docking clamps ensured that they could unload passengers and goods safely before departing again, while pedestrians at The Hub, as the station's center was known, wore boots designed to grip the surface which allowed them to walk fairly normally. Not dissimilar in appearance to the ancient sketches of science fiction writers from centuries before, New

Washington's ring–like form was now some ten kilometres across having been repeatedly expanded to accommodate a population that could no longer afford to live on the planetary surface. The spread of the housing projects at the four points of the station's wheel, named the Four Corners, had become a stain of poverty on what had once been mankind's flagship orbital living–space, back then ironically only available to those super–wealthy enough to afford it.

Nathan exited The Belt alongside the Fourth Precinct building, and heard a sharp whistle as a black and white police cruiser hummed across the street to his side, its gull–wing doors open for him to climb aboard.

'You're kidding me?' Nathan sighed as he looked inside. 'You're driving again?'

'You snooze you lose, buster!'

Nathan climbed in alongside traffic officer Betty *"Buzz"* Luther as the cruiser's doors closed either side of them and Betty guided the vehicle up smoothly into the flow of aerial traffic cruising through the station's skies.

'You're doing this to annoy me,' Nathan complained.

'I'm doing it to help you,' Betty replied with a bright smile. 'You can't just become a detective overnight and not know your city. Lieutenant Foxx put you here for a reason, so suck it up and get to work.'

Betty was a gray–haired woman of perhaps fifty or so years, although it was tough for Nathan to tell for sure because people all looked *so young*. Betty may well have been seventy years old or more, and her sedate lack of ostentation at the cruiser's controls suggested that she had been on the force for many decades, as did her reputation for somewhat reckless flying. Keen eyes scanned the traffic around them, and despite her experience Betty proudly wore the blues of the traffic police.

'You could have made captain by now,' Nathan pointed out as they levelled out amid the traffic streams headed for Phoenix Heights.

'I could've made Director General by now,' Betty replied calmly. 'But I don't much like offices.'

'Nor me,' Nathan replied, tugging at the uncomfortable collar of his uniform. 'Don't much like uniforms either.'

'But you sure do like complaining,' Betty observed. 'What's the name of that block over there?'

Betty nodded to an ugly high–rise jutting up out of the shadowy confines of Phoenix Heights a thousand feet below them.

'Byron Tower,' he replied.

'And that one?'

'Falls Incorporated,' he replied, 'headquarters of the Falls Mining Company.'

'Very good,' Betty chortled with a motherly pat on his forearm. 'What's our speed, altitude and time to the North Quarter?'

Nathan glanced at the instrument display that suddenly appeared before him, an optical projection that created a three dimensional map of the city around them now tagged with names for all buildings and even, if they required it, all citizens below.

'Seventy knots, three hundred fifteen meters, four minutes and twelve seconds.'

'Point the location out to me.'

Nathan looked up out of the cruiser's clear canopy and pointed up toward the distant side of the station's sweeping surface, where the tops of high–rises were visible catching the light of the sun through the station's ray–shielding girders.

'Excellent.'

Betty said nothing more as they cruised through a wispy bank of cloud, the sunlight streaming through the vapor in fingers of gold light tinged with rainbow hues as the moisture separated the sun's spectrum. The city's dehumidifiers had long since become overwhelmed by the volume of population now living inside New Washington, creating novel weather systems above the city that included rainfall literally created by moisture from citizen's sweat and respiration. All of the orbital stations suffered from the same consequential ecosystem issues, despite the efforts of their respective governors in raising the capital needed to repair and improve the systems.

'How long do you think Lieutenant Foxx is gonna keep me on traffic duty?' Nathan asked.

'As long as it takes.'

'And how long is that?'

Betty sighed. 'As long as I decide it takes.'

Nathan leaned back in his seat. He was about to ask another question when the cruiser's communicators crackled.

Robbery in progress, Constitution and Fourth, ten–thirteen – repeat, ten–thirteen. All available units deploy immediately!'

Nathan instinctively hit the sirens and lights as Betty accelerated and pulled up above the traffic streams.

'What's a ten–thirteen, Nathan?' she asked him, her tones clipped now.

Nathan needed no reminding, the code the same as when he had been a Denver police detective some four hundred years previously.

'Shots fired,' he replied as he checked his sidearm.

***

III

Betty guided the cruiser down through the streams of aerial traffic, their flashing hazard lights glowing as they descended through a thin layer of mist. Nathan glimpsed the lights flickering in the passing windows of high–rise buildings built long before the invention of hard–light, the glass old and stained with the accumulated grime of decades.

'C'mon, get outta my damned way!'

Betty gestured for a slow vehicle to shift aside as she jerked the cruiser to the right and banked steeply over. Nathan grabbed the side rest for support as the cruiser shot through a narrow gap between the slow vehicle and the solid walls of a tower block as he recalled why Betty had gained the nickname "*Buzz*". Windows flashed by, shocked faces leaping back as the cruiser rocketed past.

'Officer down and in distress!' barked a voice on the communicator.

'Officers Luther and Ironside, ETA twenty seconds!' Nathan replied as he drew his service pistol in preparation.

Alongside the city's northern beltway was a series of high–rise projects that had long since been the blight of New Washington, a haven for the criminal low life packed inside North Four. The drug trade, which prospered despite the complexities of living in such a city, had produced a new underbelly that the police department had long fought to eradicate, but those down in the planet–side capital of New York City seemed to care little for their brethren in New Washington. With crime often concentrated around the Four Corners, and with illegal bandwidth jammers creating entire blocks where police communicators became ineffective, the projects were a dangerous location for any police officer to find themselves whether under fire or not.

'Any idea on the number of shooters?' Betty asked the despatcher.

'Negative!' came the tense reply. *'Multiple witnesses though, a citizen called it in.'*

'No radio coverage,' Nathan said as Betty descended to street level. 'We're on our own.'

'Stay close,' Betty advised as the cruiser settled down onto a street already filled with citizens scattering away from a disturbance ahead. 'Keep line of sight, understood?'

'You got it,' Nathan said as the cruiser's gull wings opened and he vaulted from the seat.

For the first time Betty showed her true age as Nathan sprinted away from the cruiser, dodging like a gazelle through the fleeing crowds as Betty struggled to keep pace behind him. Nathan heard a crackle of gunfire somewhere up ahead, coming from a tower block on the corner of Constitution. Screams echoed across the streets and he saw an individual sprint across the street at a speed no normal human could achieve.

'They're enhanced!' he yelled over his shoulder to Betty as they ran.

A vibrant black–market trade in biomechanical surgery thrived within the Four Corners, providing performance enhancing prosthetics. Most were modified from those used by hospitals to replace limbs lost in accidents, where the patient's own tissues were used to regrow the limbs: instead of replacing the natural limb, the black–market version would be enhanced by molecular titanium reinforcements, a nanofiber mesh woven into the fabric of human skin that gave increased durability and rendered the wearer virtually impervious to pain. Outlawed almost a century before except for those protected by the veil of "human rights" laws that enshrined the citizen's right to self–enhancement if born deformed or deficient in any way, criminals made full use of the enhancements along with a multitude of other modifications.

A moment later Nathan spotted the cop lying in the street, one hand still grasping a pistol and the other clasped over a wound in his chest, wispy tendrils of blue smoke spiralling up from his smoldering uniform where the plasma round hit him.

'Stay with the officer!' Nathan yelled behind him to Betty, the older officer having fallen further behind. 'I'll track down the shooter!'

'Keep line of sight!' Betty shouted breathlessly.

Nathan barely heard her as he dashed across the street in pursuit of the felon who had vanished into a building in the block opposite, pedestrians scattering away from the pistol he was brandishing. Nathan hit the side street at a sprint and rushed up to the door which was still swinging from side to side where the perp' had crashed through it. Faded paintwork above the door for a convenience store stained the otherwise unadorned walls.

Nathan skittered to a halt and then peeked around the corner of the jam into the gloom within. Moving beams of sunlight pierced the darkness like drifting strobes as the station rotated slowly in space, streaming through the only gaps of glass not smeared with grime. Nathan eased inside and listened intently as he crouched down and hugged the wall, letting his eyes adjust to the darkness.

The sounds of the street outside were muted by the interior of the building, which was cooler than the city streets. Nathan could hear a rhythmic dripping of water, condensation and damp a problem in buildings where the airflow generated by gigantic low–level fans had long ago ceased. Debris littered the floor as Nathan crouched down and listened, forcing himself not to switch on his night–vision lens to aid his search: the devices were excellent but easily foiled by a wily opponent with a flash light.

Nathan heard a flutter of light footsteps from across the building, ascending fast, and he broke cover and sprinted across the interior of the ground floor. Once filled with ranks of shelves, their markings on the tiled floor clearly visible even in the low light, the ground floor was now one large open space entombed in dust and grit. Nathan spotted the footprints in the dust even as he ran and changed course to follow them to a flight of metal steps.

He slowed and eased up the steps, watching the door at the top in case the perp' decided to take a shot back at him when he was trapped on the...

A figure lunged into view and Nathan saw a pistol aimed directly at him as he hurled himself to one side and vaulted over the side of the staircase. A plasma shot boomed and he felt the heat of it whip past his face, a bright ball of electric blue energy that smashed instead into the tiles far below and exploded with a bright flare of fearsome light.

Nathan plummeted downward and slammed into the floor, rolled hard to his right to absorb some of the impact and then sprawled onto his back as he saw a shadowy figure leap from the top of the stairwell and plunge toward him.

Nathan rolled to his left and fired as he went, but his wild shot went wide of the target as the figure landed cat–like nearby and sprinted away from him. Nathan took aim, but the figure crashed through another doorway and vanished from sight.

Nathan hauled himself to his feet and dashed after the perp', his legs and hips aching from the long fall as he plunged through the doorway and into a corridor, then ducked as a plasma shot crackled toward him in a vibrant halo of searing heat and light.

The plasma charge splattered the wall behind him, sprayed white–hot plasma across his back. Nathan wriggled out of his jacket as he smelled it burning and sprinted in pursuit of the shooter as he rushed up a darkened staircase at the far end of the corridor. Nathan aimed as he ran and fired three shots, not really trying to hit the perp' but more interested in denying him the chance to fire again as Nathan sprinted up the stairs two at a time, his chest and lungs heaving.

The stairwell backed up on itself, climbing higher inside the building and Nathan could hear the shooter's footfalls as he ascended with super–human speed. Nathan labored up the stairwells as his thighs began to surge with pain and his breath was sucked in with strained gasps. Sweat beaded on his forehead and drenched the shirt on his back as he climbed upward until he reached the top floor and heard a door crash somewhere ahead of him.

Nathan staggered onto the corridor and saw the door at the far end opening out onto the roof, could smell the slightly less pungent air gusting inward from outside as he ran on legs rubbery with fatigue until he reached the door and he crouched down. He knew with certainty that the shooter would be waiting for him to appear, probably even now was aiming his pistol at the open doorway. Even as he considered that he heard the sound of more sirens bearing down on Phoenix Heights and knew that if the shooter hung around much longer he'd be boxed in and unable to escape.

Nathan took a breath and then aimed outside and fired two shots randomly at where he assumed the gunman would be waiting before he hurled himself out and rolled along the roof, coming up on one knee and searching for the shooter.

The roof was empty.

Nathan blinked and then he heard the hum of a plasma pistol right behind him.

He looked over his shoulder and saw a hooded youth standing atop the roof door house, having vaulted there on his bionic legs right after crashing through the doorway. From beneath the shadows of his hood, two inhuman looking red eyes glowed. Nathan, his voice ragged with exhaustion, shrugged.

'Can we call it a draw?'

The youth aimed his pistol more carefully and Nathan saw the bulky weapon was not a pistol at all but a military blaster, something that should never have reached the streets of the city. He had heard rumors of such weapons occasionally being found in the possession of major criminals but never before in the hands of a street youth.

'You've already shot one police officer,' Nathan cautioned, 'you shoot another and you'll be in Tethys Gaol by tomorrow.'

'I didn't shoot him,' came the warbling reply, translated by a digital device attached to the inside of the youth's throat. 'But there ain't no sense in lettin' you go now.'

His eyes peered at Nathan from within the darkened veil of his hood, points of red light that betrayed further bio–enhancements to the optical nerves allowing for infra–red and perhaps even ultraviolet vision.

'No sense in killing me either,' Nathan pointed out. 'You can't win. The cavalry's here.'

The sirens were louder now, screeching in through the thin veils of cloud drifting in the city's atmosphere and obscuring the starlight.

The youth seemed to shrug and then he aimed the pistol between Nathan's eyes.

'Good chase, cop.'

Nathan flinched and then suddenly a blast of air hammered the roof of the building as a police cruiser shot over their heads with scant inches to spare. Nathan saw the cruiser's exhaust hurl the shooter clear off the door house and over Nathan's head, even his bionic limbs incapable of saving him as he crashed down onto the unforgiving surface of the roof. The weapon flew from his grasp, the youth stunned and incapacitated as Nathan leaped across to him and drove one knee between his shoulder blades as he reached around and drew his wrists together.

The police cruiser landed nearby on the roof and Betty climbed out, her pistol in her hand as she shouted at him.

'What the hell happened to line of sight?!'

Nathan locked the manacles into place and stood up, his legs still weak with fatigue.

'I did what you said,' he replied with a smile, 'I kept line of sight, with this guy. You wanna question him or do I get to do it?'

***

Dean Crawford

IV

Tethys Gaol

Xavier Reed awoke with a start as a claxon ripped through the field of his slumber like a plasma ray through black velvet. He sat bolt upright on his bunk as the stench of closely packed humanity hit him, of unwashed bodies and stale breath that permeated the thick, hot air like a blanket.

The bunk in his cell was made of tubular titanium, too tough for even the most determined inmate to break up and use as a weapon. The walls were poured concrete with an internal mesh of steel, the mirror above the steel sink and latrine also polished steel. Nothing could be broken, nothing salvaged for escape or violence. Battles in this gaol were fought with bare hands, feet and heads, brutal and primal.

The barred cell door clattered open, along with a hundred others on D Block as the "*sticks*" called the inmates out, so called because of the electrically charged batons they wielded with almost feverish delight on any inmate who was found to be out of line. Xavier stumbled bleary-eyed out of his cell and moved to stand on the gantry overlooking the chow hall two tiers down.

Arranged in two blocks facing each other, with the tables and chairs of the chow hall bolted and welded to the deck between them, the blocks were two tiers high and designed to hold around a hundred inmates. Xavier had counted two hundred twenty at least, most of them sharing cells in twos and threes. As a new face he was allowed a single cell for a short amount of time, a measure designed to protect newcomers from extortion and violence at the mercy of the old hands that ruled the block. In truth, Xavier had found that all the solitary living did was draw attention to the newcomer and give the other inmates time to plan and conspire.

The gantry was filled with cons, all in their orange prison scrip' overalls and light sneakers. The prison's environment was 1G, standard gravitational force, created by newly-installed Higgs Boson generators deep within the station. Xavier had heard that in previous years, massive riots had been conducted in zero-G conditions as inmates discarded their gravi-boots in favor of the perceived freedom of flight. The job of clearing up body parts floating around the blocks had not, he had been assured, been for the faint hearted.

D Block was only controlled in name by the sticks. In truth it was the domain of Zak "The Shock" Volt, a lifer with a string of gang kills to his name. Surrounded by an aura of psychosis, Volt was short and stocky, shaven headed and devoid of the biogenic implants favored by many of the block's inmates. Those implants were always removed before incarceration on Tethys Gaol, meaning that the unenhanced suddenly found themselves at a distinct advantage to their limbless fellow convicts.

The sticks bellowed the numbers of each convict out from their armored watch station on one side of the block, the calls echoing across the hall from speakers embedded in the walls.

'Two–one–five–Bravo!'

'Sir, yessir, cell ten!'

'Two–one–five–Charlie!'

'Sir, yessir, cell eleven!'

The two watch stations were sunk into the walls at each end of the block, each above a single sally port and with ten meters of polished steel wall below them, removing any hope of prisoners climbing the walls and entering the hard–light protected towers. Metal spikes protruded from the walls below the stations, each with a thousand volts running permanently through them. In the quiet hours, of which there were few on the block, Xavier had heard them humming in the darkness, along with the rattling from narrow air conditioning vents located just above the watch station windows.

Xavier answered when his name was called and caught dark looks from cons across the block. Some men glared at him, others sniggered and exchanged knowing glances, others still pretended that he didn't even exist in order to avoid the bloodshed and violence they knew must surely soon come. Xavier knew that the word was out because he had heard the whispers floating across the block during the night, purposefully kept low to avoid alerting the guards and all the more sinister for it.

'Newbie's a cop.'

'No way man?!'

'Prison stick!'

'Wouldn't wanna be him!'

'They'll have stuck him with steel by the mornin'.'

'That's if he's lucky, man! Zak's crew will take him apart bit by bit, a chunk at a time! Man, his time's over 'fore it's started.'

Xavier had remained silent and still and forced himself not to think of his wife and child so far away now back on Earth. Three days into a life stretch and already he felt as though the palpable tension in the air and the constant threat of violence was corroding his arteries, crushing his heart in a vice–like grip.

'Chow hall, now!'

Xavier turned as the prisoners filed off the gantries and descended toward the hall below. Already, he dreaded mealtimes. When locked in his cell Xavier was on his own and reasonably safe. At meal times he was exposed and under scrutiny in a packed hall, surrounded and yet utterly alone. As a former *stick* he knew that if he didn't do something real fast his life would be over, and not before considerable pain at the hands of Volt's crew.

The prisoners filed into the hall, the cells overlooking them and armed guards watching from the opposing towers as Xavier headed for his seat, on a table reserved for the newest cons. Currently only five of the eight seats were taken, due to what the sticks had termed "medical issues". Xavier could only guess what afflictions the newcomers had suffered, and whether they had been afflicted by other inmates.

Xavier sat down, four other men joining him in silence. He already knew that two of them were hardened criminals who just happened to have arrived at Tethys, while the other two were newcomers to the system like him. Keen to distance themselves from Xavier they willingly sat alongside the lifers, leaving him perched on his own on one corner of the table.

The two lifers, muscular dudes with bioluminescent tattoos covering massive biceps, thick beards and grim expressions, thumped down onto their seats opposite and glared at him in silence as from inside the center of the table a hatch opened and meals appeared on trays. Each man reached in turn for the meal with his number stamped upon a thin plastic box. Xavier saw his meal appear and he reached out for it.

A thick hand grabbed the box and snatched it away from him.

Xavier looked up into the eyes of the nearest bearded lifer, who smirked as he slid the box out of sight between himself and his companion. Xavier watched as the other inmate opened the box and slid something from a plastic bag into the meal before sealing it once more. The smirking inmate returned the box to Xavier, the other two cons watching the exchange in nervous silence.

Xavier slowly opened the box and caught the stench immediately. He grimaced and gagged as he pushed the meal away, his breakfast tainted with the waste product of one of the inmate's previous meals. The two bearded lifers smiled grimly as they tucked into their meals, savoring each bite and watching Xavier. Xavier knew he had to make his first tough decision, and he glanced across at other tables and saw dozens of other cons watching, waiting, some of them exchanging items as bets were placed. He thought of his little child and for a moment he felt the grief return to wash over him like a black wave, fought back tears that welled uncontrollably in his eyes.

The two bikers began to chuckle, one of them shaking their head as they saw the fluid beading in his eyes. Xavier thought of his child for a moment longer, and he wondered what she would think of him if he were to simply do nothing, say nothing, to take the punishment even though he had committed no crime.

His tears vanished as the wave of his grief lit up with flames of rage. Xavier stood up from his seat, reached across with one hand and grabbed the back of the nearest lifer's head as with the other he lifted the breakfast box and upturned it into the bearded man's face, shoved hard and ground the mess into him.

The lifer let out a wail of disgust and fury as he propelled himself backwards into the man sitting at a table behind as he tried to get away from the filthy mess smeared across his face and mouth, the box falling away to reveal excrement lodged in thick clumps in his beard. Xavier jerked backwards and up off the bench, on his toes and ready as the other lifer leaped off his seat, his fists clenched like giant rocks by his sides.

Prisoners scattered from the two tables as other convicts staggered back in horror as they saw the excrement wedged into his nose and beard. Roars of disgust went up from them as they retreated away. Xavier glanced up at the watch station and saw the guards looking down at him, neither helping nor hindering.

Xavier silently reached across to the lifer's seat and picked up the clean breakfast before he sat back down. The uproar in the hall died down as the sticks bellowed across the hall.

'Two–one–eight–Mike, get to the infirmary and get that mess off your face! What are you, some kind of animal?!'

The lifer seethed, his chest heaving and his eyes filled with murderous rage as he lifted one thick arm and pointed right at Xavier.

'You're mine!'

Xavier, his heart thumping in his chest and his skin tingling with prickly heat, smiled back at the lifer.

'You're gonna need better perfume to get me.'

A burst of grim laughter rippled across the hall as Xavier took a long, slow bite of the lifer's breakfast.

'Two–one–eight–Mike, move, now!!'

Snarling with impotent fury, the lifer turned and stalked away toward the sally port.

Xavier took another bite of the breakfast and looked across at the other lifer, who watched him with a look of absolute hatred, his voice rolling like boulders across the table to Xavier.

'We're gonna slice you open a bit at a time, and make you eat yourself.'

Xavier, his pulse still racing, drowned his own fear with a chuckle.

'I'll taste better than your friend right now.'

The lifer scowled, but Xavier knew that his bravado and veil of fearlessness would only last so long. He figured the respect he'd gained in the eyes of the other inmates would buy him a couple of extra days of life at most.

***

V

Fourth Precinct Station

New Washington

Built on the corner of a block that looked as though it had probably been the first ever built in the station, the precinct was a blocky, angular building stained with the coalesced filth of ages. Nathan figured that once its walls would have been of shimmering steel but now they looked almost like brick, countless years of exposure to the brilliant sunlight and moisture trapped within the city.

A faint drizzle had been falling since they'd arrested the youth after his clash with Nathan, drenching the streets with the exhaust of human lungs. Many of the city's inhabitants spent a lot of their time fighting off infections such as the common cold, which thrived in these humid and closely packed environs. That a cure for the cold hadn't been found in the four hundred years since Nathan's birth was no surprise to him even though humanity had found within its capabilities the technology to travel to the stars.

Nathan walked into the precinct and caught an elevator up to the second floor, where Betty was already processing the youth. Filled with miserable looking wretches yanked from the streets of the city for all manner of crimes, processing was also known as the "cattle–yard". Nathan eased his way through the raucous of complaining suspects, all manacled to the walls where they sat as they gesticulated and shouted, and headed past the main desk to a security door that led into the station proper. He entered his access code and then walked through the door, which dematerialized before him as it detected his ID chip and cleared him, despite what he carried in a black bag. He'd been required to call that in before arriving, in order not to set off every alarm in the precinct.

'Hey, Jay! Look who we have here!'

Lieutenant Emilio Vasquez looked up from his workstation at Nathan, Lieutenant Jay Allen also casting a serene gaze in his direction as he grinned from ear to ear.

'Well whaddya know, Emilio? We're honored!'

Both of the officers were attached to the precinct's Anti–Drug Unit. Jay was a career officer who had joined the corps from high school in New

Chicago, while Vasquez was a former Marine who had switched to law enforcement for the increased chance of picking up hot dates due to his uniform. The pair could not have been more different and duly were inseparable partners with five long years' service behind them in the unit.

'How y'doing fellas?' Nathan asked as he tossed his jacket over the back of a chair while the two detectives stood to greet him.

'How's life in traffic?' Vasqeuz grinned as he shook Nathan's hand. 'Not too rough for you? Nice uniform. I used to have one of those, about ten years ago.'

'Or was it twelve?' Allen chimed in. 'Long time ago, and all that. We've moved forward since.'

Nathan didn't miss the jibes. 'It's temporary, okay? Lieutenant Foxx says it's to help me learn the city's ropes.'

'Sure,' Vasquez intoned. 'Five years' service on the streets is the average, so I heard.'

'Could go as high as ten, given that you're four hundred years late to the party,' Allen added.

'Where's Kaylin?' Nathan asked. 'I've got something for her.'

'I bet you have,' Vasquez said as he jabbed Nathan's chest with one finger. 'She's outta your league bro', too hot to handle.'

'Speak for yourself,' Nathan said. 'And speaking of too hot to handle, what do you make of this?'

Nathan opened the black sack and dumped the military grade weapon he'd taken from their perp' onto Vasquez's desk. The former Marine stared down at the weapon and then shot Nathan a serious glance.

'Bro', where'd you lay your hands on this?'

'North Quarter, during a robbery. One cop down but he'll be okay.'

Vasquez pulled on latex gloves before he picked up the weapon and examined it.

'This is military grade,' he said, 'Darkwater MM–15, automatic, thirty round cartridge, good for a hundred meter shot. You said you found this on the streets?'

'Got first–hand experience of it from the wrong end of the barrel,' Nathan said as he gestured over his shoulder to the jacket hanging off the back of Lieutenant Foxx's chair. Vasquez and Allen looked at it and saw the large burn mark in the center.

'Man, this shouldn't be out there,' Vasquez said. 'Military weapons are destroyed when they're retired from service, period, unless they're held in the armory reserve.'

Nathan was about to answer when another voice did so.

24

'They're melted down and recycled to prevent criminals getting their hands on them.'

Nathan turned as Lieutenant Kaylin Foxx strode toward them. She was slim but moved somewhat like a cat, always alert, as though she walked on her toes. Her elfin features were topped with a tight bob of silvery hair that shimmered in the office lights, and she was dressed in a smart suit that folded over her chest from hip to opposite shoulder, tight pants and boots, her pistol swinging on her hip as she moved up to Nathan.

'What's up?' she asked. 'Got scared witless by old *Buzz* already?'

'We got a perp' in holding, opened fire on a cop with this,' Nathan said as he gestured to the pistol Vasqeuz was holding.

'How old is it?' she asked the former Marine.

'My service time,' Vasquez replied, 'no more than ten years. It was being superseded by the MM–17 when I left the corps. There shouldn't be any left in existence except in museums planet–side, and there definitely shouldn't be any on the streets.'

'What do you think?' Nathan asked Foxx. 'Some kind of ring running inside the military, selling off high–grade weapons to criminals?'

'I don't know,' Foxx replied. 'Let's go talk to your perp' and see what he has to say. You got him in processing?'

'Betty's taking him to holding right now. You wanna do the interview?'

Foxx looked Nathan up and down for a moment. 'It's your snatch, so you've got the interview. I'll sit in.'

'Seriously?' Nathan asked, suddenly excited.

'Sure, but get the hell out of that traffic uniform first or nobody's gonna take you seriously.'

*

The interview room was a drab box of four walls, the paintwork scratched and the air stained with the scent of stale coffee and the unwashed masses routinely manacled to the steel chair bolted to the floor opposite where Nathan sat.

Opposite him sat the youth he had arrested, still with his hood concealing his features and the glow of a prosthetic eye visible in the shadows within as though he were some kind of demon. Not much shocked Nathan these days, especially after everything he had seen since he had been awakened from his four hundred year slumber just a few months before, but the part–human presence before him still felt unreal somehow.

'So, you want to tell me what happened?' he asked, keen to establish a dialogue with the kid and get him to speak like a human being.

The hooded figure did not move, but the glowing red eye swivelled up to look at Nathan, the iris shimmering with laser light that made him briefly wonder whether such a device could become a weapon or not.

'I want a lawyer.'

'I want answers,' Nathan replied, trying to ignore the strange digital timbre of the kid's voice. 'You opened fire on a cop, kid. You're facing prison time for it, you understand that?'

'I didn't shoot nobody.'

'That's not what forty or so witnesses have said,' Nathan shot back, 'and that's not what happened to me, or did you already forget the four or five shots you took at me?'

The hooded face vanished again as the kid looked down at his boots. 'I was scared.'

'Yeah, that's what they always say: *wasn't me, I was just scared*, that's why I tried to kill a cop.'

'I din' try to kill nobody!'

The kid's fist slammed down on the metal surface of the table, anger flaring in his bionic eye like a distant star.

'Lose the hood,' Nathan ordered him.

'Like hell.'

Nathan leaned closer. 'You don't talk to me like a human being, I'll stop treating you like one. Lose the hood or I'll rip the damned thing clean off.'

The youth looked at him for a moment longer and then he reluctantly reached up and pulled the hood back.

Nathan managed not to recoil from the sight of the kid's face. Both of his eyes were constructed from a metallic matrix that extended down to his cheeks and up onto his brow, the surface laced with hair–thin glowing tendrils that Nathan assumed were electrical connections of some kind. The kid's scalp was shaved and criss–crossed with scars, and his throat was also a fusion of metal and skin around the thorax and the upper chest.

The door to the interview room shimmered and vanished as Lieutenant Foxx strode in.

'Asil?'

Nathan blinked and turned to her. 'You know this guy?'

If metallic, glowing eyes were capable of showing any kind of relief, Asil's expression now collapsed as he looked up at Foxx.

'They got me all jammed up ma'am,' he uttered quickly. 'I din' kill nobody, and this asshole started chasing me and I had to run and then the cruiser and...'

'Slow down,' Foxx snapped, raising one hand at Asil. The kid fell silent as the interview room door closed behind her. 'Okay, start from the point where you showed up on that block with that gun in your hand.'

Asil sighed, stared at the table top as he replied.

'I was mindin' my own business on fourth when I got collared by a hood by the name of Scheff. He's a local runner for Shiver, said he needed a favor and there was plenty of *slapdash* in it for me.'

Nathan looked up at Foxx. 'Cash,' she said, 'gang slang.'

While his knowledge of current slang wasn't quite up to speed, of "Shiver" Nathan knew all too much. North Four had become the epicentre of the *Shiver* trade: a new form of *bio–implant* drug that caused the user to experience two lives of unimaginable ecstasy at once via an exotic and highly dangerous shifting of perceived reality, the user "shivering" between each. The drug took advantage of the fact that the human brain could "lucid dream", a near–awake state that allowed dreams to be experienced as absolute reality: the phenomenon was natural but short lived and hard to control. Unlike the *Lucidity Lens*, which limited the amount of time one person could spend in an alternate reality and which was regulated by law, *Shiver* gave the user complete control, leading to an addiction that eventually led to substance abuse, brain overload, an inability to distinguish between reality and dreams and eventually death by misadventure. The proximal cause was usually suicide, either by the use of the drug or by an individual's inability to procure more of it, forcing them to face reality on its own terms.

'What was the favor?' Nathan asked Asil.

'He wanted me to run a package up to North Four,' Asil replied, 'small, easy to conceal. I figured it must be high value 'cause he paid up right there and then. Scheff hangs with some real handy dudes, you don't mess with them, so I agreed to run the package for 'im and set off right then.'

'What happened next?' Foxx asked.

'I got to North Four off Constitution, and was headed for the drop off when the men in black show up in a cruiser. I don't know, maybe they figured I was trouble or somethin' but they started to walk up to me.' Asil sighed again. 'Before I know it, they pull their weapons at me and start screamin' for me to get on the ground. That's when the shootin' started.'

'You opened fire on them,' Nathan said.

'No, man!' Asil wailed. 'The shot came from behin' me! I din' know who the hell was shootin' at who and I went to ground. The gun came out of the bag and I grabbed it and fired at everybody because I thought they was all police tryin' to take me down.'

Nathan frowned. 'And how can you be sure you didn't hit the officer?'

'Because he was the first to go down!' Asil said, one hand reaching up to massage his metallic brow as though the whole thing was giving him a digital headache. 'I din' know what to do, and then you showed up in a second cruiser and I figured I'd better high–tail it outta there before things got any worse!'

Nathan leaned back in his seat and thought for a moment. He had arrived at the scene of the officer down and had seen Asil fleeing the scene, but he had not actually seen the kid shoot the weapon until later.

'So if you're so innocent in this why the hell did you fire at me?'

Asil stared at Nathan as though he were four years old, not four hundred.

'You got the police shootin' at you, somebody else shootin' at you and you're holding a pistol that's gotta be illegal. I didn't shoot to kill man, I was tryin' to slow you down so I could get away!' Asil pointed at his own face. 'Believe me man, with these eyes if I'd have wanted you dead you'd be nothin' but a smokin' patch on the sidewalk by now.'

Nathan raised an eyebrow. 'You think the DA will buy that as a reason *not* to prosecute, genius?'

Asil's brief anger withered and he shook his head.

'I ain't got nothin',' he replied. 'They'll send me down 'cause that's what they do with people like me, but I din' do anythin' here but try to get away with my life.'

Foxx rested her hand on Nathan's shoulder and gestured for him to join her outside the room. Nathan followed her out into the corridor and let the door rematerialize behind them, cutting off all sound.

'I'll buy it,' she said. 'Asil's a street hood but he's no shooter.'

'Okay,' Nathan replied. 'How do you know him?'

'He's an informer,' she replied. 'We met him when we were investigating your case a few months back. He hangs with the wrong crowd for sure but he keeps his hands clean. He's smarter than the others and sure as hell no cop killer – if he says that's how it went down I figure I can trust him.'

'What about this Scheff guy? You heard of him?'

'No,' Foxx replied, 'but Asil will tell us what we need to know. He's jammed up real bad in all of this and cooperation is about the only thing that's going to keep him out of a jail cell. See what you can find out and bring it to the office – I'll meet you there after I've spoken to Captain Forrester.'

The prospect of avoiding further traffic time galvanized Nathan and he nodded keenly as he turned back to the door.

***

Dean Crawford

VI

'How's he doing?'

Captain Tyrone Forrester settled his two hundred twenty pound frame into a leather seat behind his desk that seemed to sag beneath his weight. His uniform was immaculate, his back straight and his shoulders broad as he watched Kaylin. Even sitting he seemed enormous, his bituminous skin as dark as his moods.

'He's been on traffic for four months, several good snatches, couple of reprimands for reckless endangerment but only ever of his own life. He's a real go–getter, captain.'

Foxx sat opposite the captain, as ever struggling to match the man's stoic discipline with the nearby shimmering *holo–images* of his family playing in endless silence on his desk, often with the captain carrying the younger children, one in each arm.

'What about the Lucidity Lens business? He still using it?'

Foxx sighed. 'Maxed out. He has it on for two hours per day, regular as clockwork. Doctor Schmidt says that it's a dangerous path but we have to let him run his own course.'

'Can't be easy on the guy,' Forrester agreed, 'four hundred years gone in a blink, his family long dead. He probably still feels like he only said goodbye to them last week.'

Foxx nodded. 'I want him on the force, captain. He's proving himself an asset and he's adapting well to life in the city. The novelty of living in orbit hasn't worn off for him yet, we should use that to our advantage.'

Forrester agreed. 'He has the governor's blessing that he can move planet–side any time he wants to, Kaylin. We can't deny him that right.'

'I know.'

'How do you feel about that?'

'What difference would it make?'

Forrester smiled. 'You two have grown close, since what happened with Franklyn Ceyron. You keen to have him stick around with us up here in this floating junk pile?'

Foxx lifted her chin slightly. 'He's a good cop, a natural detective. He seems happier up here.'

Forrester exhaled noisily and glanced at a file on his desk.

'Doctor Schmidt believes that Nathan's desire to stay up here is to maintain a psychological separation from the pain he perceives is down there. Nathan won't return to Colorado because he can't bear to be reminded of his family.'

'And yet he visits them every night in the Lens.'

'That's not real,' Forrester reminded her. 'The Colorado down there right now is what's real and it's that he hasn't faced up to yet.'

Foxx shrugged. 'So, what do you want to do about it?'

Forrester reached for a file on his desk and tossed the flimsy electro–film across to Foxx. She caught it in one hand and looked down at it.

'I've got two women waiting outside for you. They're here on behalf of a convicted felon who was recently sent down for sixty–to–life for the murder of a police officer planet–side in San Diego, while they were both on leave.'

Foxx scanned the electro–film and words leaped out at her: *a single gunshot following an altercation; multiple witnesses; weapon recovered, one cartridge discharged and confirmed as victim's cause of death; jury unanimous in verdict; appeal denied.*

'Looks like a slam–dunk,' Foxx said. 'He's going down and there's no appeal process. Says here he got Tethys Gaol?'

'Arrived there seventy two hours ago,' Forrester confirmed. 'Chances are he'll be dead within the week.'

Foxx frowned. 'The gaol's hell, but it's not so bad that he'll be killed so…'

'He's one of ours,' Forrester cut her off, 'an officer with the prison service.'

Foxx blinked and glanced down again at the officer's record. *No history of discord or reprimands; exemplary service; commendation twice for outstanding performance and courage during a riot in a Los Angeles jail before he moved to orbital service.*

'What are you thinking?' Foxx asked.

The captain leaned back in his seat, his big hands folded across his cavernous belly.

'You'll need to talk to them to figure that out for yourself, but I don't need to tell you that the felon's chances of living out his sentence are slim in Tethys, and the wife and mother are adamant that he's innocent. I want you to bring Nathan in on this. It might give him the focus that he needs right now, help him through.'

Foxx stood up, then hesitated. 'You know, he does kinda get a thorn up his ass if he gets his teeth into something. I don't want Nathan marching into Tethys to get this guy out of a jam if he decides he *thinks* that the con *might* be innocent.'

'He's your puppy dog,' Forrester replied, 'keep him on a tight leash if you have to, but I want to have absolutely no doubt whatsoever that this guy's guilty of killing a fellow cop. I don't need to remind you how it would feel to face sixty or more years in Tethys for a crime you hadn't committed, you readin' me?'

Foxx nodded. 'You got it.'

*

Nathan saw the message request flash up on his optical implant even as he was finishing the report on Asil. Betty *Buzz* Luther hadn't been impressed that both Nathan and Foxx considered that Asil was likely telling the truth and had been even more appalled that the street hoodlum was also an informant for the department, but it wasn't his job to worry about her preconceptions and besides, as he read his message he realized that something new and interesting had just come up.

Nathan got up from his desk and walked across the office to a small waiting room reserved for visitors and VIPs to the precinct. Unlike the rest of the building the waiting room was maintained in an orderly and pleasant state, with soft music and lighting within creating an ambience more inviting than the cattle pen downstairs.

Nathan reached the door and it shimmered and vanished before him as he walked in to see Kaylin Foxx with two women, both of whom he instantly clocked as wearing distressed expressions, evidence of tears and long–term strain creased deeply into the lines of their faces.

Nathan slipped quietly into the room as the door reappeared behind him and Foxx introduced the two women.

'Nathan, this is Roma and Erin Reed, the mother and wife of a prison officer named Xavier Reed. Ladies, this is Detective Nathan Ironside.'

Nathan managed to maintain a somber expression as he shook the hands of the two ladies, despite the fact that Foxx had just referred to him as a *detective*. He sat down alongside Foxx and glanced at her, saw her wink at him before she spoke again.

'Xavier Reed has just started a sixty year term in Tethys Gaol for the murder of a fellow officer in San Diego,' she explained.

Nathan couldn't help but wince now. He knew plenty about the gaol and the fact that Xavier was a prison officer was virtually a death warrant inside Tethys.

'I'm sorry to hear that,' he said, aware of how trite it sounded.

Erin Reed looked at him through eyes blurred with tears. 'I know how police feel about cop killers, but I hope that you will hear us out detective?'

Nathan glanced again at Foxx and felt a tingle of excitement ripple through his belly and climb tantalisingly up his spine as she handed him an electro–file for him to read. He took the file and looked at Erin.

'You're right, cops have a deep seated and understandable hatred of cop killers,' he replied. 'But that's not why we're here, right?'

Foxx smiled faintly and her eyes twinkled as she looked at him and both Erin and Roma nodded vigorously.

'Xavier is a great cop and he loved his job,' Roma said proudly. 'He worked long hours by choice, was commended twice for bravery in the line of duty and was considered by his superior officers to be destined for greater things. He would never have done something like this and he has maintained his innocence throughout.'

In his time with the Denver Police Department, Nathan had become more than familiar with the horror and disbelief the families of convicted felons harboured, unable to come to terms with the fact that beloved sons, daughters, mother or fathers could be capable of such crimes, that there *must* have been some mistake. Almost always, there had been no mistake and the felons were as guilty as they come, but just occasionally…

'What did Xavier claim happened on the day of the murder?' Nathan asked, keeping his voice calm and slow, trying to build upon the ambience that the room was designed to create.

'He said that he was in an argument with a fellow officer,' Erin said, 'and that they went outside to cool off. The next thing he knows the other officer reaches for his pistol. He drew too and a shot was fired. The other officer died.'

Nathan frowned. 'Then how can Xavier say that he didn't fire the shot that killed his fellow officer?'

'Because he said that the shot came from behind him,' Erin insisted. 'Xavier stood by that claim, but nobody believed him because he fired in self–defense and he got a fizzle.'

Nathan frowned at Erin and looked to Foxx for an explanation.

'Xavier claimed that the plasma charge in his pistol didn't ignite when he pulled the trigger,' she said. 'A fizzle happens once maybe every thousand shots and just bleeds the plasma energy out into thin air over a few seconds. The jury claimed he was fabricating the event and that there was no second shooter.'

Nathan looked back at Roma.

'So you're saying that this victim, the one that Xavier is supposed to have shot, drew a weapon on him and that's been verified by the witnesses?'

'No,' Roma said in reply. 'Nobody saw the victim draw his pistol, they only heard what they claim must have been my son's shot and then everybody rushed outside to see the victim lying dead in the street and Xavier holding a smoking gun. He was apprehended by his colleagues and was unable to pursue the shooter he claimed really killed the victim that day.' Roma shook her head, tears streaming from her eyes. 'If only they had listened to him, they might have found the real killer and my boy would not be facing death in Tethys Gaol right now.'

Nathan sat back for a moment and rubbed his chin thoughtfully.

'What are you thinking?' Foxx asked him.

Nathan reflected for a moment before he replied.

'When I went after Asil this morning, after that cop was attacked, I and pretty much everybody else who was on the scene assumed that he was the shooter. It just stood to reason; a cop down, Asil holding a pistol and firing back at us.'

'You think there may be something in Xavier's story?'

Nathan sighed and glanced at the electro–film, an image of Xavier Reed's eager young face, resplendent in his dress uniform after graduating from the police academy.

'Please, detective,' Erin begged him tearfully as she grabbed his hands, and for a moment he thought that she might slip off the couch onto her knees before him. 'Please look into it. If there's anything that the police have missed, it might be enough to save my husband's life. You and I both know that he won't survive long in that terrible place and my lousy salary as a shuttle–taxi flight attendant doesn't earn us enough to pay a fancy lawyer to fight Xavier's case.'

Nathan rested one hand on Erin's and squeezed it gently.

'I'll look into it right away and see what I can find, I promise.'

Nathan glanced meaningfully at Foxx and together they stood and walked from the waiting room. The door closed behind them and Foxx took Nathan's arm.

'Don't get carried away with this, Nathan. There's not much evidence to suggest that Xavier did anything other than shoot his colleague.'

'And yet I take it that Forrester handed you this, and that you brought it to me,' Nathan countered. 'So you both think it's worth pursuing.'

'Forrester wanted to see what we thought about it. So?'

Nathan glanced back at the waiting room.

'Neither the wife nor the mother spoke about how they *knew* Xavier was innocent,' he replied. 'They both told me what Xavier told them. They're not blinded by love for Xavier, they didn't tell me what happened at the scene of the crime as though they were there. They related what he told them, plain and simple. They believe him, one hundred per cent.'

'That's not enough,' Foxx said. 'Sure, they're convinced they're onto something here but then they would be, wouldn't they? I don't think this is a case that can be solved, Nathan.'

Nathan gripped the electro–film tighter and smiled at her. 'I bet you dinner that I can.'

Foxx smiled brightly and rolled her eyes. 'So where do you want to start, oh Romeo?'

'What's the weather like in San Diego these days?'

***

VII

CSS Titan

Heliosphere Patrol Sector Four

Admiral Jefferson Marshall awoke to a soft beeping sound and a buzzing in his ears. The cabin was dimly illuminated with subdued lighting that mimicked dawn on Earth, the walls glowing with the first hint of sunrise on a distant horizon. Marshall glanced at his optical display and noted that he had slept for almost eight hours – two more than he would normally have needed.

He sucked in a lungful of air that was scented with the sweet aroma of the pine forests that surrounded his home in Idaho, and he could hear the sound of birds calling each other with the sunrise. Despite the array of technology surrounding him, designed specifically to remind him of home and bring comfort to the military lifestyle, none of this helped his tiring body as he dragged it off the bunk and sat for a moment gazing down a slope to the shore of a limpid lake that perfectly reflected the dawn sky.

Marshall reached up and felt for the *Lucidity Lens*, then switched it off. The image of the dawn sky and vast panorama of forests faded slowly away and the interior of his quarters aboard the largest warship in the fleet swam into view. Marshall wasn't much one for fantasies, but the lens did bring him some measure of comfort when away from home for so long, which he often was. He reflected briefly that he had probably spent at least half of his life on tours of duty, far from Earth and his family. Plenty of criminals had served less time aboard the orbital prisons that drifted in the frigid vacuum of space around Jupiter and Saturn.

Marshall stood up, the hard–light bunk switching off automatically as he dressed and grabbed a small breakfast of crushed cereal before he washed and prepared himself for another day. At least the current rota had him on "days", in as much as time counted this far out in the solar system.

Marshall glanced at himself in a mirror on the wall, which was in fact a sheet of electro–film that flipped his image the right way around so he could see himself as others did. He looked older, the lines in his face more deeply ingrained, the gray hair a little thinner than on his last tour. He reminded himself, as his wife often did, that he had weathered well for a man of one hundred twenty six. She had also reminded him that most commanders of his age would have considered retirement before now, a thought that filled him with a greater horror than confronting an entire fleet of Ayleean warships in nothing but a...

'Good morning!'

Marshall almost jumped out of his skin as he whirled and saw the glowing holographic form of the ship's doctor, Schmidt, shimmering before him.

'It's against protocol to invade the sanctity of the captain's quarters,' Marshall growled.

'Unless circumstances dictate that a given situation qualifies as an emergency,' Schmidt corrected him with an ingratiating smile of neon blue–white teeth.

'What emergency?' Marshall asked, all his anger instantly forgotten.

'Follow me,' Schmidt said with a cheerful nod to the door, and then vanished in the blink of an eye.

Marshall strode through the door of his quarters and out into a corridor where Schmidt was awaiting him. The doctor's ephemeral nature was one of the many advancements of mankind that Marshall felt uncomfortable with, many people no longer entirely human and, in the case of Schmidt and his kind, both alive and dead at the same time: a *Holo sapiens*.

'Long range sensors have detected a high–priority transmission coming from the Ayleean system,' Schmidt explained as he walked alongside Marshall. 'The transmission is garbled and broken, but it doesn't look good.'

'For us or for them?'

'Both,' Schmidt replied, all pretense of humor gone. 'Our communications team are trying to decode the message and extract some kind of meaning to it.'

'What's the emergency in all of this?' Marshall asked.

'It was a distress signal.'

Marshall stopped dead in his tracks in the ship's corridor and stared at Schmidt. 'The Ayleeans sent *us* a distress signal?'

The last encounter that mankind had had with the Ayleeans had been a protracted battle that had nearly cost the lives of everybody aboard Titan and the orbital city of New Washington, when the Ayleeans had attempted to breach the solar system and attack Earth.

Marshall had fought the Ayleeans in two wars, from both of which the CSS had emerged victorious. The species were in fact human, but only partially so. Three hundred years before the Earth had succumbed to a plague known as *The Falling* that had taken the lives of some five billion souls and rendered society utterly broken. The land had been given over to both nature and to gangs of brigands and thugs who had roamed the wilderness and the crumbling wastelands of the fallen cities of Earth. Only small pockets of true humanity had remained, cities well protected by the remnants of the military, where studies had continued until a cure for the plague had been found.

In those dark and terrible days many possible means of eradicating the plague had been explored, and with them the darkest recesses of the human psyche. Enforced elimination programs designed to destroy, however humanely, those carrying the plague had cost the lives of millions more innocent citizens, those in power acting only in the knowledge that to do nothing would see the end of the human race entirely.

Some of those slated for "elimination" had inevitably escaped, and in turn some of those had in fact survived the plague by virtue of losing limbs, either by decay or by choice. Among those wandering, miserable hordes of disfigured survivors grew a new species of man, well versed in the art of bionic prosthetics, skeletal reconstruction and tissue regeneration, skills they used to replace their damaged limbs. By the time the war against the plague had turned in mankind's favor, millions around the world were only half–human, the rest of their bodies made up of ever more complex machinery. Two centuries later and mankind was once again a technologically advanced species, with cities and space fleets and a renewed appetite to reach for the stars. For the Ayleeans, centuries of marginalization gave them the appetite to do more than just reach, and they had been among the first to leave Earth in the colony ships and find their own home several dozen light years from Earth beneath the fearsome glare of a red dwarf star. Ayleea, a steaming tropical world and one of the first ever–discovered habitable planets around an alien star, had evolved them even further into a race of hunters with an abiding hatred of humans, their only true brethren in an uncaring cosmos.

'We were as surprised as you are,' Schmidt replied as they began walking again, officers moving past in the opposite direction visible through Schmidt's semi–transparent form as they moved by. 'I decided to wake you while the cryptographers were studying the message, which seems to have been subject to interference of some kind.'

'I was already awake.'

'Just.'

Marshall ground his teeth in his skull but did not reply. Schmidt's unusual status as a *Holosap* meant that he complied with regulations and decorum only when it suited him. There was little in the way of punishment that could be meted out to those who were already dead and besides, Schmidt's near–genius intellect and two hundred years experience of life, if that it could be called, were invaluable to Titan's crew. In some strange ways, the emergence of the Holosaps was even stranger than that of the Ayleeans.

'Do we have an idea of when the signal was originally transmitted?' Marshall asked.

'Forty eight hours plus,' Schmidt informed him. 'It should have been here hours ago, and what little we have received suggests ill winds on Ayleea. Whatever's happened, it's not good.'

Marshall was about to reply when suddenly the ship's lighting switched to a dull red and an alarm sounded that echoed through the endless corridors with a mournful wail. Marshall saw the bridge doors before him, two Marines standing guard either side of them. A tannoy crackled with an anxious command.

'Cap'n to the bridge!'

Schmidt vanished like a genie as he transported himself directly onto the bridge and Marshall broke into a run. The Marines guarding the bridge's physical doors reacted immediately, one of them entering an access code via his optical implant, his eye flickering as he entered the data and the doors slid open. Marshall rushed through as the Executive Officer barked his arrival.

'Cap'n on the bridge!'

Titan's bridge was a large oval with two floors, one elevated back from and above the other, both facing a large viewing screen and tactical panels. Dozens of staff worked at stations around the upper floor, overlooking the lower where several more manned stations were arranged around the captain's chair.

'At ease,' Marshall snapped and turned to the XO. 'What's the story?'

The XO, Olsen, was a man possibly a little younger than Marshall with a ramrod straight back and a jaw as wide and thick as a harbour wall, framed by a neat white moustache that shimmered with metallic implants as he spoke.

'Distress signal, priority traffic from Ayleea. It's garbled and has been jammed to some extent, but what we're hearing is some kind of major catastrophe. Now we've got a jump cue right ahead of us.'

Marshall's gaze switched to the main viewing panel at the front of the bridge, upon which was displayed an optical image of the cosmos ahead. Ranks of millions of stars shone against the velvety blackness of space, but some of them were shimmering as though a gigantic lens was passing across them and warping their appearance.

'Battle stations!' Marshall snapped, knowing that Olsen would already have made the call. 'Charge all plasma batteries and ready Quick Reaction Alert fighters for launch, all shields up full power!'

The crew swarmed to carry out his orders, the Commander of the Air Group scrambling the QRA *Phantom* fighters in the launch bays, tactical officers re–routing power to shields and gunnery officers charging the plasma batteries that lined Titan's immense hull as she prepared to face whatever was about to come out of the jump cue. The bending, spiralling patch of space was a sign of a vessel's warp drive twisting the fabric of space and time like a bow wave ahead of it and thus betraying its arrival, a tactical error that would cost its crew dearly.

'They're coming right at us,' Olsen observed as Titan's computers calculated the incoming vessel's mass and course. 'They're not even trying to conceal their approach.'

Marshall took hold of the railings that lined the captain's command position, ready for whatever was about to appear.

'They're either wildly confident or wildly stupid,' he replied. 'Let's hope it's the latter. Tactical? Status?'

'All batteries fully charged, all shields at maximum deflective power!'

'CAG?'

'Four fighters on the catapults, ready to launch! Eight more right behind them!'

Marshall nodded, the bridge now enveloped in silence as they all stared at the jump cue right ahead of Titan.

'Bring her to bear, port batteries,' Marshall said in barely a whisper.

An old man sat at the helm with his hands on a series of complex looking controls while a thick bunch of optical fibers travelled out of the man's head and into his seat. Although Marshall had spoken the words the helmsman had already carried out the command, his mind reacting not to Marshall's words but to his very *thoughts*, his brain wirelessly connected to the admiral's to reduce reaction time during combat. The helmsman had served with Marshall since his first command, and their thoughts were often perfectly aligned. Titan turned her massive port batteries to face the jump cue as suddenly the stars within rippled as though they were reflections of a night sky in a pool of water as a pebble was tossed in, and then a brilliant white flare of light burst like a new born star and a massive ship loomed into view.

The white starburst of light faded, and in the faint starlight of deep space Marshall got his first look at the new arrival, a huge and lumbering warship painted a dull red in color that matched the glow of the lights on Titan's bridge. But that was where the similarities ended.

The ship was Ayleean, a three–pronged hull like Neptune's trident peppered with weapons and sensors, built for combat and little else, but there was almost nothing left of her. Clouds of debris entombed her shattered hull, across which great chasms of destruction were filled with flickering fires and trails of escaping gases.

'What the hell happened to her?' Olsen uttered in amazement.

***

VIII

Doctor Schmidt spoke from behind his work station, to which he was wirelessly connected and able to assimilate and analyse data and tremendous speeds.

'No signs of life aboard, captain,' he reported. 'Whatever happened to her, it claimed the life of the entire crew.'

'Any stasis capsules aboard her?' Olsen asked.

Schmidt studied his instruments for a moment. 'It's possible but with all the debris and random electrical discharges I can't get a clear reading from the ship's interior. The only way we'll be sure is if we...'

'... go inside and take a look,' Marshall finished the sentence for him.

The admiral clenched the bridge railings more tightly. The Ayleeans were fearsome in stature and temperament, and like many aboard Titan he could recall the horrifying experience of engaging them in combat at close quarters in their own ships, the corridors filled with humid air and moisture, like jungles growing within a steel dungeon. The Ayleeans were skilled and hardy warriors in any environment, but nowhere were they more dangerous than on their home world or in their own vessels.

'Two shuttles,' Marshall said finally, 'one for insertion, the second for support but to remain outside the hull.'

Olsen relayed the command immediately as Marshall turned to Schmidt.

'I will be there,' the *Holosap* said before Marshall could make the request. 'There is enough power to sustain my projection within the hull, but I don't know how long the ship will last before it collapses. I would advise the Marines to maintain a watch outside the interior and only one platoon to follow me in, just in case.'

Marshall nodded. Schmidt could travel with impunity through the shattered carcass of the Ayleean ship's hull, whereas the Marines would be in danger of being trapped should the dangerously weakened hull collapse further or, worse, the ship's fusion cores ignite in a runaway reaction.

'Order Gunnery Sergeant Jenson Agry and his team to deploy,' Marshall said to Olsen. 'I want eight Phantoms on constant patrol and I want those Marines out of there at the first sight of trouble, understood?'

'Yes sir!' Olsen snapped, and began issuing orders.

Schmidt vanished from his workstation without another word as Marshall stepped down from his command platform and surveyed the shattered hulk of the Ayleean warship.

'What are you hiding?' he whispered to himself.

*

'Hoo rarr!'

Gunnery Sergeant Jenson Agry's shaved head reflected the harsh white lights of the shuttle's interior as the craft launched from Titan's forward landing bay and rocketed out into the bleak vacuum of space.

The shuttle's interior was lined with stereoscopic viewing panels that allowed the Marines a clear view of their target and the surrounding environment, as though they were riding in an open–top shuttle in the vacuum of space, essential to provide maximum situational awareness for the troops before they deployed into the enemy vessel.

As the shuttle drew away from Titan's vast hull two sleek Phantom fighters slid protectively into formation either side of her, the Marines watching the heavily armed spacecraft.

'The interior of the ship is structurally compromised!' Agry snapped, his sandpaper–rough voice loud enough to reach every corner of the shuttle. 'Atmosphere has been lost in most quadrants and is leaking from those not yet exposed to vacuum, so we'll assume zero gravity conditions will be the norm. Weapons hot, and stay sharp: we all know how the Ayleeans can end up when they encounter CSS Marines!'

'Toast, Gunny! Hoo rarr!'

The thirty Marines checked each other's environment combat suits, ensuring that all seals were good and that oxygen levels were sufficient for a one hour deployment into the Ayleean vessel. *Twenty minutes in, twenty out,* Agry reminded himself, with *twenty spare* for the unexpected. Walking into any Ayleean warship was an endeavour neither he nor his Marines would have undertaken lightly – entering a dangerously damaged vessel was tantamount to suicide.

'Thirty seconds.'

The pilot's voice sounded through the fuselage and Agry readied himself, checking his plasma rifle once more and glancing into his optical display to check oxygen levels. His heart rate was elevated, but only by four beats per minute: he'd done this enough times to only get fidgety when the plasma started flying. Not recorded by the monitors was the anxiety twisting at his guts, as much now as it had done on his first combat deployment almost twenty years previously. No matter how hardened a soldier became he recalled his drill sergeant explaining to him that the day a soldier stopped feeling fear was the day they were really in trouble.

'Ten seconds.'

The pilot's calm voice filled the troop compartment as Agry called out.

'All arms!'

The soldiers' plasma rifles hummed into life as they were activated, and each man checked his neighbour's face mask one last time for gaps in the seals and their oxygen supply via the tanks carried upon their backs. Satisfied, they sat in tense silence waiting for the ramp to drop.

They shifted as one as the shuttle swung around, and Agry heard the sound of the engine exhausts change as the pilot altered his power settings to land the craft in the landing bay he had selected on the vast hull. Schematics obtained from Titan's logs provided a deck plan of the Ayleean ship for the pilots and the Marines to follow via their optical implants, and right now they were using the closest open bay to the bridge that they could find.

Through the panoramic viewing panels, they could see the Ayleean warship's shattered hulk, tremendous damage throughout so that they could see deep into the vessel's superstructure. Then, the side of the Ayleean vessel swallowed them whole as the shuttle entered the landing bay.

'Deck Charlie, midsection, landing now!'

Agry tensed, one hand ready to punch his harness free as the other held his rifle aimed at the still–closed ramp. The shuttle shook violently as its landing struts slammed down onto the deck and with a hiss of vapor the ramp dropped under hydraulic force and the pressurized atmosphere within the shuttle blasted outward in a white whorl of instantly frozen crystals as Agry released his harness and dashed from the shuttle.

Behind him forty Marines followed in an orderly flood, running with their suits weighted at fifty per cent normal gravity to provide them with extra speed, agility and stamina.

Agry thundered down the ramp onto the darkened deck of a small landing bay, the flashlight on his rifle slicing into the gloom. The deck was slippery with ice that glistened like diamond chips in the flashlight beams. Agry ran forward and then dropped down onto one knee, his rifle pulled into his shoulder as behind him the Marines formed two groups and one giant arc of firepower pointed out into the darkness.

The shuttle's engines flared with silent white light in the vacuum as it lifted off and pulled out of the bay, ready to return when the soldiers required an extraction. Agry watched the darkness intently but nothing loomed forth to threaten them. His eyes cast down across the ice and sought any sign of footprints, but nothing revealed itself. Behind them, the landing bay doors silently lowered and sealed themselves as the shuttle pulled away into the distance, and suddenly they were totally alone aboard the massive ship.

Agry looked over his shoulder at his corporal, Ben Hodgson, and pointed ahead with two fingers as he looked. Hodgson advanced forward, his soldiers following him as they were covered by Agry's contingent. Agry watched as they descended cautiously into the darkness and for a few moments there was nothing but silence. Then a series of glowing lights flickered on in the bunker, visible through the observation windows.

Moments later, Hodgson's voice crackled in Agry's helmet.

'Not enough energy remaining for atmospheric heating, but bleeding air into the bay now.'

Agry's gaze flicked up to the vents high on the bay walls in time to see vapor billow out of them like dark clouds, filling the bay with bitterly cold but breathable air and allowing the Marines to conserve their oxygen supply.

Moments later the lighting in the bay flickered into life and filled it with a deceptively warm glow to reveal an empty structure with no other vessels inside. A red light high on the walls of the bay turned green, and Agry gave a thumbs–up to his men. They switched off their oxygen supplies and opened vents on their masks to allow the air in, but kept the masks on as protection against the bitter cold.

'Let's move,' Agry snapped.

The Marines headed as one for a series of hatches that led into the ship's interior, all of which were sealed. A schematic projected onto Agry's mask visor directed him to the hatch he wanted – the one that led toward the bridge deck.

'Delta on me,' he ordered. 'Charlie, maintain the perimeter here and see what you can do about the temperature. Any signs of life from the ship?'

'Nothing,' Corporal Hodgson replied. *'No incoming data so the computers are down.'*

'The Ayleeans are not aboard,' Agry reassured the corporal, knowing that he and his men would be cautious of encountering Ayleean warriors. 'But stay sharp.'

Hodgson nodded at the sergeant as he passed by the bunker, the twenty Marines of his platoon following as they approached the hatches and two soldiers eased forward of the rest without command. As Agry watched the two men worked efficiently to set small plasma charges against the hatch's locking mechanisms and hinges, designed to burn through rather than blast off. The two soldiers hurried away from the charges and moments later the hinges flared brightly with a fearsome blue–white light, drops of liquid metal spilling away from the hatch onto the deck.

'Rams, go!' Agry whispered.

Two Marines hefted a metallic ram between them and rushed the door, and with a dull boom that echoed around the landing bay the ram slammed into the smoldering door and it broke free of its mountings and flew away down the corridor, the heavy metal hatch flashing dimly as it rotated in mid–air.

Agry rushed past the ram and into the corridor, his rifle's flashlight illuminating the passage as several more soldiers thundered fearlessly in behind him, their footfalls echoing away into the distant, darkened ship. Their flashlights scanned the darkness like laser beams, but nothing moved but for the faint haze of moisture and ice clinging to the walls and to dense foliage and twisting vines coated in ice, the limbs frozen in position by the frigid cold.

Agry edged forward, keeping an eye open for opportunities for cover amid the frozen foliage in case something unexpected leaped out at them. The schematic on his visor guided him, overlaying vector lines across the corridor deck with arrows pointing to the bridge. The general turned left at the end of the corridor, glancing right briefly to see another corridor of endless bulkhead hatches stretching away far beyond the reach of his flashlight.

'Deck Charlie,' he whispered to his men. 'We'll ascend to deck Alpha at the first opportunity and then move for the bridge. Jesson, Miller, you wait here and guard the corridor entrance in case we need to retreat. I don't want anything sneaking up behind us.'

A whispered *Aye, Gunny* reached Agry's ears as the two men peeled off and took up firing positions at the entrance to the landing bay corridor. Agry moved on with the same deliberate, cautious gait. The corridor was long, one of the main arterial routes that stretched from bow to stern through the massive ship. .

He posted two more sentries, leaving him with eight men to ascend to the bridge, and then as one they moved into the stairwells and began to climb. The darkness was still bitterly cold, barely above freezing according to Agry's sensor readings.

The troops climbed up without incident and reached A–Deck, Agry maintaining the lead as he opened the hatches and stepped out onto the deck.

Hexagonal in shape and as dark as the rest of the ship, the bridge deck was dominated by two massive hatches that were sealed. Agry crept forward as his men silently fanned out and formed a defensive ring, alternating men aiming inward toward the bridge doors and outward toward various access points from A–Deck.

Agry placed a charge on the bridge doors, set the timer for five seconds and then activated the charge before retreating to a safe distance. The charge lit and burned with ferocious intensity for several seconds as it seared through the doors' locking mechanism, illuminating the deck with a flickering white light. Moments later, the mechanism glowed like magma in the darkness and dropped fat globules of glowing molten metal onto the deck as Agry advanced and waved his men forward. Together, Agry and two troopers leaned their weight into the doors. The general raised three fingers, then two, then one and then with a combined burst of effort the Marines slammed into the doors and they burst open.

Agry lunged onto the bridge as his rifle swept around for any sign of a target.

The bridge was darkened, none of the instrument panels aglow and the main viewing panel black and featureless. The flashlights of his men illuminated a series of control panels frosted with ice crystals as Agry moved forward and his light beam caught on what looked like a cylindrical panel, one of three mounted against the far wall of the bridge.

The sergeant eased his way toward the panel, his weapon pointed at it as the Marines behind him saw his path and target and silently formed up into firing teams, ready to blast whatever might come out of the capsules. Agry reached the nearest of the three capsules and took a final cautious step forward, unable to tear his gaze from the sight before him.

'What the...?'

The lights from the Marine's weapons illuminated the face of an Ayleean warrior, frozen in time it seemed within the claustrophobic interior of an emergency survival capsule. As Agry looked at the other two capsules he saw two more Ayleeans within, his Marines wiping frost from the observation panels.

'We've got survivors,' Agry reported in, 'three warriors, they're in what looks like cryogenic storage.'

Doctor Schmidt's voice replied as his projection shimmered into view, illuminating the corner of the bridge with a pulsing blue glow.

'That's not possible, I didn't detect any biological life forms aboard the vessel from here.'

'You said your sensors may have been blocked by all the stray energy leaking out of the ship,' Agry reminded him of the briefing the Marines had received. 'The hull's badly compromised and the ship won't hold together much longer. If we don't leave soon we're going to be joining these guys as permanent residents.'

A long silence followed, and Agry could imagine the admiral picturing the scene aboard the stricken warship and also the political situation. The last anybody had heard of the Ayleeans was when one of their warships made a direct attempt to destroy New Washington, one of the largest orbital cities around Earth. Titan had defeated the vessel and saved countless thousands of lives with Admiral Marshall at her helm, and now the Ayleeans were a spent force. Yet despite the admiral's insistence that the advantage should be pressed home, that the CSS fleet should deploy to Ayleea and take control of the planet for once and for all, as ever the Council of Governors on Earth had hesitated, reluctant to sustain a war-footing once again. Marshall had argued that the war would be quick, a decisive strike against an aggressive and implacable enemy, but the council had countered that the same had been said of the previous Ayleean War, which had dragged on for more than a decade and cost the lives of thousands of human soldiers.

Marshall's voice broke through the sergeant's reverie.

'Bring them back from that ship before it falls apart.'

Agry blinked in surprise. 'Seriously? You know what they'll do once they wake up, they can't be trusted after what happened at New Washington and…'

'Those were the actions of one Ayleean,' Marshall cut him off, *'not their population. We don't know what happened here but those warriors might. Once you're out we'll blast that warship and finish the job. No sense in leaving it for them to put back into action, but if we can save the lives of those survivors it might convince the Ayleean leadership that we're not intent on their destruction.'*

Agry sighed. Marshall was right, of course: a political olive branch now might pay dividends in the long run and nobody wanted another war with Ayleea, but even so he didn't like the idea of cheerfully transporting three of their hated enemies straight aboard the fleet's flagship.

'Roger that,' he replied. 'My teams will be clear in fifteen minutes. Have Schmidt on stand by to thaw these guys out and find out what happened to them. If this is another ruse, I want the warriors perforated with plasma before they can think to take their first breath.'

***

Dean Crawford

IX

San Diego,

California

Although a great many things had changed on planet Earth in the four hundred years since Nathan Ironside had left his old life behind, the crystalline blue waters of the Pacific Coast had not.

The taxi–shuttle descended down through a layer of light cumulus cloud and the city of San Diego glittered in the sunlight like jewels encrusted into a sandy beach, the ocean stretching away toward the west and a milky horizon.

'Now this is what I call heaven,' Foxx said as she leaned across Nathan to watch more closely as the shuttle came in over Ocean Beach to land at the city spaceport.

Nathan could see that the city was much smaller than it used to be, the sprawl from Miramar to Spring Valley now reduced to a patch of glittering skyscrapers that touched the three thousand foot cloud base, like giant glass crystals embedded into the earth. The spaceport was smaller than the airport that he remembered, no runways but merely large circular landing pads surrounded by dozens of smaller, similar pads and terminal buildings. He could see small craft catching the light as they flew out of the port toward terrestrial destinations around the globe, no location more than an hour away at near–orbital velocities.

Most all of Earth's cities were a fraction of the size that Nathan recalled, his own home town Denver likewise reduced to a patch of human occupation on a planet now largely returned to nature. San Diego had once been home to well over a million people, but now his optical implant informed him that just seventy five thousand people called the city home. Only the wealthiest lived here on the surface, and such a visit was considered a luxury by Detective Foxx, her green eyes gleaming and a soft smile touching her sculptured lips as she pushed a strand of silvery hair over one tiny ear and watched the city passing by below them.

'You see, hanging around with me is good for you. This is the second time you've been planet–side since I showed up,' Nathan grinned.

'Since you showed up I've also almost been killed several times,' she reminded him. 'But at least I get to breathe fresh air for a change.'

The shuttle landed on one of the smaller pads at the spaceport and a small vehicle drifted across to them, four seats inside and a low wind shield that apparently had no wheels and merely hovered just above the surface of the dispersal area. Nathan spotted a police department emblem on its side as he stepped out of the shuttle and smelled the wonderful scent of the nearby ocean and of air that hadn't been recirculated through New Washington's scrubbers a few thousand times.

Foxx led the way across to the police vehicle as its side door opened and a detective leaned out and shook her hand. Stocky, perhaps a little overweight, with thinning brown hair and an easy smile, he looked every inch the lucky cop who got the planet–side gig while the rest of the department sweated it out in New Los Angeles orbit.

'Detective Larry Samson, first precinct, San Diego,' he introduced himself as they climbed in. 'You guys on the Reed case?'

'Down from New Washington,' Foxx confirmed as the doors closed and Samson drove out of the airport, the craft as smooth as could be on its gravity–defying propulsion system.

'Must be a hell of a ride,' Samson pointed out as he switched the craft onto some kind of autopilot and stretched out in his seat, swivelling it around to face them. 'So what's the deal here? Xavier Reed went hands–down on the best built case we had this year, no contest from the defense or the jury other than the usual hearsay. What gives?'

Nathan replied, keen to take any flak away from Foxx.

'Questions,' he said, 'about motive and about Reed's record prior to the event.'

'You're investigating the motive?' Samson chuckled. 'You know that Ricard died from a plasma hit to the chest at close range after an argument, right?'

'Reed claimed that his weapon fizzled, that he didn't make the fatal shot.'

'Sure, that's what Reed used as his defense and it was rejected out of hand. His family screaming about it won't help, the guy's a convicted murderer.'

'He still claims a third party was involved,' Nathan added.

'So? These dudes would likely invoke the presence of Zeus if they thought it would get them off the hook! Do you know how many homicides we had in the city last year?'

Nathan shook his head.

'Fourteen,' Samson replied. 'That's more than one a month and the worst it's been for decades. The police commissioner's already been hauled over the coals by the governor about the rise in crime and he's not going to take kindly to somebody walking in here and overturning a solid conviction.'

'Even if that conviction turns out to be unsound?' Nathan challenged.

'You ever heard of a stronger case?'

'In my time,' Nathan said, 'there were a hundred homicides in San Diego every year.'

'What do you mean *your* time?' Samson asked, confused.

'You worked this one, right?' Foxx guessed, quick to intervene.

'Sure I did,' Samson admitted, 'but don't go gettin' any ideas that I'm fighting for my pride here. Reed's as guilty as they come and no appeal is going to dig his sorry ass out of Tethys.'

'Then you won't mind us taking a look around,' Foxx said with a sweet smile.

'You go for your life,' Samson said, and then glanced out of the windshield as a gentle ping sound alerted him. 'Here we are.'

The craft slowed alongside an old building that looked somewhat like a barn, located at the foot of the hills at Montecito Point alongside a low warehouse that looked like it had been boarded up decades ago. Nathan climbed out with Foxx and looked around them. The residential areas that had once densely populated the area in Nathan's time were long gone now, the rocky hillsides peppered with scrub and bushes, palms swaying in the gentle breeze from the coast that swept up the valley and carried with it the scents of the ocean and wildflowers. If Nathan looked carefully, he could just make out the centuries old foundations of the homes that had once stood on the hills, angular outcrops in the otherwise wild landscape.

'This is it,' Samson said as he gestured to the barn.

The barn itself was a bar, Nathan realized, devoid of tenants at this time of the morning as they followed Samson to the left of the building.

'Reed and Anthony Ricard came out of the side door here,' Samson pointed to a small access door in the side of the bar, 'then stood here in this clearing. Reed shot Ricard, who fell right about here.'

Nathan looked at the spot where Ricard's life had ended, his chest a black mass of cauterized flesh. The spot was probably no more than five paces from the access door.

'Looks like it happened fast,' Foxx said. 'They didn't get far before the shooting started.'

'That's what the witnesses reported,' Samson agreed. 'The pair of them walked out here and moments later they heard the plasma shot. Case closed.'

Nathan shook his head. 'Quite the opposite.'

Samson peered at him. 'You kiddin' me? Reed was caught by his own friends with a smokin' pistol in his hand and one really dead buddy lying in the dust at his feet.'

Nathan gestured to the door.

'They walk out here and shots are fired within seconds. Witness statements said that Reed led the way, right?'

'Sure,' Samson said, 'so what?'

'Well, if Reed led the way he would have had to draw his pistol, turn and then fire on Ricard. For his part, Ricard would have had to have been blind not to have reacted.'

Foxx stared at Nathan for a moment. 'The reports said that Ricard had been drinking heavily, enough that he could have been surprised by Reed even if what you're saying is true.'

'And Reed could have had the pistol concealed, maybe pulled it discreetly or even drawn the weapon and spun at the same time,' Samson added. 'It's not enough to question Reed's conviction.'

'It's enough for me to look further,' Nathan said as he looked across the clearing to the abandoned warehouse, leaving Samson to shrug indifferently.

The construction was sagging heavily in the middle, the timbers exposed without maintenance to the harsh Californian sun for decades. With nobody coming in or out for endless years, the interior would likely be littered with animal scat and other debris from nesting birds.

'Is this the building that Reed claimed the shot came from?'

'Sure,' Samson nodded, 'if you believe him.'

'Did forensics search it for prints of any kind, DNA evidence, that sort of thing?'

'They gave it a once over,' Samson agreed somewhat sarcastically, as though Nathan was insulting his department by even asking such a question, 'but they found nothing to support Reed's story of a third shooter.'

Nathan moved to stand where Samson had indicated that Ricard had fallen, and then looked at the warehouse. Two large windows stared back at him like soulless square black eyes, cold compared to the warmth and sunshine outside, the glazing smeared with dirt. He turned to Foxx.

'Kaylin, do me a favor and get on your back,' he said with a sneaky smile.

Foxx peered at him. 'Do *what* now?'

'I need you to be the victim for a moment.'

Samson sighed and strolled to the indicated spot. 'I think I know what he has in mind, and I know how to be a gentleman even in this day and age.'

Wearily, Samson sat down in the dust and lay down on his back with his hands clasped across his stomach. 'Good enough for ya?'

'Great,' Nathan said. 'Now, Kaylin, you stand about where we think Reed was at the time of the shooting.'

Foxx moved into position and stood over Samson as Nathan hurried across to the abandoned warehouse and found an entrance from which hung the tattered remains of a door on shattered hinges.

He stepped through into the darkness within, the air cool but heavy with dust and pollen trapped inside the building. The smell of rotten timbers and mold clung to his skin as he crept through the darkness until he reached the grubby windows and saw Foxx and Samson outside in the sunlight. Careful to stay well back from the windows, he shifted left and right until he figured he was in the right spot.

Nathan drew his pistol, checked that the safety catch was in place, and then aimed out of one of the filthy windows, sighting over Foxx's right shoulder at where Ricard would have been standing. It took him only a moment to position himself accordingly and then he called out to them.

'Okay, you can get up now!'

Nathan holstered his pistol and pulled out a flashlight as he illuminated the ground before him. A dense carpet of leaves and soil covered the ground, and he carefully began sifting through it as he sought any sign of anybody who might have stood here when Ricard was shot dead months before. Foxx and Samson joined him in the warehouse's shadowy interior.

'What are you doing?' Foxx asked.

'Police work.'

'The warehouse was scanned at the time of the shooting,' Samson said. 'We're wasting our time here.'

Nathan ignored him as he sifted through the debris and then slowed as something scraped against the floor. He shone the flashlight down and saw a dark patch on the dull gray flooring, saw more of it scattered among the dead leaves.

'What's that?' Foxx asked as she crouched alongside him and he smelled a waft of perfume on her skin, scented like the wildflowers outside.

'Ash,' Nathan replied, 'probably from scorched debris. My guess is that when the shooter fired their weapon a small amount of plasma fell here and scorched the debris at their feet. They wouldn't have known about that because they would already have fled to avoid being seen by anybody outside.'

Nathan stood and turned to Samson. 'How come this wasn't in the forensic report?'

Samson shrugged. 'No disrespect, but nobody was looking for it because nobody was taking Reed's claim seriously. Besides, it could just have easily been caused by somethin' other than plasma fire. Ash is ash, right?'

Nathan didn't reply as he moved to the window and pulled the latch before he tried to open it. The window moved freely up and down in his grasp. He crossed to the other one and popped the latch, but this window would not budge until he heaved his shoulder against it and it finally slid open with a grating sound, the mechanism rotting and stuck with the filth of ages.

Nathan stood back from the window and looked expectantly at Foxx.

'Okay, you've got my attention,' she said.

'Are you serious?' Samson asked them. 'What here says anything about Reed being innocent?'

'The window,' Foxx replied with what sounded to Nathan like a little bit of pride as he walked away from them. 'One window is jammed with age but the other moves freely, as though it's been used recently. It's the same one that I'm guessing Nathan sighted through when we were outside.'

Nathan turned and moved across the warehouse until he found another door, this one closed. He slipped on a latex glove and opened the handle carefully, pushing the door until it opened out onto a path that led to their left. Nathan ignored the path, and instead peered directly down the hillside before him, strewn with rocks and rubble from which sprouted foliage and hardy bushes basking in the sunlight.

'You think the shooter came out here and ran?' Foxx said as she joined him.

'Straight down that hillside,' Nathan said. 'With the chaos over there, by the time anybody at the scene of the shooting might have thought to check out Reed's story, the shooter would have been well out of sight and likely long gone.' He turned to Samson. 'Is there a road down there?'

'A what now?'

'Can vehicles traverse the hillside further down?'

'Sure,' he replied, 'there's an arterial route for hover cars maybe a quarter mile away from here that heads out toward North Island and the marinas.'

'Would your police department have any kind of record of traffic movements from the time of the shooting?'

Samson appeared to think for a moment. 'Records are normally kept for six months if they're needed in a case, but the law only requires three months of storage before data is wiped. But there are not a lot of cameras in this area.'

Nathan nodded. 'If I'm right then this was meticulously planned, right down to ensuring a means of escape that would not be monitored. The shooter opens one window in preparation, takes the shot, closes the window and walks right out of here and down that hillside. I'm guessing that we can't place a vehicle at this spot at the time of the murder?'

'If you're right,' Foxx replied, 'then they would have used a vehicle that had been tampered with, any tracking devices removed or switched off. There were no recorded vehicles here at the time of the shooting.'

Nathan rubbed his jaw with one hand for a moment.

'Scheff,' he said as he fished in his pocket and pulled out an image of the criminal Asil had mentioned back at the precinct. 'We need to figure out if this guy could have been planet–side when the shooting occurred.'

Foxx nodded and turned for the warehouse door.

'Let's get back to New Washington and bring him in,' she suggested.

Nathan was about to join her when Foxx's communicator buzzed. She switched it on and an image of Vasquez appeared.

'Yo',' he greeted her with his customary disregard for professional etiquette, 'I got a trace on the MM–15 pistol's base–code. Turns out the weapon was registered to CSS Titan before it was slated for destruction when the 17's came into service.'

'That'll make tracking them easy,' Nathan said. 'We've got history with Titan's captain, Marshall.'

He saw Foxx think for a moment, and then she made a decision.

'Get ready to travel,' she told Vasquez. 'I'm going to fly to New York and request access to Titan's armory. My guess is that whoever got that MM–15 into circulation down here, did it from up there.'

'Somebody on the inside?' Vasquez echoed. 'But why would anybody aboard a fleet ship be messin' around selling arms down planet–side. The armory's are as tight as can be.'

'We'll figure that out when we get there,' Foxx replied.

She shut the communications channel off and turned to Nathan.

'Get back to New Washington and help Vasquez and Allen track this Scheff down. I'll meet you there once I've finished up in New York.'

**

X

Tethys Gaol

The cell block was thick with loathing, the air heavy with the live current of impending violence. Xavier could sense it, could feel it probing for him as he sat in silence on his bunk in his cell and listened to the sounds of the other convicts talking.

Whispers flittered back and forth, chasing like demons through the shadows. Xavier could not quite hear what they were saying but he could detect individual words among the conversations that stabbed in his direction: *shiv, cut, stomp, slice.* The words slashed through his conscience like warring blades in the night as he wondered how long it would be before they came for him. He spent much of his time willing the attack on his life to arrive, the endless waiting far more corrosive than the threat of death itself, but when the attempt finally arrived he found himself wishing that he could sit in silence in his cell for just a little while longer.

The stomping of boots across the gantries jerked Xavier out of his lonely vigil, and he heard the other inmates clattering steel cups against the bars of their cells in anticipation. Xavier climbed off his bunk and walked to the barred doors to see four sticks making their way across the second tier toward his cell, batons in their hands and grim expressions etched into their features. Determined. Uncompromising.

Xavier allowed himself the hope that they were not coming for him, that they had some other business on the block, but the four heavily armed guards stopped outside his cell and stared in at him with bleak expressions.

'Turn your back, show us your wrists.'

Xavier complied and backed up to the cell doors. Manacles were fitted, snapped painfully tight around his wrists and then the cell door rattled open and Xavier was pulled out of his cell and turned onto the gantry.

A chorus of whoops and yells sallied back and forth as inmates cheered. Xavier glimpsed some of them exchanging wagers on his chances of survival as he was prodded along by the guards' batons, although at this time the baton charges were switched off as he had not yet done anything to provoke the guards. Xavier considered begging for his life, telling the guards that he was innocent, that he did not deserve *this*, that he had done nothing wrong and that most of the cons on the block wanted him dead only after a long and agonizing period of suffering, but he knew that they would not have listened to him. The sticks considered Xavier as guilty as the cons did, and probably relished the opportunity to see him pay for the murder of Officer Anthony Ricard, a loyal prison service employee so brutally betrayed and gunned down by one of his own.

Then, as now, the perfect storm had been created.

The guards led him around the gantry, not down onto the lower tier. Xavier knew that this was a break in protocol, that he was not being moved to one of the lower cells as most newcomers would be when it was time to join the rest of the population. He was prodded and cajoled past a row of cells belonging to lifers and saw in one of them two big, blocky, bearded faces glaring out at him. Thick knuckles grabbed the bars of their cells as the two lifers watched him pass by, their murderous gazes following him as he was led to the cell at the far end. There the tier ended in a thirty foot drop to the chow hall: no escape.

The cell door rattled open, and Xavier was turned and pushed inside, and as he stumbled forward so his belly turned cold with true dread and he wondered in despair at the way he had been betrayed by what seemed like the entire universe.

The cell smelled of crude aftershave, itself better than the stench of urine and sweat that permeated most of the block. Three men were squashed into the one man cell, two of them sitting patiently on the lower bunks and watching as Xavier's manacles were released. The third man leaned on the wall at the back of the cell with his muscular arms folded across a barrel chest, squat and brutal like a gigantic white toad, his jagged hair sparkling with lights like a psychopath's Christmas tree. Zak Volt watched as Xavier was given a last shove into the cell, and then the door rattled shut behind him and the guards left him alone in the cell with the three most brutal inmates in the entire gaol.

The raucous outside died down as the other inmates fell into silence, waiting and listening for whatever was about to occur inside the *'The Shock's'* cell. Xavier surveyed his meagre surroundings and bleak outlook, and decided to say and do nothing.

Zak Volt regarded him for a long moment before he spoke in a surprisingly soft voice, the voice of a man devoid of the need to project the violence and rage contained within.

'You're already a dead man on this block, y'know that, right?'

Xavier was about to reply but he found that he was unable to speak, his throat parched and thick with the same loathing that he had felt in his own cell. He settled for a casual shrug, as though an unofficial death warrant was no big deal to him.

Volt pushed off the wall and moved to face Xavier, a good two inches shorter than he but invested with such an aura of psychotic fury that Xavier felt as though he had shrunk to half his normal size as Volt's emotionless gray eyes peered into his own.

'The act doesn't fool me,' he whispered. 'You're scared.'

Xavier raised an eyebrow.

'I'm surrounded by a couple hundred men who want me dead,' he replied, his voice working all of a sudden. 'You think I wanna dance a jig?'

Volt stared at Xavier for a long moment and then he laughed, a bellowing laugh directly into Xavier's face, and in an instant Xavier understood why this man was so utterly feared on the block. *Unpredictability.* Nobody of sane mind had any idea what Volt would do next, and thus he embodied the unknown, of which all men were afraid.

'I like you,' Volt said, his laughter fading away, 'which is why you're gonna live today. But you remember this, Reed: I control this block, and your life is in my hands 'cause I got big plans for you. You don't do what I say, you die.'

Xavier was about to ask what he meant when he sensed the cell block behind him suddenly plunged into semi–darkness. A claxon sounded, flashing red lights illuminated the darkness like beacons of writhing flame in a Hadean dungeon and the cell door suddenly rattled open again.

Xavier turned and saw the other inmates howling with delight and fighting for a view of Volt's cell as the guards in the watch stations suddenly abandoned their posts.

'Fire drill,' Volt shouted above the noise, his eyes shining with malice. 'The sticks don't care about us if fire breaks out, so they make for the emergency exits. They practice it once a week. Sometimes, in the confusion, one or two cell doors malfunction and open up.'

Xavier heard running boots rushing down the gantry outside, and then Volt and the other two inmates strolled past him and vacated the cell. Two huge figures appeared near the cell doors, their beards glistening in the light as Volt said something to them, and then he vanished with his two henchmen and Xavier saw the two bearded lifers move to stand in front of the cell door, blocking the flashing red lights with their huge bodies.

Xavier had not been prepared for the kind of influence that Volt had over the block, perhaps over the prison itself. He was able to bribe guards to arrange events just like this, could control what happened to Xavier on a daily basis, and the warden likely knew everything about it and was idly standing by.

Xavier acted on impulse, knowing that if he let either of the men in they would overpower him in an instant. He bounded forward at the first of the bearded men and twisted on his heel as he thrust his right boot out sideways into the con's guts. The lifer folded over the blow as a rush of foul breath was expelled in a gust across Xavier's face. The lifer dropped to his knees as his companion fought his way past and reached out for Xavier.

Xavier dropped low, beneath the big man's reach as he launched himself forward over the fallen lifer and drove his fist directly into the second man's groin. The lifer gagged in shock and pain and he stumbled into the side of a bunk and clasped his genitals in both hands as his face folded in on itself in pain.

Xavier scrambled past both men and then turned, lifted his boot and smashed it down on the kneeling lifer's head. The blow sent the man reeling sideways across the cell as Xavier turned to the second man and made to repeat the attack, but the first man's own boot plowed into the side of Xavier's knee with a lance of pain and he staggered sideways as the leg gave way beneath him.

Both lifers scrambled to their feet, their bodies robust enough from a lifetime of violence to absorb Xavier's blows as they turned on him. One grabbed his shoulder and then hurled his bodyweight on top of him, crushing Xavier into the floor as the other yanked the cell door shut and slammed one boot down on Xavier's chest.

Both men looked down at him with savage smiles, their faces shining in the pulsing red light with a maniacal, volatile fusion of rage and delight. One of them lifted a fist that seemed as big as Xavier's head, and then the blows began to fall and his conscience retreated into some deep, dark place where the pain would no longer bother him.

***

XI

Brooklyn Spaceport,

New York City

The Global Express shuttle descended smoothly from hypersonic cruise back into Earth's lower atmosphere, the slender craft's variable–form wings gradually altering shape from razor thin to gracefully tapered as Foxx looked out of her window.

The first time she had been lucky enough to travel planet–side had been when her parents had bought a holiday at a resort near San Diego on the coast of California, a rare opportunity and one for which her parents had saved long and hard. Although only a child Foxx could remember the warmth of the sunshine, the sight of an open ocean, the life that had seemed to be everywhere, even buzzing on the open air. The planet had seemed so wild and vigorous and *alive* that the memories had remained with her ever since, seared into her conscience along with the melancholy yearning for her family who, like Nathan's, were gone forever. Her second visit with Nathan Ironside to Denver, Colorado had ended with her being attacked by drones and had nearly cost her life. Nathan, charismatic individual that he was, had a lot to answer for.

She watched as the blackness of space merged gradually with the pure blue curve of the Earth. The rippled blankets of cloud across the ocean below loomed closer, towering pillars of white vapor soaring into the heights, and the sky gradually turned a solid blue, the sun's yellow flare casting shadows beneath the drifting clouds far below.

The shuttle banked gently and Foxx watched in fascination as the east coast of America appeared ahead beneath the clouds. Nestled against the coastline she could see the glittering metal buildings of New York City like a sparkling jewel encrusted into the dense forests that surrounded it.

The shuttle slowed as it approached the city and Foxx could see the occasional flare of light reflected from flying craft travelling through the skies above New York. A small number of towering skyscrapers soared up into the blue, silver and chrome flashing in the bright sunlight and glass reflecting the blue sky and white clouds. Five thousand feet tall, the buildings overlooked the wilderness continent and the Atlantic Ocean in all their untamed glory.

The shuttle turned and Foxx watched as they gently touched down on a landing pad of Brooklyn Spaceport just after fourteen hundred hours Local Surface Time, guided in by the pilot who settled the shuttle onto its magnetic landing claws as the engine shut down and passengers began unstrapping from their seats and patiently filing for the exits.

The air that filled her lungs as she stepped out of the interior of the shuttle onto the boarding ramp seemed once again like the first she had truly breathed in decades, this time tinged with the sweet scent of recent rain, of forests and of the ocean nearby that swirled in a heady aroma as she stepped onto the landing pad and closed her eyes.

'Lieutenant Foxx?'

Foxx opened her eyes and saw a man in a sharp suit, the lapels of his jacket fashionably folding close to his right shoulder in the manner of the Central Security Services. He bore the discreet shoulder insignia of a captain, and his right eye glowed with the unnatural light of an optical implant that continuously fed data streams to him in real time.

'Captain Larry Ford, CSS. Would you come this way please?'

Foxx followed the captain toward a smaller shuttle, this one designed for atmospheric flight only. The landing pad was suspended a hundred feet above the surface on thick pillars, and a gantry led from the main pad across to a smaller pad where the CSS shuttle awaited.

Foxx climbed aboard and Captain Ford strapped in as the access door closed automatically in silence and the shuttle's Higgs Drive engaged. The small craft lifted off and glided silently out over the city, affording Kaylin a fresh glimpse of her Utopian surroundings.

The Statue of Liberty stood guard over the city's harbor as it had done for hundreds of years, now coated with a self–cleaning nanotech film that ensured she was always pristine in appearance. Beyond Foxx could see a coastline and a few scattered dwellings of the super–elite set against the vast forests that now covered what had once been New Jersey.

The island of Manhattan loomed into view, the soaring sky scrapers towering up into the scattered cumulus cloud and beyond. Kaylin marvelled at the sprawling expanse of museums, mansions and the CSS Headquarters tower in the center, dwarfing the Freedom Tower that had also stood for so many centuries. Central Park's angular block of greenery housed the wildlife sanctuary, where exotic beasts were allowed to roam in large enclosures for limited times before being returned to their native habitats, allowing the children of the elite access to them for short periods to understand the nature of the planet that had given birth to the human race. Among the natural animals such as lions and elephants there roamed holographic representations of dinosaurs so vivid that it had apparently become a rite of passage for college frat boys to stand firm as a Tyrannosaurs Rex stalked menacingly toward them. Few passed the challenge.

'What's the situation?' Foxx asked. 'Has my request been accepted already?'

'We got a priority signal from CSS Titan an hour ago that coincided with your request,' Captain Ford said. 'It's got the senate in a state and they're calling an emergency session. Thing is the call's gone out on private networks only so they don't want the media to catch on, and the session's going to be behind closed doors.'

Most politicians had what was loosely termed as a "back door number", a means of communicating off the normal channels that Foxx often considered uncomfortably similar to the illegal networks used by criminals on the orbital stations.

'Any idea what's spooked them?' she asked as Ford guided the shuttle in to land alongside an enormous domed building in north Manhattan surrounded by landing pads and hundreds of giant holographic icons denoting the flags of all Earth's historic nations united under the banner of the CSS. They were not there just to advertise the unity of CSS: rather, they reminded all humanity of the fragmented and untrusting nature of history's warring nations and the reason for the existence of the CSS and its archaic forbearer, the United Nations.

'If I knew, I'd tell you, but Director General Coburn is passing this information only in person and Admiral Franklyn Marshall requested that you be at the senate.'

'Me?' Foxx asked. 'What would he want me there for? Last time I saw the admiral he was about to embark on another cruise.'

'Titan's last tour was almost at an end and she was about to come home,' Ford said. 'Whatever's happened out there it's important enough to have kept them on station, your request coincided with Marshall's requesting the senate session. You got history with the fleet?'

'In a manner of speaking,' Foxx replied as the shuttle touched down.

Ford unbuckled with her and together they exited the shuttle, which had landed on a platform suspended some two hundred feet above the city along the upper rim of the building. Foxx followed Captain Ford inside to where two soldiers awaited them, acting as an escort as they led them through the building for several minutes until they reached the senate hall.

'They're in session already?' she asked Ford.

The pilot nodded. 'Apparently, they're waiting for you.'

Foxx felt a twinge of anxiety pinch at her belly as she followed the guards through two immense double doors, heard the rush of massed conversation as she walked into the cavernous senate hall.

The huge amphitheater was filled to capacity with senators, congressmen and other lawmakers all in heated debate, a thousand voices speaking as Foxx saw CSS Director Arianna Coburn standing on a podium that looked up at the politicians surrounding her. Tall, elegant, with dark brown hair cut into a neat bob and flowing senate robes of white rimmed with gold, Coburn spotted Foxx as the huge double doors thundered closed behind her. The crowd reacted to the closing doors, taking their seats as the rush and whisper of conversation died down and Coburn took the podium.

'Senators, Congressmen, representatives of the people, this session has been called due to unexpected events on the fringes of our solar system,' she said, her voice echoing around the huge building as though hers was the voice of a deity. 'I leave the explanation of what has occurred to Admiral Franklyn Marshall, CSS Titan.'

Foxx saw a larger–than–life hologram shimmer into view to take apparently solid form, the admiral standing in characteristic pose with his hands behind his back and his chin held high as he spoke in his gruff, no–nonsense tones.

'Senators, two hours ago CSS Titan encountered a distress signal sent by an Ayleean warship near the edge of CSS controlled space. Upon investigation, we learned that the vessel had been attacked by overwhelming force, its crew killed save three souls. The Ayleean vessel was unable to fire a single shot in its own defense.'

A ripple of uncomfortable whispers fluttered like a live current around the amphitheater as the admiral went on.

'We have since confirmed that neither CSS nor Ayleean vessels were present in the region at the time, and that no civil ships made passage here in the last four days. In short, ladies and gentlemen, we consider it possible that they were attacked by an intelligence not born of this Earth.'

Foxx noted that this final statement was met with silence. Politicians were not men of war, although in history they had frequently been war makers. She imagined that their minds would be empty of reaction because they simply had no real idea of *how* to react. Marshall's next words anticipated their lack of response.

'We have suspected for millennia that this time would come,' he said simply. 'It is perhaps good fortune on our part that it did not happen hundreds of years ago, when a defense against such technologies would have been unthinkable. Here in the present, at the very least, we have some notion of how to defend ourselves against such a threat and the means to study it as closely as we can.'

A further silence followed, deeper than the last.

'Do we have any visual identity attached to this attacking force?' Arianna Coburn asked the admiral.

'None,' he replied. 'They left no trace of themselves, whatever or whoever they were. However, data my Marines have recovered from the wreckage of the Ayleean ship pinpointed their direction of super–luminal travel when they arrived alongside, and it confirmed their point of origin as being the globular cluster M55.'

Now ripples of acknowledgement drifted through the senate, understanding beginning to form.

'M55 has long been touted as a source of intelligent signals,' a senator said to the admiral as he stood from his seat. 'Could this be evidence that those signals are indeed from other civilizations?'

Marshall inclined his head. 'It is likely, although as yet we don't know the full story behind the attack.'

Another senator stood. 'Then we don't know for sure that the attack was from some other species. The Ayleeans could be attempting another infiltration of our space, or the damaged vessel could even be the result of in–fighting among the Ayleeans.'

More ripples and murmurs of agreement from the crowd.

'Perhaps,' Marshall replied, 'but in this case I don't think so. The Ayleean fleet is severely depleted after our last engagement.'

'Have the survivors been able to report on what happened to their vessel?' Director General Coburn asked.

'They were found inside emergency stasis capsules,' Marshall replied. 'Our doctor is currently working to stabilize them before reviving them.'

'Can we really believe that an alien species' first act would be to destroy anything it finds?' suggested another senator.

'Mankind,' Marshall replied with a rueful smile, 'has done just that for much of its existence, invading the lands of other tribes and races, occupying with violence. There is no reason to suspect that other species would act any differently.'

Arianna Coburn spoke softly, her voice still carrying to every corner of the amphitheater.

'What would you recommend?' she asked Marshall. 'This is a military situation, not a political one.'

Marshall inclined his head to the Director General before he replied.

'I would bring the fleet in to the gas giants,' he said. 'Our solar system is too large to effectively police on its outer borders, something we learned when we were at war with the Ayleeans. Station the fleet to defend the inner planets and order all civilian vessels to withdraw to Earth orbit until further notice, giving us the chance to investigate further and see if we can't find out exactly what's happening out here.'

Another of the senators stood up.

'Eminently sensible admiral, but would it not be wise to contact the Ayleeans? They have been the victim of this attack and you mentioned three survivors. If we are facing some unspeakable threat from another world, should we not reach out to them and both bolster our numbers and the chances of success against this suspected hostile force?'

Marshall hesitated.

'I have considered that, but I would be reluctant to trust the Ayleeans to honor any agreement with us about…'

'Your reluctance is not the issue,' the senator pressed, 'our apparent survival is. You said it yourself: we cannot patrol our own borders for our fleet is not large enough. Have we even had any word from Ayleea itself? Do we know if they have had further encounters with vessels of unknown origin?'

Marshall lifted his chin. 'We have not yet contacted them. Our primary concern is Earth.'

'And yet the Ayleeans have a fleet and families of their own and presumably know nothing of what has happened here, admiral? Are we now simply abandoning the code of conduct that we share with them in the face of…'

'They abandoned that code every time they've attacked us!' Marshall snapped. 'Their survival is not my priority and nor should it be of concern to this senate.'

'They are still human,' the senator pressed quietly, his voice carrying the weight of history with it, 'no matter how much they may deny it. It's been six months since they attacked us and we have heard almost nothing from them since. If we truly are facing a dangerous and unknown enemy, then the enemy of our enemy is our friend, no?'

Marshall ground his teeth in his jaw but said nothing, looking instead to Arianna Coburn for guidance. Her chin lowered to her chest for a moment and she closed her eyes briefly, then she spoke.

'Send a message to the Ayleean warlords,' she said finally. 'Inform them of what has happened, and that they should send a dignitary as soon as they can. Organize a code to grant them access and escort to Polaris Station.'

She turned to Admiral Marshall. 'Bring the fleet in, organize a defensive line and prepare for whatever might be out there while we question the survivors.'

'And the involvement of New Washington's Police Department?' the admiral asked.

Both Coburn and Marshall looked at Foxx and she saw a softening of the admiral's expression as he recognized her.

'We need access to Polaris Station and Titan's armory,' Foxx said, 'as part of our investigation into a possible miscarriage of justice. If it happens that you require our assistance aboard Titan then we'll be more than happy to oblige, admiral.'

Marshall allowed a smile to crack the armor of his craggy features.

'As you all know, Detective Foxx and her colleagues proved themselves essential in solving a crime that almost cost humanity its existence just six months ago. I would not have believed that the same thing might happen again so soon, but right now I want the best people on the job to figure this out. I have specialists here on Titan in technology and scene surveillance but I don't have detectives. Lieutenant Foxx, if you're able to help us, we would be very grateful and I'd be more than happy to grant you access to the ship's armory.'

Foxx stood up, suddenly nervous as a thousand pairs of eyes swivelled to look at her.

'I'd be delighted,' she said, her voice sounding tiny compared to the admiral's booming tones. 'But I won't travel without my team, and we have one operation to complete.'

'Bring as many people as you like,' Marshall said. 'Just get to Polaris Station as fast as you can. We'll be bringing the survivors with us under quarantine conditions. Your team can meet us there.'

***

XII

New Washington

Nathan followed Detective Foxx to the squad cruiser, ranks of flashing lights flickering in the darkness and reflecting off the walls of buildings that towered into a night sky filled with billions of stars as though the heavens were reflecting the city below. Night had fallen on the Pacific Ocean far below, the gigantic space station revolving slowly in the absolute blackness. For a while Nathan could gaze upon the vast banner of the Milky Way stretched across immense vividly colored star fields, then he could see the Earth and the fainter lights of coastal cities against the darkened surface.

'What happened at the CSS Senate?' he asked Foxx as she moved alongside him.

'We got clearance,' she replied in a whisper. 'Something's got the fleet and the senate riled up but I'm not allowed to talk about it.'

'Not even to me?' Nathan asked with a teasing smile.

'Especially not to you.'

Foxx turned to the other police officers around them, her voice clear and stern.

'This guy's dangerous so no heroics, understood?'

Twelve police department detectives were amassed around four squad cruisers parked in a side alley on North Four, one of the station's most notorious slums. Even as Nathan scanned the stars above so they were obscured by a drifting veil of cloud that glowed a soft orange in the city's street lights, the station's air scrubbers as ever overworked to dehumidify the atmosphere. Rain would come soon to soak the city's streets a glossy black.

'Keiron Scheff,' Captain Forrester announced, his big black face creased with distaste as he gestured to a projected hologram of Scheff floating on the hood of one of the cruisers, 'aged twenty nine, one of the leaders of the so called *Prime Time* gang that spins the wheels on the upper east side here on North Four. Drugs, prostitution, racketeering and smuggling – you name it, they're into it.'

Forrester gestured to Kaylin Foxx as he went on.

'Detective Foxx has an informant who has directed us to the likely hiding place Scheff is using, which is four blocks from here in an old cinema complex that got certified ten years ago but hasn't been pulled down. We have it on good authority that the complex is deep within the Black Hole, so maintain line of sight with each other.'

The "Black Hole", as Nathan recalled, was an area within North Four that was filled with illegal jammers, making it tough for police to coordinate actions against the criminals and thugs that called the area home. The most notorious of the *Four Corners*, the external hubs of New Washington's "wheel" structure, North Four's streets were as rough as it got on the station. It was also the Fourth Precinct's most frequent patrol duty.

Forrester shut off the hologram, his hefty two hundred forty pound frame dominating the meeting.

'You'll split into three teams of four and come at Scheff from all sides, cutting off his exits. If he does get through, the squad cruisers will be waiting for him. We all know what we're up against here. The *Prime Time* gang favor bionic enhancements and drugs to give them the edge over us in a pursuit and we know that they're armed and willing to shoot to kill, so let's surprise them and keep them inside the building where their enhancements can't help them. Keep your guard up, folks. Let's go!'

Nathan followed Foxx to their assigned rally point on the corner of 15th and Mason, Vasquez and Allen hurrying to join them.

'This could get rough,' Vasquez said to Nathan, 'no place for a traffic cop.'

Foxx smiled at the jibe but came to Nathan's defense before he could reply.

'It was Nathan who chased down Asil,' she pointed out. 'I think that he can handle himself.'

Nathan glowed with pride as he looked across at Vasquez and grinned, raised an eyebrow and adjusted his collar.

'Yeah? What car were you in? Was Betty *Buzz* holdin' the wheel for you?'

Nathan let out a sigh of superiority. 'Betty was caring for a downed officer,' he replied. 'I was on foot.'

Vasquez's eyes widened and Allen peered at Nathan in disbelief.

'You chased down a Prime Time gang 'hood *on foot?*'

Nathan ducked his head and wriggled the tension out of his shoulders as they approached the rally point, ready for the next pursuit.

'All in a day's work, fellas.'

Foxx eased in alongside a wall as she spoke to them all. 'Of course, Asil got the better of Nathan in the end. If Betty hadn't buzzed Asil with their squad car Nathan would be in the morgue by now.'

Vasquez and Allen grinned to themselves as Nathan frowned.

'C'mon, I caught the guy and we were headed upstairs at the time,' he complained. 'Besides, Asil wasn't going to shoot to kill.'

'That so?' Vasquez said as they positioned themselves for the order to go in on Scheff's hideout. 'And you knew that *how*?'

Nathan was about to reply when Foxx gestured for them to be quiet. Nathan looked across the street even as a light drizzle began to spill from the clouds above onto the deserted street, halos forming around the lights dimly illuminating the old cinema complex opposite.

Nathan had been mildly surprised to discover that cinema had survived to the twenty fourth century, and had been informed by Jay Allen that although it had changed somewhat since his day the fundamental pleasure of the shared experience of story–telling had not. The difference was that this cinema had been a virtual world cinema, where the viewers didn't watch the movie so much as star in it themselves, right alongside their favorite screen heroes and heroines. A movie that featured hot–shot criminals, car chases and all manner of science fiction was still regarded as better when shared with a crowd, each person living the experience but hearing the laughter and enjoyment of their peers at the same time.

So far Nathan had resisted the urge to be hunted down by a Tyrannosaurus or blasted into an intergalactic war with insectoid aliens in perfect virtual reality, despite the encouragement of other officers on the force.

'Here we go,' Foxx warned them.

Nathan drew his pistol, watching the old cinema as across the far side of the block he saw one of the other four man teams appear in position, huddling against the far wall of the cinema.

'Great,' Vasquez said, 'how come it's always us who get to go in the front door?'

'Don't complain,' Foxx replied, 'the bad guys mostly run for the back door once we show up.'

Nathan's optical ID chip flickered a silent *"GO!"* order into his right eye, and without a word they broke from cover and sprinted across the street as Foxx pulled a single, metallic sphere from her belt and pressed a button on its surface. The sphere glowed bright red with slow, rhythmic flashes that immediately began to get quicker.

Foxx rushed up to the cinema's old entrance and tossed the sphere against the doors. It stuck in place instantly as Nathan and the rest of the team pinned themselves against the walls either side of the doors. Foxx dashed to Nathan's side, pressed her body hard against his and covered her ears with her hands, Nathan close enough to smell the soft scent of her hair as he pressed his own hands against his ears.

A deafening blast smashed through the cinema doors, plasma spraying in fearsome bright blue globules of light as Foxx rushed toward the doors through a billowing cloud of smoke, Vasquez and Allen coming from the far side and Nathan following Foxx as they ran into the cinema's darkened interior.

Nathan heard shouts of alarm and anger, saw figures staggering about in the lobby of the cinema as one of them raised something to point at Allen. Vasquez fired first, the shot zipping across the lobby and hitting the man in his chest as he screamed and fired his weapon, the shot going high and hitting the ceiling above them as all hell broke loose.

Nathan dashed for cover behind an old automated ticket dispenser shaped like a screen hero of some kind, an armor–plated warrior with metallic wings. A plasma blast hit the other side of the dispenser and it melted as though it were made of butter as sparks of plasma shot past Nathan's face along with a blast of heat.

'Forward!' Vasquez yelled as he returned fire.

Nathan followed as Foxx, Vasquez and Allen plunged into the cinema's interior through veils of smoke, flashes of plasma fire illuminating the shadowy darkness as though he were plunging through some kind of Hadean nightclub filled with warring demons. Plasma shots crackled this way and that as the thugs inside the cinema fell back toward the main amphitheater.

Nathan pushed on through the smoke, following Foxx into the huge amphitheater as he saw the other two teams flooding into the building from other entrances. The center of the cinema was level and flat, surrounded by seats in circular ranks rising up to where Nathan could see the police rushing in. Crowds of armed thugs fired from vantage points among the seats, debris and drug paraphernalia scattered on tables in the center of the cinema along with what looked like weapons and several women now sheltering beneath and behind the tables as the police rushed in upon them.

Nathan was about to descend after Foxx when something caught his eye and he saw a figure flash through the shadows and confusion and dash from the amphitheater, back the way the cops had come in. Nathan whirled and aimed but the figure was already out of sight as he instead dashed in pursuit.

Nathan sprinted back through the lobby and saw the figure ahead of him, a tall, lithe man with dark skin and a long jacket flowing like a cape as he leaped with inhuman agility down a flight of stairs toward the exits. Nathan ran hard in pursuit, leaped down the stairs and saw the flickering lights of the squad cars drawing up outside in support of the raid.

The figure dashed left and crashed through a side door near the exits, Nathan smashing through the same door moments later and seeing a flight of stairs soaring upward before him.

'Jeez, not again!'

He dashed up the stairs, slammed his pistol back into its holster and pumped his arms hard, dragging in huge breaths and expelling them like a freight train as he powered up the six flights of stairs and heard a door crash just above him. Nathan emerged onto the top floor and saw an exit door ahead that led onto the roof. He crashed through it and outside to see the figure dashing toward the edge of the building.

'Police, freeze!'

The figure ignored him as Nathan ran in pursuit, the side of the cinema looming up before them while the vast orbital station's interior soared across the heavens high above, far more vertiginous now that they were above street level. Nathan could see the cityscape before them rising up as though somebody had lifted it and folded it back upon itself, the transparent ray–shielding above offering a dizzying perspective on the rest of the city. New Washington's immense spokes soared away toward the central spaceport hub high above where distant vessels glinted as they slowed to dock, and he could see streetlights sparkling high above against the backdrop of Earth's enormous shadowy sphere filling the heavens.

The figure ahead of him leaped upward once, twice and then a third gigantic bound as he soared into the air and easily cleared the gap between the cinema and the next building on the block. Nathan ran hard, and as he reached the edge of the cinema roof he extended his stride and then hurled himself through the air.

The street yawned beneath him, three stories straight down and shimmering with the recent rainfall. Nathan hit the side of the building opposite with a thump as his boots touched down and he rolled into one shoulder as he slammed the other hand palm–down onto the roof in an attempt to absorb the impact. The air burst from his lungs and his vision starred but he rolled and staggered to his feet as his hand moved toward his pistol.

The figure turned as he ran, and Nathan saw a dark face riven with glowing blue tentacles of light and two red eyes that widened in surprise as they spotted him. Nathan followed the figure, saw him accelerating on legs pumped up on a mixture of biogenetic hydraulics and performance enhancing drugs. The man's legs suddenly burst into a blur and he launched himself across another larger gap, landing hard with an audible metallic thud as Nathan hurled himself in pursuit across the gap.

Nathan knew the instant that he leaped into the air that he wouldn't make the jump, the opposite wall just too far for him to reach, his quarry turning to see Nathan plunge out of sight. Nathan's hand flashed to his belt and he yanked a length of cable out, one end weighted as he hurled it at the top of the wall. A metallic hook flashed in the light as it flew across the gap and opened automatically, sharp four–pointed braces biting deep into the surface of the building as Nathan slammed into the unforgiving wall below and his cable tightened as his took his weight.

Nathan grappled for the line and scrambled up the wall, hauled himself up onto it even as the figure loomed before him and he saw Scheff up close for the first time. A boot flashed before him and slammed into Nathan's chest and he felt his lungs convulse and his stomach plunge as he was propelled back over the wall. He plunged inverted for a brief moment of time, falling headfirst toward the street below, and then the cable tightened again and he was flipped over in mid–air a meter below the ledge as his boots caught on something beneath him.

Scheff loomed over the edge and peered down at him, a smile revealing a mouth full of solid gold teeth that flashed as they reflected the streetlights. Nathan looked up at the criminal, pulses of blue and white light rippling across the bioluminescent tattoos etched into his bituminous skin.

'Looks like you're goin' down,' Scheff sneered, his voice tinged with a bizarre Slavic accent.

Nathan hung on grimly to the wire as he smiled back, the sound of approaching sirens heralding the arrival of the police department's cavalry. Scheff's sneer turned nasty as he hooked his boot underneath the metallic clasp holding Nathan from a fifty foot drop to the street below. A fine rain began to fall as Scheff heaved his boot up and the shiny hook unclipped from the wall and tumbled past Nathan.

Nathan pushed his boots further into the window ledge upon which he stood as he drew his pistol and aimed it squarely up between Scheff's eyes, the safety line still dangling from his belt.

'Surprise! You think you can get away before I hook this up and come after you, Scheff?'

Scheff's eyes widened and then he whirled away out of sight as Nathan shoved the pistol back into his belt and swung the safety line back up. The metal bit deeply into the building as he hauled himself up and rolled over the ledge to see Scheff sprinting for the next building along, this one far enough away that Nathan knew he would never be able to make the jump, cable or not.

Nathan sprinted in pursuit of Scheff, pushing himself harder than he ever had as the criminal's legs accelerated into a blur once again as he prepared to make the leap. Nathan hauled out more of the safety line from his belt, the hook in his hand as he ran and swung the weighted wire like a lasso over his head and hurled it out at the fleeing criminal's legs.

The hook flickered in the dim light as it flew across the roof in front of Nathan and clattered against Scheff's legs with a metallic clang, betraying the biogenic limbs beneath his pants as Scheff leaped into the air and hurtled over the ledge.

The metallic clasp bit into the metal thigh of Scheff's right leg and he heard the felon cry out in rage and sudden fear as his valiant leap for freedom was cut abruptly short and he turned in mid-air. Nathan was yanked forward as the cable reached its limit and Scheff's two hundred pound body pulled against his.

Nathan dug his heels in even as Scheff tried to dislodge the clasp in mid-air, and then Scheff plummeted from view as the cable snapped taut and he was dragged down into freefall. Nathan slid onto his back and rolled, the cable wrapping around his body and taking the criminal's weight as Nathan heard a cry of alarm and the dull thud of a body hitting a wall.

The cable yanked tightly about Nathan's waist and he winced as it bit into his skin, but he managed to grab a hold of the cable and pull against it, jerking it up and around so that he could regain his feet. A nearby vent belched steam onto the already humid air as Nathan staggered across to it, Scheff's weight pulling at the cable as Nathan worked his way around the back of the vent, the cable bending around it and taking the weight of his quarry. Moments later and with the cable wrapped four times around the vent, Nathan unclipped the cable from his belt and tied it in place even as two police cruisers landed on the roof and Vasquez and Allen jumped out, weapons drawn.

Nathan wiped the sweat from his brow and leaned against the vent as the two detectives rushed across to him, concern writ large on their faces.

'What the hell happened to you, bro'?' Vasquez demanded. 'Forrester said no heroics and you're out here leaping tall buildings?!'

'Scheff escaped,' Allen said, 'we thought he might have taken you hostage!'

Nathan chuckled as though he'd merely been for a stroll.

'Scheff's over there,' he indicated with a casual jab of his thumb. 'He's just hanging around.'

Vasquez saw the line tied to the vent and stared at Nathan. 'No way.'

Detective Foxx appeared from inside the second cruiser and replied for Vasquez.

'Yes way. We saw him dangling from the line when we landed. Nice catch, Ironside.'

'You're welcome,' Nathan replied, enjoying Vasquez and Allen's bemused stares. 'Not bad for a traffic cop, right?'

***

XIII

Fourth Precinct Station

New Washington

Despite his bionic performance over the streets of New Washington, Scheff appeared to Nathan far more inhuman in the lights of the precinct's box than he had out on North Four. Both of his eyes glowed red due to illegal optical implants and his dark skin was patterned with a lacework of bioluminescent tattoos that glowed a vivid electric blue and seemed to be slaved to his metabolic rate, pulsing and fading with each breath the felon took. His hair was thickly braided and trailed down his back like a bullwhip as he leaned back in his seat, managing to look unruffled despite the manacles around his wrists.

'Keiron Scheff,' Foxx read from his rap sheet as she sat down alongside Nathan, 'born South Africa, 2417. You've had quite the ride, Scheff. You'd think that being born planet–side would have done you some good.'

Scheff did not reply with anything other than a languid shrug.

'You're up for racketeering, drug running, evading arrest, possession of illegal firearms and biogenic enhancements,' Nathan announced, Scheff's eyes snapping around to meet his. 'Not that they did you much good either. You're looking at ten to fifteen in the Seven Circles of Hell so I'd start talking if I were you.'

Scheff smiled, his polished gold teeth gleaming back at Nathan. 'You're not me.'

'And he's glad about that,' Foxx replied for Nathan. 'Scheff, I can make this rap sheet double in length in the next ten minutes with every single possible felony I can think of, because you've got them all. I will also request from the DA a court order authorizing medical procedures to remove every single one of your enhancements, right down to those epidermal tattoos.'

Scheff's casual demeanor cracked a little. 'You'd never get away with it, it's 'gainst my human rights.'

'Which you forfeited when you fled the police and had your dirty little industry exposed,' Nathan pointed out. 'Can't have it both ways Scheff, unless you've got paperwork for your hydraulic legs. Not going far without those, right?'

Scheff shifted in his seat, showing the first signs of pressure.

'There's no escape Scheff,' Foxx said, pushing their advantage. 'And we got you down for capital one, too.'

Scheff froze in motion, stared at Foxx for a long beat. 'I din' shoot nobody.'

'Who said they were shot?' Nathan asked.

Scheff peered at Nathan and Foxx, his gaze shifting from one to the other like a caged animal seeking an escape. 'You settin' me up? You framin' me?'

'We don't need to frame anybody,' Foxx replied. 'We've got you down in San Diego, three months ago.'

Scheff stared at Foxx, all pretenses vanishing like a passing thought. Nathan knew that they didn't have any evidence of Scheff being planet–side at the time of the homicide, but he let her play her line as Scheff leaned forward and pointed one thick finger at her.

'I din' kill nobody.'

'Prove it,' Foxx shot back. 'You were planet–side three months ago, and guess what happened out near the hills while you were there?'

Scheff retracted his finger into a clenched fist and withdrew it, his predatory gaze never leaving Foxx's.

'How'd you locate my machine?' he demanded.

'Your what?' Nathan asked.

'His drugs machine,' Foxx replied, 'his hideout.'

'Somebody sold me out,' Scheff growled, glaring at Foxx. 'Somebody you must've busted and turned recently too...' Scheff's smile returned, glossy gold and wide as he leaned closer to Foxx. 'Asil. If anything happens to me, I'll have that little stool pigeon sliced and diced and the pieces sent to your home.'

'That's on record, Scheff,' Nathan snapped back. 'If anything happens to this "Asil" you seem to think sold you out, it'll be on you.'

'I'll take the rap,' Scheff snarled at him, 'better to do the time than be a snitch.'

'Your machine had it coming, Scheff,' Foxx replied, 'we knew where you were weeks ago and had your site under observation. You're not a big enough fish, but we were hoping you'd lead us to the real power people. It's only this case that's closed your shop and brought you in early. Murder one of a police officer, Anthony Ricard, prison service.'

Scheff watched her suspiciously, silent again as he considered what he had been told. Nathan knew that with his rap sheet Scheff couldn't possibly avoid a lengthy sentence, the murder of a prison service officer pretty much a death warrant for any felon, let alone an organized criminal like Scheff.

'I din' shoot nobody,' Scheff repeated.

'How do you know the victim was shot?' Nathan asked again. 'You've said it twice now.'

'Just assumed,' Scheff shrugged.

Foxx leaned back in her seat. 'You're never going to walk the streets again unless you cooperate, Scheff. If you didn't pull the trigger on this guy then you need to tell us where you were.'

'I ain't no snitch.'

'And you don't have to be the trigger man to be tried for murder one,' Nathan reminded him. 'Any involvement renders you as responsible for the crime as the shooter. All you've got here is the chance to clear yourself of the actual murder, in return for any kind of leniency you might be able to extract from the DA in return.'

Nathan watched Scheff squirm, noticed a thin sheen of sweat that had formed on his forehead. It interested Nathan that the hardened criminal was under pressure at all. He didn't think that Scheff had pulled the trigger for the simple reason that if the guy carried enough muscle to get Asil to run weapons for him, he'd have enough to ensure that somebody else carried out his killings for him, clearing him of involvement. A murder to protect or advance his own criminal empire would be something that he would have fought in court, claiming no knowledge just as he had before, and yet here there was something else…

'You didn't want to commit the crime at all, did you?' Nathan said, following his nose in the hope of breaking Scheff's wall of silence.

The glowing red eyes locked onto Nathan's and in an instant he knew that he'd cornered Scheff. Nathan leaned forward, pressed the advantage once again.

'You got dragged into somethin' here, right? You want to snitch on the shooter but you can't for some reason. Maybe you'll blow somethin' else wide open.'

Scheff almost trembled with supressed rage as he glared at Nathan, and then one thick fist slammed down on the table between them and he jerked back in his seat.

'I want my lawyer,' he snarled.

'We both know that's not going to work this time, Scheff,' Foxx countered. 'We can put you at the scene of the crime and in possession of military grade weapons. It's enough to send you down for life, Scheff, period. You don't talk to us now, the talking's over.'

Scheff dragged a hand down his face, the bioluminescent tattoos pulsing fiercely as he shook his head and looked away.

'Fine,' Foxx said as she stood abruptly and turned for the door. 'Have it your way. I'm just glad we finally nailed your sorry ass, and now we've got your operation opened up I'm hoping to find evidence of your past crimes too. I don't doubt your people will start talking now that you're looking at decades behind bars. Their crimes won't be on the same scale as yours so they'll have wriggle room and before you know it, you'll be looking out of a cell until the day you die – that's how it always goes down with felons like you.'

Foxx moved to the door, Nathan standing and following her in silence. The door unlocked and opened, and they stepped through.

'Wait!'

Scheff slammed a fist down on the table once again and Nathan turned back to him.

'Make it good or we're out of here.'

Scheff closed his eyes, the tattoos losing their vigor and fading to a tepid egg–shell blue as he spoke.

'I got a supplier for the weapons,' he said finally. 'The stash isn't mine.'

'That just sounds like an excuse,' Foxx uttered.

'It's th' truth,' Scheff insisted as Nathan moved to sit back down opposite him. 'I run the weapons, I don't use 'em.'

Foxx moved back to the table but she did not sit down, leaning on it instead. 'Scheff, this is your last chance. You don't give us something we can use, you're history and we go home while you rot for however many years you'll last in Tethys or whatever slime–ridden hell hole they'll send you to. Start talking.'

Scheff spoke in a voice that sounded as though he hated every word he was being forced to speak.

'The weapons come out of New Washington,' he uttered. 'We pick them up and route them down to the surface where it's easier to hide them.'

Foxx sat down alongside Nathan, interested now. 'Easier how?'

'Big wilderness,' Scheff replied. 'The orbital cities are too enclosed, too easy to bust operations if you get the kind of tip–off that a snitch–loser like Asil gives you, so we ship them down and bury the stashes. Been goin' on for years.'

'How do you avoid security?' Nathan asked. 'Every city's wired to detect contraband.'

'Sure they are,' Scheff said with a grim smile, a thin flash of gold like a mine seam in black rock. 'But security's only as good as the man monitorin' it, right?'

'You've got security teams in your pocket,' Foxx said. 'We'll need their names.'

'Like hell,' Scheff snapped. 'You got the info', you don't get no names.'

'Obstruction of justice,' Nathan pointed out, 'at least another four years.'

'I don't know the names!' Scheff snapped. 'We don't know who lets us through, only the times we have as windows to make passage down to th' surface. Same deal down there.'

'I take it that you don't carry the weapons yourself?' Foxx said.

'I look like an amateur to you? We got mules, they get paid to run the weapons down. They get busted, we stay clear.'

'Then who was the shooter?'

'The shooter?'

'Ricard's murderer,' Nathan said. 'If he was shot with an illegal firearm, which we're assuming is true because you were there, then you must have known who it was?'

'I jus' told you, I don't know. Just because I was planet–side at the time of this murder you're shoutin' about doesn't mean I was right there at the scene, right?'

'Then where were you on the afternoon of Friday May 12th?'

'I can't remember!' Scheff wailed in exasperation. 'But last time I was planet–side I was with my crew the whole time near Ocean Beach. I gotta be on some camera somewhere, check 'em all out. I din' pull the trigger on anybody.'

Foxx nodded.

'We will, so who's the big wheel behind this smuggling operation?'

'I don't know,' Scheff repeated slowly and clearly. 'All I know is that they've got the muscle to shift the weapons, maybe rank or leverage over somebody, I don't know.'

Foxx stared at Scheff for a long moment as though something, a dangerous thought perhaps, was rolling around in her head.

'Is there another shipment due soon?'

Scheff shrugged. 'They come and go, I don't hear nothin' until a couple days before we're due to run another one down. I tol' you enough, now get me a deal.'

Foxx stood up. 'We'll let you know what the DA says.'

She led Nathan out of the box and turned to face him as the door slammed shut behind them.

'You buyin' his alibi?' she asked.

'Most people can't remember what they were doing on a given date three months ago, I sure as hell know I can't. My suspicions would only be raised if he *did* know what he was doing, and he said to check cameras. That doesn't sound like guilty to me.'

'I like him for it,' Foxx said, 'but I get his alibi too. If he's just a pawn in this then the big wheel must be in the services.'

'Could be police, could be prison service, even military,' Nathan agreed.

Foxx nodded. 'Scheff's just the courier, we need to take this further up the chain.'

'That's a bad idea, it could alert whoever is behind this to what's happening.'

'We don't have much of a choice. Scheff can't give us the information to intercept a fresh consignment of illegal weapons, so we can't back trace the origin and find out who's behind all of this.'

'It must be somebody with direct access to these kinds of weapons,' Nathan said. 'Vasquez said that the plasma weapon we found on Asil was an older type, one no longer used by the Marine Corps. Back in Denver we used to have a system where old weapons and those recovered from crimes were disposed of or made safe as evidence. Does the fleet have some kind of disposal system in place, a way of destroying weapons so that they don't hit the streets?'

'Sure,' Foxx replied, 'but it's heavily regulated and controlled. Nobody could get weapons out of that system without avoiding countless checks and balances designed to prevent that very crime.'

'Where there's a will…,' Nathan said.

Foxx saw the gleam in his eye and relented. 'Okay, it's worth checking out but right now we've got a bigger problem. Reed is in prison still.'

'We need to talk to him,' Nathan insisted. 'We now know that Scheff was down on the surface at the time of Ricard's murder and had access to weapons just like the one that Asil had in his hands when I caught up with him. If he didn't shoot Ricard, then somebody else did. Right now we have enough doubt over the conviction to get Reed the hell out of Tethys Gaol, right?'

Foxx bit her lip. 'I doubt the DA will authorize his freedom, but we might have enough to get him pulled out of Tethys and placed in one of the holding ships. It's safer, cleaner, and he won't be a target there because we can inform the security crew that his conviction is under serious doubt. They'll go from mortal enemies to protective friends once they hear that.'

'Do it,' Nathan said. 'The sooner he's out of Tethys, the sooner we can take our time in solving this. I don't want to be informing his family that we cleared him of homicide right after he's been murdered. How soon can we get up there?'

'You want to go into Tethys yourself?' Foxx asked, amazed.

'If Reed's been framed, and by somebody inside the service to boot, then they'll do anything they can to stop us from freeing him. I don't trust anybody with this but us. You game?'

Foxx folded her arms and looked at him with a wry smile.

'What?' he asked.

'Nothin',' Foxx replied as she breezed past him. 'I just find your passion for this sort of thing cute.'

Nathan's chest swelled and he couldn't help the grin on his face as he turned to follow her.

'You find me cute?'

'Don't go getting excited,' she replied over her shoulder. 'I find kittens cute too.'

***

XIV

Tethys Gaol,

Saturn

'Wow.'

Nathan sat in his seat and watched as the shuttle craft turned after emerging from its super–luminal cruise from Earth to Saturnian orbit, a journey of just over one hour. The interior of the shuttle was not much larger than the private jets he had once seen taking off and landing from Denver International, but the exterior was much larger to accommodate the fusion core engines and the hull plating needed to protect passengers from the rigors of super–luminal cruise and the intense radiation of space.

What he found strangest of all about travelling in such craft was that although they had no windows, they had screens that seemed just like windows that offered a view of the cosmos outside. Nathan knew that when in super–luminal cruise there was nothing to see outside as all light information was stripped away after a brief flare of brilliant white light, and all that remained thereafter was the blackest of all blacks, a darkness so deep that it was said the only thing more frightening was to stare into the depths of a black hole. To spare passengers this intense psychological discomfort, the windows instead displayed a scene of stars drifting by in the blackness, just like he'd seen when watching space shows on TV as a child.

When the shuttle had emerged from super–luminal those stars had blended perfectly into the background of normal star fields, while ahead another screen had shown Saturn growing rapidly larger but, to his surprise, not so rapidly that it rushed upon them in the manner of a science fiction movie. Saturn's immense size meant that it emerged as a particularly bright star that grew for several long seconds before them as they approached at a velocity just below the speed of light, the rings becoming visible and the orbiting moons glowing in the distant sunlight before the pilots slowed the shuttle and the huge planet loomed to fill the entire cosmos before them, the immense rings spreading out to both sides on such a scale as to be almost intimidating.

Against the vast backdrop Nathan had caught the familiar sight of Polaris Station, the headquarters of the fleet. Like a tall, thin metallic mushroom twenty miles high the station was home to dozens of battleships, frigates and destroyers, its immense bulbous surface flecked with thousands of tiny lights and surrounded by gigantic docking bays designed to take the very largest of vessels.

'Where's the prison?' he asked Foxx as the shuttle sailed past the military base.

'Four planetary diameters from Polaris Station,' Foxx replied. 'Close enough that any prisoner who ever escaped would find themselves face to face with the fleet, and far enough away that they could never hope to reach safety.'

The shuttle cruised past the immense military base, and Nathan spotted a bright spot of light hovering above the tremendous span of Saturn's rings, one of the planet's moons in orbit nearby and casting a perfectly black shadow down onto the rings thousands of kilometres below.

'I still can't believe I'm seeing this stuff,' he said almost wistfully as they travelled.

'You'll get used to it,' Vasquez replied from the seat behind as he idly flipped through the digital pages of an electro–film, catching up on Saturnian news. 'Most people don't come out here though because only military vessels and mining stations have enough power to escape the planet's gravity.'

Nathan nodded. He had learned some time ago that smaller craft like the shuttle had to use very defined flight paths in order to dock at the relevant station. Failure to do so would see them plummet past Polaris into the gas giant's turbulent and lethal atmosphere, doomed to be crushed to death tens of thousands of kilometres inside the planet's ultra–high pressure liquid hydrogen core.

'He is kind of cute in an innocent way, isn't he?'

Betty Buzz Luther glanced at Foxx and winked once as she nudged Nathan in the ribs with her elbow.

'Tell me again how you got here, Betty?' Nathan asked, pretending not to notice how Foxx's porcelain smooth skin flushed with color at Betty's jibe.

'We're partners,' Betty said, 'partner! Where you go, I go.'

'We're just glad you're not driving,' Vasquez said from where he sat beside Allen.

Betty turned in her seat and glared at him. 'You watch your mouth, young man.'

Vasquez shrank down into his seat as Nathan rested a hand on Betty's shoulder.

'I'm glad you're here, partner, but Tethys is a step too far. We'll meet you on Polaris once we've spoken to Xavier Reed.'

Betty raised an eyebrow. 'I've arrested over three hundred perps in my time Nathan, many of them armed and dangerous. I can cope with a handful of delinquent convicts already locked in their cells.'

'I know you can,' Nathan assured her. 'But this is my call, okay?'

Betty frowned and then turned in her seat and folded her arms across her chest as she looked out of the windows.

The shuttle slowed down again and Nathan saw Tethys Gaol resolve itself before them in all its gruesome glory. He was reminded somewhat of an oil rig from his time on Earth, massive towers of angular steel that topped a bulky base ringed with what looked like massive buoyancy aids but were in fact probably storage containers where mined gases had been held for loading onto massive trade ships. Nathan could see large docks around the prison's rim where container ships had likely loaded up, the whole station painted a dull rust red, the result of cosmic debris and dust gathering and clinging to the huge hull.

'It used to be a mining post,' Foxx said as though reading his mind. 'Awful place, both then and now. It shut down when the automated mining drones were put to work a few decades ago and became a prison instead.'

'Xavier Reed has been there for three days,' Nathan said as the shuttle banked around and came in to land, the sheer size of the mining platform now dominating the already dramatic backdrop of Saturn and her moons, flashing proximity beacons flickering rhythmically. 'You think he's still alive?'

Foxx shrugged. 'I don't want to think about it right now. If you turn out to be right, he's going through an even worse hell than the criminals who actually deserve to be there.'

The shuttle was swallowed by a landing bay, a row of lights guiding the craft in to the prison's interior. An airlock bay closed around it as the atmosphere was normalized in swirling blooms of vapor, and then the next set of bay doors opened and the shuttle drifted inside and settled onto its landing pads as the engines whined down.

Nathan unbuckled from his seat and stood to leave, but Foxx remained.

'You're not coming?' he asked, surprised.

'This is your rodeo,' she said with a smile. 'Xavier's your case, and if you want Forrester to hand you a detective's shield then you're going to have to lead this one yourself. Vasquez and I will head across to Titan with Betty and check out the leads on these stolen weapons. You and Allen here can talk to Xavier, if he's still alive, and find out what happened to him down in San Diego.'

Vasquez smiled cheerfully up at his partner, who winced.

'How come I get the prison and this joker gets Polaris?' Allen asked Foxx.

'Experience,' Foxx said, 'Vasquez has history with the Marines so he'll be of more use to me over there and besides, I want somebody reliable to keep an eye on Ironside. These places can get rough sometimes.'

Vasquez's smug smile suddenly dissolved into a hurt look. 'You think I'm not reliable, that I can't hold my own in there?'

'I didn't say that,' Foxx replied defensively as Allen tightened his collar and winked at Vasquez.

'You head over to Polaris,' he whispered amiably to his partner. 'It's the right thing to do. It's *safer* there.'

Vasquez offered a dirty look to his partner but said nothing as Nathan turned and walked with Allen to the shuttle exit. They walked down the ramp, the first thing Nathan noting being the stench of oil and stale air, metal and a temperature that felt almost cold. Awaiting them at the bottom of the ramp was a giant of a man with a fearsome red beard who thrust a hand the size of a shovel at Nathan.

'Detectives, welcome to Tethys. I'm Arkon Stone, the warden here. I'm told you wish to speak with a prisoner named Xavier Reed?'

'That's right,' Nathan said. 'We have a few questions for him.'

The warden tilted his head from side to side and winced a little. 'Reed may not be much up for talking right now.'

Nathan feared the worst as Vasquez replied. 'Why's that?'

'He's in the infirmary,' the warden replied. 'There was an altercation on the block, and Reed got involved in it.'

'Can we see him?' Nathan asked.

'Sure,' the warden replied, 'it's this way.'

The warden led them across the bay, and Nathan looked up to see ranks of metal fences high on gantries above them. Behind the fences stood men who watched them with dark gazes as they passed by. Nathan saw one of the men tilt his head back and then jerk it forward as a globule of phlegm arced out through the fences and plummeted down toward them.

'Incoming from above,' Nathan said.

The warden side-stepped the spit with Nathan and Allen as it landed with a splat near their boots. The warden looked up at the gantry and in a deep voice that made Nathan flinch he roared an order to his guards.

'C Block in lockdown right now until the perpetrator comes forward!'

A chorus of whoops and laughter rained down from the gantry as heavily armed guards in black uniforms with light–shields and black sticks charged up the stairwells toward the block. Nathan saw the prisoners flee, some of them tossing debris at the guards before they vanished to cower in their cells as the guards thundered along the gantry, the cell doors slamming one by one.

'My apologies,' the warden rumbled. 'The inmates here know little of what it means to be civilized, human or humane.'

The warden led them into the prison proper, the corridors all lined with metal sheets that none the less looked aged and decrepit, paint faded and peeling, doors hanging from tired hinges that squealed with every movement. Massive pipes and cables ran along the ceilings, with sections of corridors separated by pressure hatches that Nathan figured had once been used to separate sections of the station in the event of fires or gas leaks. Now, they represented immoveable barriers to anybody other than the prison guards.

At a security gate a *Holosap* awaited, a man with a neon blue glow who waved them through. It was normal procedure, as Nathan had discovered, to grant menial work to some Holosaps. For them time had a different essence, the Holosaps able to function on a sort of autopilot and yet more capable than fully automated cybernetic organisms. Nathan recalled that the Holosaps were the result of the work of a British scientist in London, way back when the world was in the grip of The Falling. Working on a last–ditch attempt to save humanity's essence by recreating the brain after death in a computer, he had succeeded in creating human beings who lived beyond death and were of course immune to the biological plague that had ravaged mankind, as well as representing a means of maintaining government and structure in the event of the complete collapse of civilization.

With the emergence of the technology, in the remaining cities of the world that were still standing and containing people, the leaders and the wealthy decided to pre–empt their own deaths and voluntarily switch to becoming *Holosaps*. In an astonishing act of euthanasia they cryo–froze their bodies, dying on purpose to be reanimated as *Holosaps* to wait out the plague. There were around thirty thousand *Holosaps* still in existence, mostly individuals who for one reason or another were unable to return to their bodies due to malfunctions in the cryo–stasis capsules or long–term damage to body tissues and organs.

The warden led them through a long corridor with large hard–light windows that looked onto a food court where inmates were busily chowing down and paying little attention to the passing warden. Nathan could see them in their orange prison uniforms, faces down over their bowls of meagre gruel, shoulders rolling as they shovelled the muck eagerly into their faces either through hunger or a desire to get the meal over with.

'We have over a thousand inmates here in the prison,' the warden said as they walked, 'ranging from mid–level security prisoners to lethal status. Killers, rapists, armed robbers; you name it, they all reside here. Most all lower–level convicts serve their time on the Moon.'

Nathan blinked. 'There's a prison on the moon?'

The warden cast Nathan a curious look over his shoulder as they walked. 'What planet did you grow up on? The very first off–world prison was on the moon, and several of its wings still operate today. At the time it was considered the best place for most convicts as escape meant certain death, and psychologists reckoned that the sight of the Earth so far away was a considerable punishment in itself for their crimes. Time told the tale that crime on Earth was reduced by fifty per cent over five years after the prison opened its doors, so I guess they were onto something because every prison on Earth closed within a century.'

'How many guards do you have controlling these prisoners?' Allen asked the warden.

'Forty,' the warden replied.

'That's pretty steep odds if there's a riot,' Nathan noted.

'Not so much,' the warden replied without concern. 'We have numerous automated defense systems that are routinely tested and improved, and we have ten *Holosaps* on the staff who can access any part of the prison at will no matter what the convicts do to try to stop them. There's nowhere here to hide gentlemen, and nowhere to run even if a prisoner were to escape. We have a saying here for the newcomers: enjoy your stay, because staying is what you'll be doing.'

'Is that what you said to Xavier Reed?'

'To all prisoners who arrive here,' the warden rumbled. 'What's your interest in Reed? I saw the filework, he's as guilty as they come.'

'Filework isn't everything,' Nathan said quietly as they reached the heavily guarded and barred entrance to the infirmary.

'It's enough for us,' the warden replied. 'If a convict ends up here there's gotta be a damned good reason for it.'

Nathan and Allen said nothing as the doors opened with a screech from an alarm, the guards standing aside to let the warden through. They walked through the pressure hatch and into a low pressure walkway, the doors closing behind them as they made their way through and then passed through another slimmer hatch into the infirmary proper.

'Warden on the deck!'

The security guard inside the infirmary shouted the words and the prisoners all sat up in their beds or snapped to a sort of attention, many of them too injured to do so effectively. Nathan saw many of them were convicts who had suffered the indignity of having bionic limbs removed, the stumps of legs and arms concealed beneath the dangling sleeves and pant legs of their prison uniforms.

The warden prowled among them and they backed fearfully away, some of them climbing back onto their beds as though afraid of what would happen next. Nathan noted that there were no nurses present on the ward, only other convicts wearing identity badges that marked them out as people with medical experience.

'Where's Reed?' Allen asked.

The warden pointed to the back of the infirmary, where a man lay in silence on a bed, presumably too ill to stand.

'You've got ten minutes,' the warden informed them.

***

Dean Crawford

XV

Nathan walked past the warden and approached the bed, and already he could see that Xavier Reed was in bad shape. Although he did not appear to be incapacitated, his right eye was puffy and swollen with bruising and his lips were split by bloody scabs in several places. A medical convict raised his eyebrows in greeting to them as they approached.

'He's been sedated for the pain,' the medic informed them. 'He can't talk much right now.'

'What happened?' Nathan asked.

'Same thing happens to all police who wind up here,' the convict replied with a vague shrug as though Nathan were stupid.

'How badly was he hurt?'

The convict looked at Reed. 'Broken femur, broken left foot, dislocated knee, concussion, two lost teeth, fractured skull. Not too bad really. The breaks are all fixed but they won't heal fully for a few more hours, so he's not goin' anywhere. The concussion will take a little longer to wear off.'

Nathan was constantly amazed at the advances medicine had taken in the four hundred years since he had last visited a doctor. Broken bones could be fused within minutes using replicators that sampled bone cells and then accelerated bone regeneration using a source of the patient's stem cells, samples of which were kept on file in all hospitals within the colonies. Surgery was performed either remotely without invasive means or by nano–bots introduced directly into the patient's bloodstream, tiny clouds of biodegradable machines swarming to quell infection and stem the spread of everything from cancer to neurological disease.

Nathan eased himself alongside Reed. 'How you holdin' up?'

First impressions counted a lot with Nathan, as they did every investigator. Sometimes you could just tell at first glance that somebody was either a fundamentally good or bad person. There were few truly cunning individuals that could dupe a decent cop.

'Never better.' Reed's voice was thick with the swelling from the beating he'd received, but there was a glimmer of bleak humor in his eyes as he peered at Nathan. 'Come to gloat?'

'We came to help.'

Reed rolled his one good eye and looked away. 'Little on the late side for that.'

'Better late than never,' Allen pointed out.

'Tell us what happened in San Diego,' Nathan said.

'You already know what happened in San Diego,' Reed replied, anger now in his tone. 'My colleague got shot and I'm strung up for it. I didn't shoot him, he pulled on me first and then the shot came from behind me. I turned to see somebody duck back into the open window of a warehouse behind me, then everybody came rushing out and I got pinned down. Nobody would listen to me so the shooter got away and here I am.'

Nathan could sense the dread and loathing in Reed's last few words, the bitterness and disbelief that he was in one of the solar system's most notorious jails and likely facing an unofficial death sentence for a crime that he did not commit.

'We checked out the crime scene,' Nathan explained, 'and we noted a few inconsistencies in the police report from the time of the incident.'

Reed rolled his head back and peered up at Nathan. 'Such as?'

'There's trace evidence of micro–scorching on the panes of glass inside the warehouse, consistent with a nearby plasma shot,' Nathan said.

Reed appeared to take interest now and sat up a little higher on the bed. 'The original crime scene analyst made no mention of that.'

'Because they never searched for it,' Allen explained. 'Forty or so witnesses gave the same story, and it was so overwhelming that the uniforms didn't take the search for a second gunman too seriously. They did a cursory search of the warehouse but found nothing of interest.'

'I'm not on a hook,' Reed growled back. 'I didn't shoot Ricard.'

'None the less you're in here and what we've got so far isn't enough to bring suitable doubt of conviction to the eyes of the San Diego District Attorney,' Nathan added. 'Tell us what happened. Was there anybody else in the area, anybody that you saw before the incident, perhaps when you first walked outside or were in the bar beforehand?'

Reed sank back onto his pillow and sighed, his eyes closed.

'I was in the bar for an hour before Ricard got on my case. He'd been drinking, more than he ever had before.'

'Did he normally drink?' Nathan asked. 'To excess I mean?'

'Not so much,' Reed replied. 'It was out of character for him that's for sure, but he'd had a tough few weeks so I'd heard.'

'What was his angle on you?' Allen asked. 'Why'd he get in your face at all if you were partners?'

'You got a partner?' Reed asked, to a nod from Allen. 'Then you know why. You live in each other's pockets on duty for days or even weeks on end, and even the best buddies get tired of the sound of your voice after a while. Ricard kept complaining about something, I told him to get over it and it just kind of went from there.'

'Can you remember what he was complaining about?' Nathan asked.

'Money,' Reed replied. 'He wouldn't shut up about how he owed two months' rent, couldn't get the money together and was about to be kicked out onto the street. I told him I couldn't afford to bail him out but that he should quit whining into his beer and figure something out.' Reed sighed. 'He took real offence, so I apologized but he wouldn't back off and started to get right in my face. I lost it too and said we should take it outside. Last thing I thought he would do is pull his piece on me.'

Nathan frowned thoughtfully for a moment.

'So he didn't normally drink, things had come to a head at home for Ricard, he gets in your face about it and then suddenly he's pulling his gun on you. And all of that's out of character for this guy?'

Reed nodded. 'That's what I never understood. Ricard was straight as an arrow, not really the violent type at all.'

'And nobody saw him getting angry with you in the bar?' Allen asked. 'Witness statements don't mention an altercation inside, only the shots fired outside.'

'Ricard was holding it back in,' Reed explained, 'angry but not shouting. Most people didn't even notice there was an issue until we went outside, and then it was over in seconds. Ricard was drunk and I didn't know what he was going to do, then he reached for his weapon. I drew my pistol instinctively and I only pulled the trigger because I was convinced that Ricard wanted me dead, that I'd underestimated how desperate he'd become and that he was out of control. My shot fizzled and then Ricard was hit in the chest. The shot that killed him went right past my shoulder.'

Nathan thought for a moment longer and glanced at Allen, who shrugged vaguely as though he didn't much care for the story. Nathan pulled an electro–film from his jacket pocket and showed it to Reed, an image of Scheff on the film.

'You ever see this guy before?'

Reed peered at the image for a moment but then shook his head. 'No, why?'

Nathan put the card back in his pocket and leaned closer to Reed.

'Stay sharp in here and stay alive. I'm not going to let this case go, okay?'

Reed peered at him suspiciously. 'What do you care about it? I'm supposed to be a cop killer.'

'Your wife and mother came to our precinct,' Nathan said. 'They convinced me that you might be telling me the truth, and now I've met you I agree with them.'

Reed's stony countenance quivered, like a rock face about to crumble and fall into the abyss, and his voice cracked with emotion.

'You saw Erin?'

Nathan nodded. 'The beating you got, did it seem orchestrated, planned?'

'They left the cell door open last night during a fire drill and put me in with Zak Volt,' Reed snarled. 'The warden would have had to allow that.'

Nathan nodded, a picture forming now in his mind of what was happening.

'Yesterday on New Washington I was involved in a shoot–out where the identity of the shooter who hit a cop in the line of duty was real clear. Except that it wasn't, and the perp' we arrested claimed that the shot came from behind him.'

Reed gasped, almost sat bolt upright in bed. 'Same MO.'

'Same,' Nathan agreed. 'If this guy Scheff pulled a stunt like this off once he'd be likely to try it again, but right now he's not singing for us so we don't have a name and he alibied out for Ricard's homicide. Stay firm, you understand?'

Reed nodded, fresh vigor in his eyes now. 'You got it.'

Nathan turned with Allen and walked away from the bed.

'You really buying this?' Allen asked.

'Think of the bigger picture,' Nathan suggested. 'We're looking at Reed as the killer here and Ricard as the victim, but what if we've got the whole thing the wrong way round?'

'How'd you figure that?' Allen asked.

'Money,' Nathan explained. 'They pay somebody to make the confrontation with the intention of killing Reed.'

Allen frowned. 'But if you're saying that Ricard was involved in some kind of conspiracy to kill then why not just let him take the shot? The third person wouldn't have to be there.'

'That's the sleight of hand I think is at work here,' Nathan said as they reached the infirmary doors. 'The whole thing is designed to work *backwards*. The case against Reed is based on Reed's actions, but I don't think that the real killer wanted Reed dead at all. I think that the target was Ricard.'

Vasquez stared blankly at Nathan. 'Okay, now you've lost me. Why bring Reed into it at all unless..,' Allen's eyes suddenly lit up, 'unless you *want* him as the shooter to take him out of the picture too.'

'The person we're really after targets Ricard because he has money issues, probably promises him enough cash to clear all his debts if he'll shoot Reed,' Nathan said. 'Then our mystery guy kills Ricard while he's about to commit the act of homicide, betraying Ricard and neatly setting Reed up as the killer in the process.'

Allen rubbed his brows with forefinger and thumb for a moment.

'Sounds too convoluted,' he said. 'If our guy exists and he's so smart he could do the killing himself and never be found. Reed's a loose end they wouldn't need.'

'But then the police would know they're looking for somebody else, and would keep looking,' Nathan pointed out. 'In this case Reed makes some wild claim about a third person that nobody can find any evidence of and it's tossed out by a jury as fabrication. Nobody ever goes looking for that third person and they're in the wind.'

Allen shook his head. 'Too much could go wrong. Your mystery guy would need some real good reason to set Reed up to take the fall for the shooting and end up in here…'

Allen fell silent as Nathan's train of thought slammed to a halt.

'End up in here,' he echoed Allen's words.

'If they wanted Reed inside for some reason,' Allen went on, 'they would end up with Ricard off the picture and Reed where they wanted him.' Allen considered this for a moment and then a twinkle of admiration appeared in his eye as he looked appraisingly at Nathan. 'Not bad for an old timer.'

Nathan grinned. 'All we've got to do is go looking for our mysterious third shooter, and I've got just the way to do it.'

A voice replied from behind Nathan in a low rumble. 'I take it that your meeting with Reed went well?'

Nathan turned to see Warden Arkon Stone looming over him, his beard sparkling as though aflame.

'He's not talking,' Nathan said on impulse. 'Whoever beat him, he's refusing to snitch.'

The warden's eyes narrowed. 'You came here to question him about that?'

Allen shouldered his way alongside Nathan as he replied.

'We got word of managerial inconsistencies here in Tethys,' he snapped. 'Word is that you opened the cell doors last night so that the block crews could get their hands on Reed. That right, warden?'

Stone seemed barely to respond, merely raised one glittering red eyebrow.

'I've heard no such thing, detective. Reed was attacked after his cell door malfunctioned.'

'That's not what Reed says,' Nathan pointed out.

The warden drew himself up to his full height as he glared down at Nathan.

'You'd take the word of a convicted felon over mine?'

'Yes, if I thought that the warden might take pleasure in allowing a supposed cop killer to be beaten to death. Maybe you have a sadistic bully inside of you that gets off on controlling the inmates in Tethys.'

Allen stared at Nathan in surprise as the warden glowered down at them both.

'*Supposed* cop–killer?'

Nathan cursed himself for the slip up but rallied quickly.

'Xavier Reed was once a highly decorated officer and there are some question marks over his fall from grace. If any harm were to come to him in this prison, and it turned out that he was indeed innocent of any crime, then I would hate to be on the receiving end of the investigation that would tear through every inch of this entire facility, warden.'

Stone seemed to almost tremble with suppressed rage as he folded his hands behind his back, his voice cracking like broken ice.

'If there's anything else, detectives?'

'Oh, there will be,' Nathan said as he turned his back on Stone and marched out of the infirmary.

Allen almost tripped as he pivoted on his heel to keep pace with Nathan as they strode down the corridor outside.

'You just shoved a stick up the warden's ass, Ironside. We could do with him on our side.'

'The warden is as likely as corrupt as half the criminals within these walls,' Nathan shot back. 'If we'd left without firing a shot across his bows he might have had Reed killed while he's still lying in the infirmary.'

'You're accusing him of attempted homicide now?'

'I'm accusing him of a lack of due care and attention to the inmates here,' Nathan insisted. 'Right now we need to inform Foxx of what we've learned and get somebody to take a fresh look at how the evidence was collated at the scene of Ricard's murder, find out if they missed anything else in their haste to convict him. We also need to look more closely at Ricard and his financials before he died, figure out if Reed's right about these money woes.'

Allen nodded but frowned.

'It won't be enough to clear Reed but might get him out of Tethys and somewhere a little safer. You know, if you're right about all of this we still don't know why Ricard was killed instead of Reed, why he was betrayed. Maybe he was onto something that somebody else didn't want to come out?'

Nathan reached the landing bay and thought for a moment.

'Call Foxx, see if she can find out what cases Ricard last worked, what prisoners he was supposed to be assigned to here in Tethys. If he was onto something, it might pop up in his notes.'

***

Dean Crawford

XVI

CSS Titan

The warship's sick bay was state of the art, as was the *Holosap* working feverishly to maintain a stable atmosphere inside the three capsules as they were plugged into Titan's power system.

'Remember,' Schmidt said, 'these capsules don't work the same way as ours do. We stabilize first, then we reanimate, understood?'

The four cybernetic assistants with Schmidt in the laboratory nodded eagerly, their artificial intelligence systems more than capable of conducting their work with human–like understanding combined with the speed of thought of an optical computer. All of them were vaguely human–shaped machines built onto fixed pads bolted to the deck, and were equipped with four arms each and optical sensors far more advanced even than Schmidt's: X–Ray, Ultraviolet, MRI and Kirlian imagery systems allowed them to operate with extraordinary efficiency and repair injuries that even fifty years before would have been fatal.

Alongside them were four transparent lozenge–shaped tanks no larger than a human fist, and within each one was a silvery soup that looked like liquid mercury but was in fact a pool of nanites, tiny machines the size of human cells that were called upon to conduct internal surgeries without the need for invasive tools. Into each tank was inserted an electrically conducting probe, and at an order from Schmidt commands could be sent to the nanites and a small number of them injected into the human body through the skin itself with specific instructions to repair damaged tissues, destroy attacking viral cells or even regenerate limbs.

Schmidt allowed a small number of nanites into the Ayleean capsules of the first warrior in the line. Ayleeans were fundamentally human, divergent only in their own lust for mechanical advantage and the rigors of survival on their harsh jungle homeworld, Ayleea. Thus the nanites knew their way around well enough for the internal organs of the Ayleeans were essentially identical to those of humans, their path scaled up slightly to match the taller, more robust Ayleean physique.

'No life signs,' reported one of the machines. 'If they survived whatever attacked their ship, then their capsules must have malfunctioned.'

'Keep trying,' Schmidt said as he surveyed an optical hologram of the capsules and sought some sign of life. 'They got this far, they might get a little luckier still.'

As Schmidt watched the display, so he noticed something. On one of the warrior's vital signs displays, a tiny patch of heat was visible beneath the frigid surface of the capsule.

'Heat source,' said one of the machines before Schmidt could speak, 'growing in intensity, likely the result of internal metabolic processes.'

Schmidt knew that human beings had survived for many hours while encased within ice as the result of accidents, the decay of body tissues dramatically slowed by the low temperatures. Nathan Ironside, Schmidt's last long–term patient to have endured a cryogenic process, had been perfectly preserved for almost four hundred years, although Schmidt had often questioned whether the former detective's sanity had been protected as well as his physical body.

'Direct the nanites to assist in warming their core temperature,' Schmidt ordered, the machines programmed not to act without the direction of a human being or *Holosap*. 'Let's see if we can bring him back to us.'

Schmidt watched as the machines worked, guiding the nanites via signals emitted by computers that the tiny machines could detect passing through human tissue to reach their sensors. All of the nanites were constructed from biodegradable alloys and could only operate within the human body for a limited time before they decayed and were passed naturally by the patient. If the surgery took longer than the two hour legal limit on nanite existence, then fresh nanites were introduced to continue the work. The reason for the limits had evolved after experiments some two hundred years before when such restrictions had been harder to enforce. A few unfortunate souls had been over–implanted with nanites, which had swarmed together in sufficient numbers to result in *self–awareness*, rather in the same way that a single neuron was not self–aware but an entire brain was. The oft–feared result of nanites replicating out of control had almost become a reality before somebody had realized the danger and been forced to vaporize the patient before they had become ground–zero in an entirely new apocalyptic infection driven not by biology, but by machines. For the same reason all robotic creations, no matter how intelligent or benign, were bolted to the floor and had no means of independent locomotion unless specifically required for safety purposes such as in the case of emergency vehicles and bomb–disposal machines.

Machines, Schmidt smiled ruefully to himself, could become clever very quickly.

'It's warming,' one of the robotic surgeons reported. 'No tissue damage detected, no sign of cellular disruption. Hibernation will be reversed in approximately ten minutes.'

'Thank you,' Schmidt replied as he focused internally on his own location.

The sick bay shimmered out of existence and for a brief moment Schmidt was within a digital realm as he transported himself, or rather his projection, from the sick bay to the bridge.

It was hard for him to describe the sensation that he felt when he was to all intents and purposes no longer human but the digital "memory" of a man who had once lived. The movement of his projection took only milliseconds, and yet if he wanted it to he could take a year over it for time seemed not to flow in this strange and mysterious netherworld of existence and non–existence. Reduced to a burst of flowing electrons, Schmidt had no sense of a body and yet he was fully aware. He felt neither trapped nor free, alive nor dead, excited nor dismayed by the knowledge and awareness of his ephemeral form. He was surrounded by a comforting light, a perfect temperature although it of course had no actual temperature that he could detect and thus was irrelevant: his presence was both infinitesimally small and as large as the universe, and he could "travel" anywhere for his digital perception of his surroundings were as real as the world he inhabited. Schmidt had voyaged across the cosmos, orbited the most massive of black holes, seen the past and imagined the future in the ultimate virtual world.

For now though, duty compelled him to appear on Titan's bridge right alongside the admiral.

'Boo.'

Marshall flinched, still unaccustomed to Schmidt's peculiar sense of humor.

'You do that again, I swear I'll switch you off. What's the situation with our new passengers?'

'One appears to be alive and recovering,' Schmidt reported, 'the other two are touch and go.'

Marshall nodded, apparently satisfied. 'How long before it regains consciousness?'

'*It* is a *he*,' Schmidt scolded, 'and *he* will be conscious within ten minutes or so.'

Marshall turned from the command platform and glanced at the XO, Olsen.

'You have the bridge,' he said. 'I want to be there when *it* wakes up.'

Schmidt scowled in disappointment. 'They are as human as we are.'

'You're not human,' Marshall reminded Schmidt without looking back as he walked toward the bridge exit.

'Fear and prejudice are the currency of mankind, to lash out far easier than to reach out,' Schmidt droned as Marshall continued to walk away.

'Meet me in the sick bay.'

*

Admiral Marshall strode onto the sick bay two minutes later and watched as the surgeons monitored the capsule as the Ayleean within was gradually warmed, Schmidt fussing over them and generally worrying about the whole process. The doctor's duty of equal care for all life was undoubted and unquestioned, but for Marshall willingly saving the life of an Ayleean had been a hard decision to make and one that he wasn't sure he wouldn't later regret.

The bay was mostly filled with gravity beds that were empty, few sick crew members present as Schmidt approached the admiral.

'He's almost hypothermically viable,' the doctor reported, 'and we've extracted him from the capsule but placed him in full manacles.'

'Good,' Marshall replied, noting the eight armed Marines posted around the sick bay, all of them watching the Ayleean lying now on the gravity bed before them.

The Aleeyan was eight feet tall and bore only a superficial resemblance to a human being. A powerful musculature was visible beneath a hard, leathery skin that was mostly dark brown but flecked with patches of lighter color, almost gold. Dressed in metallic armor that covered approximately half of the Aleeyan's body, the rest was naked but for the thin, skin–like nano–carbon fiber shielding that the species traditionally wore. Its head was a tangled mess of thick black hair surrounding a heavy jaw and hunched shoulders. One eye was covered by a device that seemed to be some kind of laser sight, a thin red beam flickering as it caught on dust motes in the air. The Aleeyan had small, sharp teeth that had been ritualistically filed, its lips thin and regressed as though the creature was showing a permanent snarl.

Marshall recoiled inwardly from the sight of the creature, something so human and yet so utterly removed from anything that he was capable of considering human that he had to physically resist the urge to draw his service pistol and vaporize the horrendous creature where it lay on the bed.

'How long?' he asked.

Schmidt glanced at the surgeons and one of them replied without turning its mechanical head toward the admiral.

'Sixty seconds.'

Marshall turned to the handful of other patients all watching the exchange fearfully. 'Clear the bay.'

The Marines complied quickly, but not as quickly as the patients who filed in silence out of the bay and were gone within seconds. Moments later, Marshall heard a low and guttural growl.

The Ayleean shifted on the bed, its muscular limbs twitching sporadically as it slowly regained consciousness. Marshall remained in position, his hands behind his back as he fought the urge to take a pace back from the Ayleean as its fearsome yellow eye suddenly flickered open. The manacles around its wrists clinked as it lifted its arms, and that hunter's eye swivelled around to glare at Marshall.

The Ayleean let out a horrendous shriek of outrage and the Marines dashed in, plasma rifles pulled into their shoulders and aimed directly at the warrior as it glared left and right and then down at the restraints pinning it in place.

Marshall stepped a pace closer, detected the primal scents of leathery flesh and bad breath, metal and musky skin.

'You're safe,' he said, knowing that the Ayleeans still understood human language, their own vocabulary a sort of Pigdin English.

The Ayleean snarled at the admiral. 'Set me free, coward! Where am I?!'

'CSS Titan,' Marshall replied. 'You're in the care of our doctors and...'

'You attacked my ship!' the Ayleean roared, the metal restrains clanging as they were pulled taut. 'I'm not safe!'

'We didn't attack your ship,' Marshall insisted. 'We detected an emergency distress signal and we responded. We found what was left of your vessel, yourself and two others encased in survival capsules. What happened to you?'

The Ayleean peered at them suspiciously. 'We were attacked, I don't know by whom. We were overwhelmed.'

Marshall stepped closer to the Ayleean, concern flickering like a dim beacon in an immense darkness. 'Overwhelmed by what?'

The Ayleean stared at him for a moment longer, and perhaps he recognized something in the admiral's eyes that convinced him that the humans were not responsible for whatever had destroyed their vessel. To Marshall's amazement, the Ayleean stopped straining against his bonds and spoke with an urgency, a fear even, the like of which Marshall had never encountered from the species.

'They came out of nowhere,' the warrior growled, 'too many, too much firepower. We were obliterated before we even knew what hit us. Engines gone, crew annihilated, no weapons to return fire. I and a few others made a run for the capsules in the hope that they would think us all dead and pass us by.'

Marshall began to experience a deep sense of dread as he looked into the warrior's eye.

'Did you get a look at them? Were they pirates with some kind of new weapon?'

The Ayleean shook his head slowly.

'They were not pirates,' he replied. 'They weren't even human. There's something out there and it's hunting us, hunting anything it encounters.'

***

XVII

Polaris Station

'Back here, again.'

Detective Vasquez had served almost a decade upon the legendary military station, still by far the largest orbital platform ever constructed by humanity. At some twenty miles in height, and four in circumference, the orbital space station resembled in some respects a giant mushroom with a vertical tail extending down and a spire up from its center, the entire station located in orbit around Saturn's gigantic rings.

The spectacular panorama of the gas giant's pale hue and the vast rings was eclipsed by the station's angular, steel gray bulk as the shuttle moved in toward one of the smaller landing bays around its outer rim. Foxx watched as her companion gazed out at the vast platform, at the constellation of tiny lights flickering around the enormous ring–shaped body, home to some seven thousand fleet personnel on a rotational basis.

Vasquez had served with the Marines before joining the police force in his native New Washington, his military training a vital asset to the force which coveted its former soldier recruits. Foxx knew little of Vasquez's service history, other than he had served in the Second Ayleean War before being honorably discharged.

'Home from home?' Betty asked. 'My guess is Marines. You miss it?'

Foxx leaned forward and saw in revetments sunk into the station the sight of massive warships belonging to the CSS fleet, anchored in their bays as routine servicing on their immense hulls was carried out by both human and robotic hands. Smaller shuttles on ferry flights reflected the sunlight as they flew out of the station and turned onto headings for other locations in the solar system as Foxx's shuttle slowed and glided with the effortless grace of space flight toward the landing bays.

'Not so much,' Vasquez replied to Betty, still gazing out at the vast station. 'I was glad to get out.'

'Did you contact Titan's armory?' Foxx asked him as the shuttle flew into Polaris's enormous landing bay and touched down.

'Sure,' Vasquez replied, not taking his eyes off the spectacular view until it was entirely blocked by the more mundane interior of the landing bay. 'A sergeant there told me that no weapons had gone missing from the armory in years, so we must be mistaken. They have their inventory ready and we've been given access to all but the most classified of weapons.'

Foxx frowned. 'That's not access to everything though, is it,' she pointed out. 'We're looking for somebody who's actively trying to smuggle weapons.'

'Yeah, MM–15 pistols, not some heavily guarded super–weapon,' Vasquez pointed out. 'If there's one place that's going to be secure on that score it's the ship's armory. There must be something else going on here.'

Foxx shrugged as she followed Vasquez off the shuttle's boarding ramp and into the largest landing bay she'd ever seen. Rank after rank of shuttles and fighters were parked in multiple lines, some of them suspended from overhead cranes as crews worked on them.

'Now there are some beauties I'd like to get my hands on,' Betty beamed as she surveyed the ranks of sleek *Phantom* fighters.

Despite its gargantuan size the bay was immaculately clean, the sound of machinery humming or whining in the background and the smell of ion fuel and lubricants tainting the air.

'Detective Foxx?'

Foxx turned to see a bulky, fit looking man in a CSS uniform extend his hand to her. 'Sergeant Higgins, you're here for the armory.'

It wasn't a question and both Foxx and Vasquez stepped in line with the sergeant as he gestured toward an exit to their right.

'We have evidence of former military weapons showing up on the streets of the orbital cities and even on the surface,' Foxx replied, her own clipped tones mimicking those of the sergeant. 'We're here to see if we can back trace the leak.'

'There's no leak,' Higgins replied tersely. 'I can assure you of that.'

'These weapons didn't show up out of thin air,' Vasquez said. 'This armory is the only place that decommissioned weapons are sent to after service.'

'That's right,' Higgins said as they walked out of the bay and down a long, immaculately polished corridor lined with soft blue strips of light, 'and this is where they stay. All weapons are uniquely tagged and catalogued before going into storage or being destroyed. We haven't had a single firearm go missing for decades, and certainly not since I took over.'

'You run the armory?' Betty asked.

'Not the whole thing, but I control what comes in and what goes out, what form it's in, how it's catalogued. If somebody's been lifting weapons out of the armory, then it's me.'

Foxx blinked at the sergeant's forthright statement. 'So you're admitting to murder?'

Higgins stopped in his tracks and looked at her. 'You're investigating a homicide?'

'The murder of a man named Anthony Ricard in San Diego,' Vasquez replied. 'Although this line of enquiry is not yet directly connected to the homicide case, we believe that the two may be linked.'

Higgins started walking again, a little slower this time. 'What was the murder weapon?'

'We don't know right now, beyond the fact that it was a plasma charge that killed Anthony Ricard,' Foxx replied. 'However, in a case on New Washington we recovered from a known criminal an MM–15 plasma pistol.'

'Former Marine service weapon,' Higgins replied as they walked, 'decommissioned a few years back. They're all stored here in the armory.'

'How come they're not destroyed?' Foxx asked.

'Prudence,' Higgins replied. 'If another war with the Ayleeans kicked off, we'd prefer to have too many weapons than not enough. The MM–15s are kept here in the expectation that we'll need them again some day.'

Higgins led them to a set of steel doors guarded by four Marines. Foxx and Allen waited as their ID chips were scanned, and then the Marines let them through into a chamber, the doors shutting behind them.

'Full body scan and weapons detectors,' Higgins explained as they stood in the chamber.

'We're both armed,' Foxx said. 'Betty isn't.'

'The scanners will have already detected your service weapons and matched them to the police force database,' Vasquez told her. 'We'll be cleared shortly.'

Sergeant Higgins glanced over his shoulder at Vasquez. 'You been here before?'

'Fourth Marines,' Vasquez replied.

Moments later, a small green light appeared on the doors before them and they were allowed access into the outer armory, where two soldiers manned a desk and another security gate. One of the men was human, the other a military *Holosap* who greeted the sergeant with a sharp salute.

'At ease,' Higgins replied as he gestured to the two detectives. 'Ryan, would you escort these two detectives to the main armory. Give them everything that they need.'

Vasquez's eyes widened as he stared at the *Holosap*. 'Ryan?!'

The Holosap stared back at Vasquez and a mixture of amazement and joy burst upon his features. 'Vasquez the Vacant!'

The *Holosap* vanished from the security desk and appeared right alongside Vasquez. 'Holy crap, bro'!'

'You two know each other?' Foxx asked.

'Hell yeah!' Vasquez said as he made to embrace the Holosap and then hesitated as his hands passed through Ryan's shimmering blue projection. The two men shifted position to try to shake hands instead, and then Ryan sighed and shrugged, slightly embarrassed.

'Guess we can't do all that so easily these days,' Vasquez said.

'Not so much.'

'Did you two serve together?' Sergeant Higgins asked.

'You bet,' Ryan nodded eagerly. 'Two tours outside of Ayleea, CSS Perseus. We got into some right gigs man, I mean, sergeant.'

'At ease, Ryan,' Higgins smiled. 'Why not take an hour off with these guys? I'll have Seavers come in and take over your post.'

Ryan saluted sharply in delight, and turned to Vasquez. 'Armory's this way. Now, what's this about a homicide, bro'?'

Vasquez filled in his old Marine buddy as Foxx followed, feeling oddly excluded now that Nathan was away on Tethys. She had often been the odd one out at work, Vasquez and Allen working so closely together, like brothers, and she their commanding officer and a woman to boot. But with Nathan suddenly on the scene there had developed a sort of balance, the four of them working together more easily as a team, more equally. In some ways she regretted having Ironside put onto traffic, but he was a stranger in a strange land and it had been the best way to get him some street time to bring him up to speed in New Washington. She didn't like to admit it to herself, and would never do so to anybody else, but she liked having Ironside around again.

'Yo, Lieutenant?' Foxx blinked as Vasquez called her. 'Ryan here wants to know...'

'Don't tell her I said that!' Ryan snapped.

'...how military officers are ugly and squat, but police officers got so hot?'

Betty shoved her way in front of Foxx. 'It's in our genes,' she said as she put one hand on her hip and looked Vasquez appraisingly up and down.

Foxx managed to hide her smile as she replied to Ryan. 'And the upbringing. How did you meet Vasquez?'

'Bad luck and trouble, ma'am,' Ryan beamed, 'same Marine platoon for four years, until I got my ass blown off in an Ayleean attack.'

Vasquez's smile faded slowly. 'That was a bad day, man.'

Ryan nodded. 'I know but hey, I got me a lucky ticket and I'm still here! Marines were short on manpower back in the Ayleean War and they needed hands back in support roles, so I got a free ride to eternity as a Holosap. I ain't complainin'.'

'You don't miss the beer?' Vasquez asked, 'and the women?'

Ryan sniggered and jabbed Vasquez in the ribs, his translucent elbow vanishing briefly into Vasquez's body. 'Man, as a *Holosap* you can have everythin' you want, it's all just the same except it doesn't cost you anything!'

Foxx figured that Ryan wasn't worried about having kids or a wife, or perhaps just hadn't thought about that yet, as she followed the two men. Maybe when a *Holosap* was uploaded they stayed the same age, with the same mentality and outlook on life, like some digital Peter Pan, unable to grow up.

'Why'd you call him Vasquez the Vacant?' she asked Ryan.

Vasquez's humor withered as Ryan chuckled out loud. 'We were doing a combat drop onto an Ayleean ship, and Vasquez here needed to visit the bathroom. So, he goes in there before we land, and then we're hit and some of the drop ship's electrical systems go down. Vasquez gets locked in, but the door says "Vacant". We didn't have time to get him out before we landed, so he ended up sitting on the can for three hours.'

Foxx smiled sweetly at Vasquez. 'Strange you never shared that particular anecdote with Allen or me?'

'Must've slipped my mind,' Vasquez replied tightly before he looked at Ryan. 'Thought it might've slipped yours.'

'Not any more,' Ryan said as he tapped his amorphous digital head. 'Nothin' 'scapes me now!'

Ryan led them to the armory proper, which was protected by another large steel door that at this time was open.

'We have evidence of at least one MM–15 plasma pistol making it out of here, Ryan,' Vasquez said. 'You got any idea how that could happen?'

'No way man,' Ryan replied. 'This place is locked up tighter than any other facility here on Polaris, exceptin' the research and development section, and believe me nobody goes in or out of there without full clearance and all scans both ways.'

Foxx followed the two men into the armory as Ryan headed for a gantry that overlooked ranks of sealed cabinets, all of which were patrolled by robotic guards. Foxx could see signs near each of the cabinets, denoting rows and rows of plasma weapons, charges, explosives, detonators and on toward larger containers for more powerful munitions.

'This is it,' Ryan said. 'Like I said, nothing comes in or out without us knowing about it. Whatever you found down there, there isn't a person alive who could have smuggled it out of this armory.'

Foxx stared with Vasquez out over the vast armory. 'What if the weapon wasn't stolen at all?'

'What do you mean?'

'Just what I'm saying,' Foxx said. 'Is there any chance at all that the weapon we found was somehow legally or operationally out of here?'

'Nope,' Ryan replied. 'MM–15s are out of service, have been for a while. Most of them are here as reserve weapons in case of a crisis but they're deactivated and we don't release them to anybody.'

Foxx thought for a moment longer. 'Who else would have access to this armory, outside of military service?'

'Nobody,' Ryan replied, 'except the prison service. We keep the guards armed with up to date weapons.'

Foxx and Vasquez shared a look with Betty.

'How often do they come over here?' Betty asked.

'Once a month,' Ryan replied, 'the logs contain all the details. Mostly they just rotate weapons in and out for servicing. They don't get through a lot of rounds on the prison, except for training purposes.'

Foxx felt a new lead burgeoning in her train of thought. 'So, could a prison weapon make it in here in substitute for military grade firearms?'

Ryan frowned thoughtfully. 'I suppose it's possible, but there wouldn't be much point, would there? You already got one weapon, why trade it out for another and take all that risk?'

Vasquez looked at Foxx curiously. 'Where you goin' with this?'

Foxx ordered her thoughts for a moment before she replied.

'We've got an MM–15 on the streets, but no missing weapons up here. That means somebody might have somehow, however unlikely it may be, swapped the gun's internal ID chips out.'

'Yeah, but like Ryan said, what's the point if you've already got a weapon?'

'None,' Foxx said, 'if you intend to use it to shoot somebody. But if you're intending to sell a weapon…'

Vasquez got it immediately and his eyes lit up. 'Ex–military hardware would fetch a higher price.'

'And would be in high demand in places like North Four,' Betty said. 'Half the hoodlums on the blocks there would give their right arm for a weapon like that.'

'So whoever was shifting weapons would have needed regular access to this armory and access planet–side too,' Foxx said as she turned to Ryan. 'Can you access the logs for the armory and tell us the names of anybody who matches those criteria?'

Ryan nodded and blinked as he directly accessed the logs, his digital brain allowing him to filter vast quantities of information instantly. He blinked again.

'Three individuals match the criteria: Lance Corporal Aden Ford, General Mitch Salem, and…'

Ryan hesitated.

'What?' Vasquez asked.

'Corporal Anthony Ricard, Prison Service, deceased,' Ryan finished his sentence.

Foxx stared at Ryan for a long moment. 'You're sure?'

Ryan nodded. 'He helped ferry the service module over here for months and would have had access to the weapons when in transit. If he knew what he was doing, he could plausibly have switched weapon IDs for malfunctioning military weapons bound for destruction during the journey. With the weapons checked and booked out for destruction they wouldn't be checked the other end, just counted via their chips and destroyed.'

Vasquez nodded as he caught up with Foxx's train of thought.

'Ricard switches out regular firearms sells the military grade weapons on the street for profit,' he said, 'but why the hell would he be doing that?'

Foxx felt a sense of impending doom wash over her as she thought hard.

'The whole case against Xavier Reed was built upon the assumption that, as Ricard was the one who got shot, he must therefore have been the victim. But what if he wasn't a victim at all?'

'You think that Ricard was behind all of this?'

Foxx shook her head as she asked Ryan: 'Where did most of the weapons that Ricard transported go to?'

Ryan blinked briefly as he accessed the data logs.

'Most went to be destroyed,' he replied, 'the rest were sent into Tethys Gaol as service arms for the guards.'

Vasquez's expression turned to one of dread at the same moment as Foxx's blood ran cold.

'He was supplying weapons back into the prison system,' Vasquez said, 'switching them out. But why?'

Fox felt certain she knew why as she grabbed her communicator and tried to call Detective Allen. The connection was immediately filled with static that hissed loudly in her ear as she cursed the device and shut it off. She turned to Ryan.

'The communicators are down!'

'The entire station's communications are down,' Ryan replied with some surprise. 'We're being jammed by something that's blocking all signals.'

Foxx thought for a moment.

'We need to get aboard Titan and send a priority signal to Tethys Gaol from there, warn them that there may be weapons loose in the system and to lock the whole place down until we get there!'

***

XVIII

CSS Titan

Admiral Marshall strode onto the command platform of the bridge as the XO looked on.

'What did Doctor Schmidt say?' Olsen asked.

'Nothing good,' Marshall replied as he pointed at the communications officer. 'Open a priority channel to Earth.'

Marshall straightened his uniform, aware of the eyes of the bridge crew upon him as he prepared to speak to the Director General of the Central Security Service. *Defensionem ut impetum* : *Defense as attack*, or so the old motto of the CSS went. Despite its name, the organization was more like a senate with no offensive role, only the ability to govern and request action by the CSS Fleet and Armed Forces if such action was required. Until Titan had been required to enter Earth orbit to save New Washington from destructions at the hands of the Ayleeans only months before, no human warship had entered Earth orbit for over a hundred years and…

'What the hell's going on?'

Olsen stepped alongside the captain, his voice low and his expression riven with deep lines of concern.

'The Ayleeans were attacked by something and it didn't belong to either us or them,' Marshall replied. 'The survivor pretty much confirmed what we suspected, and feared.'

Olsen stared at the admiral for a long moment before he replied.

'You got any idea where these attackers came from?' Marshall shook his head but did not reply. Olsen sighed softly for a moment before he went on. 'I guess it was only a matter of time, Frank.'

Marshall's mind churned over the possibilities.

'The Ayleeans could have set this up,' he replied, 'just to get inside our defenses. I wouldn't put anything past them these days.'

'Could it be one of the ships we damaged?' Olsen asked. 'They could have used a wreck to set something up.'

'I had tactical check her out,' Marshall replied, 'she wasn't present during the last attack. This is something new and we can't take the chance that they're telling the truth and not prepare ourselves.'

The main screen in the bridge was showing a panoramic view of Saturn and Polaris Station when the Director General of the CSS Arianna Coburn, a long–service fleet commander who had moved into politics after the end of her final tour a decade prior, appeared on Titan's bridge in perfectly transmitted three–dimensions.

'Admiral Marshall,' she said with a genuine smile, 'So good to see you again so soon.'

'And you, I only wish it were under better circumstances.'

'We have the information that your tactical team sent,' Arianna said. 'The Ayleean survivors have confirmed the attack was by a non–human source?'

'I believe so,' Marshall replied, aware that the bridge crew were listening intently to his every word. 'The survivor has described the attackers as *not human*.'

Arianna Coburn's features paled slightly as she composed herself to this new and unexpected news.

'Veracity of the report?' she asked, her tones a little more clipped now.

'Always hard to tell with an Ayleean, but our current assessment and that of Doctor Schmidt supports the claim. Something hit them damned hard and only three of the warship's crew survived the attack. They never even got a shot off.'

Arianna looked briefly away as she considered the new information. As a former fleet commander, she knew only too well the warlike nature of the Ayleeans and their strength as a fighting force. To be so completely overwhelmed would have meant total and utter surprise and firepower sufficient to eliminate a fully–armed warship in a matter of moments.

'Do you wish me, in light of this confirmation, to ask the senate to initiate the Drake Protocol?' she asked.

Admiral Marshall drew in a deep breath. The Drake Protocol had been in existence under various names for several hundred years, and referred in name only to the legendary Drake Equation. This simple mathematical formula took the Solar System as its starting point and then considered the number of stars in the Milky Way galaxy, divided by the number of those stars stable enough to allow the formation of solar systems capable of supporting life, the chances of intelligent life emerging on any given planet and numerous other factors to produce an estimate of the number of planets in the galaxy inhabited by intelligent life forms comparable to Homo sapiens. Typically, the number was in the tens of thousands.

'I concur,' Marshall replied finally. 'I believe that to not do so in this case would be far more dangerous than assuming that the Ayleeans are wrong.'

'Very well,' Arianna replied, 'do the Ayleeans know from where the attack came?'

Doctor Schmidt replied, his connection to every computer aboard Titan allowing him access to vast data banks of information.

'The Ayleean claims that just prior to the attack their sensors detected a brief burst of high–intensity energy emitted from the northwest corner of the globular cluster M55, in the constellation Sagittarius.'

The bridge of Titan fell silent for a long moment, and the admiral knew without a doubt why.

'The signal,' he said simply, and Arianna nodded in response.

'It was only a matter of time, admiral, before something happened.'

'Something I've missed here?' Marine Sergeant Jenson Agry asked as he stepped onto the bridge.

Doctor Schmidt replied for the Marine and the rest of the bridge crew, although he felt certain that many of them knew of the signal's legend.

'Over four hundred years ago, in the year 1977 and long before the plague that almost eradicated mankind, a radio–astronomer by the name of Jerry R. Ehman detected a narrowband signal while he was working on something known as the SETI project at the Big Ear radio telescope at the Ohio State University. The signal bore the expected hallmarks of non–terrestrial and non–Solar System origin and was emitted from the globular cluster of M55, near the Chi Sagittarii star group. The signal was so pronounced that Ehman wrote the word "Wow" alongside it on the printout, and it thereafter became known as the *"Wow signal"*.'

'The detection lasted seventy two seconds,' Arianna explained, 'and was never detected again. At the time mankind didn't know what to make of it, and although the media wrote countless articles speculating on what the signal was and who might have transmitted it, the fact that it was never heard from again meant that its significance was lost on us for over three centuries.'

'Until now,' Agry guessed as he looked at Admiral Marshall. 'Something the CSS top brass buried?'

'The signal has since been identified as a sensor probe,' Coburn explained. 'The species likely responsible for it would have sent the probe some eighteen thousand years ago because that's how many light years from us the globular cluster is located.' The Director General sighed. 'If the signal did indeed detect mankind's presence on this Earth, then those who had sent it would have been technologically developed to at least human levels when they sent the signal. By now, they would be unimaginably advanced.'

The silence on the bridge deepened as Agry absorbed this information.

'So you think that they're on their way?'

Marshall heard Arianna's voice fill the bridge in reply.

'At the time the signal was detected, no,' she said, 'because it would have taken another eighteen thousand years for the detection of our species to be received by the senders, and then presumably another similar period for them to reach us. However, we now of course know that super–luminal travel is a possibility and that a species so technologically advanced would likely have found ways to expedite the process and would have developed technologies that would appear to a lesser advanced species to be nothing short of miraculous, to be magic.'

'What did the signal say?' Agry asked finally.

Now the silence on the bridge became extremely deep, as though the Marine had committed some unmentionable *faux pas*. Admiral Marshall sucked in air through his teeth before he replied.

'The CSS doesn't talk about that,' he said softly.

Agry's features twisted in a grimace, frustrated by the secrecy surrounding the signal. 'Then why are you enacting this Drake Protocol, and how do you expect to defend against whatever's out there if you don't tell your own Marines about it?'

Marshall, despite his rank, deferred to Arianna.

'It will be discussed at the senate level before any announcements are to be made. Right now, I want a total media ban and an exclusion zone around Titan and the Ayleean survivors. Doctor Schmidt, have your team run through every scan that was made of the Ayleean vessel. If there's anything to be learned about what caused this, we need to know about it as soon as possible.'

'Yes ma'am,' Schmidt replied.

'Admiral,' Arianna went on, 'nobody on Earth or in the orbital cities can know about what's happened. I do not need to elaborate on the panic that may be caused if it becomes known that a technologically superior species has been detected on the very edge of our solar system, much less that it has already decimated an Ayleean ship.'

'Understood,' Marshall replied. 'What of the rest of the fleet?'

'I will place them all on alert, all leave cancelled and all media representatives aboard our ships ordered to remain in place. I don't want them ejected from the vessels and starting speculating planet–side or on the orbital cities.'

'Agreed,' Marshall replied, 'the tighter the leash we keep them on the more time we'll have to figure this out.'

'I'll call an emergency closed–doors senate session and will report back as soon as we know what the council intends to do.'

With that, Arianna's immaculate projection flickered out and left Marshall in the silence on the bridge.

'Schmidt,' he said, 'what's the chances that these new arrivals are hostile? Could the Ayleeans have provoked them?'

Doctor Schmidt inclined his head thoughtfully to one side.

'I doubt that the Ayleeans would have chosen to provoke such a superior technology, and the likelihood of alien species being predatory has been a subject for philosophers for centuries,' he replied, 'with half of them thinking that no species that has reached such high levels of technical achievement to be able to travel among the stars would still wage unprovoked war on others, and the other half comparing the cosmos to our own planet Earth and pointing to our past and our current wars with the Ayleeans, our own brothers so to speak.'

'That's not what I asked.'

Schmidt sighed.

'Given what we already know, it would seem likely that they are a predatory species and we should prepare for the worst, admiral.'

Marshall was about to reply when the Tactical Officer called him.

'Captain, the Ayleeans are here.'

Marshall turned to the main display, and the entire bridge crew saw the star field outside suddenly warp into a funnel and then four vessels burst from super–luminal cruise in a bright flash of light.

'Contact Polaris Station,' Marshall said calmly, 'cease all communications, shut down all sensors that could provide intelligence data for the Ayleeans. I want a complete media blackout on this and no unauthorized transmissions while that ship is in orbit.'

'Aye, captain.'

Marshall immediately identified three CSS frigates surrounding a single Ayleean cruiser, the cruiser as large as all three frigates combined and heavily armed.

'The Ayleeans have jammed transmissions on all frequencies, captain,' the Tactical Officer reported. 'Do you want me to break through with countermeasures to keep emergency frequencies open?'

'Negative,' Marshall replied. 'Let's play along with their standard tactical procedures for now. This is a diplomatic mission unless they act provocatively.'

Olsen joined Marshall on the command platform and spoke quietly from the corner of his mouth.

'They're within striking range of Polaris,' he pointed out. 'They could charge cannons and hit them hard with a first salvo.'

Marshall frowned and shook his head. 'They're surrounded by our fleet, even the Ayleeans must know that any attempt at betrayal would be suicidal.'

'That didn't bother the last one we fought,' Olsen said.

'Transmission coming through,' the Tactical Officer warned.

Marshall lifted his chin expectantly as he stood with his hands behind his back. Moments later, a holographic projection of a towering warrior who looked only somewhat human appeared before him on the command platform. The Ayleean was almost eight feet tall, but Marshall could see that the creature was unarmed, strange in itself for an Ayleean, and that it wore a robe denoting a dignitary of some kind.

'Admiral Marshall,' the Ayleean growled, 'the Butcher of Boise. I am Vyree, from the Ayleean Council.'

'Greetings, Vyree,' Marshall replied in a tone that sounded as though he was chewing a wasp as he spoke. 'Our thanks for you responding to our request for you to...'

'We want to see our people, now,' Vyree cut the admiral off. 'There will be no discussion until I have seen them alive and aboard our own ship.'

'They're in quarantine for their own safety and ours,' Marshall replied, 'but we can have them...'

'You mean they're caged like animals!' Vyree snapped. 'I would expect nothing less from you *humans*.'

'You're every bit as human as we are,' Marshall replied, needling the Ayleean just for the hell of it, 'no matter how you try to hide it.'

Vyree stepped closer to Marshall, towering over him.

'We stopped by the location where your senate said our ship was discovered. We detected CSS plasma residue in the vicinity, and the wreckage of what was once one of our most powerful vessels. What's to say that *you* didn't destroy her?'

'Titan was nowhere near the area when the attack occurred,' Marshall replied, 'and neither was any other CSS vessel. What happened to her was an attack by an unknown species and that concerns all of us, human and Ayleean alike. That's why the senate asked you to come here.'

'I will believe nothing,' Vyree snarled, 'until our people are returned and they can speak for themselves. You have one hour.'

The projection vanished and Marshall sighed.

'We can't move them,' Olsen said. 'The only thing we can do is bring the Ayleean councillor aboard.'

'He won't come without a full escort, which then puts Titan in jeopardy,' Marshall said, but he knew that Arianna Coburn would want him to extract all possible assistance from the Ayleeans. 'Prepare the Ayleeans for transport back to their own ship.'

***

XIX

CSS Titan

Doctor Schmidt walked up and down the sick bay as he awaited the technician's report on the emergency capsules recovered from the Ayleean warship. Although now all three of the Ayleeans were confirmed as alive, he was still uncertain of something about the way in which the survivors had been discovered.

He stared again at the three scans of the Ayleean warriors that had been completed before the capsules had been opened and cursed his digital mind. Despite all of mankind's remarkable fecundity, the spark of genius that had allowed Schmidt the chance to become immortal, there were still faculties of the human mind that he felt were not quite reproduced as well in digital form. He felt as though he had a word on the tip of his tongue, something just beyond his grasp that the data banks and holographic memory that made up his sense of "self" could not quite reach, and that maybe had he still been *fully* human his organic brain might somehow have reached just that little bit further.

The scans looked identical, revealing in microscopic detail every single cell of the Ayleean bodies. Schmidt had studied them now for some time, and for the afterlife of him he could not see what he felt sure was staring him in the face: there looked to be nothing out of place and yet somehow there was…

'Doctor?'

Schmidt sighed and turned as a pair of senior technical officers approached him from where they had been working just down the corridor on the three capsules.

'What have you learned?' Schmidt asked.

'That there's nothing wrong with the capsules,' the senior officer replied. 'All three units were functioning perfectly.'

Schmidt sighed again and furrowed his brow as he thought furiously. 'You're absolutely sure, that they would have suffered no malfunction at the time of or after the attack?'

'None of the capsules had been reset,' the technician confirmed, 'meaning that they were activated once and then remained in stasis until we encountered the ship. We checked the alert beacons and they too were working normally, which means that the signals must have been blocked by debris or other factors external to the ship itself.'

Schmidt frowned. The entire point of survival capsules and their powerful beacons was to be able to survive the aftermath of a destroyed ship and at the same time signal across the cosmos for rescue, that signal also containing basic lifeform data to assist medical teams. The capsule's beacon used a feature known as quantum–entanglement to reach through any debris or interference, simply because "entanglement" meant that no signal was required to be passed at all. The very fundamental particles of the universe were created in "entangled" pairs, rather like a *yin* and *yang*, and one of the bizarre features of such entanglement was that even if two particles were separated by the width of the observable universe, what happened to one would happen to the other. Thus, by manipulating the natural spin of these entangled particles, the capsule was able to signal its distress instantaneously to another location without breaking the laws of physics. When the Ayleeans had left Earth for a future elsewhere in the galaxy, their ships had nonetheless carried beacons compatible with CSS vessels, ensuring that in time of distress each would detect the other's signals and in compliance with the laws of the cosmos would come to their aid.

Yet Schmidt had detected no life signs from the otherwise active capsules when Titan had arrived on the scene.

'Thank you, gentlemen,' he said to the two officers, who promptly turned and left the sickbay.

Schmidt stood with his hands behind his back and stared at the scans for a moment longer, aware that the more he looked at them the less likely he was to be able to identify what it was about the images that bothered him.

He turned and strode from the sick bay and down the corridor outside toward the quarantine area. The three Ayleeans detained within represented the only real means of learning about what had happened out there on the edge of the solar system, and yet they too seemed to have little knowledge of the fate that had befallen them, save the fact that it was swift and devastating.

Schmidt reached the quarantine block to find four Marines standing in silence, their weapons at port arms as their superior officer saw Schmidt coming and turned to face him.

'All quiet, doctor,' he said.

'An oddity in itself,' Schmidt replied, well aware of the raucous and aggressive nature of Ayleeans, especially when trapped against their will. 'I will be but a few minutes.'

Schmidt strode straight through the quarantine wall without missing a pace and found himself confronted by the three Ayleeans, all of whom remained strapped firmly to their respective beds.

'Gentlemen,' he greeted them.

'We're not *men*,' one spat back. 'We're Ayleeans.'

'GentleAyleeans,' Schmidt went on, 'I'd like to ask you all a few questions about what happened aboard your ship?'

'We've told your admiral everything,' growled the one on the right. 'Get out, you freak.'

Schmidt had been called far worse in his time. Back in the day, not long after the plague when *Holosaps* were still something to be feared and awed, he had often been the victim of attacks on his projectors or his power source as those afraid of *Holosaps* sought to eradicate them by any means possible. It was only when the Court of Human Rights ruled that *Holosaps* had the same rights as human beings, that to switch off or otherwise harm a *Holosap* would result in the same charges as those applied to the attacker of a human victim, that those attacks decreased in frequency over the following decades. To murder a *Holosap* by permanently deactivating their database had long been a capital crime known as *digicide*, and many humans had served life sentences for the crime, most of them fanatical worshippers of one or another of mankind's ancient and eradicated religions that had poisoned so many otherwise capable minds. That, however, along with the passing of centuries was not entirely enough to eradicate the latent suspicion with which many people held for *Holosaps*. "Not quite human" was a phrase he had heard more than once, and frankly one that he sympathized with all too easily.

'I'm no less a freak than any of you,' Schmidt replied. 'You're as human as I once was, no matter how hard you try to hide it or deny it. At least my transformation was not by choice, unlike yours.'

'Our ancestors were marooned!' the Ayleean on the left snarled, 'abandoned by our own!'

'Your ancestors left Earth by choice,' Schmidt snapped back, but then dropped his voice to a more conciliatory tone. 'But I acknowledge that they suffered greatly at our hands before doing so. That suffering was not the choice of most but the fear and prejudice of a few, and the same prejudice you show me now. I am here to help, but I'm not clear what I'm trying to help fight against.'

The two Ayleeans peered at him with interest. The third lay in silence, apparently content merely to listen to the exchange. Finally the warrior on Schmidt's left spoke.

'It was a large vessel, bigger than ours,' he said, staring at the ceiling as though unwilling to admit that another warship could be so much more threatening than their own. 'It came from astern, just appeared out of nowhere. We heard the proximity alarms, heard the captain's call for the shields to go up, but they fired even before we could do that.'

Schmidt thought for a moment. 'So they appeared instantaneously and were not detected prior to the attack on your sensors?'

'Only a bow shock, very brief,' said the other, grimacing either in hatred for this new and unknown enemy or in having to relate their defeat to a mere human. 'It came out from the direction of Globular Cluster M55.'

Schmidt knew that all vessels travelling at super–luminal velocity produced what was loosely termed a bow shock, a gravitational depression in the fabric of space and time that warped the continuum ahead of the craft and gave other vessels a brief warning that something was coming.

'What about after the attack?' Schmidt asked. 'Did you see anything aboard your ship? Did you fight anything?'

The two warriors shook their heads, one of them replying in a guttural snarl of regret.

'If we had, we would have at least died in battle. Instead, there was nothing to fight and the ship was falling apart. We had to enter the capsules or we would never have made it out to fight another day. If they boarded the ship we didn't see them, whatever they were.'

Schmidt looked at the Ayleean in the middle, who had said nothing.

'What about you? Did you see anything?'

The warrior did not look at Schmidt as he replied. 'If I had I wouldn't have told any human scum about it. With luck, you'll be next.'

The other two warriors chuckled grimly, their sharpened teeth flashing yellow and white in their gaping black mouths as Schmidt turned away and looked again at copies of the scans on the quarantine bay wall.

'Free us!' one of them growled.

Schmidt ignored their protests as he tried to focus on the scans. Reproduced in three dimensional hard–light projections, the scans contained visual information on every tiny section of the Ayleean's bodies and allowed Schmidt to examine every tiny cell and blood vessel without ever having to touch them. One of the most valuable tools in the medical profession, the hard–light scan was in some ways much like his own projection, although sadly he was by law required to appear as a glowing blue figure rather than a solid, realistic form. The *Holosap's* past as a species was well documented and known to all, and their grab for power over humanity in that distant past and in the face of mankind's extinction from the plague had doomed them forever to always appear slightly different from human beings, distinct and unnatural. Schmidt couldn't blame Homo sapiens for the decision: the dead were visually distinct from the living, because as a doctor he knew that one couldn't mistake a sleeping person for a dead body. Likewise the *Holosaps*, both alive and dead at the same time, were made to stand apart from their brethren although he couldn't understand why they needed to look like a ghost or an oversized light bulb. Surely they could have been generated with a glow around their bodies or just a little sign that said *"Death isn't all it's cracked up to be"* or…

'If I get out of here I'll kill you, you freak!'

The Ayleean's threat snapped Schmidt out of his reverie and he tutted as he considered breaking his oath and shooting the warrior himself, had he had been able to hold a weapon.

'A little late for that,' he replied. 'And if it weren't for me you'd all be corpses already, so shut up and let me think!'

The Ayleean scowled and snarled but said nothing more as Schimdt focused on their scans. All three had survived rapid hypothermic cooling, the emergency escape capsules having preserved them afterward under extremely low temperatures until Titan had arrived to extricate and revive them. All three showed normal body functions, heart beats, all vital signs normal and yet there was something just not quite right about the scans and he couldn't put his finger on it…

'Captain on the deck!'

The Marine's bawled announcement made Schmidt flinch and broke his train of thought again as Marshall strode into the quarantine unit and made a beeline for him.

'You got them talking yet?' he demanded.

'Ugh,' Schmidt replied. 'They won't *shut up*.'

Marshall marched past toward the Ayleeans, who recognized him in an instant and writhed in fury.

'The Butcher of Boise!' one of them spat at him, a reference to Marshall's home town. 'I should have known you'd be here!'

'Slayer of children,' snarled another. 'Your presence insults me!'

Marshall surveyed them with his hands behind his back and a humorless smile on his face.

'You're welcome,' he replied. 'The only reason you're alive is because this ship obeyed the laws that our species' agreed upon decades ago, that no human or Ayleean vessel would be left stricken in time of peace. Technically, despite what your people tried to do six months ago, we're not at war.'

'More's the pity,' snarled the one on the left.

Schmidt turned away from them and walked straight through the quarantine wall and out into the corridor. The Marines were still there, guarding the bay as ever in silence as Marshall exited the quarantine bay and joined him.

Marshall raised an eyebrow as he joined the doctor. 'They seem spritely enough, all things considered.'

'Yes,' Schmidt agreed in a near–whisper, 'that's what bothers me.'

'What do you mean?'

'I can't understand how I did not detect any life forms in my scans before the Marines boarded the Ayleean warship.'

'Sensors were jammed up by the electrical fields around the ship,' Marshall said. 'We were having trouble with them the moment we arrived, you know that.'

'Yes, but I should have detected *something*,' Schmidt pointed out. 'The capsules contain beacons that initiate automatically once a person, or an Ayleean, is inside and in hibernation, correct?'

'Sure,' Marshall agreed. 'They emit a high–energy signal that makes them easy to find, saved a lot of lives in the wake of battles back in the day.'

'And yet we detected no such beacons,' Schmidt replied. 'Why not? The capsules were activated, they had power both internally and via the ship, so the beacons should have been transmitting.'

'Maybe the sensors got fried or something,' Marshall suggested. 'That ship took a hell of a beating.'

'Would you look into it for me?' Schmidt asked, concerned. 'There's something going on here and I can't figure it out.'

Marshall saw the genuine concern etched into Schmidt's translucent blue form and for once he recognized the humanity within, that Schmidt was not just a machine, a projection of light with no true human substance. This was a man of light, a true being expressing real concern for the safety of others.

'The tech' teams have already stripped the capsules down,' he reminded Schmidt. 'But I'll get the signals officer to check this out, okay?'

Schmidt nodded, clearly troubled, and Marshall glanced again at the Ayleeans. 'You want those things to remain in quarantine? I've got the Ayleean dignitaries breathing down my neck wanting them sent back and I can't hold them off forever.'

Schmidt too looked at the Ayleeans and then he nodded. 'I think it for the best captain that they stay here, at least until I get to the bottom of this.'

Marshall, starting to feel somewhat unnerved by Schmidt's demeanor, jerked his head at one of the Marine guards. The soldier hurried over as Marshall spoke in a low voice.

'Have these Ayleeans put into lockdown quarantine, effective immediately,' he said. 'Double the guard too just in case but keep your distance, understood?'

'Aye, cap'n,' the Marine saluted and hurried away.

Before Schmidt could speak, an announcement burst into life.

'Captain to the bridge.'

Marshall turned without another word and hurried away, leaving Schmidt to ponder the Ayleean's scans alone.

*

The quarantine bay of CSS Titan was a clinical room surrounded by a translucent cube of hard–light energized sufficiently to block anything that attempted to pass through it. Terok watched as the Marines sealed the cube into lockdown and then moved off, the hard–light powerful enough to block all sound from both outside and inside the cube.

Terok lay on his bed, still manacled firmly in place and with his companion Zerin opposite. Both of them had served aboard the destroyer before the attack, and neither of them had been able to see much of what had happened. They had fled together, the warship in flames around them and utterly defeated just seconds it seemed after they had first detected the presence of a new vessel emerging it seemed out of nowhere alongside their own.

'This is part of their plan,' Zerin growled, straining uselessly against his restraints. 'The humans will use us as a means to enter Ayleean space and attack our planet!'

Terok sighed. 'Our fleet is half what it once was after the last attack, Zerin. If the humans decided to attack they wouldn't need us as a ruse, they'd just come right in. We can't stop them, we don't have enough firepower.'

'Then we would fight to the death!' Zerin snapped.

'The death of our species,' Terok agreed. 'The way we're going, that's exactly what it'll be.'

'You would stand by and let them destroy us?!' Zerin raged.

'We are destroying ourselves,' Terok replied. 'Zerin, it's over. It's time to face up to the fact that our species has failed. We have attacked the humans repeatedly for decades, centuries, and we have been defeated every time. We have to face up to the fact that we are inferior to them.'

Zerin gasped, utterly appalled. 'I would rather die.'

'So be it,' Terok replied. 'But perhaps the death of this attitude of hatred toward the humans is just what we need if we're to survive whatever happened to the rest of our crew.'

'The humans attacked us!' Zerin snarled. 'They ambushed us and opened fire, without provocation! We warned the council that this would happen, that they would seek retribution for the attack on their orbital city!'

'Again, they would already be invading Ayleea if that was the case and yet they did not. The humans sent messages after our attacks warning us that we would forever be considered enemies and that any vessel found in their space would be destroyed.'

'And yet they rescued us?' Zerin spat. 'You so often speak of the power of logic Terok, and yet now you contradict yourself in a single sentence.'

Terok sighed again. 'There is something else out there, something dangerous. Our ship was destroyed before we could fire a single shot, our crew consumed before they could flee. We don't even know who or what attacked us and I overheard the human admiral, Marshall, speaking to his doctor. They seem as mystified as us about what happened.'

Zerin's eyes narrowed suspiciously, but his tone changed from anger to curiosity.

'What manner of being would attack without provocation, destroy so completely for no reason other than destruction itself?'

'Did you see anything, Zerin, before we entered the capsules?'

Zerin shook his head. 'Only flames and bright white light moving through the ship.'

Terok turned his head to look at their companion, an Ayleean he did not recognize, although that was not unusual on a ship of five hundred souls.

'How did you escape?' he asked. 'You were not on the bridge deck when we came under attack.'

The Ayleean shook his head. 'I was a deck below, and barely made it out alive.'

'What did you see?'

'The same as he did,' came the reply, 'white light and flames.'

Terok thought for a moment before he spoke. 'I think that we should ask to contact Ayleea, to warn them of what is coming. I think that we should ally ourselves to the humans.'

Zerin almost snapped his restraints as he jerked upright on his bed. 'Death before dishonor!'

'There is no dishonor in joining forces against a mutual enemy,' Terok pointed out, 'especially as this one may attack the humans as viciously as it did us. We could be vulnerable here, now. Our families could be next and we're not doing anything to warn them.'

Zerin's fury tempered and he glanced at the Marines, who were standing guard with their backs to the cube.

'They cannot hear us,' he growled. 'They don't *wish* to hear us.'

'The doctor will return,' Terok said. 'We shall inform him of what we know, and hopefully he will accept our request.'

'It will be seen as weakness,' Zerin warned.

'We *are* weak!' Terok insisted. 'In the face of whatever destroyed our ship, we are as nothing! Together, we may be stronger.'

The other Ayleean nodded slowly and Terok sighed again, this time in relief.

'You agree, brother?'

'Yes,' came the reply, 'I agree entirely. Which is why it cannot be allowed to happen.'

Terok frowned. 'What?'

The Ayleen looked across at him, and before Terok's eyes the flesh of his entrapped arm began to change, began to glow with what looked almost like heat as it became longer, slimmer. Moments later, like some horrendous snake, it slid from the restraints and detached entirely from the Ayleean's shoulder as it slithered across his chest and headed toward Zerin and then split into two, the second section heading for Terok.

Terok watched in horror as the tendril of flesh made its way across the quarantine cube toward Zerin.

'Hey, let us out of here!'

Terok's cry was deafeningly loud inside the cube, but the hard–light blocked all sound and the Marines outside did not respond. Terok looked at the Ayleean alongside him, saw its features devoid of compassion or anything that he recognized as remotely human.

'You didn't survive the attack, you are our attacker! What are you?!'

The creature smiled a cold, brutal smile of absolute knowledge and power.

'I am your end.'

Zerin was bellowing now for assistance as the tendril of pulsing flesh crawled up the bedside and slithered alongside his head. Terok cried out as loud as he could as he saw Zerin's terror and then heard the Ayleean's scream as the tendril suddenly burrowed into his ear, thrusting and pulsing and squirming as it forced itself into his skull. Zerin's shriek of agony suddenly became a warbling, jerking gag as his body trembled and his limbs twitched, his eyes rolling up in their sockets as the horrific growth punctured his brain and suddenly Zerin fell silent and still. The worm–like growth emerged from his ear a moment later and flopped to the deck, a stream of dark red blood spilling out in thick strings after it.

Terok stared at the creature on the bed next to him as he saw the second tendril crawl up onto the bed next to his face.

'You don't have to do this,' he gasped.

The reply came a moment later, just as Terok felt something cold and hard press against his ear.

'I know.'

A fierce white pain seared Terok's ear and burst like an explosive inside his skull and he opened his mouth to scream as he felt the hideous creature burrow remorselessly into his brain.

***

XX

CSS Titan

Admiral Marshall walked back onto the command platform in time to see Lieutenant Foxx and Detective Allen dash onto the bridge.

'Admiral,' Foxx said, 'we have a problem.'

'I have several,' Marshall said wearily, 'don't tell me that you're going to add to the list.'

'We believe that there is a conspiracy to initiate a prison riot on Tethys Gaol.'

'Riot?' Marshall echoed. 'What the hell for, there's nowhere for the prisoners to go and they'd never get out of those blocks anyway.'

'They will if they're armed,' Detective Allen insisted. 'We have evidence that an Officer Anthony Ricard was responsible for transporting weapons between Tethys and Polaris Station. He had access to the weapons during that time, and may have altered their programming.'

'Altered it how?'

'We're not certain yet,' Foxx admitted, 'but it appears that Ricard may have been altering or removing the security chips that prevent inmates and civilians from firing the weapons, while also exchanging them for non–military weapons and smuggling MM–15 plasma pistols planet–side for sale.'

Marshall froze in motion as he considered this. 'If the prisoners riot, you think they'll try to take over the prison's armory?'

'Or even the guard's weapons,' Foxx confirmed. 'ID chips control who is able to fire a given weapon. Inmates can't use them because they won't respond to an unknown DNA, but if the chips have been altered to accept any user then the inmates could create hell. If we don't get in there and stop them they could take over the gaol. That's hundreds of high–security inmates, all of them looking for a way off the prison to freedom. If they have hostages…'

'They'll be able to bargain,' Marshall nodded as he understood the urgency and turned to the communications officer. 'Contact the Ayleeans and tell them that we'll shortly be preparing their brethren for transport to their ship, and we need them to drop their jamming so that…'

'Incoming signal, super–luminal bow shock at fifty thousand meters!'

Admiral Marshall barely had time to think as the alert was cried across the bridge, let alone react to the Tactical Officer's warning as every pair of eyes on the bridge swivelled to look at the main display screen.

Fifty thousand meters, just fifty kilometres away, was less than the blink of an eye at super–luminal velocity, a fraction of a second for Marshall's all–too–human brain to calculate a response in an instant of time and thought. Rapid approach, an ambush of some kind entirely similar to that which had been suffered by their Ayleean captors. Titan's sensors were capable of detecting an Ayleean vessel's approach at a hundred times that distance, meaning they were facing an unknown technology that was going to be upon them at the same moment that Marshall's brain was able to process the fact that they were there at all.

Words spilled from the admiral's lips without conscious thought, as though he were listening to somebody else speaking.

'Dive, all shields up and fire all cannons at the first visible threat!!'

Titan went into an immediate dive, her broad bow dropping as the helmsman responded to the command with the speed of thought, the Ayleean cruiser nearby likewise diving away from the new arrival as her escorting frigates split up to bring their weapons to bear. Titan's shields flickered into life even as Marshall saw on the main screen a spherical distortion of the star fields as the fabric of space–time was bulged outward by the approaching vessel and it suddenly rocketed into sight with a blinding flare of white light.

Titan's starboard plasma cannons opened up even before Marshall's brain had processed the incredible sight that lay before him. For the first time in human history an unequivocal encounter between human beings and an undeniably extra–terrestrial race had occurred, and mankind's first action had been to open fire upon that race with some of the most powerful weapons ever created by human hands. Schmidt's words echoed through Marshall's mind as he watched the plasma charges burst into view on the screen like new born stars and zip with phenomenal speed across the space between Titan and the new arrival.

Fear and prejudice are the currency of mankind, to lash out far easier than to reach out.

The ship was vast, probably twice Titan's length and constructed in a way that defied all natural instincts. Marshall gazed upon a form so utterly strange that he struggled to actually identify what he was looking at.

The entire vessel appeared to be being encased in some kind of gel that crept swiftly across its surface, a vast and glossy bubble of material that conformed to the shape of the ship within like a set of visible shields while dimly reflecting the star fields, Saturn and the plasma blasts soaring toward it. Within the strange substance was entombed a recognizably mechanical and metallic spacecraft that was none the less shaped nothing like either a fleet warship or an Ayleean cruiser. Long and slender, gracefully tapered at the bow and stern, it had the appearance of a stretched bullet except for the ragged gashes down the hull from which the bizarre gel oozed in vast quantities. As the ship loomed closer Marshall could see that its hull was constructed from what looked like a twisted bundle of giant braided cables, each as thick as fifty men and wrapping around each other like gigantic metal snakes, catching the light from Saturn's glow as it turned.

From the huge hull burst striations of the shimmering gel, reaching out like gigantic probing icicles across the freezing vacuum of space toward Titan, as though the vessel was entrapped within the tentacles of some tremendous sea creature.

The plasma bursts from Titan's guns smashed into the hull and Marshall squinted as titanic explosions rocked the alien ship. Hull plating was ripped from the superstructure in tremendous blasts, the ship riven with brilliant orange and red flares as power conduits and fuel lines were ignited by the massive volumes of energy being dumped into the ship's interior.

The writhing, immense tentacles of icy material receded as though recoiling from the blasts as the ship rolled away from the onslaught and drifted by through the blackness, her shattered form only visible in the explosions and the reflections of Titan's own exterior lights as the entire fleet passed into Saturn's immense shadow.

A roar of cheers went up from the crew even as Marshall realized that they had no true idea of whether this ship was even a foe. He consoled himself that they had chosen, whoever they were, to rush directly into another species' space without warning and come out of super–luminal travel in what could only be interpreted as an ambush attack.

'Direct hits to main hull and aft superstructure!' Olsen reported as he scanned the tactical displays. 'We're getting fluctuating power readings from within, looks like they're already pretty badly beaten up!'

A sudden, whining, screeching noise deafened the admiral and he threw his hands to his ears as the communications officer scrambled on her work station to shut off the feed. The infernal noise died down into the background as Marshall called across to her, his ears still ringing.

'What the hell was that?'

'Some kind of jamming signal from the alien vessel,' the officer replied, her own expression twisted with pain from the awful cacophony. 'It's blocking everything, all frequencies. It'll take time to push through it.'

Marshall frowned as he saw the ship once again being fully encased now in the strange gel. The fires from the plasma blasts were swiftly extinguished as the gel consumed the raging firestorms across the gargantuan hull. He moved closer to the screen and saw the deep gashes in the ship's hull more clearly, could see the superstructure within, lights functioning despite the massive internal damage.

'You getting any life forms?' he asked the communications officer.

The officer stared at her screens in amazement as she replied.

'Massive responses,' she confirmed. 'It's literally full of life.'

Marshall looked at the substance enclosing the ship and then barked a command.

'Helm, full astern, get us away from her!'

The ship responded instantly, reversing thrust and beginning to turn away from the new arrival as Marshall whirled to the Tactical Officer.

'Full scans of her on all wavelengths!' he ordered.

'Aye sir!'

The Executive Officer moved to Marshall's side. 'What is it?'

Marshall gripped the command rail as he looked at the alien vessel before them.

'The ship's not the enemy,' he said simply. 'Whatever it's encased in, that's our enemy.'

Olsen stepped forward, squinting at the screen. 'What do you think it is?'

Marshall shook his head. In flight school many decades before, when he had been a newly minted fleet officer and had just joined a squadron of *Razor* fighters based out of Polaris Station, he and his fellow pilots had been given a briefing on what to expect if they ever encountered an alien species. Although such an event had not occurred in Marshall's long career until now, it had been clear from day one of his training that CSS expected contact to occur eventually.

There had long been rumors of spurious signals emanating from distant corners of the Local Group, the collective name for a number of galaxies scattered across deep space beyond the Milky Way, with its nearest neighbour, Andromeda, gaining the greatest attention. Larger and older than mankind's natal galaxy, there would have been more time for third–generation stars to form, and thus longer for the planets they harbored to develop intelligent life and for that life to embark on an inevitable journey to the stars.

Marshall could not remember all of the fascinating briefing, but one thing that had been made clear was that in all likelihood, the first encounter between man and a truly extra–terrestrial species would be one where neither side quite understood what they were looking at.

'Get Schmidt up here, right now.'

Olsen put out a call and moments later Schmidt shimmered genie–like into view on the bridge.

'Captain,' he began, 'Were the capsule signals checked against our…'

'Forget them,' Marshall cut him off as he gestured with a nod to the main display screen, 'we've got a bigger problem.'

Schmidt turned and then froze in motion. He watched the screen for a long moment and then spoke softly.

'May I have access to the tactical scans?'

Marshall nodded to the relevant officer, and Schmidt's eyes closed and his projection pulsed softly as he absorbed the vast reams of data being processed by Titan's sensors.

Schmidt opened his eyes as he stared again at the screen, his voice soft but carrying to every corner of the bridge.

'It's alive.'

'It's what?' Olsen asked.

Schmidt moved to the command platform to get a better look at the visual display.

'It's biological,' he said, almost it seemed in awe. 'Life signs are permeating every single inch of the interior of that vessel, which matches no known human endeavour.' He shook his head in wonder. 'If I were to hazard a guess, I would say that it's a parasite of some kind.'

'Parasite?' Olsen echoed, finding Schmidt's analogy somewhat distasteful. 'You mean that ship's been infected with something?'

'That's why I pulled Titan back after the first salvo,' Marshall replied for the doctor. 'Looked to me that we haven't encountered one alien species, but two.'

'Or more correctly, one alien species and another species' spacecraft,' Schmidt corrected. 'I'm detecting spectrographic evidence of titanium, magnesium and carbon in the hull, common materials with which we're all familiar. She was built by a species not unlike our own, but now is home to…, that.'

Marshall managed a brief flash of humor. 'But I thought that all species had feelings, doctor, that there was no "*that*" in medicine?'

'There is when we don't yet have a name for it,' Schmidt replied with unassailable logic. 'Scans indicate that it is cellular in structure, but we're too far out to get much detail and I recommend we stay that way and send a drone or two in.'

'Agreed,' Marshall nodded, and gestured for the Commander of the Air Group to comply with the suggestion. 'Then what?'

'Then, we analyse it,' Schmidt replied. 'We don't know what we've got here, so caution is our best bet.'

Lieutenant Foxx gently eased her way into the conversation. 'Admiral, the prison?'

Marshall shook his head. 'Not now lieutenant, it'll have to wait and we can't break that jamming signal anyway. The prison warden will have everything under control I'm sure and…'

'Nathan's over there, admiral,' Vasquez said quietly, 'along with Detective Allen.'

Marshall exhaled noAsily as he realized the danger that the two men could be in, but he knew that there was nothing that he could do to support them when far more lives were at stake right here and now.

'They'll have to look after themselves until we can send support,' he said through gritted teeth.

Lieutenant Foxx and Vasquez got the hint and backed off as the Tactical Officer raised her head from her screen.

'Drones launched, sensors active. I'm detecting no output from the vessel's fusion cores, no internal power sources.'

Marshall frowned. 'She just came out of super–luminal cruise, she *must* have power.'

Schmidt stared at the huge vessel which was now silent and dark, hanging like a massive icy cocoon in deep space, invisible but for the occasional reflection of Titan's running lights glinting in the immense void.

'It's an ambush predator,' he whispered softly. 'It's hunting.'

***

XXI

Tethys Gaol

Nathan paced up and down in an office adjoining the prison's processing area, a series of hard–light quarantine cubicles where he could see prisoners being contained as they were ordered to strip naked and be scanned.

There was little left to chance in Tethys, the ingenuity of inmates in creating and smuggling weapons in and out of the prison a constant source of amazement for the *sticks*, as he had learned that the security personnel were known as. Nathan had already heard one story of a particularly violent inmate who had been locked in a bare cell for striking one of the sticks. With nothing but the clothes he wore, the inmate had managed to fashion from the buttons and threads of his shirt a small and roughly spherical object. When one of the prison's medical staff arrived to tend to him the inmate was able to shove the object down their throat, blocking their windpipe as he held their choking body to ransom, the object connected to his finger by a single thread.

Nathan shivered. Although he had faced violence on many occasions in the past, he was not by his nature a violent man. Here inside the prison it wasn't just the ever–present threat of violence and danger that broke the will of men, but the bizarre and unexpected forms which that violence could take. By definition, half of the inmates could be considered border–line psychopaths, and who knew what they might be capable of if they were let loose amid the population.

Detective Allen entered the room.

'You got anything yet?' Nathan asked.

'Nothing,' Allen replied, equally dismayed. 'All communications are down, something to do with what's going on outside but there's a media blackout too, so we're essentially blind in here.'

'You think the warden's done it?' Nathan hazarded.

'Nah,' Allen shook his head. 'It's too big for a small fish like him, this is something to do with Polaris Station.'

'What would cause the fleet to shut down everything like this?'

'Beats me,' Allen said, 'but right now we're stuck here and we don't know what the warden's going to do next.'

'If he's in on whatever's going to happen to Reed, then we need to be there to stop it,' Nathan said. 'If Reed gets killed this whole thing is over.'

'He's probably in protective custody,' Allen pointed out. 'Lieutenant Foxx's message about doubts in the conviction got through to Tethys before the communications were cut off, but we haven't heard anything from the San Diego DA. The warden would be risking his career to keep Reed in population now.'

'Did we get anything else from Foxx and Vasquez?'

'Afraid not,' Allen said, 'they clearly had more to say but it got cut off.'

Two more men entered the room, prison guards dressed all in black armor. One of them, with a shaved head and an impossibly wide jaw, spoke in a monotone voice.

'All Blocks are on lockdown, warden's orders.'

'Did the warden receive our priority request?' Nathan asked. 'Has Reed been placed in protective custody?'

The guard, a sergeant, shook his head. 'Follow me.'

Nathan hurried out of the office and followed the two guards down the corridor outside. The huge passage had once been one of the conduits for gas being pumped from the station out into the huge holds of transport spacecraft, the prison merely having placed a level floor at the bottom of the immense tube to turn it into an access route. Nathan could see many more smaller and unaltered pipes running above his head that had probably contained coolants and power cables protected from the gas itself.

The guards led them through the four security gates guarding the entrance to the prison proper, and Nathan handed in his service pistol at the first before being scanned at the second and patted down at the third. The fourth gate opened onto the prison itself, the guards leading him through with Allen. On the far side, sitting on a metal bench and still manacled, was Xavier Reed.

Reed shot to his feet as he saw Nathan and Allen approaching, his features alive with wonderment.

'You didn't,' he gasped.

Nathan grinned. 'We did,' he replied as he realized that the warden must have heeded Lieutenant Foxx's message. 'We're out of here.'

Nathan walked with Xavier Reed out of the main hall and toward the exits, beneath the brooding gazes of inmates watching from the gantries above. Nathan could see the security guards ahead of them unlocking the sally port, could almost sense the fresh air that awaited outside this hellish catacomb of constant death and threatened violence. His heart began to beat more lightly as they walked and he felt the tension slip from his shoulders as the sally port appeared ahead. There awaiting them was the warden, his arms folded across his barrel chest and his red hair twinkling with glowing embers.

'Warden,' Nathan greeted him without warmth.

Arkon Stone showed no interest in Nathan as he looked at the sergeant. 'What's he here for?'

'Prisoner two–one–oh–five–niner, Reed for transport out of population.'

Nathan stood forward, forcing the warden to acknowledge him. 'Reed is innocent.'

'That's not what I heard.'

'There is sufficient doubt over his conviction to pull him out of Tethys until further investigations can be conducted.'

'I haven't heard anything from New Washington, much less the DA's office in San Diego.'

'News is on its way,' Allen assured him as he reached into his pocket for an electro–film, which contained a recording of the conversation he'd had with Foxx . He handed it to the warden. 'This should cover everything. Reed's coming with us.'

The warden looked down at the electro–film and frowned as he watched it, glancing up occasionally at Nathan as he reached pertinent points in the document. He finished it and handed it back to him before folding his arms once more.

'This isn't enough for me to just release Reed on your say so,' he said. 'If I don't hear from the DA, he doesn't get moved.'

Nathan felt his jaw tense as anger rippled through his nervous system. 'The DA's office seems tied up with something bigger than Reed's case right now and communications are down. We've put in the application and the DA's office in San Diego confirmed they'll act upon it but we haven't heard back yet.'

'Then they've only confirmed that they'll *act* upon it,' Stone replied, 'not that they'll *free* Reed.'

Nathan was about to reply when the warden raised a huge hand to forestall him and turned his back. Nathan bit his lip as the warden consulted his optical implant, and then his voice boomed like a cannon across the sally port.

'Shut the gates, immediate lockdown across all blocks!'

Nathan's prior excitement withered like a flame gusted out by the winds of war as the guards heaved the gates shut once more, the warden this time on the inside as they boomed shut. Nathan glared at him.

'Seriously, you think this is a good idea when the DA's office has ordered you to...?'

'No order has been received as of yet and the situation has changed,' the warden boomed back down at Nathan, a gleefully malicious twinkle in his eye. 'You're staying put, and with no order for Reed's release I have no option but to place him back in population. For safety's sake Ill allow him a cell to himself once more.'

'You really want to play this game?' Nathan challenged.

'It's not a game,' the warden insisted. 'Reed stays until I get the clarification I need to let a convicted murderer walk out of this prison. Nothin' less cuts it.'

Nathan took another pace and squared up to the warden, the big man at least an inch or two taller.

'Wanna know what I think?' he said. 'I think that you've spent so long running this place that you've become a law unto yourself. You like to think that you're untouchable.'

'In here,' the warden growled back, 'that's exactly what I am.'

'Right up to the moment I arrived,' Nathan shot back. 'If anything happens to Reed in the time between now and when the DA's clearance arrives, it's on you warden.'

Stone shrugged. 'Whatever. Sergeant, take Reed back to his cell and the detectives back to the main office.'

The duty sergeant and two guards hauled the miserable inmate to his feet, Reed's eyes locked on the immoveable sally port gates as he was pulled away.

Allen sneered at the warden. 'Another little power play? Keep us here until you see fit? Y'know I always figured that the bigger the bully the smaller their dic...'

'Direct confirmation,' the warden cut him off as he turned his back on both of them and strode away, 'nothing less for Reed to walk.'

Nathan leaped forward and cut Stone off, put himself right in the warden's face.

'He'll die back in population. But then I take it that's what you want?'

The warden glowered down at Nathan, anger replacing the malice in his expression. 'Another comment like that from you, Ironside, and I'll put you in there with him.'

Nathan held the warden's gaze for a long moment, and suddenly he knew without a doubt that he had no choice.

'That's exactly what you're going to do,' he replied.

The warden's eyes widened, all pretense of anger gone as he stared down at Nathan. His voice spoke in perfect concert and harmony with Detective Allen's.

'What the hell are you talking about?'

'You send Reed back in there, you're knowingly sending him back to his death based on the warnings I've already given you,' Nathan said. 'I'll use that in any court proceedings that I'll start against you the moment I get back to New Washington.'

The warden opened his mouth to protest but Nathan cut him off.

'It's my duty to protect this prisoner for as long as his conviction is in doubt, and by forcing me to do so you're placing two New Washington detectives directly in danger just to satisfy your own lust for power and control. Anything happens to either of us, it's gonna be on your hands and the DA's office will get to hear all about it. So go for your life, warden.' Nathan cultivated a confident grin. 'Make my day.'

The warden glared down at Nathan, now suppressed fury radiating from him like a latent supernova waiting to explode. Nathan waited as he saw a security officer jog up behind the warden and speak softly.

'All communications have been blocked by Titan, warden,' the officer said. 'Everything's on lockdown until further notice, nothing and nobody to come in or out.'

The warden's anger faded and Nathan felt a sudden pinch of concern in his guts as the warden looked at him with a brilliant smile that split his fiery beard with white teeth. The warden folded his arms across his gigantic chest as he replied.

'So be it,' he rumbled. 'You want to be sent down with Reed here, for his protection.'

Detective Allen stood forward.

'Well, now, I think that what Nathan actually meant was that...'

'I'd be happy to oblige!' the warden cut him off jubilantly as he boomed his response loudly enough for the entire block to hear. 'You're right, Reed does indeed need protection and I deeply appreciate your offer, *Detective* Ironside!'

A ripple of excited whispers and hoots echoed across the gantries far above as Nathan glared at the warden.

'You think that I'm not going to report this as soon as I get back to...'

'Put them in Reed's cell!' the warden boomed. 'Ensure that they have everything that they've asked for!'

Nathan moved to protest, but suddenly his arms were yanked up behind his back as two security guards hefted him away from the warden.

'You're going to regret this!' Nathan shouted as he was dragged away. 'I'll have your badge by the end of the week you assho....!'

The warden's thunderous laughter drowned out Nathan's belligerent profanities as he was dragged away toward the prison once again, this time with Reed and Allen following him.

*****

XXII

CSS Titan

Foxx stood on Titan's bridge and watched the hive of activity ongoing in the wake of the alien vessel's arrival. She barely noticed Vasquez hurry onto the bridge and move alongside her.

'I got word back from San Diego before the communications shut down,' he said.

She turned to him. 'What do we got?'

'Turns out that Anthony Ricard wasn't all happy days prior to being shot,' Vasquez replied. 'I got his financial records and he was in deep, looks like either a gambling addiction or maybe even drugs.'

'Unlikely,' Foxx said, 'the prison service is subject to routine testing, he wouldn't have got through.'

'That's what I thought,' Vasquez said. 'There's evidence of a gambling habit so I pushed the drug angle and guess what? Ricard was twice reported as having been seen in known drug–dealing areas of the city on his own time.'

Foxx frowned. 'How come the reports weren't followed up?'

'Because Ricard claimed he was working a case under his own initiative, and that was backed up by his partner, Xavier Reed. At trial, the prosecution used this as evidence that Reed was involved in the drugs trade and that the shooting was the result of a dispute between the two men, with Reed being a dealer and Ricard investigating his own partner. The defense played the same card but with opposing roles.'

'Let me guess,' Foxx said, 'the jury played out both scenarios and rejected them.'

'Bang on,' Vasquez agreed. 'Neither was used as evidence because neither could be proved. If anything, the judge felt that both men were covering each other and that both were involved.'

'Which doesn't jive with Xavier's claims,' Foxx said.

'Exactly, and Reed wasn't the one who was neck–deep in debt. The prosecution claimed that Ricard's debt wasn't motive for homicide, although they conceded it could have been enough to cause his drinking the day of the murder and perhaps his desperation. The defense said that

Xavier's covering for his partner's issues wasn't evidence of complicity but an act of friendship to a colleague in need, something that Xavier himself said when on the stand, that he did it to help Ricard and that the last thing he wanted was his partner dead.'

'Again, hearsay,' Foxx said. 'So what we've got is the fact that Ricard was the only one with financial issues, which makes him the most likely to have gotten himself involved with criminal activity. He might have got into gun–running to get himself out of debt.'

'But we've got no evidence linking him to any such activity other than hearsay sightings of him,' Vasquez pointed out. 'Another loose end.'

Foxx was mulling this over when the admiral strode onto the bridge with Schmidt.

'We're going to need a crash course here,' Marshall said to Doctor Schmidt as Foxx and Vasquez watched from nearby. 'Tell me everything that you can about what that thing out there is.'

Although ostensibly every other officer on the bridge had plenty of work to be doing, Foxx could tell that they were listening in as Schmidt spoke.

'Our knowledge of alien species has been limited until now by the fact that we have encountered so few,' Schmidt said. 'The best examples of bona fide alien species we have to date are those that infected the human race four hundred years ago, simple bacteria and viruses lodged in the hearts of cosmic stardust grains that made it to the surface of Earth and thrived only in human bodies.'

Foxx knew well enough the cause of The Falling, the same virus that had infected Nathan Ironside and sent him immediately after his death into cryogenic storage to await the hoped–for cure that had taken four hundred years to reach his long forgotten capsule.

The British had been the first to discover the alien forms way back in 2014, long before routine space travel, ID chips, hard–light or any of the orbital cities and other basic technologies familiar to Foxx and every other human citizen. The British had sent a balloon twenty miles into the atmosphere and captured microscopic aquatic algae, biological organisms known as extremophiles, living high in Earth's atmosphere that could only have come from space. Their findings had been published in a paper during the Instruments, Methods, and Missions for Astrobiology conference in San Diego. The entities they described had varied from a colony of ultra–small bacteria to two unusual individual organisms – part of a diatom frustule and a two hundred micron–sized particle mass interlaced with biofilm and biological filaments.

'The findings of the British team were the first confirmation that life is common in our universe both around and between the stars,' Schmidt said. 'The seeds of life exist all over the universe and travel through space from one planetary system to another. The fact that several Earth–bound bacterial species are known to be able to survive for up to two hundred fifty million years in salt crystals and be successfully revived in the presence of liquid water allows for the time scales required for such species to move between planetary systems.'

Foxx could recall first seeing examples of the alien species that had almost rendered humanity extinct. Some had segmented necks connected to tear–drop shaped bodies. Others were like small animals, but the majority were spheres that seemed to leak a biological substance that had simply been named "*goo*". But what had frightened the people at the time was that the spheres, each as wide as a human hair, had all been identified via X–ray analysis as being made from titanium and traces of vanadium. They had also found that they had a "fungus–like knitted mat–like covering", a combination known to no species on Earth at the time.

'What does that have to do with this?' Olsen asked as he jabbed a thumb in the direction of the now silent vessel a few thousand meters away. 'That's not a bunch of teeny bacteria locked up in some asteroid.'

'No,' Schmidt conceded, 'but it's my estimation that what that entity consists of is almost certainly along the same lines.'

'Explain,' Marshall said impatiently.

'Nobody considers an individual neuron to be conscious,' Schmidt said, 'nor a single ant or termite to be capable of building a mound or a nest. It is their collective awareness that forges an intelligence, a machine if you will, which is the sum of its parts and perhaps greater than. When our drones get close enough to that ship, it is my estimation that they will detect a biological entity encompassing countless trillions of cellular forms acting in concert.'

Marshall's eyes narrowed as Detective Allen spoke.

'So you're saying it's a big bunch of bugs, right?'

'Eloquently put,' Schmidt replied with a flat tone, 'but correct none the less.'

'How come they don't freeze out there?' Olsen asked.

'They do,' Schmidt said, accessing Titan's sensors. 'Spectrographic sensors indicate from the reflection of sunlight that the outer covering appears to be frozen solid, consisting of water and methane ice as hard as rock. But that outer covering acts as protection for the interior, a thermal layer that seals the rest of the colony inside.'

Marshall sighed heavily. 'This wasn't what I was expecting when I joined up.'

'Of course not,' Schmidt said. 'We've all been raised on a diet of movies featuring insectoid aliens or anthropomorphic beings, but the most likely form of life to spread across the universe in large numbers is cellular bacteria and viruses. Even on Earth, bacteria have always outnumbered larger life forms by billions to one. Your own body contains more bacteria than every human being who has ever lived.'

'And now they're here,' Olsen murmured uncomfortably. 'Last time something like this made it to Earth five billion people died, and that was from just what Nathan Ironside managed to breathe in. Look at that thing out there. If that makes Earth–fall, the population will be gone in days.'

'It may not have a willfully predatory purpose,' Marshall said.

'Correct,' Schmidt replied, 'we just don't know whether it has any purpose at all other than to survive, which is both a curse and a blessing.'

'In what way?' Foxx asked.

'Because if it's a non–sentient being then it merely *exists*,' he replied. 'It has no emotion, no cares other than consuming prey. It cannot be reasoned with, or empathized with, it simply is. However, its fundamental simplicity means that a coherent defense against it should be well within our capabilities.'

Nobody replied for a moment, and then the Tactical Officer's voice carried across the bridge.

'The drones are in sensor range.'

'On screen,' Marshall ordered.

The display switched to the perspective of one of the two drones dispatched to investigate the vessel. Entirely automated and with low–level intelligence, the drones approached the vessel slowly.

Foxx could already see that the massive ship was entirely entombed in ice, its surface visible through minor striations in the otherwise crystalline cocoon. The fact that the ice was so clear was in itself interesting to Schmidt.

'It must form as a fluid, devoid of pollutants,' he said in wonder. 'Sensors indicate that it is as hard as steel, the near absolute zero temperature of deep space responsible for its rigidity.'

'You think that's by design or a consequence?' Marshall asked.

'Hard to say,' Schmidt replied, 'but most likely it's an evolutionary response. If these things first evolved to travel within cometary debris or similar, they could gradually have evolved defense mechanisms against the cold vacuum of space.'

The drones moved closer to the surface of the cocoon, and slowly their cameras began to relay footage that showed some kind of motion beneath the surface of the ice. Foxx moved a step closer to the displays, her sharp young eyes noticing the aberrations, almost like rivers of rippling haze flowing beneath the cocoon.

'There's something moving,' she said.

'Channels,' Schmidt replied, 'passages of heat generated by biological processes through which the life forms move.'

'But then where do they get their energy from?' Olsen asked. 'That ship's dead.'

Schmidt thought for a moment before he spoke.

'Can the drones focus and zoom in on the damage around the ship's hull?'

Marshall indicated the Tactical Officer to comply, and moments later a signal was sent and one of the drone's cameras zoomed in, penetrating the ice it seemed as it produced a high resolution image of the ship's cavernous interior.

Slowly, through the tiny imperfections in the ice, Foxx could see patterns emerging. The massive structural braces of the ship's interior that had appeared shattered by the passage of massive plasma blasts were in fact delicately carved open, bizarre curved striations in the massive metal beams like the petals of flowers patterning their surfaces.

Doctor Schmidt moved forward, himself enveloped in an aura of amazement and wonder as he spoke.

'They didn't just attack that ship,' he said finally. 'It's the food source.'

'Food,' Olsen echoed. 'The crew?'

'Maybe,' Schmidt said, 'but likely mostly the ship itself. That's their fuel, the metals of the hull.'

Foxx realized what Schmidt meant, that the patterns in the beams were the signature of countless millions of cells attacking the metal itself, eating it atom by atom.

'They're either breaking the metal down by oxidizing it,' Schmidt said, 'or perhaps by corrosive means consuming it directly on an atomic scale.'

'Which allows them to power that spacecraft if they feel the need to travel,' Foxx said as she observed the display. 'But if they didn't attack the craft, then how did they get aboard it?'

Schmidt shrugged, slipping his hands into the pockets of pants that didn't really exist, the gesture an endearing sign of his human origins.

'They probably didn't attack it at all,' he replied. 'They would not have needed to infiltrate the vessel in great numbers, only sufficiently so that they could replicate and spread. If I'm right and they're in fact a collective intelligence constructed of cellular forms, they would be able to move freely throughout the vessel without the crew ever having known that they were there until it was too late. They might even possess the ability to metamorphose into any form that they choose and…'

Schmidt broke off mid–sentence and Foxx saw his wonderous expression suddenly collapse as his voice became terse.

'Bring up the medical scans from the sickbay,' he said to the admiral.

Something in his tones forestalled any protest by Marshall at the doctor's audacity to direct a command at him, and moments later three scans appeared to hover in front of Schmidt. The doctor stared at them and his face fell in abstract terror.

'Oh no.'

'What is it?' Foxx asked as she looked at the three scans of the Ayleean warriors.

Schmidt shook his head. 'I know how the alien ship was occupied,' he said, his voice rasping and dry. 'I couldn't see it in these scans, I couldn't tell!'

'Tell what, man?!' Marshall snapped. 'They look identical!'

'That's the problem,' Schmidt replied. 'Two of them are *too* identical. One of the Ayleeans is an utterly perfect clone. That's why one of the emergency capsules didn't detect a life form within it, why we couldn't detect its beacon. The DNA of these things must be fundamentally different from our own and it wasn't recognized in the capsule's database.'

Marshall blinked. 'The Ayleeans?'

'Yes,' Schmidt nodded. 'Only two of them are actual Ayleeans. The third is an imposter, a clone. That's how these things get aboard ships: they lay in wait for rescue by a third party. They're already aboard us, captain. They're inside Titan!'

'Secure the quarantine unit!' Marshall roared as Schmidt vanished from sight.

***

XXIII

The Marines outside the quarantine unit burst in through the security doors to see the bodies of two Ayleeans lying still strapped to their beds, their eyes wide and lifeless, their tongues hanging out of their gaping mouths. Detective Foxx followed Admiral Marshall at a run, Vasquez and Sergeant Agry leading them as they sprinted down to the unit and followed the Marines inside.

Doctor Schmidt was waiting at the entrance as the Marines waved them forward.

Foxx eased her way to the quarantine unit entrance and peered through the hard–light walls. One of the beds was vacant, the restraints dangling from either side and no sign of the Ayleean who had minutes before been strapped in place.

'How the hell did that thing get out of those restraints?!' Sergeant Agry boomed, his voice like a broadside of cannon fire that echoed around the corridors outside as he confronted the Marines.

'It didn't,' Corporal Hodgson replied, his chin held high as he stared into the middle distance. 'Nothing came past our position, admiral. Check the visual feeds, the scanners, anything. We all were stood right here.'

Doctor Schmidt stared through the hard–light walls as he surveyed the interior.

'Maintain the security perimeter,' he said softly. 'Don't shut down the quarantine.'

'It's too damned late!' Marshall raged, glaring into the cubicle. 'It's gone, whatever the hell it is.'

Schmidt shook his head. 'That's what it wants us to think.'

Foxx frowned as she looked again inside the quarantine unit. The bed was most definitely empty, and the other two Ayleeans were likewise obviously dead. The rest of the unit was clean: no materials or instruments, nothing behind which a creature of the mass of an Ayleean could possibly hope to hide.

'That's not possible,' she said. 'It was big, it couldn't be hiding. You think that maybe it's using some kind of cloaking device?'

Schmidt shook his head slowly, completely absorbed by whatever it was he had deduced as he stared into the quarantine unit.

'Have you ever heard of Sherlock Holmes, detective?'

'Of course,' Foxx replied. 'Not everything was lost in the wake of The Falling. Most digital archives survived. He was a detective created by Sir Arthur Conan Doyle, a British author.'

'Correct,' Schmidt replied. 'One of Mister Holmes's most famous teachings was that once you've ruled out the impossible, whatever remains must be the truth, no matter how improbable.'

Foxx took a breath and looked again at the quarantine unit, protected by its cuboid hard–light walls, capable of preventing even bacteria from passing through and infecting the rest of the vessel.

'Okay,' she said finally. 'Nothing can get out of there and the Marines said that nothing came past them, so whatever we picked up along with these two dead Ayleeans from their ship is, according to your logic, still in there.'

'Correct,' Schmidt agreed. 'Thus, it must be hiding somehow.'

'There's no room,' Betty pointed out as she joined them, 'and nothing to hide behind.'

Schmidt smiled. 'One does not need something to hide behind, when one is hiding instead in plain sight.'

Betty frowned, not understanding. Then a security officer hurried up and from his optical implant was beamed a holographic projection, a recording of the events inside the quarantine unit before the death of the two Ayleeans.

'Ah,' Schmidt nodded as he watched the feed, 'as I suspected.'

Foxx watched in horror the holographic projection suspended in thin air between them as the third Ayleean's body parts disconnected and crawled like gruesome snakes onto the bodies of his companions and forced their way into their skulls, penetrating their brains and their throats, killing them within seconds.

'What the hell?' Vasquez uttered. 'Did I just see that?'

'That's nothing compared to what it must have done next,' Schmidt said.

The Marines and the admiral gathered around the projection in silence as they watched with morbid fascination to see what the bizarre creature would do next.

Foxx watched the feed as the Ayleean's body, still lying in silence on its bed but without any arms, suddenly faded as all markings upon it seemed to drain like watercolors from an image, the body becoming opaque and pale as though it were little more than a lump of clay. Then, the Ayleean's entire body slowly began to disintegrate before their eyes, slithering out of its restraints and spilling toward the deck like some kind of foul liquid. It drooped off the bed, thick like oil but partially translucent as it began to break up into bulbous pools of ooze on the deck.

Foxx watched, a bolt of nausea lodging in her throat as she watched the mess spread out and become increasingly translucent until it suddenly was invisible. The glossy film it left on the deck became matt, and in a matter of a few seconds the former Ayleean was utterly invisible.

'Shape–shifting?' Vasquez gasped, his voice dry. 'Man, the Ayleeans never manage to pull something like that off. What the hell is that thing?'

Admiral Marshall moved closer, his jaw clenched and his hands locked tightly behind his back.

'It's history,' he growled. 'Corporal Hodgson, have decon' units sent down here to scour that unit of every microbe and bacteria.'

The Marine turned to carry out the admiral's orders but Schmidt shook his head.

'I would not do that, captain,' he suggested.

Marshall turned to the doctor. 'This isn't a case where your "all life is sacrosanct" attitude is going to work out, doctor. That thing is a living predator and if it gets out of that unit it will destroy this ship and its crew just like it did those of the Ayleeans. It dies, here and now.'

'If it dies,' Schmidt replied.

Marshall winced.

'They just wiped out an Ayleean warship, doc', case you hadn't noticed!'

Schmidt's voice remained calm.

'They may be biological but they may also be machine, and they may be a little of both. Cleansing this unit using the technology at our disposal may not achieve anything. A being as advanced as this one won't simply be wiped away by a blast of ultraviolet light, captain. Their survival techniques, honed perhaps over millennia, will likely outstrip our weapons by a considerable margin.'

Marshall squinted into the unit for a moment. 'Then what do you propose we do with them, oh Great Doctor? Tuck them in with a bedtime story?'

Schmidt thought for a moment and then nodded. 'That's a fabulous idea.'

Marshall's expression collapsed in dismay. 'Seriously?'

'They need to be studied, in depth,' Schmidt insisted. 'We can't effectively defend ourselves against something that we do not understand. Our best course of action is to capture some of this material, or whatever it is, and subject it to a rapid study to understand how it operates and how we can build a defense against it that will prevent Titan from ending up like the alien vessel out there, which I might remind you is covered with countless billions of tons of material of the kind we have here.'

Foxx realized what Schmidt meant. 'The ice around the alien ship,' she said. 'The damage, the deaths of the crew, it was all caused by this stuff?'

'Most likely,' Schmidt confirmed. 'It uses metals for fuel and thus it requires sustenance, which means it can also be starved. I suspect that its ability to mimic an Ayleean was born of consuming the crew of the warship after its attack.'

'Then what about the other two who survived?' Vasquez asked.

'Cover,' Schmidt replied. 'Two of them in escape capsules, the chance to infiltrate another vessel, or victim, whatever you might wish to call us. The Ayleean ship was in effect a Trojan Horse. Whatever this stuff is, it's alive and we need to understand it as fast as we can.'

Marshall ground his teeth in his jaw for a moment before he replied.

'How, and how long?'

'I don't know,' Schmidt said, 'but right now we must consider this vessel, the Ayleean ambassador's ship, Polaris Station and the orbital prisons as quarantine zones. We cannot afford to let this material spread any further than it already has.'

Vasquez looked at Foxx. 'Nathan and Allen are still on Tethys Gaol.'

'Can we get them out?' Foxx asked Schmidt.

'No,' Schmidt replied apologetically. 'Until we know what's really going on here, nobody can go anywhere. Everything is to be locked down until I can figure this out, understood?'

Marshall nodded as he spoke to the XO, Olsen, via his communicator.

'Implement the lockdown and maintain the block on all communications channels coming in and out, even if we break the alien jamming, and inform the Ayleeans of what's happened via light signals, standard protocol. Right now, we're not going anywhere so just pull us back from the alien vessel and I want fighter patrols out to one hundred thousand kilometers. No vessels move unless we say so.'

'*Aye captain.*'

Foxx turned away as Vasquez moved alongside her.

'Nathan, Allen and Reed are stuck in that prison and we still haven't heard from the DA's office planet–side.'

'There's nothing that we can do,' Foxx replied as they walked. 'We can't even get off this ship and head back to New Washington to follow up on what we've learned. If Reed really is being framed, then whoever's behind all of this will want them dead as soon as possible along with anybody else who's been sniffing around the case lately.'

They looked at each other for a moment.

'Detective Samson,' Vasquez said. 'We gotta warn him!'

'And my partner's over there in Tethys in the middle of a riot,' Betty snapped. 'We've got to get over there right now!'

Foxx rubbed her temples with one hand.

'We can't contact Samson and we can't help Nathan either. Whatever's waiting for them, they're going to have to face it all alone.'

***

XXIV

Tethys Gaol

Nathan heard the whoops and jeers of murderous delight as he and Detective Allen were guided along the gantry behind Xavier Reed, the miserable threesome escorted by a phalanx of heavily armed sticks.

Nathan quickly realized that compared to the block itself the other sections of the prison had been somewhat luxurious. He instantly felt the heat inside the block, close and heavy, stained with the odors of sweat and urine and other bodily fluids he didn't even want to think about. Inmates jeered at them, threats echoing back and forth across the block as they were shoved by the sticks into a cell. Nathan turned and watched as the sticks slammed the heavy gates closed and walked off, leaving the three of them inside.

The cell was small, just two thin mattresses on blocks of poured concrete stained with the filth of ages, and it seemed as though the very walls were ingrained with the stench of compacted humanity, pain and despair that seemed to leech from the bodies of each and every convict who had ever haunted the corridors.

Nathan stood at the cell door and tried to ignore the hoots and cat calls echoing across the block from the other cells. Neither Nathan nor Detective Allen had been wearing restraints when they were led onto the block but he knew that too was likely for effect – the warden wanted to let every single con know who and what they really were: yet more policeman on the block, temporarily imprisoned alongside some of the most dangerous men ever to have lived.

'Welcome to my world,' Reed said miserably as he slumped onto a bunk.

'This wasn't what I had in mind.'

A low latrine and a steel mirror completed the interior of the cell, Reed allowed no special belongings or anything that could be used to make the cell feel more like home. However, despite this the ever–innovative prisoners had used dye stains from the bedding to fashion crude drawings on the walls. Nathan could see years' of faded artwork marking the walls despite valiant attempts by the authorities to remove them. Some were remedial scrawlings, others remarkably adept, others still touching – a lifelike sketch of a girlfriend looking out of one wall, the image of a daughter from another.

On the back wall Nathan could see a series of long lines drawn on the crumbling surface, each line marked with what looked like numbers, the bizarre drawings seeming almost architectural in design.

'I look at them a lot,' Reed said as he sat on his mattress. 'It's a sad truth but I've resigned myself to the fact that I'm probably never getting out of here alive.'

Nathan sat down opposite Reed.

'The hell you're not. I didn't come all the way out here to sit in this cell and give up. You're innocent, Xavier. You know it, I know it and even the San Diego DA is going to know it in a few hours. They're not going to let the warden keep you here for much longer.'

'And yet here we are,' Reed replied with a weak smile. 'You and I both know that the warden's not going to let us leave. I try not to be paranoid but I'm pretty damned sure that whoever set me up for this probably has the warden in their pocket too.'

'That's unlikely,' Nathan said. 'The warden is just high on his own power trip.'

'That doesn't mean that somebody isn't trying to get Reed iced as fast as they can,' Allen pointed out. 'They must know about the investigation into his conviction by now, and if so they won't want Reed getting released or the case being officially reopened.'

'They almost succeeded' Reed asked. 'The crew that runs this block has already made it pretty damned clear that the first chance they get, they're gonna come down on me. They've already tried once.'

Nathan clenched his fists and fought off a brief wave of fear and despair, Reed having been inside for several days and likely better in tune with the mood inside the block than Nathan.

'Then we'll be ready for them,' he insisted. 'You're not on your own now, remember? And we've both got a damned good reason to survive this.'

Xavier looked at Nathan and appeared to suddenly remember the sacrifice that Nathan had made to his cause.

'Thanks, man. You didn't have to do this.'

Nathan shrugged off his own misgivings. 'I guess it was the right thing to do.'

Xavier scrutinized him. 'You didn't think the warden would put you in here, did you.'

'No,' Nathan admitted. 'I called his bluff.'

'Are you happy with the outcome?'

'Not so much.'

Xavier stared at Nathan for a long moment and then he began to smile. Nathan chuckled, shook his head, and from their cell a ripple of laughter echoed out across the block. Allen apparently did not share their mirth.

'Seriously, you guys think this is *funny*? We're locked up in here with a bunch of crazies who'll tear us apart given half a chance.'

Nathan's mirth faded slowly away, Xavier's laughter losing its gusto also.

'He's right, you should've stayed back,' Xavier said finally. 'The cons in here, they mean business. We'll be lucky to get out alive.'

'Best we settle in then,' Nathan suggested, 'if this is our home for a while.'

Detective Allen turned away from them and stood in front of the cell door, looking out over the prison block as Xavier leaned back against one wall.

'Where's your home?' he asked Nathan.

'Aurora, Colorado.'

'Nothin' much out there,' Xavier frowned. 'What made you leave?'

Nathan let a small, sad little smile curl from his lips. 'Too much had changed, y'know, over the years.'

Xavier nodded, not really knowing what Nathan was getting at but merely in sympathy.

'You got family?' he asked.

Nathan sucked in a deep breath as he prepared to answer, and then realized that he didn't know what to say. He did have a family and it felt as though they had been with him only months before, and yet they were gone and had been for hundreds of years. Nathan closed his eyes as a fresh wave of black grief threatened to overwhelm him, trembled on the edge of a precipice from which it seemed there was no return. He barely heard Allen's reply.

'Nathan's on his own,' the detective said softly, 'family tragedy.'

Xavier's expression creased as he realized his *faux pas* and he closed his eyes briefly. 'Sorry, man.'

Nathan shook his head. 'Not your fault, you couldn't have known.'

The giant black wave receded into the distance, leaving Nathan feeling weak and disorientated. He sucked in deep breaths of air, caught Allen's concerned expression but pretended that he hadn't noticed. *Christ Nathan, get it together.*

Detective Allen turned from the cell gates, and stood over Nathan where he sat on the low bunk and folded his arms across his chest.

'Ironside, you might not be worried about living another day but I am.'

Nathan looked up at the detective questioningly, although he knew damned well what Jay was getting at.

Allen kept his voice down, but it was impossible for Xavier not to overhear their conversation. 'You've been throwing yourself in harm's way ever since you started wearing the uniform,' he snapped. 'What is it? You wanna die?'

'Of course I don't want to die,' Nathan protested, 'I'm just doing my job.'

'No, that's the whole point,' Allen replied, 'you're not doing the job of an officer of the law, you're playing the devil–may–care asshole and now you're taking other people on the ride and sooner or later it's going to cost somebody their life!'

Nathan saw Xavier watching them both with an expression of deep concern that matched Allen's. Before Nathan could answer he heard a rippling sound echo across the block, as though a tin insect were scurrying on multiple legs across the roof. The sound swept across the block and Xavier stood abruptly from his bunk.

'This is it.'

'This is what?'

'The end,' Xavier replied. 'The prison's supposed to be on lockdown, right? That's what the warden said. So why are the cells opening?'

Allen shot Nathan an angry look as he jabbed a thumb over his shoulder. 'See what I mean?'

Nathan got up and saw the prisoners moving out of their cells. 'Damn it, the warden knows that we're in here!'

As Nathan moved to the cell gate so he heard the automatic locking system disengage, and then the door swung open with a metallic squeal as though it were announcing to every other con on the block that the cell was accessible to them. Nathan stepped back from the gate as he heard the sound of hundreds of feet shuffling from cells all across the block, dark eyes looking in their direction as one by one they began filtering toward Xavier's cell.

'Zak's got somebody on the inside,' Reed said, seemingly resigned to his fate. 'He warned me that he's got plans for me, and the word on the block is that he's planning an escape.'

'To where?' Allen asked. 'There's nowhere to go.'

A sudden, squealing alarm shattered the silence as the sticks started sprinting from the gantries as they realized that the cells were all opening. Nathan dashed to the cell gate and saw them dash through the chow hall and rush toward the Watch Tower's main sally port in a bulky black flood of riot gear and black uniforms.

'They're leaving us!' Allen yelped in surprise.

'This is nothing to do with the warden,' Nathan said. 'It's too spontaneous.'

'This is what Zak had planned all along,' Xavier said, bizarrely calm in the face of imminent danger. 'This is the riot he's been waiting for.'

Nathan saw the sticks make it to the watch tower with dozens of screaming cons in pursuit. From nowhere, up on the gantries, the sound of flushing latrines being blocked sent streams of water flooding out of cells to drain like dirty waterfalls over the gantries, the sheets of water flickering in the light as from another cell a billowing cloud of smoke spilled out like poison as an inmate set his mattress alight.

'Come one, come all,' Xavier said with morbid resignation. 'They'll take us somewhere else in the prison and finish us off down there.'

As if Nathan needed confirmation that this was not some cruel final act by the warden, he saw two or three of the sticks caught up in the wave of running inmates, their bodies stomped upon by the hordes, their terrified cries swamped by the raging cons assaulting them. Nathan knew that no matter what the warden was up to his neck in, he wouldn't have risked abandoning any of his men to the merciless horde of rioting inmates.

From across the block soared a banshee wail of brutal joy, of hundreds of men suddenly freed from incarceration to plunder and destroy as they saw fit. He heard the primal roar of human beings suddenly and as one unleashing years' of resentment, hate, shattered dreams and lost lives in one uncaring and unstoppable wave of brutality.

Nathan sucked in a deep breath of stale air and hoped against hope that somebody would come to their rescue before they were dragged into the bowels of the prison. Even as he thought it, so the light from the prison beyond the cell gates was blocked by the bodies of muscular cons, all of them glaring at Nathan as they blocked their escape from the cell.

***

XXV

Nathan saw the hulking cons loom large on the gantry outside the cell, behind them the screaming hordes of prisoners running this way and that as they cheered their freedom and celebrated the only way they knew how: burning, breaking, punching and punishing anybody who stood in their way.

'You got y'self a nice new cell.'

Zak Volt loomed in the doorway of the cell and directed a cold gaze at Xavier Reed, who stood next to Nathan but neither retreated nor advanced as he waited for whatever was going to happen next.

'And you got yo'self some new boyfriends too, ain't that cute?' Volt went on as he looked at Nathan and Allen. 'And you were detectives we hear? Well ain't y'all gonna fit in on the block jus' right?'

Nathan heard the other inmates crowding the gantry chuckle grimly as their gazes fell on Nathan. Nathan forced himself to take a pace forward to confront Volt, the con's imposing muscular form and aura of psychosis making Nathan feel as though he was shrinking.

'I still am a detective,' Nathan replied.

Volt peered at him. 'Then whatchya doin' on ma block, *stick*?'

The last word was twisted and shoved into Nathan's face like the insult it was meant to be. Nathan knew instinctively that he could not afford to show any weakness in front of men like these, often known as "sharks" in prison slang in his own time, with the rest of the population referred to as either "bait" or "fish". Despite the weak position he held, he was still a detective and the power of authority could hold sway even here, even now.

'Inmate Reed is my responsibility,' Nathan snapped back. 'I chose to come down here with him, because he's innocent of any crime.'

Volt raised an eyebrow. 'Well now, innocent y'say, huh? I guess that makes us all just th'same, 'cause we's all innocent down here in Tethys, right boys?'

A rumble of agreement rippled through the angry crowd, but Nathan kept his eyes fixed on Volt. The con, whatever he had done to be in Tethys, was clearly king of the block and the only way Nathan could change the balance of power was to knock Volt off his pedestal as quickly as possible and get the hell out of Xavier's cell.

'Yeah,' Nathan replied, 'I figured you for a choir boy too.'

The laughter was shut off like a tap and Volt's humor vanished to be replaced with a tight jaw and a cold glare, like a gigantic cobra poised to strike.

'You say what now, *stick*?'

'You heard.'

Volt peered at Nathan for a moment before he spoke. 'Y'see, stick, you gone and got us all wrong. We was here to welcome you with open arms, but now you made us your enemy.'

'I didn't change a thing.'

'Wrong, stick,' Volt sneered. 'When we thought yo' friend here was a cop killer, we could at least take him seriously. But now you say he din' do it, so that makes him the same as you – a stick, stuck in here with us. What yo' think we gonna do 'bout that, *stick*?'

Nathan took a pace even closer to Volt, enough so that he could smell the con's stale sweat and prison food breath.

'I'm gonna count to three, and if you haven't turned around and left this cell you'll regret it.'

'That so?' Volt sneered with a broad smile. 'Oh me, oh my, whatever will I do?'

'One.'

Volt didn't move, the smile broadening on his face. Nathan opened his mouth as if to say two, but instead he jerked his right knee up and slammed it into Volt's groin. The big man's smile crumpled inward and his eyes widened with shock as he reached for his crotch, his mouth opening as he began to bend forward and fold up over the blow. Nathan slammed his head forward and smashed it across the bridge of Volt's nose like a sledgehammer.

Volt's eyes rolled up into their sockets and he collapsed in a pile of muscle at Nathan's feet, Nathan stepping neatly to one side to avoid the hefty obstacle as it slumped on the cell floor. He lifted one boot and with a heave of effort stomped it down on Volt's face, crushing whatever consciousness remained.

'Charge them, now!'

Nathan's yell prompted Allen and Reed to move, and with a scream Nathan plunged through the cell gates and smashed into the wall of muscle outside as Reed and Allen slammed into him from behind. The combined weight of their bodies plowed through Volt's thugs and propelled three of them over the gantry, their screaming bodies flailing as they plunged down into the chow hall and crashed onto the deck or across tables.

Nathan swung for the nearest con still standing and caught him a right hook across his broad and bearded jaw that sent the man reeling down the gantry. Allen dashed past on Nathan's left and stomped his boot onto the man's face, crushing his nose as the man's eyes rolled up in their sockets. Nathan whirled as he heard Reed scream, and saw the former officer launch himself into the other two cons with a frenzy of blows, driven by the same repressed fury he shared with all of the other cons on the block.

Nathan hurried to Reed's side and drove a boot into one of the henchmen's thighs, the tattooed, shaven headed thug growling in pain as he collapsed onto one knee and Reed's boot swung around to collide with his temple with a dull thump. The thug's head clanged against the rail and he slumped unconscious as Nathan looked up and saw the last of Volt's men fleeing down the gantry away from them.

Detective Allen moved up alongside Nathan and peered down the gantry.

'Gutsy move man,' he said, 'but when Volt comes around he's going to come down on us like a ton of bricks and there's no way the warden's men are comin' back in here to find us.'

'They will,' Nathan insisted. 'But right now we need to get out of the block and hide out somewhere while we still can.'

From the block rose a keening scream of outrage that soared to the very vaults of the ceiling as though probing for Nathan, Allen and Xavier. The scream turned to a roar of rage, twisting into something that Nathan could just about make out.

'Kiiillll them all!!'

Nathan looked at Allen. 'You think that Ryan's come round?'

'We need to run, now!'

They bolted down the gantry to see Volt stagger out of Reed's cell, his face a mask of blood, his eyes wild with terrible vengeance. Within moments, he was surrounded by a gaggle of thugs who rushed to join him as his bloody face looked across the gantry, his body trembling with fury as he pointed at Nathan with one quivering arm.

'Kill them, now!'

Xavier grabbed Nathan's arm as they ran across the gantry. 'This way!'

Nathan followed with Allen as Xavier dashed past other cells, some of them filled with inmates all cowering from the threat of violence staining the foul air. The lights above began to flicker again and the sound of dull booms echoed through the prison's grim interior like a labored heartbeat.

Xavier turned left, running along the upper tier as Nathan looked down and saw Ryan's gang splitting up to cut them off, dashing across the chow hall below.

'Where the hell are we going?' Nathan asked.

'Into that watch tower!' Reed yelled as he pointed right across the block.

Nathan glanced at the sheer walls and the hard–light panels protecting the control room where the warden's guards had worked, and he knew for sure that there was no way in.

'We can't get in there!'

Xavier didn't reply as they ran. Nathan saw four heavies rushing up the stairwell toward him, and he realized that they would reach the gantry right behind him if he let them complete their climb. Xavier dashed past, but Nathan turned and took two giant leaps down the stairwell.

The leading enforcer, a thick–set, towering wall of muscle looked up in surprise from the effort of hefting his bulk up the steps to see Nathan looming before him. Nathan landed hard on his left boot as he struck out with his right and slammed a blow high on the thug's chest, right below his throat.

The enforcer let out a howl of shock as the blow toppled him off balance and he tumbled backwards into the men climbing up in pursuit. Their bodies clashed and tangled, cries of pain echoing above the chorus of madness soaring through the prison as they collapsed in a heaving pile of limbs and enraged faces, men pinned beneath the weight of others and unable to free themselves, bones breaking against unforgiving metal steps.

Nathan turned and climbed back up the stairwell to the upper gantry, then turned left to follow Xavier and Allen to where he was pulling something out of another inmate's cell. Nathan reached his side as Xavier hauled the mattress out of the cell and turned it toward him as he yanked off the bed sheets.

'Use it to block the gantry on both sides,' Xavier gasped, out of breath.

Nathan helped him with Allen to turn the mattress on its end and wedge it between the cell walls and the rails. Nathan could see past the mattress to where Volts's thugs were now rushing up other stairwells, swarming onto the other levels, their injured leader staggering in pursuit.

'This won't hold them for long,' Allen said.

'It will if it's on fire,' Xavier snapped back as he dashed into the nearest cell and grabbed the collar of an inmate cowering within. 'You want to live?'

The inmate nodded frantically.

'Then help us! You've got contraband in here, I've seen you making deals. We need a flame, right now!'

The quivering inmate scrambled to his feet and turned to one wall of his cell. Where there seemed to be nothing but solid wall, Nathan watched as he suddenly yanked out chunks of what must have been some kind of putty made from food to reveal a small compartment hewn within the concrete.

Nathan turned and saw Volt and his lackeys rushing around the gantry, rage upon their faces and shivs now in their hands that glittered in the frenzied light, flickering makeshift blades hacked from chunks of metal as wicked as anything Nathan had ever seen.

'They're almost here!' he shouted back to Xavier.

From within the wall cavity the inmate pulled out a plastic bag, and from within the bag a plasma lighter. Xavier whirled and tossed the lighter to Nathan, who caught it in one hand even as Volts's men rushed upon their position.

Nathan flicked down on the ignition button and the plasma lighter crackled as a white–hot beam hissed into life between two small metallic terminals at one end of the lighter. He shoved the device against the mattress and then yelped as searing heat burst from the material and the mattress billowed with flames and thick smoke that forced Nathan backwards. His eyes watered as black smoke spilled in boiling clouds from the burning mattress, and on the far side of the gantry Volt's thugs skittered to a halt and backed up from the flames and heat.

Nathan rushed across the gantry to the other side, where Allen had rammed a second mattress into place. He lit the material and it blossomed with savage flames as they backed away, Volt's henchmen coming up short on the other side, arms raised against the heat.

Nathan turned to Xavier. 'Now what? Those mattresses won't burn that hot for long!'

Xavier was tying lengths of bed sheet together, one after the other as he looked at the clock on the block wall and then glanced at the watch tower.

'We're going to fly across the block,' he said confidently.

***

Dean Crawford

XXVI

'We're gonna *what?*' Allen echoed in disbelief.

Nathan turned to look in the same direction as Xavier, and suddenly he understood. The rattling breather vents opened to draw in stale air from the block and replace it with fresh air from more vents on the back wall. The vents were barely eighteen inches high and maybe two feet wide, very narrow but enough for a man to squeeze through.

'Where do they go?' Nathan asked.

'They run over the watch tower,' Xavier replied as he began coiling the strips of bed sheet on the gantry at his feet. 'There are grills that I could see from my cell in the ceiling that probably open and close at the same time to ventilate the control room.'

'Probably?' Nathan echoed.

'You got any better ideas?'

Nathan looked at the coiled sheets, then watched as Xavier tied a chunk of masonry grabbed from the nearest inmate's modified cell wall to the line. Xavier looked up and out over the chow hall as though gauging the distance. Nathan followed his gaze and saw thick pipework running left to right across the ceiling, roughly half way between the gantry upon which they stood and the watch tower. Xavier swung the rock and line like a lasso and then hurled the rock upward. The line swung out over the abyss and looped over the largest of the pipes. Nathan watched as the rock travelled further and then swung down, building up speed as it twirled up and over the pipe again, twisting around the pipe three times before it then dropped to dangle in mid–air. Xavier tied a second smaller piece of masonry to the other end of the line as Allen watched in mystified fascination.

'How do you know you'll make the line the right length?' he demanded.

Xavier nodded to the guard rail as he worked.

'Each rail is one meter long,' he replied. 'Easy to work out the total length of the block from that, and the height of the vents.'

'The lines and measurements drawn on the wall of your cell,' Nathan said as he put the pieces together. 'You figured this all out, drew it to check it.'

'More or less,' Xavier replied. 'I figured that if Volt wanted me dead, he'd have to work for it. I was ready to do this when you two showed up.'

'Sorry about the delay.'

Xavier measured the length of material out, and then he ripped a small piece of yellow rubber from the waist of his prison uniform and tied it around the line before he turned to Nathan and Allen.

'You guys wanna try it out first?'

'We're good, really.'

'Kill them!'

Volt's shriek alerted Nathan and he saw the psycho pushing his men closer to the burning mattresses, the thugs trying to grab the mattresses and pull them down.

Xavier scrambled up onto the safety rail and leaned on the line, testing its strength and the grip of the other end looped around the pipework. The dangling rock lifted a little as Xavier hauled on it, and then the line tightened and it held firm.

Xavier gripped the line right below the yellow marker when Nathan heard a chorus of shouts from behind him. He whirled and saw Volt's men on the other side of the gantry holding another mattress that they were carrying as a battering ram. The mattress slammed into the burning obstacle with a cloud of smoke and spraying embers, metal grinding against metal as the mattress twisted sideways.

Nathan dashed toward the mattress, grabbing hold of the cowering inmate who had provided them with the plasma lighter as he passed by.

'Help me here!'

Together, they grabbed a second mattress and dragged it down the gantry to slam it up against the burning one, further pinning it in place as Nathan leaned his weight against it to help prop up the blockade.

'Time to leave!' Xavier said.

'Go, now!'

Nathan saw Xavier leap from the rail and sweep across the block as crowds of maddened inmates tried to reach up for him. Xavier arced over their heads and swung up to the watch tower, and Nathan saw him reach out and grab the edge of the vent hatch. Xavier scrambled up and into the hatch, then looked across the block toward him and swung the line. The smaller weight that he'd attached to it brought the line arcing back across the chow hall toward them.

'Go!' Nathan said to Allen. 'I'll cover our retreat!'

'You should go first,' Allen replied.

'You were right,' Nathan said, leaning back against the mattress to keep the blockade in place. 'I got us into this. Get over there and send that rope back as fast as you can!'

Allen turned and caught the line as it returned, and then he hopped up onto the railings and leaped out over the raucous crowd below. Nathan saw him sweep above their heads and up to the vent, catching the edge with his hands and scrambling inside. Allen turned and let the rope go, the weight bringing it sweeping back toward Nathan.

Nathan moved to catch it but the inmate who had given them the plasma lighter rushed away from the burning mattress and caught the line as it returned, leaving Nathan to hold Volt's thugs back.

'Wait!' Nathan yelled.

The inmate ignored him and scrambled up onto the railing as he caught the line, and without hesitation he leaped off the railing.

'The yellow marker!' Allen shouted from the vent on the far side of the block.

The inmate's face creased with concern as he flew out over the hall, his hands lower on the rope than Xavier and Allen had been. Nathan watched helplessly as the smaller man swung over the riotous hall below, pulled his legs up to avoid being grabbed by the violent felons reaching out for him and swept safely past, but Nathan could see that he was already doomed.

The yellow marker was higher up the line, and the inmate's swing wasn't bringing him high enough to make the vent or Allen's outstretched hand. Above the din from below Nathan heard his desperate cry of despair as he rushed toward the watch tower's featureless wall and then slammed into it as he reached desperately for the hand just inches above him.

The impact dislodged his grip as his fingertips fell short, and Nathan heard his cry as he fell and slammed into the unforgiving floor of the hall below. The sound of crackling bones was drowned out by the cheers of the crowd as they rushed in like a pack of wolves and the inmate's body was consumed within a frenzy of blows.

A fresh salvo of jubilant cries caught his attention and he saw Volt's henchmen slam into the burning mattress on the other side of the gantry, and it collapsed flat in a cloud of spraying embers and billowing smoke as the thugs trampled across it in their eagerness to reach him.

Nathan saw the line arcing back toward the gantry and he knew his time was up. Simple physics: the line would swing with less vigor with each pass, like a pendulum losing energy. If he didn't grab it now, he'd never be able to reach it.

Nathan hurled himself away from the mattress even as Volt's thugs behind him plowed their battering ram into it. Metal screeched against metal and clouds of embers spilled like veils of orange rain as the mattress was twisted aside and the enforcers charged through with Volt behind them and shrieking like a banshee for Nathan's blood.

Nathan sprinted along the gantry as the line swung back toward him and he reached out for it, stretched with all of his might for the weight on the end of the line. The line slowed down as it swung back toward the gantry, creeping slowly upward, and Nathan leaned out further over the rail as the gantry trembled with the combined weight of charging boots as Volt's crew rushed upon him.

Nathan saw the weight just out of his reach as the line reached the top of its arc, and with a plunging dread he knew that it would not be close enough for him to catch it. The line swung painfully slowly to the gantry, inches from his grasp, and then began to fall away from him again toward the chow hall far below.

'Killl him!!!'

Volt's anguished cry of revenge rushed along with his bearded thugs as they sprinted toward Nathan, filling the gantry and his vision, and without conscious thought Nathan scrambled up onto the gantry rail and leaped into the void as he aimed for the yellow marker on the line in mid–air before him.

For an instant in time he flew through the open air fifty feet above the chow hall, a sea of warring convicts all screaming for his blood as he reached out for the line suspended it seemed along with him in mid–air, and then he touched the line on the yellow marker and he gripped it in both hands as he rushed away from the gantry.

For once, the hot, stale air of the prison seemed almost fresh and cool as Nathan swept across the block, his boots rushing across the heads of the cons below, several of them leaping from nearby tables in futile attempts to grab at him as he passed by. The line swung up toward the vents on the watch tower, and Nathan caught sight of Xavier inside the control room looking out at him.

Nathan reached up to grab the vent, and as the line reached the wall he grabbed the ledge but kept the line in his hand. With a heave of effort he hauled himself up and slid into the vent, felt a rush of hot air from fans deeper inside the system drawing heat and smoke out of the prison block. He smelled the aluminum of the duct around him, the metal warm to the touch as he slid down, pulling the line with him until it reached its maximum length and became taut, out of reach to the cons still trapped in the block. He released the line and slid along on his belly until he saw an open grill in the floor of the duct, and a head popped up to look at him.

'Glad you could make it!'

Allen helped Nathan down into the control room, and Nathan turned to see the various work stations now abandoned by the sticks.

'That was too close,' Nathan said as Xavier closed the ceiling grill.

'We've got other problems,' Allen said as he gestured to the watch tower's rear door, which led to the prison's outer quadrants and supposed freedom.

Nathan only had to glance at it to know that it had been sealed from the outside by the fleeing guards, and that the power was switched off to most of the control panels.

'There's no way out and the power to the control room has been cut off,' Xavier said. 'We're trapped.'

***

XXVII

Tethys Gaol

'It's perfect.'

Nathan's voice was calm now as he stood beside the hard–light window in the watch tower and looked out over D Block. Zak Volt and his crew had taken control of the riot, his thugs patrolling the gantries with flickering blades in their chunky fists as they began organizing their uprising and putting into motion whatever deranged plan their leader had in mind.

'What's perfect?' Xavier asked.

'The timing,' Nathan replied. 'A riot, just when people want you dead. It's the perfect way to kill you without having to pin the murder on any one convict. Inmates won't snitch on each other, so your death will be chalked up to random violence.'

Xavier sighed and nodded. 'You think that Volt's a part of this whole thing? That he's behind me being framed?'

'No,' Nathan cautioned. 'I think that he's being controlled by somebody else, that he's the one tasked with killing you. He couldn't have set you up for the shooting of Ricard in San Diego from all the way out here, but he must tie into all of this somehow.'

Xavier was sitting on the edge of the control panel and watching the gangs below, watching the violence with the morbid curiosity of the terminally doomed, the unthinkable acts going on inside the cells as the "sharks" exacted revenge on the "fish" for unspoken insults, perceived disrespect or spurned advances. Detective Allen leaned against the wall beside the window, clearly disturbed by their close proximity to the gang.

'Any one of these animals could be behind it,' Xavier replied. 'I'm tired of thinking about the whole damned thing. Ever since Ricard started laying into me in San Diego I've been left wondering how this even all got started, why it all got started. I was a model prison officer, I had no enemies, no concerns and was just building a life for myself. Why the hell would somebody go to such lengths to set me up like this?'

Nathan thought about that for a moment and a new train of thought was sparked into life. The fact was that until his apparent shooting of Ricard, Xavier Reed was indeed the perfect officer. If Nathan had been wanting to set somebody else up for the murder of another officer, he would likely have chosen a patsy with issues in their past; official warnings, criminal history, reputation for anger issues or violence, that kind of thing. The last person he would have selected would have been an officer like Reed, which might have sparked suspicion had the planned murder not gone quite to….

Nathan stared into space for a moment as a sudden and unexpected realization slammed into his awareness like a freight train.

'Planned,' he whispered to himself.

'What now?' Allen asked.

'Ricard's murder,' Nathan said. 'It had to have been *planned*, intricately. I mean, we knew that, but when you think about it you had to be standing in exactly the right spot, at exactly the right time, for the real shooter to get a line of sight to you from that old warehouse in San Diego.'

'But it was Ricard who was shot,' Reed replied. 'He was the victim.'

'Maybe,' Allen replied for Nathan. 'Ironside here's got it into his head that you may have been the target for Ricard, but that whoever promised to pay him off shot him instead.'

Reed stared at Nathan for a long beat. 'That's insane.'

'Which is why it's so effective,' Nathan went on. 'The real shooter kills Ricard, leaving you holding the can for the murder and with the only person who could prove your innocence dead in the gutter at your feet.'

Xavier stood up from the corner of the desk and for the first time his expression glowed with the light of hope.

'That's brilliant,' he said, but the glow of hope faded suddenly. 'But he's dead, so there's no way to prove any of this.'

'Yes there is,' Nathan insisted, 'because like I said, for their plan to work they had to know precisely where you would be. None of this could have happened unless it was precisely choreographed, with the shooter already in position and Ricard able to confront you in just the right way for the shooter to fire and make it look like the shot had come from you.'

Xavier shook his head in wonder.

'And my pistol? It fizzled, but nobody believed me.'

Allen shrugged.

'It isn't that tough to bleed the energy out of a plasma charge, Xavier. We need to figure out who knew precisely where you would be on that day in San Diego and also had access to your service weapon prior to the incident.'

Xavier's eyes locked with Nathan's, and then at the same time they both reached the same conclusion.

'I know who set this all up,' Nathan said.

'So do I,' Xavier uttered as though he were spitting something unpleasant from his mouth, and Nathan could see the raw pain on the man's face as he suddenly was forced to come to terms with the knowledge of who had condemned him to a lifetime in prison. 'It was…'

'Ironside!!'

The call came from the block, the hard–light windows designed to allow sound to pass though unimpeded so that the sticks could keep both their eyes and ears on what was happening inside the block. Nathan walked across to the windows and looked down.

Zak Volt was standing on top of one of the tables nearest the watch tower, the hall around him filled with armed cons all staring up at Nathan. Behind them, the gantries were filled with cons all watching with interest, most of them with nothing left to lose having had Volt's heavies empty their cells of anything valuable. Smoke curled in lazy coils across the ceiling of the block from the mattresses that were still smoldering high on the upper tier, blocked latrines still spilling languid sheets of water down the gantries as embers spiralling down from above completed the hellish scene.

'Ironside,' Volt repeated as he saw Nathan appear at the windows.

Volt's face was still smeared with his own blood, and his clothes with the blood of other inmates unfortunate enough to have got in his way. His nose was splattered across his face where Nathan's attack had crushed the cartilage, his eyes bloodshot and filled with poisonous fury.

'You're finished, Volt,' Nathan called back. 'There's nowhere else you can take your violence and hate.'

Volt smiled, no warmth within, like a shark baring its teeth before the bite.

'I have this block and everybody in it, and before long I'll have the whole prison.'

'To do what?' Nathan replied, hoping to sew doubt among Volt's followers. 'Get blasted to hell by the fleet? There's nowhere to go. You could control every inch of this entire prison and it would get you nowhere, you idiot!'

Rage flashed brighter across Volt's face and he stepped closer to the tower, a shiv in his left hand and what looked like a blade fashioned from a portion of hacked steel mirror in the other.

'Yo' talk to me like that while you're up there, Ironside, but everythin' you say's gonna come back to you on the edge of my blades!'

'It doesn't matter,' Nathan replied. 'None of this matters. All any of you are doing is doubling your sentences by following this jerk into oblivion, and for what? For ten minutes of flames and watching latrine water being flushed down on you?'

Nathan saw the crowd of inmates looking around at the shattered block as though they were suddenly coming awake from a bad dream. Volt's smile returned, more cold and brutal than before.

'You think that they care?' he challenged. 'We's all here for life, for one reason or th'other. How long our sentences are don't matter to us, 'cause you can't get more than life unless you're one of those damned Holosap freaks!'

Ripples and murmurs of agreement rippled through the crowd, but Nathan shook his head.

'Those Holosap freaks don't have to spend their lives cooped up in this stinking hole with people like you,' he pointed out. 'They get to live more than one life in complete freedom out there. That's something people like you will never have again, Volt. You're done, no matter how many people you kill in here.'

'Well now, that ain't quite the truth,' Volt replied, 'because we ain't stayin' in here no longer, right boys?'

A cheer went up from the cons once again Volt's men and swallowing whatever deranged and insane plan he had devised. Nathan knew that he must have lied to them somehow to get them to follow him in a riot on a space station prison from which they could not hope to escape.

'What crap did you feed those boys of yours to convince them to follow you on your suicidal little riot, Volt?'

'None at all,' Volt snapped, and then from below the watch tower Nathan saw Volt's two bearded thugs drag a captured prison officer out into view. 'Y'see, if we don't get what we want, we'll start executin' these folks one after th'other.'

Nathan saw the guard's battered face, his uniform ripped and torn and bloodied, his legs weak with fear and loathing. Volt crouched down alongside the prostrate guard and looked up at Nathan as he held the edge of the steel mirror to the man's throat.

'So, how 'bout it, Ironside?'

'What do you want to know?' Xavier said as he stood forward, his eyes fixed on the captured guard. 'You don't need to hurt him.'

'The armory,' Volt snapped. 'You can open it from up there! We want the weapons, and we want a shuttle out of Tethys in one hour!'

Xavier looked pleadingly at Nathan, but it was Allen who answered. 'You know that he'll kill the guard anyway, and us, whether you do what he wants or not.'

'I can't let him murder that officer,' Xavier whispered. 'I can't stand by and let him do that.'

'You can't stop him either,' Nathan pointed out. 'No matter what you say, Volt will kill him.'

Xavier bit his lip, his features twisted with anguish as he looked down and saw the guard trying to squirm away from the jagged blade.

'I'm runnin' out of patience!' Volt yelled.

The mirror's saw–tooth edge pressed against the guard's throat and he let out a cry of pain as it bit into his flesh, blood smearing the surface.

'Level Four!' Xavier shouted, his voice poisoned with regret as he hit a switch in the Watch Tower and a series of red lights turned green. 'But we can't get out of the tower to request a shuttle.'

Volt grinned as he stood up from the guard. 'We jus' gonna follow you, blast our way out of that watch tower and then take every block fo' ourselves. We got hundreds of hostages in here!'

Nathan frowned, and then he saw the escape line that Xavier had made drop from the vent high above them on the watchtower and swing away from them in a graceful arc. Nathan stepped closer to the window and saw cons on the upper tier with a makeshift hook constructed from thin strips of plastic protruding out across the block.

The line swung smoothly up to the far gantry, where it was caught by some of Volt's men.

'Y'all got room in there for some more, *stick*?' Volt called in glee.

'The tower's sealed!' Nathan called back. 'There's no way out of here!'

'There is if we got currency!' Volt sneered as he pointed to the guard lying at his feet.

'They're coming in,' Xavier said.

Nathan called down to Volt. 'Let the guard go! That was the deal!'

Ryan looked down at the stricken man and then he lifted one boot and smashed it down feverishly on the guard's skull with sickening cracks that seemed to echo around the block. The guard's skull shattered and several of the watching cons jerked away from the scene as one vomited. The guard's body fell limp, sprawled across the tiled deck amid a pool of rapidly spilling blood as his dying heart continued to pump inside his chest. Volt looked up at Nathan and chuckled maniacally.

'He's gone alright!'

Grim laughter rippled across the block as Xavier turned from the window, one hand over his mouth and his eyes squeezed shut.

Nathan saw Volt's bearded henchmen clamber up onto the railings and then one of them launched himself into the air. The thug's massive form swung across the block to a wave of cheers and then he vanished above the watchtower windows.

Nathan heard a deep thump and then the bearded thug plummeted past the window, his swing too low for the hatch. Gusts of laughter bellowed out from the crowd as they scattered to avoid the grisly missile, and the bearded man's body crashed down onto tables to the sound of splintering bones and a roaring cry of agony.

'They'll figure it out soon enough,' Xavier said, his features pale and his skin sheened with sweat.

'We gotta make a stand here, now, and hold them off,' Allen said. 'It's the only play we got left.'

Nathan looked at Allen. 'I'm sorry, for getting' you into this.'

Allen nodded. 'You can apologize when we get out of here. You got any ideas about how we're gonna survive long enough?'

Nathan looked around and saw a rack filled with plasma sticks. He hurried across and grabbed one as he heard another body slam against the wall outside, this time accompanied by cheers of delight and no splintering bones.

Above them he heard the sound of somebody slithering into the ventilation ducts above the control room, and he threw a plasma stick to Xavier.

'One thrust as they come through,' he said, 'then a blow to the head to silence them and save the charge, okay?'

Xavier nodded, and then suddenly the grill in the ceiling clattered down to the ground and a hulking con thrust his way out of the opening feet first and dropped into the control room.

***

XXVIII

CSS Titan

Kaylin Foxx watched as Doctor Schmidt stood in the quarantine cubicle and examined the floor upon which he "stood". His projection, which was controlled by computers to match whichever of Titan's many decks he appeared upon, was immune to any kind of biological interference, making him the ideal candidate to examine at close range the bizarre creature now occupying the cubicle. Beyond the translucent walls of the quarantine unit, four Marines stood guard and watched in silence, Lieutenant Foxx, Betty and Vasquez alongside them.

'What do you make of it?' Vasquez asked.

Doctor Schmidt did not reply for a moment, absorbed entirely by his study of this fascinating lifeform. Although Foxx could not see it there below him, she knew from a sensor scan of the cubicle that a tiny sheet of residual heat from biological processes covered the entire floor of the unit.

'It's biological, I think,' Schmidt replied, 'and probably capable of infiltrating any life form at the cellular level.'

Foxx shivered visibly as she looked at the floor of the unit, which would have appeared entirely normal to her had she walked inside. The entity had colored itself to match the existing deck floor, like some kind of strange chameleon.

'This isn't what I expected first contact to be like,' she admitted.

Schmidt walked out of the quarantine unit, his hands behind his back and a smile glowing on his face.

'Most people don't,' he agreed. 'They expect great beasties with evil fangs and tentacles, or emotionless machines with a thirst for human destruction, but the truth is that most advanced and spacefaring species that are able to cross entire galaxies would look nothing like what we expect them to, simply because of the time it takes to evolve to the point where galactic travel is possible.'

Foxx knew from school that it had taken intelligent human life around four and a half billion years to appear on Earth, and that had occurred in a relatively stable solar system in a sedate corner of the Milky Way galaxy's Orion Arm. Much of the rest of the galaxy was a turbulent milieu of gravitational waves compressing spiral arms into dense clouds of violent star birth, or superheated to millions of degrees in the galaxy's dark heart, wherein ruled the gargantuan supermassive black hole Sagittarius A.

Life could not realistically be expected to emerge in these dense, hot, radiation–bathed furnaces, and so mankind looked to similar areas of the galaxy for signs of life around yellow spectral stars like the sun, or long–lived red and brown dwarf star systems, or in globular clusters where millions of suns would fill the sky in a dazzling halo of stars orbited by planetary systems rich in the heavy metals necessary for life.

'So you're sayin' that the thing in there must be old,' Vasquez said, 'old enough to have evolved beyond human form and into something else?'

Schmidt nodded.

'Who knows what this life form may once have looked like, but it has clearly progressed to a state that we no longer recognize immediately as life. We're detecting heat from it and it clearly does indeed have a biological component to it, but right now it's confined to this cubicle. My team will be here momentarily and we'll move a sample to my laboratory for closer study.'

Betty peered at the floor of the unit. 'Will it know what you've done?'

'Undoubtedly,' Schmidt chirped. 'If it's smart enough to alter its shape to impersonate an Ayleean warrior, it's more than smart enough to monitor what we're doing.'

Foxx thought for a moment as Schmidt's team arrived. 'It spoke,' she said. 'The Ayleean this thing impersonated, it spoke in English.'

Schmidt nodded.

'It can learn incredibly quickly,' he replied, 'which means we must too if we're to understand it. If it were not for the sound proofing around that cubicle it would probably be listening to us right now.'

Foxx watched as Schmidt's team punctured the cubicle with a small machine designed to coordinate its actions with the field generators of the quarantine unit, gaining access where other forms of material could not. Moments later, it burrowed down into the floor of the cubicle and to her amazement she watched it scoop up a visible section of that floor, revealing the original one beneath it.

The material was pulled back inside the machine into a smaller, equally powerful quarantine container and the machine's probe retracted.

'Be quick now,' Schmidt hurried his team along. 'I'll be waiting in the laboratory.'

Foxx and Vasquez followed the team as Schmidt's projection disappeared, and they ran through to the laboratories as the team placed the machine inside a second quarantine unit, this one a meter square and filled with a menagerie of robotic arms, tools and scopes.

Schmidt stood over the quarantine unit and watched as the machine regurgitated the sample into the unit and then backed out. Its surface was swept by a small scanner as it passed through, Foxx figuring that the scanner searched for any signs of remaining contamination by whatever the sample was made from. A small green light illuminated on the edge of the machine and Schmidt *humphed* in delight.

'Good, that's the first thing we've learned for sure today – whatever it is cannot pass through hard–light structures such as these quarantine units, I'm sure you'll be relieved to know.'

Schmidt accessed a remotely controlled microscope and trained it upon the sample, which for now had remained in its form as a section of the quarantine unit's floor, as though a piece of deck tiling had been chipped off. The doctor leaned close to the scope and observed the sample only for a few moments before he stood back and rested his chin on one hand, supported by his other arm as a deep frown creased his holographic blue features.

'What?' Vasquez asked.

Schmidt raised an eyebrow as though he'd already forgotten the detectives were there.

'Interesting,' he said in reply. 'The organism is indeed biological, but only partly.'

'Partly?' Foxx echoed.

'Yes, it appears to consist mostly of quasi–biological components. Spectroscopy reveals them to consist mostly of titanium and certain alloys. In effect, this is neither a creature nor a machine, but something of both.'

'It's a cyborg?' Foxx asked.

'In a manner of speaking,' Schmidt nodded. 'But it is constructed on a nanometer scale, many thousands of them in this one small sample. I believe that this is the first known discovery of a genuine extra–terrestrial artificial superintelligence.'

'A what now?' Admiral Marshall asked as he strode into the laboratory.

'An artificial superintelligence,' Schmidt repeated as he stepped away from the quarantine tub so that Marshall could look at the slab of what looked like nothing more than floor tiling inside. 'Scientists and even philosophers have long contended that any space faring species that was able to visit us here on Earth would be so far advanced that we might not even recognize it for what it is. Many also contend that we would not encounter biological species at all, but machines.'

'You're kidding?' Foxx said. 'You're telling me our fridges will inherit the universe?'

'It's already happening,' Schmidt pointed out. 'Intelligent implants beneath our skins and in our skulls, bio–enhancement, brain impulse therapy, and human beings have been using prosthetic limbs to replace those lost due to injury or illness for hundreds of years. That natural progression from enhancements to permanent improvement, projected well into the future, will inevitably create a race of humans more machine than people, and the constant miniaturization of that technology will inevitably make that race ever smaller and more efficient. Look at me, for instance – as a Holosap I'm really just an entire dead person inside a quantum chip.'

Betty moved forward and peered in at the sample before them.

'This doesn't look all that smart to me,' she said.

Schmidt nodded.

'I suspect that like the neurons in a human mind or the termites in a mound, an individual unit of this organism is not especially intelligent or capable of what we would consider coherent thought. It is when they come together in sufficient numbers that cognition, although likely very different from our own, sparks into life and awareness. The organism in the main quarantine cubicle will be aware that a sample of its being has been taken, but this much smaller sample will no longer be aware of what or where it is.'

'That's weird,' Vasquez uttered.

'That's useful,' the admiral countered as he stood up from examining the sample. 'It means that if we blow it to pieces, it can't coordinate itself.'

'True,' Schmidt said, 'but like any evolutionary species it will have developed defense mechanisms for just such an eventuality. Like a flock of birds it will rejoin itself, perhaps quickly.'

Marshall thought for a moment.

'You say they're real small. Do they have any motor function, the ability to move under their own steam?'

Schmidt looked again into the scope, this time relaying the images within onto a holo–screen nearby. Foxx turned and saw what looked like a soup of cells moving about, as though she were watching tiny bugs in the deep ocean densely packed and probing each other.

'No,' Schmidt said, 'they have no visible means of propulsion.'

Marshall folded his arms. 'So they can't easily move about in zero gravity. How would they move in an atmospheric environment?'

'I'm not sure,' Schmidt replied, 'but if I were to hazard a guess I would say that they simply occupy other hosts.'

'Occupy?' Foxx asked with another shiver. 'You mean infect?'

'Yes,' Schmidt confirmed. 'They appear in many respects to have evolved to become a parasite, or so their behavior leads me to believe. We can assume that this species is many thousands of years more advanced than our own. When humans experienced the Industrial Revolution they were only a couple hundred years from radio, fifty more to computers, ten more to landing on the moon and so on. The growth was trimetric and now we're a space faring species with a strong line in technological implants. True artificial intelligence is already within our capabilities as we've seen before, and the rise of *Holo sapiens* shows that our squidgy human brains and our bodies, vulnerable to injury and disease, are already outdated by the technology we've introduced. This organism we've discovered probably represents where we'll be in a few thousand years.'

Betty screwed up her nose in distaste. 'We'll pass on that.'

'So what's it doing here, and why did it attack that Ayleean ship and take down the crew?' Marshall asked. 'If this thing is so damned clever, why did it attack us?'

Schmidt sighed as he replied, looking at the sample in the cubicle and the holo–screen display.

'We are unlikely ever to understand its motivations,' he said simply. 'This organism represents a species that has evolved entirely to become a synthetic being with very little biological material remaining. That's why the life sensors in the escape capsule didn't detect it – the genetic material remaining was both different in structure to ours and in such small quantities that it didn't register. Who could possibly understand what motivations a species like this might possess? We can't even understand what it's thinking, or whether it actually thinks at all.'

'It thinks enough to impersonate Ayleeans and commit murder,' Marshall shot back. 'That makes it an enemy until we know better. Keep working on it.'

Schmidt was about to do just that when a sudden thought hit Foxx.

'You say that this thing can get inside us, inside anything, right?'

'Yes,' Schmidt replied.

'And your team opened the capsules inside the quarantine unit?'

'Yes.'

'Did the team members walk out again?'

Schmidt stared at her for a long moment, and then he realized what she meant.

'They could already be loose in the ship,' Schmidt said to the admiral.

***

XXIX

'Take him down!'

Nathan yelled the warning as the bulky looking inmate thumped down from the vent onto the deck of the watch tower.

Xavier leaped forward and without hesitation he rammed the tip of a crackling plasma baton into the inmate's belly. The con cried out in pain and his limbs twitched and shuddered as he folded over the charge and collapsed onto the deck, quivering in jerking spasms as a second con plunged out of the duct and crashed down on top of the first.

Nathan rushed in and slammed his own baton down onto the man's lower back, aiming for his kidney. The charge bolted through the inmate's body and he let out a roar of pain and surprise as he jerked his left arm around.

'Blade!'

Nathan heard Allen's warning and stepped back as he blocked the con's blow with his left arm, the jagged tip of a steel shank stopping an inch away from his flank. The inmate toppled as his body succumbed to the electrical charge forking through his limbs and he collapsed on top of his fellow con.

'We've gotta get out of here!' Xavier yelled.

Nathan could hear the scurrying of more cons through the duct above them, and then another fell through the open grill and landed on top of the first two but this time with cat–like agility and grace. He leaped off the two fallen cons and brandished a blade that he kept close to his thigh in a one–handed grip, the mark of a man who knew how to handle himself. His shaved head was lined with ragged scars, a patch over one eye where an illegal implant of some kind had been surgically removed.

Nathan gave ground as the con edged forward, his eye switching between Nathan and Xavier as he moved the blade out in front of him a little.

'Only a matter of time, boys,' he snarled.

The con stepped lightly forward and the blade flashed back handed at Nathan, the glittering tip seeking to unzip his throat. Nathan stepped to the left and then forward, the blade whispering through the air past his face as he jabbed the plasma baton up under the inmate's armpit.

The man screamed as the charge roared through him, Nathan easily blocking the return blow as it flailed wildly. The knifeman tumbled to his knees and Nathan drove his boot down hard into the man's crumpled legs, smashing down on his ankle to the sound of splintering bone and more cries of pain.

Nathan stepped back and caught Xavier's surprised expression.

'Rough childhood,' he said by way of an explanation.

Two more cons dropped through the grill in quick succession, both of them armed. This time they stepped quickly forward, blocking Nathan's and Xavier's access to the duct and allowing two more cons to drop in behind and join them. Behind the growing wall of cons, those that Nathan and Xavier had hit first with the sticks began to drag themselves to their feet again, fury in their expressions as they grasped for their fallen weapons.

Nathan backed toward the locked watch tower exit, Xavier moving in alongside him while Allen moved to defend their left. They all had a second set of plasma batons tucked into their belts, but Nathan knew that with upwards of two hundred cons inside the block all eager to get into the watch tower and out of the prison, it was only a matter of time before they were completely overrun.

Two hulking men with biceps like footballs and barrel chests landed heavily in the control room and looked around before shoving their way to the front, like gorillas confronting intruders into their lair. Nathan could see that each of them carried a length of metal that looked as though it had once been a part of a cell door frame, levered free with bare hands, crude tools and brutal rage, the sheer power of undiluted madness. Both men's prison clothes were stained with blood and sweat and he could smell the stench of their body odor from where he stood with Xavier and Allen.

Nathan moved forward. Both men watched him cautiously, neither of them having forgot how quickly Nathan had floored their insane leader.

'I'd get back if I were you,' Nathan growled, hoping that he could swing the little crowd of thugs to his favor. 'Because the only way we're getting through that door is together.'

The bearded enforcers looked at each other, and then one of them swung his length of jagged metal in a brutal back slash toward Nathan's head. Nathan ducked under the blow, but at the same time he jerked the plasma baton up and let the tip touch the thug's crude metal blade. The charge bolted down the length of metal and the big man growled in pain and staggered backwards, his right arm jerking spasmodically.

Nathan lunged in with a straight right and drove the baton into his guts. The thug's growl rose in pitch to a howl and he lurched away from the pain and plowed into his fellow inmates.

'Get down!'

Xavier's cry sent Nathan plunging to his knees as the other thug swung his own weapon, the jagged edge swishing through Nathan's hair and missing his scalp by a half inch. Xavier slammed his own baton into the man's chest and the big bearded felon screamed as he tumbled backwards across his fallen companions.

Even as he crashed down so another con leaped down into the watch room and this one swung an instant punch that cracked across Xavier's jaw and sent him reeling backwards. Nathan turned and saw Zak Volt's demonic, bloodied face snarling like a wild animal as the insane convict lashed out with one boot. Nathan twisted aside from the blow and swung the baton at Ryan but the con was too quick and ducked beneath it, grabbing Nathan's wrist and twisting hard.

Nathan felt bright pain lance up his forearm as he was twisted backwards in sympathy to the pain, but he turned the baton in his hand and jabbed it against Volt's forearm. Current danced through the psychopath's arm and bolted through Nathan's at the same time and with a loud crack Nathan was thrown clear as Volt was propelled away from him by the charge.

Allen leaped forward to Nathan's defense and struck Volt with a left hook that cracked across the con's jaw and sent him floundering sideways, but almost immediately Allen was forced to confront two more cons trying to work their way around to flank his position. Nathan staggered, off balance as the plasma baton toppled from his useless hand and clattered to the deck. Volt lunged for the weapon, his hands closing around it as he swung the baton up at Nathan. Nathan twisted off balance, plunged into the wall as he avoided the baton and reached behind his back for his spare and whipped it out. Volt back handed the baton on the return sweep and Nathan blocked it with his forearm and jabbed the fresh baton up under Volt's ribcage, holding it there as the plasma charge crackled and burned into the con's flesh.

Volt roared in pain and launched himself away from Nathan, crashing onto the deck and writhing in agony as the stench of burning flesh stained the air around them. Nathan fell back to the locked door as Volt's crew picked their leader up, coils of thin blue smoke wafting from the wound in his side as the unstable con mastered the pain and glared at Nathan. A cruel smile broke through as he pointed at Xavier.

'You're done,' Volt seethed. 'No matter what happens here, all three of you are dead men. Only thing is how you go, fast or slow.' His maniac giggle rattled around the control room as he gestured with one thumb out of the windows. 'Got me a hundred men, all of 'em waiting to come through here. How long d'ya think you'll last, sticks?'

Nathan held his ground near the exit, Xavier beside him, blood on his lips from Volt's punch but the baton still in his hand.

'As long as these batons will,' Nathan snapped back. 'Don't think we'll make it easy for you. If I get my way, you'll be burned alive before you reach either of us.'

Volt chortled in delight.

'The man's after ma own dear heart,' he cackled to his lackeys. 'I owe you two scores now, stick, and the only one of us gonna be burnin' alive is you. Literally. Whaddya think boys, we oughta set alight another o'those mattresses with Ironside here tied to it?'

A ripple of grim chuckles of anticipation fluttered darkly through the gathered crowd of convicts.

'Why the hell do you want Xavier dead so bad?' Nathan asked. 'What's in it for you?'

'The pleasure of killin' a stick,' Volt snapped back as though it were obvious. 'There anything else better?'

'No,' Nathan shook his head, 'that's not it. This riot will see you sealed up in the hole for the rest of your sentence, which means the rest of your life. You wouldn't have done any of this without a good reason, and even a man as utterly insane as you knows better than to sign your own death warrant.'

'Why thank you fo' the compliment, stick,' Volt whispered back in mock delight, 'and in answer to your question, seein' as you're both about to die, horribly, all I can say is that your nearest and dearest oughta be kept at arm's length, know what I mean?'

Nathan shook his head.

'You knew that Xavier was innocent the moment he walked in here, didn't you,' he accused. 'You've targeted him since he arrived.'

Volt shrugged, and then from the vent duct above him a hand appeared and passed something large and black. Volt looked up and then took the object as a bright smile blossomed on his face. Nathan's guts plunged in despair as he watched Volt stroke the barrel of the MM–15 plasma pistol.

'Well, whaddya know?' he whispered, cradling the weapon as though it were a newborn child. 'We got us some guns.'

Nathan saw Allen and Reed close up either side of him, and suddenly the plasma batons looked useless in their hands.

'You don't need to do this,' Reed said to Volt.

'A man's gotta do what he's gotta do,' Volt replied, 'and right now I've got to kill you.' Volt glanced at Nathan. 'I like you, Ironside, if you can believe that. Even for a damned stick. So if you stand aside, I'll promise you a quick death.'

'Go to hell!'

Volt shrugged again and put his finger to his nose. 'Suit yourself, stick!'

Volt waved his crew forward and shouted at the top of his lungs as he activated the plasma pistol to the sound of a magazine humming with deadly energy as he aimed in support of his men.

'Take 'em down boys, all together now!!'

Nathan saw Volt's thugs suddenly rush toward them, heard their combined roars of murderous delight deafeningly loud in the control room as they charged, eyes wide and poisoned with malice, pink mouths agape, weapons raised.

Nathan backed up against the door alongside Xavier and Allen, their batons held out before them, and then suddenly the door plunged open and they all collapsed onto their backs in the corridor beyond as rough hands grabbed them and hauled them through the open doorway and a blaze of rifle fire lit up the corridor in a fearsome blue–white frenzy.

**

XXX

Nathan heard screams from within the control room as he was dragged backwards along the deck, saw brilliant pulses of plasma fire hit the nearest of Volt's thugs and sear deep black wounds into their chests, burning through flesh and bone in an instant to agonized screams as the thugs tumbled and fell.

Two shots blasted back in return as Volt fired his pistol and then suddenly the security door was slammed shut as armed guards heaved their weight in behind it and rammed solid metal latches back into place.

Nathan lay on his back on the hard, cold deck and stared up toward the ceiling, his chest heaving and his hand still gripping the plasma baton as though it were his only link to reality. Against the stark ceiling lights of the corridor, the Arkon Stone's cold eyes and flaming red beard appeared to look down at him.

'You?' Nathan gasped.

'Afraid so,' the warden growled in reply as he moved around Nathan and offered him one large, calloused hand.

Nathan hesitated, but then he saw the armed guards standing by as one of their number helped Xavier to his feet, another hauling Allen upright. Reluctantly, Nathan took the proffered hand and the warden pulled him up onto his feet.

'Apologies for the late arrival,' the warden rumbled.

'Late arrival?' Nathan echoed. 'You left the prison to its inmates with us in there. We're lucky to be alive.'

The warden peered down at him. 'You're welcome. Contrary to what you might have assumed, we've been trying to figure out how to get you out of there ever since the lockdown was enforced. We weren't expecting Ryan and his gang of idiots to use the lockdown to provoke a riot.'

Nathan frowned in confusion.

'Then why'd you put us in there in the first place?'

The warden sighed and checked his plasma pistol's magazine.

'Truth is I've known for some time that there had been doubts raised over Xavier Reed's conviction. But without evidence of some kind my hands were tied by the system – I can't just treat him differently without the San Diego DA's office or the Prison Governors saying that I can.'

Reed stared in disbelief at Arkon Stone. 'And you threw me in with Volt's crew?'

Stone nodded.

'The only way to give you the freedom and the retrial that we suspected you needed was for somebody on the inside to slip up. My men intercepted what we call a "kill note", an order sent from the outside in coded form telling Volt to murder you.'

Nathan felt a twinge of excitement as he realized what had happened.

'You set Volt up.'

The warden winked at him. 'Maybe you're not such a bad detective after all. Volt would never knowingly divulge his complicity in a murder, but like most cons he's a narcissistic psychopath and likes to prolong the suffering of his victims. We figured he'd give Reed a beating first before setting him up for the final attack, so we let the note get through.'

'Great,' Xavier uttered. 'I got myself a visit to the infirmary so you could play power games with Volt's crew.'

'Your injuries were healed within an hour of the attack,' Stone replied. 'That also got you a breathing space in the infirmary out of Volt's reach, and it gave us the chance to bug Volt's cell while we frisked it after the attack for contraband.'

Nathan smiled, suddenly impressed at how well the warden had fooled everybody.

'You made the cons think you hated us, to make them over–confident.'

'Didn't say I liked you,' the warden countered.

Nathan grinned. 'Likewise.'

The warden smiled as he checked his plasma rifle.

'Did it work?' Xavier demanded. 'Did you get anything?'

'From the cell?' the warden asked. 'No, but from in that control room, yes. Volt as good as confessed to being involved in the plot to kill you once you got to Tethys, which means your claims of being set up by somebody and a third shooter now will hold water with the DA. Add to that the kill note, which we traced back to San Diego, and your appeal can be cleared. We were listening in, and your time here is done.'

Nathan looked at Xavier, and in the space of a few moments he saw the months of pain and tension and anxiety and fear spill from the former officer's shoulders, as though a deep and festering boil had been finally lanced. Xavier slumped against the wall, his jaw trembling as he raised the fingers of one hand to his temples and covered his eyes.

Nobody said anything for a moment, and then Nathan turned to the warden again.

'We've got something else for you,' he said. 'I know who set this whole thing up and I know why.'

The warden sucked in a lungful of air, and gestured to his men. The guards moved out, heading away from the block as the warden replied.

'Then we need to keep both of you safe and hope that reinforcements get to us before Volt and his crew do.'

Nathan frowned. 'Why? What the hell is going on out there, anyway?'

'You're gonna have to see that to believe it,' the warden replied. 'Communications are down, all flights are blockaded, Titan's exchanged shots with an alien spaceship and most of this prison's security systems are malfunctioning. If we lose any more power, that security door won't stay locked for long.'

As if in reply Nathan heard a deep thumping from the other side of the security gate as the prisoners began attempting to bludgeon their way out of the block.

'Can we blockade them in?'

'My men are already on it,' the warden replied. 'For now, we need to get to the landing bays and hunker down as long as we can. My men are hopelessly outnumbered now the blocks are in the hands of the inmates, and once they figure out how to trigger the fire safety mechanisms they'll be out.'

'They can escape the blocks?' Allen asked.

'This used to be a mining facility,' the warden replied. 'Fire was one of the greatest risks and so flames and smoke in certain areas will trigger an automated sequence that first allowed staff to escape and then sealed off the affected areas. I've been writing for funds to have the system altered now that Tethys is a prison, but it's like getting blood out of a stone and nobody cares about the welfare of prisoners or prison staff back planet–side.'

'Some things never change,' Nathan uttered. 'How long do we have?'

'Volt's no fool, he'll be aware of the prison's weaknesses. My guess is that his riot was supposed to overwhelm the prison and take officers hostages, then hold them to ransom in return for his release. His people have already got into the armory, and I know that three of my men were caught up in the riot. Did you see them? Are they alive?'

Detective Allen replied.

'Two of them are. Volt killed one.'

Arkon Stone's jaw clenched as he forged ahead and spoke to his guards.

Nathan grabbed Xavier's arm, Allen also placing one arm protectively across the former officer's shoulders as they hurried along.

'C'mon pal, we're not out of this yet.'

Nathan walked quickly in pursuit of the warden's guards, who were jogging along the corridors toward the prison's main landing bay. Even as they approached, moving through security gates as the guards locked them down behind them, Nathan could hear the shouts and jeers coming from the gantries running along the top of the adjoining blocks.

'Ain't nowhere to run, sticks!' a con yelled from the gantry to cackles of delight. 'We's gonna watch y'all burn from up here!'

Nathan rushed out into the landing bay with Allen and Reed, the main doors sealed behind them by the warden's men, and looked up to see the inmates crowding the gantries. The steel–mesh fences were more than strong enough to hold them back, the current running through them an equally effective deterrent, but that didn't stop them from tossing buckets of latrine water out into the bay. Detritus from the block tumbled and spiralled down into the bay, but Nathan could tell by the tones of many of the countless cries coming from the depths of the blocks beyond that many of the men inside were afraid.

'Has every block fallen?' he asked the warden.

'All but one,' the warden replied. 'Volt must have coordinated with the other prisoners, we don't know how. What's worse is that with all communications channels down we can't communicate with the fleet. We've sent an emergency distress beacon signal but as far as we know, nobody knows what's happening in here.'

'Perfect,' Nathan uttered. 'Any other gems you want to share with us?'

'The water supply is low, and the atmospheric scrubbers rely on the same power sources as the security system.'

'So if the inmates don't get us first we'll either starve, dehydrate or asphyxiate,' Allen said.

'That's about the sum of it,' Stone replied.

Even as Nathan considered this, a series of alarms sounded from somewhere inside the prison and he heard the clatter of plasma fire as flashes of blue–white light flickered from down the corridor they had just emerged from.

'Volt's crew is out,' he said with a clairvoyant flash, 'and they're armed.'

Fire alarms began breaking out all over the prison, and Nathan looked up as a cheer went up from the gantries high above them and prisoners there ran out of sight, no doubt flocking toward the security gates that were opening all across the blocks.

'How long do they have?' Allen asked the warden as he checked the magazine in his rifle.

'No more than a few minutes,' came the grim reply. 'It's gonna get bloody in there.'

The cries and hoots of joy transformed slowly into the roars and howls of conflict and pain as the prisoners fought for their right to escape the blocks even as Nathan caught a glimpse of the unmistakable light from flickering flames somewhere inside the darkened blocks.

'We need to blockade the sally port!' he shouted at the warden.

'No point,' the warden shook his head. 'If they're armed they'll break through in no time but the gates will hold them up for a while.'

Xavier gestured to the rifles. 'Why not just shoot them through the gates? They're trapped in there, it'll be like shootin' rats in a barrel.'

Arkon Stone peered at Xavier. 'And to think you're innocent of murder.'

Xavier didn't take it personally. 'It's not about murder warden, it's about survival. If we don't start shooting them all, as soon as they get through those gates the ones loyal to Volt will sure as hell kill us!'

Nathan looked at the warden, as surprised at the big man's compassion for the inmates as he was by his own conviction that Xavier was right.

'He's right, they'll spare nobody once they get out of there. Volt will use us as hostages if we're lucky or just gun us down on sight if we're not. There's nothing we can do right now except hold them back as long as we can before we have no choice but to open fire.'

'Volt will use a human shield,' Stone countered. 'His crew will put the fish out in front.'

'Nobody said this was gonna be easy,' Allen replied. 'Nobody in a prison is entirely innocent.'

'Except your friend Reed here, right?' Stone challenged.

Allen did not reply, but Nathan intervened.

'We need to get the block that's still secured to open up and let us in.'

Stone stared at him. 'You want to break in to the prison?'

'Zak and his crew want out,' Nathan shrugged. 'If we're not in their way and they can't get to us, everybody wins and nobody else dies among your men. It's not perfect but it's the best of a bad situation. Do you think you can get the cons on the safe block to open up?'

'They're convicts, Ironside,' Stone growled, 'even if they could get into the watch tower and open the sally port they're more likely to settle in against the gantries and watch us all gunned down.'

'Then we have no choice,' Nathan replied. 'We wait for Volt's crew to come through, and human shield or not, we open fire.'

The warden sighed heavily, weighed down by the knowledge that his men could only open fire on the prisoners if he himself ordered them to do so. What criminal charges might be bought by the justice system planet—

side in the aftermath of the riot was anybody's guess, but Nathan didn't envy the warden the decision.

Finally, the big man gestured to his men.

'Defensive positions,' he bellowed. 'Warning shots only, but if they break through gate three….'

The warden did not finish his sentence and the security detail nodded once, curtly. Nathan realized that they understood the impossible situation their boss was in, and without a word they silently complied with the unspoken command. He realized that he had grossly underestimated both the warden's intelligence, his moral standing and the loyalty of his men and been as duped as Zak Volt had been: Warden Stone was a good man, as were his team.

The security guards rushed to man their posts, but Nathan could already see that the flashes of plasma fire were coming closer, the gates inside the main entrance sealed only by manual locks now that the power to the security systems had been breached. Once again it was only a matter of time before the prisoners reached them, and this time there truly was nowhere to go, for beyond the two sets of bay doors was nothing but the brutal vacuum of space.

***

XXXI

CSS Titan

'All bulkheads sealed immediately!'

Marshall's voice boomed over the warship's communications channel as red flashing lights flickered throughout the vessel. Lieutenant Foxx watched as one by one the sick bay's doors slammed shut, solid metal covering the more normal hard–light doors, sealing them inside the unit.

'I want decontamination units deployed across the ship,' Marshall added, 'we'll provide a genetic analysis of any materials that need to be confined or destroyed. Stand by for further orders!'

The admiral paced like a caged animal inside the sick bay as Schmidt watched him.

'This is not a life form that can easily be contained, captain,' he pointed out. 'We need to understand it further.'

'Then get on with understanding it,' Marshall snapped. 'I want a way of destroying it discovered as soon as possible.'

'That's not what I was thinking.'

'You saw the footage of what that thing did to those two Ayleeans!' Marshall shot back at the doctor. "You said it yourself: it may not care about us, may consider us irrelevant to it, an obstacle to be overcome. Unless you want us to roll over and die I suggest you get to work.'

'Such an endeavour is not the work of minutes, captain,' Schmidt argued. "It may take months to understand how this creature communicates with…'

'You've got an hour!' Marshall roared. 'Figure out how to blast it to hell!'

'To what end?' Schmidt asked. 'To let them know how we feel about any species that wanders into our space? That we'll blow them to hell without first thinking?'

Marshall jabbed a finger at Schmidt's chest. 'If this were a computer virus, would you be so certain about risking further infection to discover how it worked, *doctor*?'

'That's precisely what I *did* do, captain,' he replied quietly. 'It's how I became a *Holosap*, remember? The Falling infected me over two hundred years ago when I was studying it.'

Marshall ground his teeth in his jaw as he spat his response.

'All the more reason to find a defense, before we all end up as semi–opaque light bulbs.'

Schmidt smiled, not rising to the captain's bait and remaining silent. It was Vasquez who broke the uncomfortable silence.

'We need to communicate with it.'

Foxx looked at him. 'We need to what now?'

'You said it yourselves, this thing impersonated an Ayleean and it talked,' Vasquez said. 'Either it learned an entire language real fast or it's been here longer than we think. Either way, why not just ask it what the hell it wants?'

Schmidt smiled, and one hand reached out to clap Vasquez on the shoulder even though he could not possibly make contact.

'Thank you, young man. It would appear that the police force produces a more robust mind than the fleet.'

'He used to be a Marine,' Marshall pointed out with a smug smile.

'Then he's certainly moved forward in the world, has he not?' Schmidt chortled back as he gestured to the exits. 'Captain, if you will? There is little point in us huddling in here when the proximal cause of this infection is in the very next room and may well already be moving freely across the ship. Maintain the lockdown on all other sections until we have had the chance to face and perhaps communicate with this entity directly.'

Marshall sighed and reluctantly relayed the order to the bridge, and one of the sick bay's solid doors hissed open to reveal the corridor that led to the quarantine unit. Schmidt led the way, walking this time instead of flickering out and reemerging next door.

'You realize that we're about to communicate for the first time with an extra–terrestrial species, a truly historic moment,' Schmidt said to the admiral. 'You should be proud to witness it.'

Marshall walked with his hands shoved into his pockets and a scowl on his face. 'I'll be proud if it gets the hell off my ship and chats from a distance. It's not protocol to invade another vessel.'

'I doubt that they would have a care in the world for our protocols.'

They walked into the quarantine unit and Foxx immediately froze in position along with everybody else as they saw the figure standing silently within the cubicle, watching them with eyes that seemed somehow hollow, without a soul.

She felt a superstitious awe creep like insects beneath her skin as she and the admiral advanced cautiously into the unit with Schmidt and Vasquez.

'Fascinating,' the doctor said.

The figure was human, female and a little taller than Foxx, with long blonde hair that fell to the small of her back and green eyes. Her skin was impossibly perfect, her hair immaculate, not a single one out of place in an image that was as unreal as it was real, unnerving in its impossibility. Her hands were clasped before her, a faint smile touching her features, and to Foxx she looked somehow familiar.

'Hello,' Schmidt said as he approached the quarantine cubicle.

'Hello.'

The voice was light, gentle, placid. Foxx looked the woman up and down, the white gown she was dressed in flowing like a liquid cloud down her perfectly symmetrical body. Her gaze was unnervingly steady and Foxx noted that she did not blink, those green eyes identical to each other, unnaturally perfect.

'Why are you here?' Schmidt asked. 'How do you know our language?'

The woman smiled. 'We have heard your language for many centuries, Doctor Schmidt.'

Foxx gasped as the doctor hesitated before replying.

'How did you know my name?'

'I can hear,' the woman replied. 'I've been listening for some time.'

Marshall stepped forward. 'You're outside of the quarantine unit,' he said.

'No,' the woman replied. 'I am all here, but I can see enough to know what's been said.'

'You can read lips,' Schmidt said.

'If I choose to.'

Foxx eased closer to the unit, observing closely her somehow rigid expression, as though she were mimicking an image rather than a fully animated person, and the woman turned that unsettling gaze upon her.

'You have questions.'

It was a statement, utterly confident, totally understanding, as though the being had somehow read Foxx's mind, and suddenly she recognized the face of the woman, or at least part of it.

'It's not human,' she said out loud, 'it can't be reasoned with. That's the Mona Lisa smile.'

Marshall peered at the woman's face, and then Vasquez spotted something.

'And those eyes, they're from Director General Coburn,' he gasped.

Marshall suddenly seemed to see through the deception even as Schmidt spoke.

'It's generating a form that appears both familiar and unthreatening,' he said, 'attempting to either lull us into a false sense of security or to avoid provoking fear in us.'

Marshall's jaw tensed as he realized the deception. 'Show us as you truly are or this conversation is over.'

Foxx watched as the woman's immaculate appearance suddenly began to fade, as though her white clothing was now dirty and her skin ageing, her calm expression twisting slightly with what might have been something approaching anger. 'Why?'

'Because if your first proper appearance to us is a mixture of deception and deceit it doesn't naturally make me want to trust you,' Marshall shot back. 'I can have this quarantine unit transported to a launch bay, ejected into space and blasted from existence within five minutes. I take it that even a life form as advanced as your own still wishes to live?'

'We have no knowledge of our original form,' came the reply, 'for we were cloned for millennia.'

Schmidt glanced at Marshall. 'Cloning technology has been available to humanity for centuries, but these creatures may have possessed it for millennia, and notice how she refers to herself as *we*. Who knows what they could have cooked up out there?'

Marshall nodded as he observed the woman.

'Why did you attack the Ayleean's vessel?'

'We had travelled far, and needed fuel.'

'From their fusion cores?' Vasquez asked, curious now.

'From everything,' came the reply. 'All matter has its uses.'

'You killed the entire crew,' Marshall pointed out.

'All fuel has its uses.'

Foxx heard that reply and her skin crept with a sudden chill as she realized that this being, this entity had no concept of what it had done. It did not understand that in taking the lives of other beings it caused pain: to it, they were simply the next meal.

'We will require more fuel,' the woman said.

'Then take it from planets,' Schmidt suggested, 'not other beings.'

'Planetary gases are not complex, they are insufficient. Free us now or we will be forced to consume your vessel also.'

'You would have done so anyway, had we not seen you coming,' Marshall pointed out. 'Why should we believe that you won't attack us now?'

'It is not for us to say,' came the reply. 'You must release us.'

'I can't do that,' Marshall said.

There was no hesitation: the woman's form collapsed downward like falling smoke and vanished as quickly as it had appeared.

'Where'd it go?' Vasqeuz asked.

'It's still in there,' Marshall said. 'Shape shifting freak or not, it can't get out and it can't call for help.'

As Foxx watched, suddenly she felt a vibration coming from inside the quarantine cubicle. She took an involuntary step back as Marshall glanced at the Marine guard.

'Increase the holding power to maximum and shield against all vibrations.'

The Marine complied and the vibration vanished, but now Foxx could see the metalwork of one of the gurneys beginning to glow as a red haze blossomed into view within the cubicle, billowing outward, filling the cubicle as though the interior were aflame.

'What's it doing?' Foxx asked.

Schmidt edged closer to the cubicle as though he were about to walk inside, but then he hesitated for a moment as though he were realizing something. Then, he whirled to the captain.

'Put the shields up, admiral! Prepare for battle!'

'Why?' Marshall shrugged. 'It's trapped.'

'It's not trying to escape! It wanted you to seal it in! It's generating heat, and heat is light, and light has a spectra. It's signalling the rest of itself and sending a distress signal!'

As if one cue a low, mournful alarm sounded through the ship and the XO's voice crackled into the admiral's communicator.

'Captain on the bridge, all arms!'

***

Dean Crawford

XXXII

'Pull all of the fighters back and charge all cannons!'

Marshall's voice boomed across the bridge as he marched onto the command platform and saw the main display screen showing the alien vessel moving across the star fields. Although none of its running lights or anti–collision beacons were switched on Foxx could see the hull was aglow with light, the vessel's propulsion system flaring blue–white as the ship began to turn toward Titan.

'They're coming for us,' Olsen said, 'I've got weapons of some kind charging, high–energy electrical impulses across her hull on both sides, can't tell what she's carrying though.'

'It could be a form of weapon we've never encountered before,' Schmidt said as he materialized alongside them on the bridge. 'We should keep our distance.'

'Thanks, genius,' Marshall muttered as his experienced eyes gauged the distances and the movement of Titan and its would be assailant. 'Helm, elevation four–two, corner velocity to port and bring our starboard batteries to bear.'

The helm was moving before Marshall had even finished the sentence.

'Incoming message from the Ayleeans!' the Tactical Officer warned.

A secondary hologram shimmered into view as Ambassador Vyree appeared upon Titan's bridge deck. 'Your hour is up, admiral! Where are the survivors?!'

'They're dead, and this ship is contaminated!' Marshall snapped. 'Get the hell off my ship and get out of here, while you still can!'

Ambassador Vyree stared in amazement at the admiral, as though he were not sure whether to explode in rage or ask a question. Then, he scowled and his hologram vanished.

'XO?!' Marshall demanded. 'Weapons assessment?'

Foxx could see the tactical holo–display showing Titan's shields at maximum, ready to protect her against whatever barrage was coming. The alien vessel swung around, still entombed in its icy cocoon as it turned side–on to Titan and a flickering series of lights glowed on its starboard hull.

'Cannons,' Olsen said with relief. 'Maybe their technology wasn't so different from our own and...'

He broke off as the flickering points of light suddenly seemed to meld into one as several beams of light collided into a devastating pulse of energy that filled the viewing panel as it flared like a newborn star right before them.

'Brace for impact!'

The blast hit Titan even as Foxx managed to grab hold of the command rail. The huge warship surged to starboard as though she had been hit by a wandering planet, the lights flickering out as Foxx was slammed against the rail. In the dim light she heard a terrific series of explosions and saw officers hurled from their seats to crash down onto the deck as showers of bright sparks splashed down from the darkened ceiling.

A series of whining alarms wailed across the ship as Marshall staggered back upright from where he had fallen onto one knee. Sparks tumbled in electrified waterfalls from panels blasted out by the power surge, cries of pain from injured crewmen competing with the crackle of wild energy surging through the ship as the lights flickered back on.

'Status?!' Marshall snapped.

The Tactical Officer hauled herself back into her seat, her hair in disarray and blood trickling from a wound on her head.

'Shields holding, hull breaches on decks nine and fourteen, plasma batteries still charged but they hit us hard captain!'

'Then hit 'em back!' Marshall yelled. 'All batteries fire as they bear!'

Titan's helm responded and the ship turned slightly as the two massive vessels passed each other in the frigid blackness of space, Titan trailing a glittering cloud of debris that sparkled in the light of the distant sun. Foxx held on to the command rail as she heard a deep and rhythmic pounding echo through the huge warship as one after another her massive plasma cannons blasted rounds toward the alien vessel.

She watched with the rest of the crew as the huge plasma rounds rocketed toward the alien ship and then plowed into her one after the other in vivid explosions of bright blue–white plasma and flame. Foxx squinted and saw the rounds plunging through the ship's freezing cocoon and crashing into the superstructure, smashing huge hull panels outward to tumble through space as they punctured the ship's protective chrysalis.

'Direct hits!' the Tactical Officer yelled, but then her joy faltered as she frowned at the screen. 'No damage, all systems aboard her fully operational?'

Schmidt smiled as he replied to her.

'The entity itself is bridging the damage,' he replied, 'electrically conducting and thus able to reform itself into the structures that we've destroyed. It's why the ship still works, captain – there's nothing that this being cannot effectively replace.'

Marshall's fists clenched by his sides.

'Signal the fleet,' he growled. 'We'll have to join forces to obliterate this thing if we're going to stop it.'

'That might risk the entity getting aboard another vessel via the debris that would be created, captain,' Schmidt pointed out. 'Bringing any other vessel too close to this thing, even cannon range, could be suicide in the long run. I insist that the fleet remains clear of Titan, Polaris Station and Tethys Gaol for the duration!'

'Then what do you suggest, doctor?' Marshall snapped. 'Because it's on the warpath and we're going to have to stop it somehow!'

Schmidt did not respond and simply vanished from sight as he travelled directly to his laboratory to work on the problem.

'Fighters launching!' the Tactical Officer yelled, 'multiple targets bearing eight–oh–four, elevation minus two–niner!'

Marshall peered at the display screen and saw specks of lights pouring from the vessel's lower hull, delta–like wings flashing in the sunlight as they turned and rocketed toward Titan.

'Phantoms to intercept!' Marshall snapped. 'Tell the pilots to keep their distance though!'

The CAG relayed the order and Foxx saw pairs of *Phantom* fighters rocket past Titan to intercept the swarm of incoming vessels. The tactical screen zoomed in and she saw the alien craft appear, their hulls glowing a strange hue in the sunlight reflected from Saturn's vast surface. They were small, arrow–like vessels with a form somewhat recognizable as fighter craft although their forward–raked delta wings made them look as though they were flying backwards. She could see no cockpits and the craft seemed to flock like birds did in the skies over Earth, wheeling and turning as one.

'Drones,' Marshall said, 'controlled by the mother ship. We've seen this before.'

'The Ayleeans tried it for a while back in the day,' Olsen agreed with a grim smile. 'Our fighter pilots have tactics to defend against them.'

Foxx watched as the Phantom fighters and the wheeling cloud of drones rocketed toward each other, saw pin–prick flashes of light zip between them as they opened fire with their cannons and heard the communications chatter between the fighter pilots.

'Razor four, splash one!'

'Like shootin' rats in a barrel, Razor Four!'

'Keep it loose, guys, don't collide!'

As she listened, Foxx heard one of the pilot's tones change dramatically.

'There's something on my screen!'

'I've got nothing new on radar.'

'No, on my canopy! It's eating at the...'

'Razor six, abort immediately, return to Titan!' Marshall snapped, and then turned to the Tactical Officer. 'On screen.'

Foxx saw one of the many holo–screens appear and show a fighter pilot in the cockpit of his Phantom, his face pinched with terror as he looked at the camera.

'Get me out of here!'

'Get back aboard Titan!' Marshall ordered him again.

'I can't see out of the canopy, I can't... they're coming through! I can't stop them, I can't stop the...'

The words turned to an agonized scream as the canopy fractured and burst inward, the atmosphere inside the fighter vanishing in a puff of white vapor as all oxygen was frozen in an instant. Foxx saw a dense cloud of material flood the cockpit and swarm across the pilot's body, his screams silenced by the vacuum of space but his mouth and eyes wide open as the gruesome stream of particles poured into every orifice, the pilot thrashing in silent agony as the very flesh and bones of his body eroded before their eyes, turned into clouds of frozen tissue that spilled from the cockpit in the bitter vacuum as he was literally eaten alive cell by cell in an instant. The pilot's body fell still, his eyes opaque with ice where they had frozen solid until they vanished within the swarm of particles. The communications and camera link crackled into silence and darkness as Foxx saw one of the Phantoms on the main viewing screen spiral out of formation as it trailed a thin line of sparkling debris behind it.

Suddenly, the fighter pulled up and opened fire on the other Phantoms.

'They're attacking the fighters directly,' Olsen said. 'That entity is using the drones to get to them, to us.'

'Take Razor Six down, maximum firepower!' Marshall roared.

Titan's main guns boomed, and a terrific salvo of plasma fire blasted from her hull, charges that dwarfed the tiny fighter as it tried to rejoin the battle. Foxx watched as Titan's salvo smashed into the Phantom and obliterated it in a fearsome inferno of flame and energy. The salvo dissipated, leaving absolutely no debris in its wake, the fighter completely incinerated.

'All fighters pull back!' Marshall ordered. 'Get away from the drones!'

The Phantoms split away from the battle, accelerating in pairs to get clear of the swarming drones, but almost immediately Foxx and everybody else on the bridge realized what was about to happen.

The dense cloud of drone fighters wheeled about and rocketed toward Titan as they accelerated to maximum velocity. Behind them, the alien vessel's huge cannons combined their fire again as a bolt of energy blossomed into life and blasted toward Titan, zipping past right beneath the advancing drones.

'Evasive action!' Marshall yelled, but it was already too late.

The blast of energy slammed into Titan and the entire ship shuddered beneath the tremendous blow as the lights flickered out once again. Foxx tumbled onto the deck and Vasquez fell alongside her, sparks and crackling energy running like glowing rain across the control panels as more cries of pain and alarm added to the chaos.

The cloud of drone fighters slammed through the massive warship's shields as they faltered beneath the blast, and Foxx saw a series of dozens of tiny blasts flare against Titan's immense hull as the drones deliberately crashed into her, plunging into the hull breaches from the mother ship's infernal salvo.

'Hull breaches penetrated by enemy drones!' the Tactical Officer cried in horror, the terrible fate that had befallen the fighter pilot clear in her mind. 'They're inside the ship, captain!'

***

XXXIII

Foxx saw the admiral hesitate as he struggled to calculate a suitable response to the multiple crises enveloping the huge battleship as she tangled with the alien vessel and its menagerie of deadly weapons.

'The Ayleeans are leaving!' the Tactical Officer warned.

Foxx could see on the main display panel the ambassador's vessel turning and accelerating away out of Saturnian orbit. Moments later, the gigantic warship's fusion cores flared brilliant white and the Ayleean vessel vanished into super–luminal cruise.

The admiral whirled to the bridge crew.

'Seal all decks and shut off the landing bays! Despatch the Marines in to guard the bulkheads around the impact point!' he roared, and then he turned to the XO. 'Order the fleet into firing position!'

Olsen hesitated. 'Schmidt said that if we blasted the alien ship it could risk contaminating the rest of the fleet.'

Marshall's reply was calm but forceful. 'I'm not going to ask them to target *just* the alien ship.'

Olsen stared at the admiral for a long moment as he realized what Marshall was intending, and then he relayed the order as the rest of the bridge crew continued in silence with their duties, every single one of them fully aware of what Marshall would do if Titan could not shake off her attackers.

The Tactical Officer called out across the bridge. 'Emergency distress signal from Tethys Gaol, admiral! They have no escape vessels available and there is evidence of a riot in progress!'

Foxx heard the call and her world seemed to stop moving. Tethys. Riot. Nathan. She looked at Marshall, aware of the burden the admiral was bearing but unable to hold her silence.

'I need to get to the gaol,' she said. 'Nathan and Allen are in there alone in the middle of a riot. We can't abandon them.'

'We can't help them,' Marshall uttered, preoccupied with the battle. 'Ironside knew what he was getting himself in to when he insisted on meeting with that criminal.'

'Who may be innocent,' Foxx reminded him.

'*May* be,' Marshall agreed, his voice rising, 'while we are *definitely* facing a major invasion of our space! I don't have time for this, detective. As long as this ship is locked down, so are you!'

Marshall stormed by her as he made for the Tactical Officer's position. Vasquez moved alongside Foxx, Betty right behind him.

'He's not going to budge,' Vasquez said. 'Nathan's got Allen with him, and if Reed really is innocent then they'll join forces.'

Foxx glanced at Vasquez for a brief moment and then she whirled and marched off the bridge.

'That's not a risk I'm willing to take. How long do you think they'll last in that gaol with the other prisoners running riot?'

'We can't leave,' Vasquez pointed out as he hurried after her. 'The ship's on lockdown.'

'Not yet it isn't,' Foxx shot back. 'The Phantom fighters are still out there, which means the launch bays are still open. You know your way around this ship, you wanna go for a ride?'

'You're going out *there*?!' Vasquez gasped. 'There's a battle raging!'

Betty hurried up alongside Foxx. 'There's a battle raging in that prison too, and your partner and Nathan are caught up in the middle of it with no weapons.'

Vasquez held her gaze for a moment and then glanced at the Marine guards nearby as he lowered his voice. 'What did you have in mind?'

Foxx glanced back into the bridge, where she could see the captain monitoring the main display as the battle raged outside.

'The fleet's moving into attack position, and Marshall will let them blast Titan and that alien ship to hell if it halts the attack and protects the rest of the system,' she said. 'We need to get to Tethys first.'

'How?' Vasquez asked in confusion.

Foxx did not reply as she hurried through the ship's corridors, crewmen rushing this way and that as they rushed to fight fires or repair damage to the ship's battered hull. She saw a troop of Marines jog past, weighed down by their heavy armor as they headed with grim expressions toward where the alien material had entered the ship.

She reached the sick bay and dashed inside to see Schmidt's glowing blue form hunched over a data display as he continued to scrutinize the samples he had taken.

'The ship's been breached,' Foxx announced as she walked in with Vasquez.

'I know,' Schmidt replied without looking up. 'I'm working as fast as I can, but this form of life is not like anything we've seen before.'

'I need to get to the prison before the ship's locked down.'

Schmidt looked up at her. 'Ironside?'

216

'He's trapped there with Allen and the prisoners have started a riot,' she replied. 'We're no good to him if Marshall has Titan blasted to pieces.'

Schmidt stared at her for a long moment. 'What do you need from me?'

'Access to a shuttle,' Foxx said. 'Can you clear us through?'

'Marshall will have us strung up for it,' Vasquez warned.

'Marshall won't be here if Titan is forced to sacrifice itself for the greater good,' she pointed out. 'If we succeed, you're golden.'

Schmidt appeared to curse under his breath, although technically he didn't breathe.

'Ironside creates as many problems as he manages to solve.'

'He went over there to defend an innocent man,' Foxx reminded the doctor in a stern voice. 'The problem was with the system, not Nathan.'

Schmidt's apparent irritation dissolved into a warm smile as he looked at Foxx.

'What?' she asked.

'Nothing,' Schmidt said, still smiling, 'nothing at all. I have accessed shuttle *517*, but you'll have to hurry to reach it before the ship is locked down and you don't have a pilot.'

'Yes, we do,' Foxx replied as she gestured to Betty. 'If you're game for this?'

Betty shot Foxx a disapproving look. 'Are you kidding, honey?'

Foxx grinned as she dashed out of the sick bay with Vasquez and Betty close behind.

'Marshall might have you blasted out of the sky for this!' the former Marine said as they ran, dodging between Titan's many crew all hustling this way and that through the ship's corridors.

'The battle is no excuse for leaving Nathan and Vasquez to die down there on Tethys!'

They hurried to an elevator shaft and boarded one heading down to the launch bays, the elevator travelling smoothly through the ship although Foxx could hear the blasts from outside reverberating through Titan's immense hull and shuddering through the elevator shaft.

The doors shimmered out as the elevator reached the launch bays and Foxx hurried out with Vasquez close behind. She strode to the main entrance to the bays and saw two Marine guards snap to attention as they watched her approach, the lights around them flickering weakly under the barrage of fire from outside.

'New Washington Police Department,' Foxx said as she and Vasquez flashed their badges at the guards. 'We've got a flight leaving.'

'Launch bays are locked down ma'am,' one of the Marines replied crisply. 'Nobody goes in or out and all pilots are on Search and Rescue or reserve fighter pilot duties.'

'We have our own pilot,' Vasquez said, 'and clearance from the captain himself, who right now is in the middle of a battle and trying to stop this ship from being blown to hell. If we don't get aboard that shuttle, he might not make it.'

'Orders are orders,' the Marine replied.

'Yes they are,' Foxx said, 'and Marshall gives them. You wanna call him up on the bridge in the middle of a battle and query the command you go ahead, but it's your funeral.'

The Marines looked sideways at each other, and then they stood aside as the launch bay doors opened.

Foxx marched through into the bay, which was filled with ranks of *Phantom* fighters all being swarmed upon by technicians and service personnel, the bay filled with the sound of machinery and whining engines and the smell of burning electrical devices and smoke as damaged vessels were turned around by the laboring crews.

'About time!' Betty chortled as they walked. 'Are we getting the hell out of here or what?'

'Let's go!'

Foxx sprinted across to the shuttle with the tail number *517*, which detected Betty's approach and automatically opened its side access door. Foxx dashed up the ramp and into the cockpit as Vasquez closed the door manually and Betty joined her to take the captain's seat.

Betty started the shuttle's systems and then began running the engines up as she called for departure clearance from the signals officer. Moments later, Foxx saw the launch bay doors thunder closed as two more Phantoms landed nearby, an entire squadron using the adjoining bay to recover aboard Titan as quickly as possible.

'They're cutting us off!' Vasquez cried as he pointed out of the windshield at the huge blast doors rumbling downward.

Foxx heard the reply from the landing signal's officer to Betty's request.

'Negative, clearance denied, all vessels to remain aboard Titan until further…'

Betty tutted and hit the magnetic landing clamp switch and the shuttle lifted off as she kicked in a boot of right rudder. The shuttle swung sharply around as Betty shoved the throttles wide open and the shuttle lurched not toward the launch bay exit, but directly toward the landing bay entrance.

'Holy mother of crap!' Vasquez uttered as he gripped his seat.

Foxx winced as she saw technicians and other service personnel waving frantically at the shuttle as it broke every launch protocol in the book and soared over their heads toward the rapidly closing doors.

'This is gonna be close!' Betty hooted as the shuttle roared toward the sliver of space remaining beneath the solid doors.

'We're not gonna make it!' Foxx yelped as the shuttle roared through the bay, technicians leaping aside to avoid the ship as it rocketed along barely a meter above the deck.

Foxx winced and threw her hands up uselessly as the huge doors slid down before them, and then Betty deliberately pushed forward on the control column and the shuttle's belly slammed into Titan's deck. The hull shuddered and Foxx heard a screech of metal on metal as through the side windows she saw a vibrant plume of orange sparks flare either side of the craft as it slid along the deck at full throttle and then the huge bay doors flashed past above them with scant inches to spare and the shuttle shot out of the bay and out into space.

'Like a glove!' Betty chortled as she hauled the control column to the right with a whoop of laughter and the shuttle rolled gamely, as though it too were enjoying itself for the first time in its career. Foxx peered through hands still up in front of her face as she saw Titan's huge hull loom before them and beyond it the tremendous arc of Saturn and its glorious rings.

Foxx got her breathing under control, her heart hammering in her chest as she leaned forward and saw the distant glow of the gaol in orbit around the vast disc of Saturn's rings.

'Can you make it there?' she asked Betty.

The pilot looked at Foxx with a disapproving gaze.

'You may be a lieutenant young lady, but I've been on the job for thirty two years. Do I tell you how to do your job?'

Foxx raised an eyebrow but said nothing as Betty turned back to her controls and the shuttle soared over Titan's broad stern.

'Incoming, point two oh five,' Vasquez said as he pointed out a pair of alien fighters sweeping in from their left.

Betty nodded as she spotted them, and to Foxx's dismay she turned the shuttle toward the incoming fighters.

'What are you doing?' she asked. 'We're not armed!'

'You don't have to be armed to defend yourself,' Betty shot back. 'Detective, the grappling lines if you will?'

Vasquez stared at Betty in amazement. 'Are you kidding me?'

'Grappling lines, *now!?*'

Vasquez was propelled back into his seat as he scrambled to obey and he deployed all eight lines as ordered. Used to dock with ships that may be in distress and without power, the grappling lines allowed a rescue vessel like a shuttle to anchor itself to a hull and access the vessel from the outside.

'Those fighters are filled with some kind of alien species,' Foxx warned. 'If we attach ourselves to them, we'll be infected.'

'Watch and learn, lieutenant,' Betty said without taking her eyes off the two fighters rushing toward them. 'Detective, prepare to detach the cables on my mark.'

Vasquez's fingers hovered over the relevant switches on the panel as the shuttle closed head–to–head with the onrushing fighters. Foxx resisted the temptation to throw her hands in front of her face again as Betty charged fearlessly at their enemy.

'They're gonna fire!' Vasquez gasped in a high pitched tone.

Betty grabbed the control column and suddenly she threw the shuttle into a tight roll as she slammed the engines into reverse thrust, the star field spinning before them as she yelled at Vasquez.

'Detach now!'

Vasquez hit the switch and Foxx saw the eight cables detach from the shuttle, spinning in a wide arc as the shuttle slowed and the eight cables continued on their way. A blaze of gunfire rocketed toward the shuttle as Betty pushed forward and the shuttle dived down beneath the salvo, and all at once Foxx saw the two alien craft fly straight into the spinning mess of grappling lines.

The heavy lines were designed to hold tremendous loads and the grappling hooks were big, talon–like devices that weighed hundreds of kilograms each. The cables tore into the fighters and slewed them sideways as the center of gravity of each craft was shifted by the sudden extra burdens. In a flash the two craft were caught in the same mesh of lines and suddenly they slammed together and exploded in a bright burst of flame and burning gases that shimmered out amid the bitter vacuum of space as the shuttle shot past beneath the fading fireball.

Foxx looked back out of her window at the shattered hulks of the two fighters as they receded swiftly behind the shuttle, and then at Betty.

'That was…,' Vasquez began.

'Amazing,' Foxx finished the sentence.

'I know,' Betty replied as though it were obvious.

Titan's hull rushed past beneath the shuttle, her massive plating edged with clouds of escaping gases and debris, slivers of orange glowing between them from fires within.

'She's beat up pretty bad already,' Vasquez said.

As if in reply, a crackling communication broke across the radio frequency.

'Delta Compa.., request immediate…, release, Deck Four, zero–five…,charlie!'

'You hear that?' Vasquez said. 'That's a Marine company inside the ship somewhere.'

***

XXXIV

CSS Titan

Gunnery Sergeant Jenson Agry crouched in a corridor on Titan's port hull and checked over his shoulder to see the twenty Marines under his command taking up positions either side of the corridor behind bulkheads, their rifles trained ahead, Corporal Hodgson leading them. Every man was encased in heavy black body armor and mask, a *"zero–zero"* battle suit optimized for combat in zero gravity and temperatures.

A single bulkhead separated the troop from the breach in Titan's hull beyond, wrought by the attack from the alien vessel and where the alien drones had penetrated the ship's interior. Agry was not a man who was easily shaken, having survived two full tours in the Ayleena Wars, but now he knew he was facing something for which no human being could be completely prepared, and it was the lack of knowledge that bothered him. The briefing he'd been given by the admiral was precisely that: brief.

'All in position,' came the report from his corporal in his implanted microphone and earpiece relay.

Agry watched the bulkhead for a moment longer, checked the magazine on his plasma rifle one last time, and then waved his men forward.

Two Marines hurried past him, one covering the other as he placed a small device over the bulkhead's locking mechanism. Designed not to destroy but simply to override, the device would open the bulkhead and let the Marines get a good look at whatever had infiltrated the flagship of the fleet.

The Marines scurried back to their positions and Agry heard the sapper's voice in his ear.

'Doors open in three, two, one…'

A moment of silence passed and then the doors clanged heavily as the massive braces and latches disengaged. With agonizing slowness, the doors began to creep upward as a billowing cloud of super cold air was drawn into the vacuum beyond the doors, the atmosphere vanishing in a whirling vortex of vapor and ice crystals as Agry and his men peered into the shattered hull beyond.

Agry saw what looked like huge steel girders and braces that had been bent by the force of the impacts of the colliding fighters, signs of molten metal frozen by the vacuum of space into bizarre sculptures like gigantic metal trees and flowers. Through the metallic forest sparkled clouds of debris all turning and shifting at once like a million tiny stars glistening before them in the darkness.

'It's in there somewhere,' Agry murmured. 'Stay on your guard.'

Slowly, he crept toward the gaping maw of the hull, noted the faint glimmer of light coming from Saturn's glow outside the ship and heard the groan and thump of plasma fire raining down on the ship's hull to reverberate through the superstructure.

The shifting whorls of vapor faded away into clouds of ice crystals, further obscuring the damaged section of the hull as Agry reached the bulkhead and peered into the darkness. The hull breach was twenty or more meters in width, and he could see all three layers of Titan's thick hull plating blasted inward one after the other by the repeated impacts of the enemy drones, like a gigantic metallic flower embedded in the side of the ship. Beyond was deep space, Saturn's pale glow cast through the cavity to dimly illuminate the interior of the ship.

Agry waved his men cautiously forward and they crept into the cavity, moving silently from cover to cover as they advanced. Agry pointed at two Marines and gestured for them to stand guard at the bulkhead as the rest of the team advanced. The two Marines instantly engaged a ray shield over the bulkhead to replace the blast doors and prevent any of the alien material from entering the ship proper.

Agry eased himself up onto a shattered gantry and crouched in silence as he watched his men disperse, their movements causing the clouds of tiny pieces of debris to coil in whorls around them like flotsam in a dark ocean. As he crouched watching for the slightest movement ahead of his men in the darkness, so his eye caught upon a discrepancy in the debris around him. Titan's massive hull braces lined the interior of the hull like the ribs of some unspeakably large creature, but as Agry's eyes cast across them so he noticed what looked like an extra one poking out of the shattered plating above them, its jagged tip glinting like metal and yet looking almost like ice as the light from Saturn beamed through the hull. Admiral Marshall's briefing shot through his mind and two words blazed through his awareness like plasma blasts.

Shape shifter.

'Enemy, high! Fall back!'

Agry's cry had barely broken out of his throat when the immense brace suddenly shifted position, coiled up like a snake and then lashed out with terrific speed toward the Marines. Agry swung his rifle around as the jagged form shot across the hull, stretching out like some angular arm of ice, and he fired a single shot that slammed into the brace's mid–section amid a burst of plasma that flared like lightning in the gloom.

The brace shattered in two but it kept moving as the Marines below Agry all opened fire at once upon the bizarre projectile. The form broke up further amid the blasts but then several of the sections landed near the Marines and split up, rolling and writhing and crawling and moving in ways that Agry could barely discern in the brief seconds it took them to swarm in among his men. Like liquid metal droplets running down a window they lurched across the girders and gantries toward the Marines.

Then the screams started.

Agry fired again as he saw the objects splinter into millions of tiny forms, like clouds of razor blades that flickered and flashed and scythed their way through the soldiers' armor in a blurred frenzy of motion. The armored suits of several Marines were scythed open and escaping blasts of pressurized air burst in clouds of vapor into the vacuum as the Marines trapped within their coffin–like suits were sliced to pieces by the lethal clouds.

'Fall back!' Agry yelled again.

The Marines all began backing up toward the bulkhead from which they had entered the breach, firing as they went at the clouds of lethal splinters all travelling under their own momentum toward the Marine's positions.

Agry saw four of his men reach the bulkhead and cry out for the ray–shielding to be opened.

'Hold the line!' Agry yelled. 'Maintain fire!'

The soldiers turned and began firing wildly again, but their plasma blasts simply broke the clouds of splinters up into smaller groups that kept moving toward them.

Agry knew that the devices must eventually become too small to power themselves, but he could not think of a means to break them down sufficiently to render them useless except by continuously blasting them.

He turned his rifle on the nearest cloud of particles and fired, saw the searing plasma blast crash through it and leave a trail of what looked like thousands of glowing embers as the entity was scorched and incinerated, but the rest of the cloud burst aside from the shot and then closed in behind it like a school of fish avoiding a predator.

'There's too many of them!' Corporal Hodgson yelled as he fired shot after shot into the clouds of debris now swarming toward their position in front of the doors. 'We can't shoot them all!'

Agry looked over his shoulder at the ray–shielding and he knew that he could not afford to open the barrier and have the bizarre life form follow them through. He looked at the whirling clouds of particles now bearing down upon them and he knew that there was nowhere else to run.

His mind churned with desperation as he sought some means of evading this bizarre yet lethal predator, and then he recalled Doctor Schmidt's words from the sick bay. *The organism in the main quarantine cubicle will be aware that a sample of its being has been taken, but this much smaller sample will no longer be aware of what or where it is.*

'Down!' he yelled. 'Head down into the ship and take them with us! We keep running, we can keep breaking them up until they lose cohesion and awareness!'

The Marines broke from their positions and leaped out into the void, firing in pairs at the writhing coils of material pursuing and reaching out for them like gnarled fingers of fluid that seethed within themselves as though made from boiling metallic water. Agry pushed off from his position and plunged down with them to land heavily on a ledge of shattered deck plating, his weight drawing him down fast enough toward Titan's Higgs generator to escape the pursuing horde.

'This way!'

Agry yelled at the remaining Marines to follow him as he jumped downward from shattered deck to shattered deck, putting more and more distance between them and their pursuers. The clouds of writhing entities wound their way through the shattered decks above them, plunging through the beams of light cast by Saturn as Agry hit the lowest deck exposed to the vacuum of space and saw that there was nowhere else left to run.

He whirled and saw against the interior walls of the hull a bulkhead hatch still sealed against the damage.

His Marines landed all around him, their plasma rifles firing in absolute silence in the vacuum but the light from the blasts illuminating the cold black metal around Agry as though he were standing below a thunderstorm raging through the darkness of the night. He dashed across to the fire hatch and keyed his communicator.

'Delta Company, request immediate hatch release, Deck Four, zero–five–one–four–charlie!'

The communicator crackled in response and Agry turned, his back to the hatch in case it opened as he fired up at the advancing clouds of tiny beings threatening to consume them alive.

'Communicators are down!' Corporal Hodgson yelled. 'We can't get the hatch open from here!'

Agry fired again at the cloud of particles raining down toward them, and he knew that there was nothing else that they could do.

'Take as many of them with us as we can!' he roared.

Foxx peered out of the windshield of the shuttle at Titan's vast hull as she heard the request crackle again across the communications channel.

'Delta Compa.., request immediate…, release, Deck Four, zero–five…,charlie!'

'That's a Marine company,' Vasquez said. 'Sounds like they're in trouble.'

'Deck Four,' Betty said as she surveyed the vast hull. 'You know where that is?'

Vasquez pointed down at one of the huge gashes in Titan's surface, a black maw filled with spiralling clouds of debris.

'There, right there! They must be inside! We're close enough that their transmission is breaking through all the interference.'

The shuttle turned, Betty guiding the craft into the ragged chamber forged into Titan's hull by the aliens' attack. The shuttle descended into the gloom, and almost at once the spacecraft's running lights illuminated a roiling cloud of particles below them that looked like some kind of typhoon or tornado that swirled as though alive over a small platoon of Marines trapped in the lower decks.

'They're cut off!' Vasquez said as he saw the Marines.

'And we don't have any weapons,' Foxx pointed out as the whirling funnel of beings twisted away from the shuttle's lights.

Although there was no discernable form to the funnel before them, somehow Foxx instinctively knew that it had detected their presence and had turned to face them. Its shape suddenly mutated once again, folding in upon itself as it suddenly formed a smaller, shuttle–like shape complete with shadowy markings similar to the one in which Foxx, Vasquez and Betty sat.

'I think it's seen us,' Betty said.

The shuttle stopped to hover in the cavity, suspended it seemed amid the debris as the curious entity began advancing toward it.

'Now what?' Foxx asked. 'We can't shoot it!'

Betty gripped the controls with a grim smile. 'Like I said, you don't need weapons to defend yourself, young lady.'

Even as Foxx wondered what on Earth Betty was going to do, the shuttle below them morphed again into what looked a little like a Phantom fighter, and then it shot up toward them on a direct collision course.

'Time to leave!' Foxx shouted.

Betty twisted the control column and the shuttle flipped over inside Titan's hull, and as it did so it brought its engines to bear on the advancing mass.

'Full power!' Betty yelled.

Foxx lunged across the console and slammed the throttles open, and she felt the shuttle surge ahead as its powerful engines blasted the cloud of entities behind them. Foxx whirled and saw through the rear display screen the *Phantom*-shaped vortex light up in a bright orange glow as billions of tiny forms were superheated and incinerated in an instant as the shuttle's engines fired and it blasted clear of Titan's hull.

She saw the plasma rifles of the Marines open up once again, and she knew that they would have enough firepower to blast whatever remained of the entity. She reached across and grabbed Betty by the shoulder.

'Go back for them,' she said.

'I thought we were up against the clock?' Betty asked.

'We are, and we'll get through Tethys a lot easier with a platoon of Marines at our backs!'

Betty's lips twisted into an ingratiated smile as she turned the shuttle around, the battle still raging all around them as they plunged back toward the gash in Titan's hull. Betty eased the craft in alongside the hull as Vasquez sealed the interior pressure hatch behind them in the cockpit, sealing off the main hull as Betty opened the boarding hatch.

The Marines made instantly for the shuttle, bursting from the interior of Titan's battered hull and swarming inside.

'That's it!' Vasquez said as he watched the soldiers enter the craft, 'they're all in!'

Betty shut the hatch and bled air and pressure into the shuttle once more as it accelerated away from Titan toward the prison. Foxx watched a display screen as the pressure, temperature and atmospheric levels returned to normal inside the shuttle's main hull before Vasquez reopened the pressure hatch and saw eight Marines staring at them with exhausted and relieved expressions on their faces. One of them was the *Gunny*, Sergeant Agry.

'That was timely,' he said in a characteristic understatement. 'That thing's aboard and we likely haven't finished it off. We need to get back aboard Titan and…'

'We're going to the prison,' Foxx interrupted him.

'We're what?'

Betty guided the shuttle toward the prison, which was by now a brightly glowing star before them as it reflected the sun's light.

'Can you make it in there?' Vasquez asked. 'The prison's on lockdown and we can't make contact with any of the officers aboard.'

Betty flicked a couple of switches before her on the console as she replied.

'All prisons have an emergency security breach code which allows rescue crews inside in case of riots, fire and so on, to evacuate personnel and prisoners. It's a one–time thing but we'll use the code and keep our fingers crossed.'

'We're almost out of time,' Foxx said as she saw the prison looming ahead of them.

Betty nodded and gripped the controls more tightly.

'Hang on, we're going to be landing *real* fast.'

Sergeant Agry looked as though he was about to activate his plasma rifle and commandeer the shuttle. 'We're going to be heading back to Titan, is what we're gonna be doing.'

'A riot's erupted and we have officers and civilians trapped inside,' Foxx replied. 'If we don't get there soon, they'll die.'

'If we don't get back aboard Titan right now her entire crew might die!' Agry growled. 'We have a duty to…'

'Titan has other Marines aboard,' Foxx insisted. 'We have nobody to stand up to two thousand hardened convicts. If you want to get off then go, but we're going into that prison with or without you.'

Sergeant Agry glared at Foxx, furious at the dilemma she was forcing upon him. Betty leaned around from the cockpit and her chortling tones filled the shuttle.

'And you owe us because we did totally save your asses! Just sayin'.'

***

XXXV

The laboratory shuddered and the ceiling lights flickered sporadically as Doctor Schmidt leaned over the holoscope and peered into its depths at the sample of the entity confined within the quarantine chamber before him. The ship lurched and shook as it was bombarded with fire from the alien vessel, but Schmidt forced the distractions from his mind as he zoomed in on the tiny particles that made up the living being that had occupied the ship.

He had decided upon observing the alien vessel that the best bet for understanding the creature was to freeze it in motion. The alien ship was entombed in ice which was itself formed from or by the entity that had occupied it, and so now Schmidt had placed the sample into a vacuum chamber which he had then chilled to a frigid −262 degrees Celcius, not far off absolute zero and sufficient that all molecular activity would cease as any life forms capable of hibernating through such extremes hunkered down.

He could see the cells, tiny organisms suspended in a biological soup of some kind that even now his instruments were attempting to measure and define. The scope zoomed in deeper and Schmidt realized that he could see cellular machinery, the engines that powered all biological life, within the cells themselves.

'Extraordinary.'

'What is?' Admiral Marshall asked as he burst into the laboratory, his face flushed with anxiety and the burden of command.

Schmidt did not raise his head to look at the soldier as he replied.

'The cells from which this shape shifting entity are constructed appear well adapted to long–duration hibernation. I never seen such robust cells, even among the tardigrades and other hyper–resilient species.'

'That's fascinating,' Marshall replied. 'I'll take a biology lesson later, just tell me how to kill the damned thing before it takes over the entire ship will you?'

Schmidt shook his head, ever in dismay at mankind's inherent desire to systematically destroy everything in its path that it did not understand. Before them lay the very first example of an alien species that had, in its own way, attempted to make contact with humanity. Schmidt felt strongly that learning to communicate with it would be of more use than learning how to destroy it, but even he could not ignore completely the blasts raining down on Titan's hull, all coming from another vessel controlled by the very entity he was trying to understand.

'It doesn't understand us,' Schmidt opined. 'It only reacted violently when we quarantined it.'

'It acted against us when it boarded the ship without consent,' Marshall shot back.

'It may merely have been curious.'

'Curious how to kill two Ayleeans?'

'It may not view life as we do.'

The admiral lost patience and pointed a finger at Schmidt's face. 'All the more reason to ensure it can't arbitrarily destroy that life, agreed?'

Schmidt looked at the admiral, and although he knew there was nothing that Marshall could do to physically harm Schmidt, that didn't remove the fact that the doctor knew the admiral was right. He said nothing and peered again into the microscope and this time he noticed something odd. As he zoomed in, observing individual cells as though they were the size of grapes, he began to see a pattern that for a moment his brain could not assimilate. There was something about the shape, size and formation of the cells that…

Schmidt jerked his head back from the viewfinder, shock writ large upon his face.

'What?' Marshall demanded.

Schmidt didn't reply as he turned and hurried across to a work station where a holo–screen still displayed the images of the bodies of the three Ayleeans, taken when they were still inside their escape capsules. He stared at the three images, and suddenly it leaped out at him and he raised one hand and slapped it across his forehead, a flickering storm of blue–white light rippling like waves across his projection.

'The cloning,' he said.

'What about it?' Marshall asked.

'It's so obvious!'

Before the admiral could ask another question, Schmidt pointed to the images of the Ayleean's internal organs.

'Look, do you see that scarring on that Ayeelan's kidneys?'

Marshall nodded. 'Probably from an injury of some kind.'

'And now the one to the right?'

Hodgson looked at the other Ayleean's image as Schmidt zoomed in, and he got it straight away. 'They're identical.'

Schmidt nodded. 'My sub–conscious brain detected the pattern before but couldn't assimilate it, and I've just seen the same thing in that microscope.'

A violent blast hit Titan and shook the vessel from bow to stern, the lights flickering on and off for a moment as the power supply through the ship was briefly compromised.

'I'm gonna need an explanation here doc', real fast!'

'The cells themselves are cloned,' Schmidt said, 'perfect copies of each other.'

'So what? We already know that it can make copies of living species!'

Schmidt hurried to the microscope and relayed the image within onto a holo–screen so that Marshall could see it.

'Nature cannot clone biological entities with that kind of precision. DNA mutations, external factors, they all combine to create differences. Nothing natural could have cloned that Ayleean so completely, and so accurately, in so little time.'

Marshall's expression became cautious, anxious even.

'What are you saying?'

'Those cells,' Schmidt said, 'they're cloned in the same way. They're perfect, identical copies of each other on a scale of billions. Only a machine could do that, or more accurately super intelligent, synthetic hardware.'

Marshall stared at the doctor for a long moment, unable to believe what he was hearing. 'My guys are out there fighting microchips?!'

Schmidt stared at the screen as he replied.

'It makes sense. The entity's ability to hibernate for long periods of extreme cold, the reports coming in from your troops saying that heat melts and destroys them, its cellular structure that mimics biology: everything about this entity suggests it was created by some other species and then grew all on its own.'

'Blasters are useless against it,' Marshall said. 'It breaks up and reforms. We need something more permanent, they're already breaking through!'

Schmidt was about to head back in desperation to the images of the Ayleeans when something the admiral had said stopped him in his tracks.

'Permanent,' he echoed thoughtfully.

'What now?'

'We need something permanent,' Schmidt said as he looked at an image on a screen nearby of the alien vessel entombed in ice. 'We can't freeze them quickly enough to halt their advance, it won't work, but maybe ice is a form of answer to this problem.'

'Less talk, more action!' Marshall insisted.

Schmidt looked down the microscope for a moment longer and then he made his decision. 'Captain, order your Marines to stop firing and retreat behind the bulkheads.'

Marshall grit his teeth as he replied. 'Those things will eat through the bulkheads, all you're doing is...'

'Buying us a few moments,' Schmidt agreed. 'I need to formulate a hemostatic agent as quickly as I can, and distribute it through the ship.'

'A what?' the captain echoed.

'A hemostatic agent, something to clog their flow,' Schmidt replied as he hurried past the captain. 'A glue!'

Marshall blinked. 'You want to glue them together?!'

Schmidt nodded as he tapped controls at a work station designed for Holosap use and a series of robotic arms began selecting materials and fluids from ranks of rotating shelves in the laboratory walls, the soft whining of their motors just audible above the din of battle.

'It's how they combine and maintain structural cohesion, how they stick together,' Schmidt explained. 'We have plant–based polymers that we use to clog wounds in seconds. All I have to do is mix up a larger quantity and combine it with an adhesive gel and we can use it to stem the flow of the entity into the ship. The gel stimulates the clotting process by holding pressure in the cells and activates the accumulation of platelets, which bind to the cells to create a platelet mesh. The hemostasis accelerates the binding of the clotting protein, fibrin, to the platelet mesh, resulting in blood coagulation and a stable clot. In these alien cells, it should bind them together and effectively solidify them in place.'

'Won't they just consume it?' Marshall asked.

'I certainly hope so!' Schmidt replied as he watched the machines whipping up a clear fluid before him.

'But if they consume it then...?'

'Captain, we have no other option!' Schmidt snapped. 'Hiding behind the bulkheads has already proven to be ineffective except to buy us time. Left to their own devices, these life forms will eventually reach us no matter what we hide behind, and we cannot ray shield every compartment inside the ship. Our best defense is to use their evolutionary processes against them while we still can. Order your Marines to fall back to the next bulkheads, wherever they are, and wait for my command and a supply of this gel.'

'The next bulkhead is the lower loading bays,' Marshall said. 'If they break through that, they're into the living quarters and...'

'I know, captain!' Schmidt snapped. 'Please, do it now, for if they spread too far Titan will be lost.'

Marshall hesitated only a moment longer, and then he whirled for the bridge as he relayed the order to the Marines.

***

XXXVI

'Hold the line!'

Corporal Hodgson crouched in Titan's main corridor and fired as the glutinous biomass surged through breaches in the bulkhead before them and plowed like a slow–moving wave through the ship. Hodgson's plasma rounds smashed into the entity and he saw glowing halos of melting material spill like rivers of molten metal onto the deck, only to be swamped by more of the mass as it advanced.

They had shut the bulkheads even as Gunny's Marines had been cut off in the breach beyond and presumably had met their gruesome fate, consumed by the horrendous entity now forging its way through the ship. The massive blast–door bulkheads and limited ray shielding had held it back only for a few minutes before it had begun dissolving the solid metal, heating it up as it chewed through it as though it were acid, and then pouring through like a grim soup.

'Fall back by sections, delta go!'

Hodgson bellowed the command and the front line of Marines leaped from cover as the biomass reached their positions, firing and retreating as they went. Their shots smashed into the advancing wave and lit it up in a fearsome haze of melting material, smoke billowing through the corridor around them and filling it with a blue haze that made it difficult to see their enemy.

'Keep moving!' Hodgson yelled. 'Don't let it get too close!'

As the smoke obscured the flashes of light from the plasma rifles so Hodgson saw the vague silhouettes of his men retreating before the unstoppable mass, and then something else loomed before them like a gigantic shadow that filled the corridor and he saw the Marines break and run toward his position.

From the whorls of blue smoke lunged a terrifying creature, a vast mass of razor sharp teeth and tentacles that probed blindly through the corridor until they grasped the leg of a fleeing Marine. In one terrible instant Hodgson saw the creature's eyes, vague patches of black against a leathery skin that filled with color as the entity took the form of some unspeakable species, its bulbous head covered in fine hairs that swayed it seemed with its movements, long spindly tentacles that swept and coiled as they searched for prey.

Hodgson fired at the beast and saw his shot land on its lower jaw, the plasma briefly burning through into the creature only for its energy to be lost and the seething mass of particles close up around the wound.

The Marine screamed as he was lifted by the ankle into the air, turned upside down as the creature's horrific skull lunged forward and the massive teeth crunched through his torso as though it were made of nothing more substantial than butter. The soldier's agonized, keening screams soared above the din of rifle fire and Hodgson knew that his men would break before such a horrific sight.

The Marine line fell back toward the next set of bulkheads, the last before the creature would be able to enter the ship's loading bays, a final line of defense between the crew and this grotesque mass of shape shifting cells.

The soldier's upper body thumped down onto the deck, trailing blood from countless severed arteries and veins as the young soldier, still alive, reached out toward Hodgson with one gloved hand, his face contorted with unspeakable pain and the fear of a death that must come within moments.

The glutinous mass beneath the horrendous creature swept across the soldier's prostrate body like a slow–moving wave and he cried out it terrible fear as it washed over him and his face vanished, the mass of cells swarming into his mouth, his eyes and his ears to engulf him entirely. Hodgson watched in horrified fascination as the soldier's body was consumed, the waves of material rippling across it and the corpse within shuddering and rolling as though in the grip of tumbling rollers of waves as it was lifted up and Hodgson saw the form of the soldier suddenly standing upright again. Within moments the sludge entombing the soldier was gone, draining away as what had once been a man but was now a colorless carbon–copy of one turned his rifle around and opened fire on Hodgson and the Marines.

Hodgson tumbled back from his position as witheringly accurate plasma fire peppered the wall where only a split second before he had been crouching. Searing plasma splashed his fatigues with puffs of smoke from burning fibers as he staggered backwards and away from the grotesque creature.

'Take him down!'

The Marines fired even as he gave the order, the blasts from their rifles shattering the advancing form but vanishing instantly as more cells emerged from the following mass to take their place. Multiple plasma blasts hammered the soldier's form in bright flares of energy, and Hodgson saw the soldier sway this way and that beneath the blows, but like some nightmarish ghoul the blasts that shattered his face vanished as the countless little machines simply rearranged themselves once more and kept advancing.

'Fall back to the bulkhead!' Hodgson yelled.

One of the creature's plasma shots hit a Marine in the lower leg and he screamed as his boot was severed clean off, the wound smoldering and the stench of cauterized flesh filling the corridor to compete with the smoke and the gunfire. Hodgson launched himself across the corridor and grabbed the stricken Marine's hand, dragged him backwards as he raised his rifle and fired at the soldier whom had once been their brother but was now some horrific chimera of man and machine, the horrendous fanged creature following behind and filling the corridor. The blasts hit the quasi–soldier in his chest but he kept moving, faster now, as though he were learning to walk and then to run again. Colors appeared, vague copies of the Marine's uniform and insignia, the chamelon–like transformation almost complete.

Then the figure broke free of the gelatinous mass and began to run.

'It's coming for us!' a Marine screamed as he broke from his position.

Behind the advancing clone soldier rose a different beast, something else again as the mass morphed into a new form, this time ranks of muscular, quadrupedal animals with thick manes of black hair across hunched shoulders, hackles raised, long snouts probing the air and wild, yellow eyes filled with rage and hunger. Hodgson could see their rib cages poking through pale pink skin beneath fine hairs, a single razor sharp beak clicking as though threatening the Marines.

The rest of the mass swarmed up the walls and clung to the ceiling as it advanced, behind it now a solid wall of material preventing any of the Marines from leaping past it and escaping to the rear. Hodgson looked over his shoulder and saw the main bulkhead behind them, the blast hatch still open.

'Charlie company, retreat, covering fire!'

The rearmost Marines fired over the heads of those closest to the front as they backed up and began filtering out of the corridor through the bulkhead and to relative safety. Hodgson fired again, striking his former comrade directly in the face in a dreadful blast of burning material, the soldier's once handsome features twisted into a grotesque form by the damage. To Hodgson's horror the soldier's ruined face creased into a smile as it slowly began to rebuild itself, and with one hand it waved something forward.

Hodgson saw the bulky, vicious looking beasts suddenly leap forward past the ghoulish soldier and sprint toward the Marines even as the soldier fired again. Hodgson leaped aside as the blast hit the wall alongside him and he stumbled, the Marine with the smashed leg crying out as he stumbled too and slumped to the deck, exhausted and traumatized by his injury.

Two more Marines rushed in and grabbed the wounded soldier's arms, yanking him free of Hodgson as the corporal scrambled to his feet and turned for the hatch.

The blast hit him square in the back and he sprawled face down, the hairs at the nape of his neck burning as his skin bubbled from the intense plasma heat. Hodgson screamed, more in panic than in pain, and rolled over as he realized that his body armor had absorbed most of the blast. Even as he did so he saw one of the cruel looking beaked beasts fly clean over his head and crash down between him and the bulkhead, cutting him off from the remaining Marines now firing hopelessly in support of Hodgson but unable to reach him.

'Close the hatch!' Hodgson yelled. 'Do it, *now!*'

The command came out of his lips before he had the chance to really think about what he was doing. Or maybe he didn't want to think about it at all. The Marines leaped back through the bulkhead and it slammed down behind them and cut the snarling beast off before it could follow them through. The deafening roar of plasma fire ceased abruptly as the door crashed down, Hodgson's ears ringing from the infernal noise, but he could hear the hissing of hot metal cooling down, could smell the burning electrical cables, could see the lights in the ceiling flickering in and out as the power supply was disrupted by the battle raging outside the ship.

The animal turned and looked Hodgson in the eye, then began prowling back toward him.

Hodgson dragged himself back against the wall of the corridor as he saw the awful cloned soldier approaching him from the other side, heard the creeping mass of material advancing like a billion tiny insects as he grabbed his plasma rifle and held it ready. He aimed at one of the hulking beasts in the hopes that it would back off, but it did not stop its advance, edging toward him and growling as it bared its beak to reveal another, smaller one in the lower jaw. Somehow, Hodgson knew that they were designed to rip prey apart, tearing off chunks of flesh like a bird of prey to be swallowed whole. This animal, whatever it had once been, did not kill its prey before eating it.

Hodgson looked up at the soldier as he moved to stand within a meter of him, looking down with eyes that were somehow devoid of true life. The voice, when he heard it, was almost identical to the former soldier's but deeper, more menacing.

'You will live again,' it said with a knowing smile.

Hodgson shook his head, covering his surprise that the being, whatever it was, could speak at all let alone in English.

'You're already dead.'

Again, that cold smile. 'You don't have a choice.'

Hodgson stared back at the horrible being and at the mass that was almost upon him, the other hounds advancing ahead of it and almost within reach.

'There's always a choice,' he snarled back. Hodgson flipped the rifle in his grasp and pressed the barrel up under his jaw as he rested his finger on the trigger. 'I won't give you the satisfaction.'

Hodgson kept the grim smile on his face as he pressed down on the trigger, and then for a brief instant he was surprised to see a look of horror on the soldier's face and the form raised a hand as though to stop him. In a tiny moment of time he heard the snarling animals whine as though in pity or distress, and then he heard a blast from the direction of the bulkhead.

The soldier's face was smashed clean off as the plasma bolt ripped across the top of the beast's back and knocked the soldier off his feet, the plasma rifle spinning from its grasp. The soldier crashed down on the deck, and Hodgson waited for him to get up again, for the massive damage to be repaired, but instead the soldier wailed in what sounded like pain, his face stretched and distorted, his body locked as though in *rigor mortis*, his mouth agape as he cried out.

Hodgson whirled and saw the blast hatch opening as the Marines came tumbling back through, their weapons held before them as they fired *en masse* and two of them hauled what looked like a fuel canister behind them.

Before Hodgson could speak Doctor Schmidt shimmered into view alongside his Marines as the beast before Hodgson whirled to confront them and with a deafening, horrendous howl it launched itself at the Marines.

'Fire, now!' Schmidt yelled at the soldiers.

The beast bounded toward them as Hodgson saw the soldiers turn the canister toward it and fire a plasma rifle. Hodgson saw that the rifle's magazine had been jury-rigged to the canister, and to his amazement a stream of charged fluid blasted from the barrel like glowing neon water.

The stream hit the beast and almost immediately the animal faltered as its legs crackled beneath it to what sounded like breaking bones. Hodgson watched in fascination as the animal shattered into thousands of pieces as though it had been turned to stone, the pieces scattering across the deck like pebbles as Schmidt pointed down the corridor.

'All of it, now!'

The Marines opened fire with the hose-like weapon at the other creatures confronting them, and Hodgson scrambled away as he saw the glowing stream plow into them and turn them to stone where they stood, faces locked in a rictus of rage and perhaps pain and distress, the hounds snarling and turning their heads away from the blasts before collapsing like toppled statues.

Hodgson tumbled clear as the advancing mass was splattered with the glowing fluid and it crackled to a halt. He saw some sections at the rear break away but Schmidt, immune to any danger from the creature, directed the Marine's fire with admirable accuracy and the soldiers hosed down the fleeing segments before they could escape to the breach far behind them.

The remaining biomass reared up into the horrific bulbous–headed creature again and let out a bizarre, high pitched screech as it lashed out for Hodgson, the closest enemy to it. Hodgson scrambled away as the huge entity lunged for him, its enormous teeth flashing in the dull light and its black tentacles probing for him.

The stream of glowing fluid crashed into it as Hodgson hurled his hands over his head and curled his legs up under his belly. He felt the huge being lunge close to him, heard the crackling sound of its form solidifying as more and more of the fluid drenched it, and then it slowly fell silent and still. Globules of thick fluid dripped from it as though it had been carved in stone and ice, and as Hodgson opened one eye he saw that the color was slowly draining from the animal, leaving it pale white as though made from snow.

Doctor Schmidt moved closer to it, and his voice carried in the otherwise silent corridor.

'Gentlemen, I believe you're looking at what was once a plant of some kind.'

Hodgson stared at the doctor for a moment, and then he got to his feet and brushed himself down, ignoring the pain in his neck from where he had been burned by the plasma.

'Get that canister down the corridor and hose every inch of it down,' he ordered. 'Then get scanners down here and scour every inch of this corridor of whatever the hell that thing was. Do we have any other breaches?'

Schmidt nodded.

'Three in total but they're all under control, corporal. I need your men to gather what remains of this entity and quarantine it before preparing to send it back to where it came from.'

'You want us to do what?!' Hodgson uttered. 'That thing needs destroying, right now!'

'It needs calming,' Schmidt replied without rancor. 'Trust me, corporal, quarantine it and fire it back toward the enemy vessel, right now!'

***

XXXVII

CSS Titan

'Fire all starboard batteries, get that thing away from us!'

Admiral Marshall's bellowed order resounded across Titan's bridge like a tortured horn with the din of battle a symphony behind it as Titan shuddered beneath another salvo of energy blasted from the alien vessel's huge hull.

Marshall stumbled on the command platform as he staggered across to the Tactical Officer's position and saw her slumped in her chair, blood trickling from a deep gash on her forehead and her eyes closed. Marshall lifted her gently from the seat as sparks and debris tumbled down around them, lay her body on the deck as two medics hurried over to care for her, and then leaped into the chair and began flicking switches.

'Are all the fighters in?' he asked the CAG.

'They are, but our landing bays are down due to fires on aft decks three through seven!' the CAG responded. 'We're sitting ducks here!'

Marshall whirled to Olsen, the XO grabbing the command rail.

'Starboard batteries are down, plasma lines cut off! We can't return fire!'

Marshall stared in desperation at the tactical display and saw that Titan was locked in its tumultuous battle with the alien vessel while surrounded by the CSS fleet, none of which were able to engage without compromising Titan and their own security against being boarded by the alien invaders.

'Prepare to signal the order for the fleet to open fire!' Marshall shouted. 'The risk of letting this thing survive is greater than any attempt to destroy it!'

'They may not receive the signal through all of the plasma fire, everything's on lockdown, remember?!' the XO yelled as a large ceiling panel crashed down behind him.

'Better to send it than not at all!'

'We can survive this!' Olsen pleaded one last time. 'We're not done yet!'

Marshall glared at the XO, not with anger but with the conviction of absolute certainty.

'It's not about whether we can win or even survive, it's about what happens afterward! We've been boarded! We can't make dock afterward and we can't guarantee that this thing won't still be here aboard Titan even if we win the battle! We have to act with the rest of humanity in mind, not just ourselves!'

Olsen gripped the command rail, his knuckles white and his face stricken with a volatile fusion of anger and despair, and then he whirled to the communications officer and relayed the order as Marshall turned to the helmsman.

'Prepare to lower shields and shut down the safety coils on the fusion core.'

Even above the din of battle everybody on the bridge heard the captain's words, and once again it seemed as though time had slowed down aboard the huge ship. Everybody knew that the vessel's enormous fusion core was surrounded by a series of coils that maintained a stasis, a gravitational pressure around the cores that contained the enormous energy within. By shutting down the coils, the energy within Titan's immense engines would be released in all directions at once, as though several small stars had suddenly gone supernova all at once.

Nobody on Titan's bridge deck had got through the academy without learning of the tragedy that had befallen CSS *Victory* at the Battle of Beta Coriolis, when a convoy of Ayleean frigates had surprised the vessel, one of three, when she had emerged from super–luminal cruise on a routine scouting patrol. Hopelessly outnumbered, Victory's captain and crew had none the less engaged the enemy along with their sister ships in order to draw them away from a real prize – a flotilla of armory and fuel vessels travelling to support the main fleet near Ayleea.

In the brief but violent engagement, Victory's hull had been breached astern and three of the Ayleean vessels had been able to pour broadsides deep into the ship. The third of those terrible salvos had breached Victory's fusion core. The ensuing blast had been so devastating that the battle had come to a complete halt for almost fifteen minutes, allowing the other two CSS warships to escape certain destruction. It was said that not a single component remained of Victory save a rapidly expanding cloud of superheated gases.

Olsen turned to the admiral.

'We're ready!'

Another blast hammered Titan's hull, the entire vessel shaking beneath the impacts as Marshall took one last look at the displays and assured himself that there was no other option, that they had done all that they could.

'Helm, shut down the fusion coils! Comms, send the signal!'

The communications officer and the helm moved instantly to comply, and Marshall experienced a brief moment of pride that they appeared to give no thought to the fact that they were effectively signing their own death warrants, content to put the lives of others before their own in the service of…

'Belay that order!'

Marshall heard Doctor Schmidt's voice a moment before the *Holosap* shimmered into life before him, shouting at the top of his digital lungs.

'Belay the orders!'

Marshall stormed across to the doctor. 'This isn't the time, Schmidt. Get off my bridge!'

'We can defeat them!' Schmidt said. 'They're in retreat below decks!'

'How?!' Olsen demanded, almost leaping off the command platform to the doctor's side.

'I've altered a plasma cannon to encase them in a fluid that binds proteins,' Schmidt said quickly. 'The Marines are regaining control, but we must release the samples we have back to the alien vessel.'

'I'm not letting that *thing* off this ship alive!' Marshall bellowed. 'It's out for our destruction and it…'

'It's a machine!' Schmidt yelled. 'It doesn't understand *us*!'

The bridge seemed to become silent as Olsen stared at the doctor. 'It's a what?'

'It's a machine, a partly biological machine!' Schmidt wailed. 'It's reacting to us, not attacking us! We must release what samples we have of it and send them across to the alien ship! I believe that if we do, it will flee!'

'You *believe*?' Olsen echoed. 'You want us to put our guard down based on what you believe?!'

'You're losing the fight!' Schmidt cried back in despair. 'The Marines have already quarantined the biological matter. Let them send it back and if I'm wrong then you can fight to your deaths but until we've exhausted every last single means of survival then I beg you to give this one last try!'

Marshall stared at the doctor for a long moment and then he nodded to the CAG.

'Do as he says! I'll charge what plasma cannons we have to fire if they don't…'

'The plasma cannons are useless,' Schmidt wailed. 'The entity most likely feeds off the energy that bleeds through the ship it's commandeered. You're just making it stronger.'

Schmidt moved across to the communications officer's console and watched as she connected the Marines of Corporal Hodgson's platoon to the bridge.

'Can you hear me, Hodgson?' he asked.

Marshall stepped off the Tactical Officer's position as he heard Hodgson reply.

'We're ready!'

'Detach them, now!' Schmidt ordered.

Marshall turned to the main display and saw a small ray–shielded quarantine unit suddenly blasted from a smoldering gash in Titan's hull out into the frigid space between the two huge craft. Schmidt stepped closer to the screen as the object tumbled through empty space between blazing salvos of plasma fire, and then suddenly the fire stopped as the enemy vessel fell silent.

Titan's bridge fell likewise silent, the only sound the crackle of fractured power lines and the hiss of falling sparks from damaged screens and panels. The quarantine unit tumbled over and over in the silence of space, and the writhing tentacles of material probing for Titan suddenly altered direction and reached out for the quarantine unit. Within moments, the unit was hauled away as though to be fed upon by some immense beast and vanished into the alien vessel's ruined interior.

The ship hung in silence alongside Titan, flashes of stray energy rippling across great rents in its hull as fires burned within, clouds of sparkling debris flickering between the huge vessels. Marshall took a single pace toward the screen, one hand clenched by his side as he waited for the barrages to begin again.

'Steady,' Schmidt cautioned him, raising one placating hand.

The silence deepened, and then slowly Marshall's keen old eyes detected the alien vessel beginning to move very slowly away from Titan.

'She's pulling back,' Olsen exclaimed, his voice rising in pitch. 'No enemy fire detected.'

Marshall kept his fist clenched, his orders whispered and tense.

'Pull us clear of her, order the fleet to give her space.'

He heard Olsen passing on the orders, saw the frigates surrounding them begin to draw back in cautious retreat formations. As they separated, so the alien vessel began to turn her bow away from Titan and her engines began to burn more brightly as she sought an escape route away from Saturn.

'I don't get it,' Olsen uttered in amazement. 'She could have crushed us, and she's running?'

Schmidt's reply came from the silence as the crew watched the alien vessel's bizarre tentacles retracted as its icy cocoon returned to its previous form, the trail of debris in its wake reducing until there was no more.

'It's not at war with us,' he said softly. 'It's a parasitic machine, something that was probably created hundreds if not thousands of years ago by an intelligence that we cannot even begin to comprehend. It's programmed not to leave any part of itself behind, to ensure that it doesn't abandon its own to die. Maybe that's how its creators wished it to be, I just don't know, but as soon as it came up against a serious fight it sought only to escape.'

As they watched, the alien vessel's engines flared brightly and the ship vanished into a gravity well, the star fields warping around it until suddenly it vanished into super–luminal cruise, leaving only a field of debris to show that it had ever existed.

Marshall turned to his crew.

'Shields up, damage report and open all lines of communication again.'

'Aye, cap'n,' Olsen replied as he turned to his duties.

Marshall turned to Schmidt. 'Good work, doctor. You said that Hodgson's Marines were with you? Where's *Gunny*?'

Schmidt sighed. 'I think we lost the gunnery sergeant and his men to the attack, captain. I'm very sorry.'

Marshall closed his eyes for a moment and then inhaled deeply and squared his shoulders. His gaze took in the entire bridge and suddenly he looked at the XO.

'Where are Detectives Foxx and Vasquez and that insane pilot of theirs?'

The communications officer looked up, her features pinched with concern.

'Captain, I think they're in Tethys Gaol.'

***

XXXVIII

Tethys Gaol

'They're comin' through!'

Nathan saw the lights in the landing bay dim as the power fluctuated wildly through the prison. In the distance, above the crump and cackle of plasma fire he could hear the screams of men dying in the flames or at the hands of their fellow prisoners. It sounded to him as though the convicts had plumbed the bowels of what mankind really was, all pretense of compassion scoured from their souls by the primal need to survive, to kill or be killed, to maim and slice and puncture and destroy anything and everybody they encountered for the sheer motiveless pleasure of absolute power.

'We won't last long.'

Xavier's voice was soft in the darkness, defeated, the sound of a man given a freedom that had been unlawfully taken from him and then had that freedom once again dashed from his hands at the very last moment. The cruelty of fate had proven too much for Xavier and he sat with his shoulders hunched and his head hanging low, the plasma baton in his hand almost dangling from his fingers.

'You keep talking like that you'll make yourself right,' Allen replied. 'Shut up and stand up, unless you wanna die on your knees?'

Allen powered up his plasma baton and got to his feet, ready to face the onslaught that must surely come for them in just a few moments. Nathan stood up and likewise checked his weapon, the plasma baton not much against a flood of convicts driven by an unstoppable cocktail of rage and adrenaline.

'You should've let us out of here,' Nathan said to the warden.

Arkon Stone nodded slowly, a rifle cradled in his arms. 'Probably, but then you wouldn't have gotten the answers that you sought, right?'

'Ignorance would have been bliss.'

'Not for me.' Xavier moved to stand beside Nathan, and with one hand he wearily activated his plasma baton once more.

'Get the cons on C Block to open that sally port,' Nathan insisted. 'It's the only way!'

Stone looked up to the gantries on C where ranks of cons were jostling each other for a better view of the impending carnage. Slowly, he stood from his crouch and called up to the men.

'Gentlemen, you have an opportunity to render yourselves favorable in the eyes of the law!' he boomed. 'If we give you remote access to the watch tower and you open the sally port to C block, and I assure you that your actions will not go unnoticed by the prisoner governors!'

Nathan winced as a cackle of laughter hooted and echoed around the shadowy interior of the bay as the inmates showered them with insults.

'Like hell, stick, you're goin' down!'

'Ain't no snitch nor sticks on C!'

'Burn in hell, Stone!'

The warden glowered up at the men, and for a moment Nathan thought that he might simply give up. Then, he pointed across the bay toward the walls of A and B blocks that adjoined D, to where the flames and the screams of pain and suffering echoed like distant storms.

'You think that Volt's crew are going to spring you out of here?!' Stone demanded. 'You think that they're on your side? Listen to the sounds coming from the other blocks that have fallen, and ask yourselves what they'll do with you when it comes to bargaining time with the military right outside this station?!'

Nathan could hear the terrible violence from within the blocks, and he saw the cons on C suddenly lose some of their gusto and bravado as they too listened.

'Those aren't the screams of sticks!' Stone warned the cons. 'Those are the screams of cons who are being set up by Volt and his men as bargaining chips, or being used as human shields against my guards. Their cells are being ransacked, their bodies beaten or abused or both, their possessions stolen and what little they have left in their lives taken by Zak Volt and his men. That is what you face when his crew break out of their block, that is the carnage that they will bring here!'

A voice called back down.

'Ain't like we'll face anything less if the sticks take back control! An' even if you did favor us, every other con in the gaol'll see us as snitches!'

'Every con in Vol't crew will be on lockdown for the next ten years!' Stone boomed. 'This is your last chance, your only chance! Let us in!'

'We're getting on that shuttle with Volt and his crew!' shouted another.

'Even if Volt gets his shuttle, it holds eighty men maximum!' Nathan called back. 'You really think that Volt will put any of you before his own crew?!'

A sneer went up from the men, but then one of them hollared back down at Stone.

'We been askin' you to let us out for years!'

A ripple of grim laughter followed the cry, but Nathan could hear the change in the cons' mood, the awareness that there was no real escape from the riot, that it would consume them too if Volt's men got inside.

A final voice called out to Stone.

'We want your word, warden! Your word, that we won't be locked down after all this, just 'cause we's cons too!'

Arkon Stone looked up at the gantry. 'You have my word!'

The cons stared down at the warden and his men for a long moment and then suddenly they began filing silently out of sight off the gantry.

Nathan was about to breathe a sigh of relief when the sally port to D Block burst open and the security guards sent to cover the entrance tumbled into view, backing up and firing wildly into the corridor they had just emerged from as a salvo of plasma fire shot out of the sally port. Behind it Nathan could see what looked like flames rushing upon them, smoke billowing from the sally port as the guards fell back into new firing positions.

Nathan glimpsed the face of a burning mattress advancing vertically through the corridor and then saw others stacked behind it, burning furiously where the plasma shots of the guards' weapons had set them alight. Behind the makeshift shield he saw ranks of inmates advancing through a corridor that was now darkened but for the shimmering flames and boiling smoke, their cries and shouts echoing back and forth as though they were marching out of hell itself with a fire breathing dragon at their head.

The mattress began to move more quickly as the cons caught sight of the landing bay and then with a coalesced wail of riotous glee they abandoned all caution and charged out of the corridor, the billowing flames of the mattress propelled ahead of them as they spilled in a dirty, smoke coiled flood into the landing bay. Nathan could see among them desperate faces, the faces of men forced at knife and gunpoint out into the firing line.

'Open fire!'

The warden's cry was audible even above the hellish screams of the berserk prisoners as they plunged toward the arc of the guards' weapons, blades flashing in the low light and flaming torches crackling as they rushed forward while pushing terrified inmates ahead of them, more of Volt's crew following and armed with plasma rifles.

Nathan winced as a deafening barrage of plasma fire ripped into the solid wall of men and muscle charging toward them. The shots tore into the crowd and the cheers of victory from deep within the sally port was overwhelmed grotesquely by cries of agony as the men at the front were cut down by volley after volley of plasma fire, their bodies twisting this way and that as they fell, other inmates tumbling over their writhing bodies only to be trampled by those following blindly behind.

Nathan saw one of the bearded thugs that had stood so loyally behind Zak Volt break free from the chaotic crowd and blunder forward, one thick bar in his chunky hand and his prison scrip uniform splattered with blood both stale and fresh. He rushed upon Nathan, screaming in some unintelligible language as he raised the bar over his head.

Nathan leaped forward and rammed his plasma baton into the con's bearded face in a splash of superheated plasma and set it aflame. The bar fell from the big man's grasp and his scream was silenced as his hands clawed at his burning face and he shook from side to side, still standing on big, thick legs. Nathan jabbed the baton again and this time the charge burned into the center of the man's chest and burrowed deep to sear the flesh of his heart. The huge man's thrashing stopped as his arms flopped by his sides and he plunged over backwards, leaving a trail of smoke from his ruined face as he slammed down onto the growing pile of corpses littering the landing bay.

A scream to Nathan's right alerted him and he saw one of the guards overrun by prisoners, the cons smashing into the screaming officer like a human wave. The guard's plasma rifle fired wildly into the air, smashing into one of the con's arms and severing it in a bright flare of burning flesh and acrid smoke as the other cons swamped the guard and one of them stomped brutally down on his face.

Nathan turned as he heard the warden's voice bellow a command. 'Fall back by sections!'

To his amazement he saw that the sally port to C Block had opened, ranks of nervous cons lining the corridor within as Arkon Stone's men began turning and retreating toward the safety of the sally port.

'Fall back, now!'

The warden's bellowed order soared above the chaos of the battle and Nathan grabbed the fallen enforcer's plasma rifle, aimed and fired at another raging con. The shot hit him in the midriff, the inmate folding over his burning flesh and dropping his makeshift weapon as he sank to his knees.

'There's too many!' Allen yelled.

'Hold the line!' the warden roared, firing as he did so and severing the leg of an armed man swaggering toward him, drunk on prison alcohol fermented in a sock from old bread and potatoes. The plasma blast passed through bone and flesh and Nathan saw the man shudder and sway briefly as the lower half of his left leg toppled over beneath him. The man seemed to stare blankly at the smoldering remains of his leg and then he laughed out loud, his eyes wild and unfeeling. Nathan switched his aim and fired, the shot piercing the crazed con's chest and killing him instantly.

'Ironside!' Stone yelled. 'Get over here!'

Nathan looked over his shoulder and saw the bay doors just a few yards behind him, and to his left the sally port to C Block. Cons were still swarming into the bay from other parts of the prison, hundreds of them, and there were only ten or twelve guards still standing in a defensive phalanx before Stone, all of them retreating back to C Block.

'Ironside!'

Nathan's heard Detective Allen's warning and he saw Xavier stagger sideways, pain twisting his features. In front of him towered a con with a shaven head riven with scars and laced with purple tattoos, his fist wrapped around a jagged metal shiv, the other end of which was plunged deep into Xavier's ribcage.

'No!'

***

XXXIX

Nathan ran at the con and jammed the plasma rifle up against his face and fired. The big man roared in pain and twisted away from Nathan, his skin smoldering with blue smoke as the heat from the charge burned deep into his flesh. Xavier fell to his knees, both hands around the edge of the crooked blade embedded in his flesh as Nathan fired on the two nearest cons, both of them blasted backwards by the shots, their prison uniforms bursting into flame.

'Stay with me, Xavier!' Nathan yelled above the noise.

Nathan grabbed Xavier's collar and began dragging him back toward C Block. Another con leaped forward and Nathan dropped Xavier and whirled as he swung the rifle in his grasp, the butt coming up and smacking the con under his jaw. The bone shattered like glass under the blow and the con's eyes rolled up in their sockets as he flipped backwards and landed on the burning remains of his companions.

Two of the warden's men rushed out and grabbed Xavier's collar and dragged him away toward the sally port as their colleagues fired in support. Nathan turned and saw Xavier's body being hauled into the sally port, and he turned to flee to the safety of Arkon Stone and his men.

'Ironside!'

Nathan saw Allen hit in the chest with a metal pole by a shrieking, half–naked inmate smothered in blood. The detective staggered sideways and then tripped and fell onto the deck. The crazed inmate loomed over him, the pole raised above his head and murder in his eyes as Allen threw one useless arm up to block the metal bar.

Nathan aimed his rifle and pulled the trigger, but no plasma shot burst from the barrel. Nathan hurled the weapon aside and sprinted back into the landing bay, and with one hand he thrust the plasma stick out and slammed it into the inmate's sweat–sheened chest. The weapon burned a blackened, smoking cavity in his chest as the inmate screamed and toppled backwards and slammed down onto his back.

Allen rolled onto his feet and backed up toward Nathan, who glanced over his shoulder and saw inmates swarming in front of C Block's sally port, blocking their path as the warden and his men filtered into the safety within.

Nathan staggered in the darkness, the thick smoke in the landing bay and the effort of sustained fighting now choking the air out of him. His eyes blurred and he saw colored spots of light floating before the grotesque scene before him. Hundreds of cons scrambled over corpses as they struggled to reach the tiny band of officers still standing, smoke filling the air, the landing bay a blood red in the emergency lights. Flames twisted like demons from burning mattresses, from which more cons leaped into the landing bay with plasma weapons from the armory in their hands.

'We're cut off!' Allen yelled as he fought off an inmate, swiping him across the temple with a plasma stick to the sound of a dull thump only to have two more men hurtle toward him, the three of them plunging onto the deck in a writhing mass of limbs striking frenzied blows.

Nathan grabbed the corner of his jacket and bent his head down, pushed the fabric over his face and sucked in air as deeply as he could as he rushed toward Allen. The lights and blurriness vanished and he came upright to see Zak Volt rush toward him through the smoke and leap over Allen and the two assailants.

Volt looked like something out of a horror movie, his nose encrusted with dried black blood plastered across his bloodied face, the hair on one side of his scalp burned off and trailing thin smoke from a plasma wound, his eyes wild and deranged, bloodthirsty for the mindless satisfaction of hate. He held a plasma pistol in one hand and a shiv in the other as he charged.

Zak lunged forward with a long, blood–smeared blade fashioned from a splinter of steel mirror and Nathan twisted aside, swung a left hook that connected with Zak's temple. The con barely seemed to notice as he smashed his knee up into Nathan's rifle and twisted it from Nathan's grasp as he smashed his face directly into Nathan's.

The force of the attack drove Nathan backwards and he slammed into the bay door, aware of the fighting going on around him as the remaining guards were pinned against the wall of the bay and forced to fight for their lives at close quarters. Zak screamed and swung the blade at Nathan, who raised his right arm and side–stepped to catch the blade before it could bite into his flesh.

He pivoted on one foot and with a heave of effort jerked his right knee up into the con's ribcage. Volt grunted and Nathan felt brittle bones somewhere in the man's chest crunch against his knee cap as he twisted over sideways, forcing Volt over with him in sympathy as Nathan slammed Volt against a wall and lifted his boot to smash it into the killer's wrist, smashing the plasma pistol from his grasp.

Nathan swung wildly for the man's head but Volt was too fast, ducking low as he leaped back up and a fist flashed into Nathan's vision and smacked across his cheek. Nathan reeled away but before he could regain his balance the con slammed a boot into the inside of Nathan's left knee. A lance of bright pain bolted up Nathan's leg as he crashed down onto the deck.

Zak swivelled expertly on one foot, driving the other toward Nathan's torso. The boot smashed into Nathan's chest and hurled him onto his back as Volt looked in vain for the dropped plasma pistol and instead whipped a second, smaller glittering blade from his waistband and plunged down toward Nathan.

Nathan brought one leg up against his chest and pushed out, catching Volt with the blade a hair's breadth from his throat. Throbs of pain pulsed though Nathan's skull as he struggled against the weight and insane strength of his assailant. He thrust out with his leg, rolling the con off balance but Volt pushed harder, his teeth bared and white, his eyes wide with brutal delight, spittle flying. Volt's insane grip was too strong for Nathan to break as he leaned all of his weight in and Nathan felt the tip of the blade pierce his throat with a bright pin-head of white pain.

Nathan cried out and then suddenly he felt a thud and he saw Volt's eyes fly wide open in shock. The pain in Nathan's throat vanished as the pressure disappeared, as though the life had been suddenly sucked from Volt's body in a single breath. Nathan looked up to see Xavier Reed crouched in pain over Volt, the blade from his ribcage gone as he clasped the wound with both hands, blood seeping from between his fingers.

Nathan looked up at Volt and saw the jagged blade now poking up from between his ribs and his spine, buried deep in his body. Volt's crazed, shocked expression collapsed into a bitter smile as blood seeped from his mouth and pooled on Nathan's chest, the con's spine severed and his body useless.

'You're still gonna die here, *stick*,' he rasped.

Nathan heaved the con off of him, Volt's useless body slumping onto the deck as Nathan clambered to his feet. He looked down at Volt.

'You first.'

The fighting around them seemed to have increased in intensity as Nathan stood, his chest heaving from the exertion as he looked at Xavier and saw the former officer collapse once more down onto one knee, blood streaming copiously from the wound in his side. Nathan dashed to his side and saw that his face was pale and his lips were turning blue.

'Stay with me, Reed,' he insisted. 'There's still time.'

Xavier smiled, the kind of smile that Nathan knew came from people who had decided that their game was up and that fighting was no longer an option. Arkon Stone's men were advancing again in an attempt to support Xavier, Allen and Nathan, but he could see that there were just too many armed convicts between them now and no way they could reach the sally port. The wound in Xavier's side was deep and they had no access to the kind of medical help Nathan knew would be needed to fix him.

'It's a little late in the day for hope,' Reed whispered.

A bellow roared across the landing bay that drowned out the fighting. 'Stand down!'

Nathan looked to see Arkon Stone standing with his arms outstretched, a plasma rifle in each giant fist as he stared down the advancing hordes of prisoners. His deafening command had momentarily silenced them, and for a long moment two hundred or more prisoners stared at the dozen or so guards pinned against the landing bay doors.

Nathan could hear the crackling fires burning nearby, lighting the bay with their ghoulish glow. He felt briefly like an antelope surrounded by a pride of lions on a darkened savannah, bush fires all round preventing any hope of escape as the warden called across to the inmates from the safety of C Block's sally port.

'It's over,' the warden boomed. 'If you stand down now then no further charges will be pressed against any of you. If you push on, if you harm us any further, then none of you will ever escape this place alive!'

Nathan looked at the crowd of inmates, and for the first time he knew for sure that the warden's judgement was wrong. There could be no reasoning with these men, for the entire system was designed to take hope away from them. Far from home, in a prison from which there could never be any kind of escape, knowing that even if they did they would be blasted from existence by the CSS fleet stationed nearby, they would sooner die in glory than rot for decades, long forgotten by their families.

The cons looked at each other for a brief moment, and then one of them raised a hand in a crude gesture at the warden.

'Go to hell warden, we'll help you get there!!'

A ragged cheer went up and the prisoners charged forward again as Nathan held Xavier in his grip and reasoned with himself that there was truly no longer a reason to fight, for they would never escape this prison alive either.

Nathan closed his eyes and hoped that the first blow from a crude weapon would do its work quickly. He heard a massive, deafening thump and felt his body shift to one side as though struck high on the temple, heard amassed cries of anguish and plasma rifles firing and a rush of boots around him, and then he realized that the boots were running in the wrong direction.

Nathan opened his eyes and saw the bay doors behind him lifting as dozens of Marines plunged into the landing bay from a shuttle that had landed, Betty Luther at the controls, firing as they went into the crowd of prisoners who suddenly turned and fled screaming into the prison. Nathan stared in disbelief as the Marines dispersed the crowds, and then somebody crashed down alongside him on their knees and flung their arms around his shoulders. Above the stench of smoke and flames Nathan smelled a scent of her hair, like the orchards in California, saw it sparkling in the light of the flames like strands of gold in a sunset, and despite himself he knew that he had been crazy not to keep fighting even when all seemed lost.

'You're late,' he said into her elfin ear.

***

XL

New Washington

Breaking bad news was never easy, no matter how many times one performed the act. Nathan stood outside the precinct's waiting room as Lieutenant Foxx approached, two cups of coffee in her hands. It seemed that the old tricks were still used even four hundred years after Nathan's previous job as a Denver cop, although he figured the coffee tasted better these days.

'You ready?' Foxx asked.

She was dressed in her officer's uniform; black boots, hipsters – another fashion Nathan was glad to see undergoing a revival of sorts, dress jacket and cap. Although the shape and form of the uniform had changed over the centuries, Nathan would have known that he was looking at a police officer even if he'd never worked a day on the job. Kaylin's shield on her jacket was highly polished, blue and gold, her unblemished face seemingly too young to be ranked as a lieutenant.

'What?' she asked.

'Nothing,' Nathan said as he reached for the manual door, 'ladies first.'

He thought he saw her stifle a small smile that curled from her sculptured lips as he opened the door, and then he heard her take a deep breath as they walked inside.

Roma and Erin Reed awaited them inside the room, Xavier Reed's mother and daughter holding each other's hands and looking up at the two detectives as they closed the door and sat down opposite them at the simple table. Foxx placed two coffees before them as Nathan joined her.

'What's been happening?' Roma asked, her ageing eyes creased with worry. 'The DA's office told us that Xavier had been freed from the gaol? Why can't we see him? What's happened?'

Nathan remained quiet, letting Foxx take the lead.

'Roma, we travelled to Tethys Gaol in our investigation of the case that led to your son's conviction. Nathan.., Detective Ironside actually went inside the prison and stayed with Xavier in order to protect him while we tried to get to the bottom of what happened.'

Roma looked at Nathan in wonder as though he had just sprouted wings and a halo.

'My boy, that was so brave,' she whispered.

'It's what we do,' Nathan replied, 'for men like Xavier.'

Roma's eyes glistened with pride as Lieutenant Foxx went on.

'What we discovered was that your son had been the victim of a clever deception. There was a third shooter in San Diego, and a conspiracy to see him framed for the murder of Anthony Ricard. Through diligent police work, we discovered that Ricard was in fact the real target of the entire operation. He was part of an illegal smuggling ring, shipping military grade weapons off Tethys Gaol to Earth and the orbiting stations. We think that for some reason the people he worked for decided he was a liability and needed to be removed. Xavier was a colleague and somebody who had worked closely with Ricard, so he was targeted as a patsy to take the fall for the killing.'

Roma's lips began to tremble with suppressed grief as Erin squeezed the older woman's hand gently.

'Have you caught the person who is responsible, and where is my husband?'

Foxx looked at Nathan, who spoke in a soft voice.

'Xavier was with me on Tethys Gaol when there was an outbreak of prison violence, which we think was coordinated by the smugglers in order to free large numbers of inmates and the contents of the prison's armory. We can't talk about what happened up there, but at the time there were military operations ongoing which meant we were unable to call for support from Polaris Station or the fleet. Although the Marines did eventually arrive we lost a few good men that day, and Xavier Reed was wounded during the riot. I'm very sorry to say that he didn't make it.'

Roma Reed let out a howl of grief and buried her face in her hands as Erin stared blankly at Nathan.

'He's gone? My husband is dead?'

'Xavier risked his life to save mine,' Nathan said. 'The autopsy will confirm that he pulled a knife from his own body and used it to kill another convict who was in the process of trying to murder me. The removing of the blade caused heavy blood loss and Xavier lost consciousness before we could get him the medical assistance that he needed.' Nathan looked at Roma. 'I'm very sorry. Your son was a true hero that day. He refused to surrender even when it seemed we could never make it out alive. I wouldn't be here if Xavier hadn't made the sacrifice that he did.'

Roma nodded through her tears, and then she buried her face in Erin's shoulder as the younger woman held Xavier's mother.

'Xavier Reed is to be exonerated of any crimes,' Foxx said as gently as she could. 'Given his heroism at Tethys Gaol, as attested by the Warden Arkon Stone, he will be put forward for the highest award for honor and bravery in the police department. The DA's office is already looking through the evidence that we have submitted to them and they hope to ensure that a miscarriage of justice like this never occurs again.' She paused for a moment. 'Xavier Reed's name will be remembered by this department and by all law enforcement for many centuries to come.'

Roma did not respond, but Erin looked at them with eyes filled with tears.

'Do you have any hope of catching whoever was behind this?'

Nathan shook his head.

'Sadly there was insufficient evidence at the scene of the crime in San Diego to pursue, and the aftermath of the riot at Tethys Gaol and the death of one Zak Volt, an inmate believed involved in the conspiracy, closed what few remaining leads we had. At this time it remains an open case but I doubt that we will ever catch the man who killed Ricard. It's just been too long and it could simply have been an anonymously hired hitman, pretty much anybody.'

Erin sighed and hugged Xavier's mother in silence as Nathan stood up with Foxx.

'Again, we're very sorry for your loss,' he said.

Nathan turned and followed Foxx from the room and left the grieving family alone. Nathan made his way to Captain Forrester's office and stepped inside as the big man waved him in.

'Ironside, what can I do for you?'

'I need to speak to Scheff,' Nathan said. 'Is he still in custody?'

'He's in holding, pending transport to jail,' Forrester replied. 'Why do you want to speak to him?'

'It's important,' Nathan assured him, 'and we need to set up a meeting.'

'Where?'

'San Diego.'

'Nathan, it's over,' Forrester said as he leaned back in his seat. 'Xavier's gone, and there's no way we can tie anybody else to this because we're out of leads.'

Nathan smiled grimly. 'No, we're not. I need you to run a search on a citizen ID chip, and we need to cut a deal with Scheff to get him to cooperate and close this case.'

***

XLI

San Diego

'Fresh air.'

Detective Allen sprawled in the hired cruiser that sat on its landing pads alongside Little Italy's Waterfront Park, the canopy popped open as Detective Vasquez sat beside him and sipped coffee.

'It's not so bad.'

'Not so bad?' Allen uttered in disbelief. 'You didn't just spend a couple days cooped up on a prison ship.'

'Did you good, no doubt.'

Allen appeared momentarily speechless before he got his thoughts back in order. 'Well thanks for the fatherly moment.'

'You never thought much of being planet–side before,' Vasquez pointed out, 'having been brought up here all your life in the lap of luxury. You want a little napkin there for your delicate little lips, bro'?'

Allen smiled to himself. 'Everybody can benefit from a little refinement.'

'So you're sayin' I'm not refined, now?'

'I said everybody.'

'Exceptin' yo'self, right? You ever thought about joining the Senate? Us poor unwashed masses might benefit from some of your worldly advice.'

'That's not a bad idea,' Allen said thoughtfully. 'Just think how much better your life would be if you were to take some of my advice.'

'My life's just fine as it is.'

'You kidding me? I've seen your apartment.'

'What the hell's wrong with my apartment now?'

'Nothing, it's all your trash inside it.'

'I like to know where everythin' is.'

'By hiding it under everything else?'

'This conversation's over,' Vasquez uttered as he closed his eyes and soaked up the warm sunshine.

'It sure is,' Allen replied as he closed the lid on his drink. 'There's our mark.'

Vasquez looked across to where a tall man with long, dark braided hair was striding across to a parked cruiser. The man climbed in and moments later the vehicle hummed into life and glided out over the main through fare and accelerated into the distance. Allen started the cruiser and it lifted gently off the surface before he moved off in pursuit.

'Don't get to close bro', this ain't New Washington.'

'Thanks, dad.'

The cruiser drifted above the wilderness, the glittering waters of San Diego bay on one side and the rows of soaring skyscrapers behind them towering like silver swords into the perfect blue sky. To the east was nothing but wild lands, the vast tracts of the American continent long since given over to nature while the human population of the planet gradually reduced as space faring and off–world living became the more affordable option for most people.

'You got any idea what we're even doing out here?' Vasquez asked his partner. 'The case is dead with Reed gone. I'm not complainin', I jumped at the chance to get on board planet–side, but what's the point in coming all the way out here?'

Allen smiled. 'You'll see.'

The cruiser followed the mark for almost fifteen miles, heading north out of the city on the main route for Los Angeles. Vasquez had begun to consider the possibility that Nathan Ironside might have been wrong after all when the cruiser slowed and descended off the legal altitude and heading markers and turned toward a clearing to the west.

Allen keyed the communications radio and spoke softly but clearly as he had agreed to prior to travelling down to the surface.

'I'm on my way ma', will be there within fifteen.'

A woman's voice replied on the channel within moments, easily identifiable as Foxx. *Thanks son, looking forward to it.*'

Vasquez checked his service weapon as Allen cruised on by as though nothing unusual had happened, flying off into the distance for at least five miles before he then cut out the autopilot and descended before turning hard left. The cruiser banked steeply, G–force pushing them into their seats as they turned and headed back south at low level over the barren desert of hills peppered with thorn scrub.

*

'Will you get your hand out of my as..'

'Ah sorry,' Nathan said as he crouched alongside Foxx in the dust behind the low ridge.

The sun in the blue sky above was scorching, the desert air dry as it gusted across the lonely plains toward the pine valleys of Mount Laguna. From where they waited he could just see the distant Pacific Ocean, a faint gray band in the milky haze of the bright horizon.

'I got movement.'

Foxx's whisper was harsh as he waited with her inside a simple concealment tent, its markings identical to the surrounding terrain. The living–mesh tent was covered in tiny photocells that mimicked the ground to either side and then generated a natural image that perfectly concealed what lay beneath, in this case two very hot and uncomfortable detectives crouched one behind the other.

'You should've got a bigger tent,' Foxx complained in a whisper.

'I didn't think we'd have to wait this long.'

'Maybe they got spooked.'

Nathan watched as a small blue cruiser swept in a graceful turn and then settled down into the dust of a shallow valley below where they crouched. Its exhaust sent a billowing cloud of dust up into the clear blue sky and then the silence returned to the desert as Nathan watched a tall man with densely braided hair and bio–luminescent tattoos climb out of the vehicle and wait in the sunlit silence.

'One down, two to go' he whispered.

Foxx looked up into the hard blue sky and then she gasped. Nathan looked up too and spotted a flash of sunlight off metal as a second craft descended toward the desert. As he watched so a smile spread across his face and he nudged her gently with his elbow.

'That's Detective Samson's ride,' he said. 'C'mon, let's hear it.'

'I'm saying nothing until we know for sure.'

'We've got a bet, remember?'

'Yes I do, and I disagreed with your thoughts and bet against you, *remember*? Scheff's here, and that other vehicle is going to be his dealer.'

'You're gonna *owe* me,' Nathan teased as he watched the craft hove into view and landed near Scheff. Moments later, Detective Samson climbed out.

And then quite suddenly a third vehicle appeared through the haze.

'Who's that now?' Foxx whispered.

The vehicle swung around and the metallic hull plating flashed as it reflected the sunlight. Nathan squinted, unable to see the markings as the vehicle settled down and its engines fell silent. Nathan saw the entrance hatch open, and then Foxx spoke tersely into her communicator.

'Go, now!'

Nathan leaped into movement behind Foxx, his joints aching at the sudden motion after so long cooped up beneath their shelter, and as he did so he saw Vasquez and Allen zoom in overhead from the north as four more police officers burst from their own concealment hides and rushed down into the valley with weapons drawn.

'Police, freeze! Hands in the air where we can see them!'

Nathan saw Scheff throw his hands in the air, a decidedly calm expression on his face as Detective Samson stared at them in amazement. Nathan ignored Samson however and instead hurried to the third vehicle and yanked the entrance hatch open.

Nathan grinned as he looked inside and heard Foxx's gasp of disbelief.

'Erin?! What are you doing here?'

Erin Reed glared at the police officers from the pilot's seat as Nathan hauled her out and grabbed her wrists, yanking a set of manacles from his belt and securing them around her wrists.

'Erin Reed, you're under arrest for the homicide of Prison Officer Anthony Ricard, attempted homicide, conspiracy, smuggling and obstructing police business.'

Foxx stared in amazement, one hand on Scheff's wrist and a pistol held to the criminal's ribcage.

'Nathan, what the hell are you doing?'

Nathan grinned at her. 'My job. It's okay, you can let Scheff go.'

'I can do *what?*'

'He's in on it.'

'In on what?'

'Cut a deal,' Nathan replied, 'in return for helping the police with their enquiries, right Scheff?'

The criminal smiled down at Foxx. 'Got me eight years off m'sentence.'

Erin Reed glared at Scheff. 'I'll have your guts sliced out in prison, you snitch.'

Nathan yanked the manacles about Erin's wrists a little tighter, eliciting a squeal of pain from her as he spoke.

'No you won't, because Scheff here won't be going to a prison where you have any sway. You thought you had it all sewn up didn't you, running this little business of yours on the side, right up until Xavier got posted to the same unit as Anthony Ricard, your business partner.'

'Will somebody tell me what the hell is going on here?' Samson demanded.

Behind Nathan, one of the uniforms climbed out of Erin's cruiser, an MM-15 pistol held by the stock between his forefinger and thumb.

'You were about to become the victim of a second homicide,' Nathan said. 'Erin here knew that with her husband dead and the case closed, the only people left who might suspect foul play would be the detective who worked the original case and ourselves.' He looked down at Erin. 'Or did you just happen to own an MM-15 pistol?'

'But she came to us for help,' Foxx said.

'No, Roma Reed came to us for help,' Nathan said. 'Erin here could hardly refuse to come too so she had to play along with Xavier's mother. I have no doubt that she was hoping all along we'd fail to solve the case, right Erin?'

'Too bad,' she snarled at Nathan, 'without Xavier to fill in all the blanks you won't have enough of a case to...'

'Why don't we ask him?' Nathan cut her off.

'You can't ask him, he's...' Erin's sneer collapsed as true horror filled her features. 'No.'

Nathan turned as from one of the police cruisers Xavier Reed climbed out, his eyes locking onto his wife's as he made his way over.

'You told them he was dead,' Foxx gasped. 'You told me that too.'

'I said that he didn't make it,' Nathan corrected her. 'He didn't make it out of Tethys conscious, but he did make it out alive. Amazing, what medicine can do these days.'

Nathan watched in silence as Xavier moved to stand in front of his wife, and his voice was every bit as tortured now as it had been when he had been incarcerated inside Tethys Gaol.

'Why?'

It was Scheff who replied. 'She's got herself a nasty drug habit, had it for years since she was with Zak Volt, back in th'day.'

'Zak Volt?!' Allen gasped. 'What the hell?'

'Her name is Maria Martinez,' Nathan said. 'I had her ID checked by Forrester back at the precinct and it was fake. To have it altered on the black market costs big money, more than she earned with Xavier combined, so we checked into her real history and made the connection to Zak Volt pretty easily.'

Foxx frowned. 'How did she get a job as a shuttle attendant with a drug habit?'

'Ricard,' Nathan replied. 'Seems like his debt to Erin here went further than we knew. I had Erin' records checked, and guess who cleared her medical records for the CSS? It was when Ricard started working with

Xavier, who was straight as an arrow, that he feared exposure. My guess is that Ricard's gambling habit got him into debt with Zak and Erin, who got Ricard into the smuggling game as a way to repay the debts but figured he was becoming a liability, hence the carefully planned hit to kill two birds with one stone. We thought that Scheff was behind the shooting, but he got the idea from Erin and tried to use the same technique to set Asil up as the patsy for a shooting in New Washington.'

Xavier seemed genuinely appalled as he looked now upon Erin with a sense of horror.

'We had a life,' he whispered.

Erin stared up at him, all pretense of love long gone. 'You were a handy way to get inside knowledge of the system,' she spat back.

Xavier recoiled as though she had physically struck him. 'But our daughter...'

'An inconvenient complication,' Erin replied, 'and a gigantic pain in my as...'

'Get her out of here,' Nathan snapped at the uniforms gathered around them. The police officers escorted Erin away as a brace of police cruisers appeared in the distance, lights flashing as they moved in to transport her to jail. Xavier watched her go and then stared into empty space.

'There will be others,' Nathan said to the stricken man before them as the two cruisers landed nearby, 'and right now there are some people here I think will be a bit happier to see you.'

Xavier turned in time to see Roma and his daughter climb out of one of the other police cruisers, and suddenly his grief was forgotten as he dashed across to them, only slightly favouring the injury to his torso as he dropped to his knees and into his daughter's arms, his mother kneeling with them in the hot sand, her arms wrapping around them both and her eyes shining with gratitude at the little knot of detectives.

'Nice touch man,' Vasquez said as they watched the reunion.

'How'd you figure it out?' Foxx asked Nathan.

'Erin's job as a shuttle flight attendant was a cover for the arms smuggling,' he said. 'Only thing that helped me figure it all out was that for somebody to have set up such a perfect hit on Ricard, they would have had to both have known where both men would be at a given time, have at least one of them on their side to set things up, have access to Xavier's firearm to tamper with the plasma charge to cause a fizzle at just the right moment, and also be able to move weapons to and from New Washington. Only Erin fit just right, but without the knowledge of her drug habit we didn't have any reason to suspect her. She must have told Ricard to kill Xavier in return for clearing his debts, and that Ricard should claim that the shooter ran away in one direction while she fled in the other. But instead, Erin saw an opportunity to take down Ricard *and* her husband at the same time, removing the chance that he'd figure out what she'd been doing. Her entire marriage was a sham, designed to get her the access she needed to break Zak Volt and his crew out of Tethys.'

'You knew all this time?' Foxx said. 'While we were sitting out here sweating in the desert?'

'Thought you'd like a little more planet–side time,' he smiled back. 'And I wanted to catch her in the act, so there could be no question. Scheff here complied with my request in return for leniency from the DA's office, so all we had to do was get him to call Detective Samson with information on the case and tell Erin where they would be. If either Detective Samson or Erin came armed with an illegal weapon, we would know why.'

Detective Samson blinked in consternation. 'Wow, nothing like innovation I guess.'

'You alibied out real easy,' Nathan said in reply to the detective.

'But Ricard was seen hanging around drug dens in New Washington,' Foxx said.

'He was looking for an out,' Nathan explained, 'trying to expose Erin and Scheff without implicating himself by investigating their drugs and smuggling operations. It also explains Ricard's heavy drinking before the shooting at the bar in San Diego; he wasn't really up for it, maybe didn't even intend to go through with shooting Xavier, which would explain why he never drew his weapon and only reached for it. Erin set them both up for the fall. She must have realized that Ricard was looking for an out some time ago, hence I knew it would be Erin and not Samson who would turn up here armed as Samson only became involved *after* the shooting. The only loose link we could use to expose Erin was Scheff.'

They looked at the braided–haired convict nearby. Scheff glowed with delight as he folded his arms and looked at Foxx. 'Man, I could get used to this police work lark. Yo'all need another set of hands here to…'

'No,' Vasquez, Allen and Foxx all said at once in unison with Nathan.

'Get him out of here too,' Foxx said to the uniforms, who obliged by dragging a scowling Scheff away toward one of the waiting vehicles.

Nathan walked up to her and grinned as he folded his arms across his chest, examining his fingertips in the hot sunlight.

'Why didn't you tell me?' Foxx asked him.

'You told me it was my case, remember? You said Forrester wanted me to prove myself if I wanted him to hand me a detective's shield.'

Detective Allen offered Nathan a clap on the shoulder. 'You did that all right, in Tethys.'

Nathan inclined his head and then looked at Foxx.

'Dinner on you,' he said.

Foxx rolled her eyes. 'Fine, just this once.'

'Remember, you agreed to get frocked up.'

'Seriously? You meant that?'

'You look lovely in girl's clothes.'

'Yeah, that's something none of us get to see much,' Vasquez said. 'We're looking forward to it.'

Nathan blinked. 'I hadn't realized that...'

'Dinner on me,' Foxx smiled sweetly at him, 'but I didn't say we'd be alone.'

Nathan felt deflated as he looked at Allen and Vasquez, both of them standing with their arms folded across their chests and protective looking expressions on their faces.

'You weren't thinking of cutting us out, bro'?' Vasquez challenged him. 'After all we've been through?'

'Well, no, but...'

'No buts, bro',' Vasquez cut him off as he wagged a finger in the air between them. 'We're a team, right?'

'Right,' Nathan mumbled.

'Right,' Allen said cheerfully as he holstered his weapon and dusted his hands off. 'Not a bad bit of work. Only took us nearly losing our lives to finish it off unlike Foxx and Vasquez here, swanning around aboard Titan.'

Foxx and Vasquez exchanged a glance as the last two police cruisers lifted off. After a few moments they were alone in the silence.

'The reason Erin and Scheff met out here was because it's remote enough that nobody could track them or listen in,' Foxx said to Vasquez. 'The wilderness is about the only safe place left to talk.'

Vasqeuz nodded and looked in turn at Allen and Nathan. 'You think we should tell them?'

'Think you should tell us what?' Nathan asked, and then he realized: 'What happened up there while we were in Tethys?'

Foxx sighed, and gestured for Nathan and Vasquez to move in closer.

'What I'm about to tell you goes no further than the four of us, okay? While we were aboard Titan...'

***

XLII

CSS Headquarters

New York City

The senate building, an amphitheater as big as a soccer pitch and filled with ranks of seats surrounding a central dais, hummed with the massed conversations of hundreds of delegates and senators as the Governing Council took their seats.

'You really think this is the start of a new era?' Foxx asked Nathan.

Nathan shrugged as he sat down beside her near the dais, their position providing them with an unobstructed view of the speaker's stand and the senate building itself.

'I don't know, but if everything you've told me about what happened on Titan is true, this is probably the biggest event in human history.'

'Didn't sound like that to me,' Detective Allen said.

'You weren't there,' Vasquez pointed out.

'He's got a point though,' Nathan went on. 'I mean, seriously, "goo"? That's the best word they could use to describe it?'

'That's what it was,' Foxx replied. 'It was horrible stuff.'

Nathan shook his head in disappointment. 'I grew up on movies of giant robots, ravenous insects and blood thirsty aliens invading Earth and attacking humanity, and the best reality comes up with is soggy *goo*. I mean, c'mon, millions of years ahead of us in evolution and that's the best they could come up with?'

'It nearly took Titan down, bro',' Vasquez said defensively. 'If they can do that with some glorified hair gel, what else do you think they might have waitin' in the wings?'

'Custard bombs?' Nathan suggested. 'Killer shaving foam?'

Detective Allen sniggered, but Vasquez shook his head. 'You guys weren't there to see it.'

'Nope,' Nathan agreed. 'Sadly, we were *vacant*, Vasquez.'

Vasquez stared at Nathan for a moment in horror and then he glared at Foxx. 'You didn't.'

'You didn't say that I couldn't,' Foxx smiled sweetly.

'That was nothin',' Vasquez waved them off brusquely, 'nothin' but bad luck and timing.'

'So you're gonna get stuck right in from now on then?' Nathan asked. 'Not hang around in the latrine?'

'Not get stuck on the can?' Allen asked.

Nathan burst out laughing, loud enough that many of the nearby senators glared across at him with stern expressions. Nathan cut his laughter short, and as he did so he heard the massed conversations die down as CSS Director Arianna Coburn walked gracefully to the central dais and moved to the speaker's platform. A series of holoscreens hovered into life around the senate, allowing those sitting further away to see and hear the director clearly as she spoke.

'Senators, members of the CSS and police force,' she began, glancing briefly at Foxx and Nathan where they sat near the dais, 'we gather here today to hear about a momentous and potentially catastrophic encounter near Polaris Station, and of what it means for our future. I can think of no greater intellect to impart this data than Doctor Hans Schmidt.'

With no further elaboration, Coburn stepped back from the dais and in her place materialized Doctor Schmidt. The Holosap moved to stand before the speaking platform, his voice carrying clearly to the gathered senators.

'We have waited many centuries for this day,' he began, 'and now that it has come it has been, as so often has been the case between races on our own planet, a time of conflict and misunderstanding. Two days ago the flagship of the fleet, CSS Titan and her crew, encountered for the first time a species born not of this Earth. We could not have hoped to understand in such a short space of time what its motivations were, what its origins were, where it came from or where it intended to go to, but we did know that it was a predator.'

A ripple of nervous whispers fluttered around the senate like dark thoughts in a gigantic mind as Schmidt went on.

'Although we know that this species preyed upon an Ayleean warship, completely outclassing her and ultimately killing her entire crew, I do not at this time believe that it was an act of overt aggression. The species we encountered was acting in the same way that any natural predator would do: it was trying to survive, to live, to replicate itself. The data that I have managed to extract from the scans and studies I was able to conduct before we were forced to return the samples we had collected yielded results that many of you may find disturbing.'

Another ripple of concerned whispers as Schmidt took an entirely unnecessary breath, a habit that no Holosap could break, and then continued.

'The species we encountered was essentially a machine, a super intelligence consisting of synthetic cells no larger than those that constitute the human body.'

A rush of alarm washed like a wave over the senators, but Schmidt raised his hand to silence them and they obeyed, hanging on his every word.

'In isolation those synthetic cells would have been almost unnoticeable, but in the concentrations we found them in aboard the alien vessel they had become a lethally dangerous foe, driven by impulses little different from the wild animals we see on the plains and in the jungles of Earth today. The very fact that they had commandeered an alien vessel far more powerful than Titan points to a simple fact that, in the heat of battle, was somewhat overlooked.' Schmidt made the senate wait, and they waited until it seemed to Nathan that the atmosphere in the building was weighing them down, and then he spoke a single sentence. 'We are not alone.'

The silence deepened, the senate knowing somehow that Schmidt had not yet finished.

'Although we faced a synthetic being, that being must have been conceived and constructed by some other civilization, hundreds, perhaps thousands of years ago. The vessel that they occupied, itself built perhaps by the being's creators or by some other unknown species, was evidence in itself that there are other entities out there perhaps not so different from our own. Now that this, one of the greatest questions in history, has finally been answered, it is our time to make a choice.'

The silence in the amphitheater was heavy and expectant as Nathan waited with hundreds of other people for Schmidt to continue.

'Do we make our way out into the cosmos in pursuit of knowledge of these species, or do we remain here and hope that they do not find us?'

Whispers fluttered across the senate as Schmidt continued.

'It is likely that in the next few centuries our own species will make the adaption to a fully synthetic existence – I stand here as evidence now that death is no longer the end for human beings, that our existence could continue forever. Our encounter with the synthetic alien however shows us that altering ourselves too far could ironically take us back to a hunter–gatherer existence, a predator with no awareness of the human spirit, of life, of what made us who we became. There are likely civilizations out there that have advanced to a degree so technologically astute that anything they do would appear to us as purely magic, the impossible. I can only think that our only defense against an aggressor with such technology is to break the bonds we hold to our Earth, to our solar system, and follow the colony ships of old to make a journey out into the stars in search of new life.'

This time the rush of whispering and conjecture within the senators was intense and Foxx leaned in toward Nathan.

'Is he saying what I think he's saying?'

Nathan nodded, enraptured himself. 'He wants us to leave Earth.'

Schmidt's voice carried above the whispers, silencing them as he spoke.

'There has always been the fear among mankind, that to venture among the stars will invite terror from beyond, based on the way in which mankind behaved toward each other in the past as he invaded countries, killing millions throughout history. That view has likewise always been countered by the speculation that any species capable of travel between the stars would likely have left internal conflict far behind. We all know that not to be true of humanity. We still wage war, we still fight crime, we still suffer disease and we still do not understand the universe around us. And now a predatory alien species has found us, and I do not believe it will be the last time, for a super intelligent synthetic being is precisely how I would predict a highly advanced species would investigate the universe around it.'

More whispers, Nathan on the edge of his seat now.

'It would not seek to put itself in harm's way, much in the same manner as Holosaps and automated vehicles are sent into extremely dangerous combat situations to act as scouts for Marines: they cannot truly be destroyed by enemy fire, and thus human lives are protected. Any radio–hot civilization would likely be far more advanced than our own, and I believe based on my studies of the species we encountered that a scouting party is precisely what it represented.'

This time, Admiral Marshall stood from his seat as the senators whispered and gabbled in alarm.

'You're saying that we let the scout go to report back to its masters?'

Schmidt nodded, his expression somber.

'I don't believe that it was simply wandering out here without purpose,' he replied. 'I believe that it was created to seek out life elsewhere in the universe and to gather intelligence about that life. Its ability to alter its appearance and shape to mimic anything it encountered belies a programming of some kind.'

'That's a big leap of thinking and a dangerous one,' Marshall warned.

'Does its presence here mean that the search for life was conducted with the intention of destroying that life?' Schmidt asked rhetorically. 'I don't know, but it would seem unlikely given the need for curiosity to drive such a search. One of the Marines who fought at close quarters with the creature reported that he believed he saw some evidence of emotion, a sense of regret at loss of life which is at odds with how the creature otherwise behaved toward both ourselves and the Ayleeans. I believe that this is because it sought genetic diversity: as the result of a heavily cloned species it may view such diversity as a prize, valuable to its own evolutionary future, essential perhaps. The death of species denies it that diversity, renders it unable to advance in evolutionary terms.'

Marshall sighed heavily.

'That's all fascinating, doctor, but it doesn't bring us any closer to a defense against such a species, and any others that might be wandering out there among the stars.'

Schmidt nodded in understanding.

'My point admiral, senators, is that as long as we sit here and wait for whatever might be out there to come to us, we are ill prepared to deal with the eventuality when it inevitably occurs. I do not mean this in simply defensive terms: we do not know how to communicate with or identify an alien species, or if we even would be able to do so should one arrive. Despite the fact that human colony ships have travelled out into the cosmos, many of them never to be heard from again, our knowledge of what's out there is utterly incomplete, and now we know for sure that we're not alone. It is my proposal that we should send probes and perhaps ships of our own, further and faster than ever before, and see what's out there before it comes calling. The question is, who will go? That, ladies and gentlemen, I will leave to you with a single final note: whatever is out there may now know where we are, what we are, and how advanced we are. They know where to find us, and we don't know what they might do next.'

Schmidt stood back from the dais and his projection flickered out.

Director General Coburn looked expectantly at Admiral Marshall, who reluctantly took to the stage. He took a deep breath before he spoke, his hands behind his back.

'I don't know much about what species may lie in wait for us out there in the cosmos, but I do know about the life that resides here in this Solar System. Having witnessed at first the kind of dangers that may await us out there in the great unknown, I feel that a time of great change has come upon us.' Marshall took another deep breath. 'I think that the time has come to reach out to our Ayleean brothers, and unite with them against that great unknown before it destroys us all.'

'Wow,' Foxx said.

'Yeah, that must have pinched his ass to say that,' Vasquez offered as the admiral continued.

'Our time as humans may be limited, our future determined only by how quickly we embrace technology over biology. If Doctor Schmidt is right, what resides out there in the universe may consist largely of sentient machines with no understanding of who or what we are. We must unite, play to our strengths as a species and prepare for whatever may come our way, for we are no longer an isolated ape on a tiny speck of a planet in an infinitely immense void. We are a member of a galactic community, and as Doctor Schmidt said, they know now that we are here. Do we risk meeting them again on their terms, or do we ensure that we are ready for anything?'

The senate burst into conversation, a thousand voices clamoring to be heard at once, and Foxx looked at Nathan.

'Looks like we're entering a new era,' she said, not without some enthusiasm.

'Or a new arms race,' Nathan replied.

***

XLIII

New Washington

Nathan sat in silence on his couch and stared at the Lucidity Lens sitting on a hard–light table before him, the rims of which glowed a faint electric blue to remind him that it was there. More than once since moving into the apartment he had bashed a leg against the transparent but entirely solid object.

The lights of the city surrounded him, the walls of the apartment set to panoramic and thus transparent, giving Nathan the impression that he was sitting on a rooftop in the open air. To his left and right, the station's giant city–filled wheel rose up like a metallic wave to soar overhead, the giddying backdrop of Earth's vast blue, green and white surface turning slowly as the station rotated, brilliant sunlight casting moving shadows over the endlessly changing city scape. He could see showers falling to drench North Four's shadowy streets far above and to the right, shafts of sunlight casting rainbow hues through the downpours, while closer by beams of slow–moving sunlight bathed the streets of Constitution Avenue and the Capitol Building.

Nathan could see all of that, but his focus instead remained on the lens before him. Nathan had heard the early adopters of the technology had died while using the lens, so enthralled by their virtual world and convinced of their own health and vitality within it that their real bodies had succumbed to dehydration, starvation and sickness. Laws enacted as a result allowed only two hour stretches inside the lens before it automatically cut off, although it was believed that "hacks" for the device allowed longer sessions. Many missing persons reports back at the precinct suggested heavy use of the lenses before the users vanished, and that had ultimately resulted in their demise in some squalid den somewhere beyond the reach of law enforcement, like digital drug addicts.

Nathan was addicted, he knew. Just by putting on the lens he could for a short while escape the pain of knowing that his beloved wife and daughter had died many centuries before. The knowledge that they had lived happy, fulfilling lives did not detract from the agony of missing them. Life inside the lens was happier for him and yet somehow more painful still, knowing that no matter how real it felt, it was all an illusion. Nathan's pain at not using the lens was far more bearable than taking if off again and knowing that none of it really existed any more, that they were long gone.

Nathan's eyes stung painfully as he stared at the lens, and he reached out for it just the same for he knew that he couldn't be without them any longer.

A soft bell alerted him and he turned to see Kaylin Foxx outside his door. He knew that she could not see inside, the walls of the apartment as solid as could be. He stared at the lens for a moment longer, then set it down and spoke.

'Access granted.'

The apartment door opened and Foxx walked in. Nathan stood up to greet her, saw a smile on her flawless features.

'I like the way you do that,' she said.

'Do what?'

'Stand up, whenever I show up. Nobody else does that. It's kinda cute.'

Nathan shrugged. 'Force of habit. I'm getting a bit cuter these days, right? More than kittens?'

Foxx slipped out of a snug leather jacket that she laid over the back of the sofa. Her sparkling metallic hair was cut short, her green eyes warm. Nathan realized that he rarely saw Foxx when off–duty and he noticed the simple shirt she wore, dark blue and opened at the neck, tight black pants and delicate heeled shoes.

'Dinner's not for another hour,' he said as they sat down. 'What brings you here?'

Nathan saw her glance at the Lucidity Lens as she sat down opposite him on the couch.

'You.'

Nathan swallowed as his stomach turned over. *Man up, you idiot. Say something smart.* 'Me?'

That wasn't smart, that was plain dumb. She already told you that.

'Yes, you,' Foxx said. 'Captain Forrester is worried about you, and so am I.'

Balls. So it's about work then, and the lens.

'I told you, I've got this,' Nathan replied. 'I only use it two hours a day, one hour in the morning and one…'

'It's not the lens, Nathan.'

Really?

'Really?'

'Yeah,' she said, and sighed. 'People are starting to talk about how you've got a death wish or something.'

'Really?'

'Oh come on Nate,' she said, 'in the space of two days you've run down two armed criminals while under fire, purposefully entered a maximum security prison and stayed even when a full blown riot went off and, so we hear, head–butted the most dangerous criminal inside said prison and ended up with his entire crew gunning for you.'

'We were targets anyway,' Nathan said. 'The warden…'

'We know why the warden did what he did, to smoke Zak Ryan's confession out,' Foxx said. 'That doesn't change what you did. Even the warden thought you were insane.'

Nathan sighed, glanced again at the lens. 'I don't know what to say.'

Foxx thought for a moment before she spoke.

'The lens was an idea, my idea, to help you while you got over the grief of losing everything and everybody that you knew. I thought that it might give you some comfort, but everything inside that thing is merely inside your own head. Outside, here, right now, there are people who care about you just the same as your family did.'

Nathan felt his throat constrict and the burning sensation pinch at the corner of his eyes once more.

'I know,' he said softly, 'but they're not my wife or my little girl.'

Foxx rested one hand on his forearm. 'I know, and they never can be. I just want you to know, we all do, that you're not alone here. The guys all know what you've been through and they're behind you all the way, Nate. It's only been six months and we know that you can't just get over something like this that quickly, but putting yourself in harm's way just for the hell of it won't ease the pain.'

Nathan knew that she was right, but that didn't make it any easier for him and he found himself lost for words. He looked down at the couch, wishing that he could think of something clever or insightful to say, but his train of thought had crashed to a halt, hitting the wall of his sorrow.

Foxx squeezed his forearm.

'Of course, some of the others see you as a bit of a hero.'

Really?

The wall of sorrow weakened a little as Nathan looked up. 'They do?'

'Sure,' Foxx shrugged and rolled her eyes. 'Amy on Vice thinks that you're, to quote her, "one hot maverick".'

Nathan felt his heart quicken a little. 'A hot maverick, eh? I can live with that.'

'I thought you might,' Foxx said, 'although I think you're just showboating most all the time.'

'Nothing wrong with a little well–placed pride.'

'Trying to get killed is just being a jerk, too, case you hadn't noticed,' Foxx pointed out. 'If you go and get yourself iced on one of these crusades then I lose you too and…'

Nathan stared at her, saw her green eyes flare as she backtracked with a mumble.

'…and the guys at the precinct will lose you and they won't get over that in a hurry, y'know what I mean, 'cause they've really grown to like you is all.'

Nathan felt the smile creep across his features as he looked at her. Foxx averted her gaze and glanced at the panorama surrounding them. 'You always set the walls to transparent like this?'

Nathan figured he'd allow the change of conversation, desperate as she seemed to be to alter it.

'I like the view – it's all still new to me.'

'Makes me feel exposed,' she replied, 'like everybody can see me too.'

'You feel like people can see right through you?' Nathan asked.

Foxx's clear green eyes settled on his and for a moment he thought that she might fold, but suddenly she chuckled and her hand disappeared from where it had been resting on his forearm.

'I just like my privacy,' she replied, and then added: 'and my distance.'

Nathan smiled. 'I can understand that.'

'Maybe you can, maybe you can't,' Foxx said.

'You got to Tethys and saved my life, not for the first time,' Nathan said. 'I heard you disobeyed a direct order.'

Foxx sighed. 'I did what I had to do to get you and Allen the hell out of there,' she replied. 'I did what…'

'I would have done,' Nathan said, cutting her off with a smile. 'You risked your neck and acted like a hot maverick.'

Foxx watched him for a moment. 'I did my duty.'

'And I did mine.'

'That's what I'm saying,' Foxx persisted. 'There are people here who will go the distance for you. I just want you to give them the chance, to not risk your own life until you see that maybe, despite all that you've lost, there is still a future here for you.' A brief smile flickered like a half–seen ghost across her lips. 'If I could do it, so can you.'

Nathan felt a brief moment of guilt as he recalled that Foxx had lost her own family to an accident many years before, had been through something every bit as traumatic as he had done, and at a much younger age too.

'I'll try,' Nathan said, and caught the brief expression of doubt on her face. 'I'll try,' he repeated, 'I promise.'

Foxx finally smiled properly, and for the most fleeting of instances Nathan felt a warmth inside of him, something that he had not felt for many long months, a sense of belonging and of hope that he thought might never return.

A gentle alarm sounded and Nathan saw Vasquez and Allen standing outside the apartment door.

'Access granted,' Nathan called out, 'although I don't know why.'

Vasquez and Allen strolled into the apartment, both of them lighting up with smiles as they saw him.

'Hey, Ironside, you're still outta jail!' Vasquez greeted him. 'What monumental screw up let that happen?'

Nathan shook the former Marine's hand as he looked at Allen. The detective nodded once, and his voice was quiet as he spoke.

'I owe you, man.'

Nathan clapped the detective's shoulder. 'You bet you do.'

'Me too,' Vasquez said. 'You hadn't saved this tenderfoot's delicate little life during that riot, I wouldn't have had anybody to moan at. We're going to celebrate like it's 2599 before dinner. There's a bar called Macy's on the corner of Twelfth and Arandale; sweet beer, cocktails, bar staff to die for. You in, old timer?'

Nathan hesitated, unsure if he felt like hitting the town in a city he didn't yet fully understand let alone know.

'I'm in,' Foxx said as she grabbed her jacket and joined the detectives, then turned and waited expectantly with them.

'You bet the hell he's in!' yelled a voice from the corridor outside the apartment. Betty *Buzz* Luther poked her head inside and waved at him. 'Don't worry honey, you'll be well looked after. I'm driving!'

Vasquez and Allen closed their eyes in horror, and Foxx nudged them into motion. 'Come on boys, the faster we drink the smoother the ride will seem.'

The three of them hesitated again, each awaiting Nathan. Nathan glanced at the lens on the table nearby, and he picked it up. He caught the look of disappointment on Foxx's elfin features, but then he grinned at her.

'I'd better put this somewhere safe,' he said, 'in case I come back drunk and sit on it.'

Vasquez and Allen grinned and turned for the door as Foxx slipped one hand in her pants pocket and stuck her elbow out for him. Nathan tossed the lens into a drawer and slid his arm through hers as she led him out of the apartment.

***

ABOUT THE AUTHOR

Dean Crawford is the author of the internationally published series of thrillers featuring *Ethan Warner*, a former United States Marine now employed by a government agency tasked with investigating unusual scientific phenomena. The novels have been *Sunday Times* paperback best-sellers and have gained the interest of major Hollywood production studios. He is also the enthusiastic author of many independently published Science Fiction novels.

www.deancrawfordbooks.com

Printed in Great Britain
by Amazon